HALO REDEEMED

A BROKEN HALO NOVEL

JILLIAN NEAL

Published by Realm Press

ISBN: 978-1-940174-47-1

Library of Congress Control Number: 2018959211

First Edition

First Printing – October 2018

To Dave

Thank you for enduring my endless emails, my random questions, and for patiently putting up with me. I could never have brought T and Maddie to life without your help. You really are the best.

CONTENTS

1

MADDIE

"I call this one Darren." The man seated across the booth from me thrust yet another photo of plant life in front of my face. "Darren the Daphniphyllum Macropodum." When he went as far as to tickle the screen of his phone and coo at the flora, I twisted in my seat searching for someone with a camera crew and a microphone. I was obviously being *Punk'd* or maybe they'd revived that old *Candid Camera* show, and I was their first victim.

Surely, Ashton Kutcher was going to pop up from behind the salad bar at any moment to relieve me and maybe tell me I'd won some prize money for enduring this insanity. No one actually discusses the names of their plants on a blind date, do they? The red glow of the exit sign over the front door beckoned.

"This plant is odd, though, kind of like you." He turned his beady brown eyes on me.

Shock slithered over my skin. "I'm sorry. What about me is odd?" Who did this guy think he was?

"Well, it's not so much you that's odd but the fact that Jenn set us up on this date. I told her I prefer well-endowed blondes and you are neither of those things. Not that you're not cute, my dear Mad."

I dug my nails into my palms to keep from scalping him. Why

hadn't I told Jenn to take her asinine bet and shove it? I could be home with T and Olivia having fun. "I've asked you three times to call me Maddie. Mad is not my name, and I am not your dear." I'd endured eleven plant pictures along with their watering schedules and being told my boobs were too small for this jerk. A woman can only take so much. This guy had to be the poster child of horrifying date Reddit subthreads. Not that I have a great deal of experience with horrifying dates, or dates in general, or Reddit for that matter. But I'm assuming, as dates go, this ranked right up there in the *dear merciful Jesus, why* category.

"Go on with what you were going to say about the plant being odd, Stevie." His mother lanced me a disapproving glare. Oh, did I forget to mention his mother had joined us on our blind date? Apparently, Stevie still lives in her basement, even though he had to be pushing forty. She was also his ride. I swirled the straw in my iced tea. The clinks of the rolling ice cubes weren't enough to drown him out, however.

"Yes, Mother." He gave her an adoring grin. "The interesting thing about the Daphniphyllum is the male stamens produce a purplish-pink bloom while the females are a light green." His uproarious laughter reminded me of a whale call. "Isn't that hilarious? They don't conform to gender stereotypes." He slapped his own leg and caused his napkin to fall to the floor. Either that or it couldn't bear another one of his plant stories and had flung itself off of his lap in protest. I couldn't be sure.

I briefly contemplated flinging myself on the floor. My four-year-old did it on occasion when she was beyond exhausted and over-whelmed. There had to be something to it, but then he might check on me.

The irritated knot in my stomach tightened with the thought of his hot artichoke breath anywhere near my face. I shuddered when he dipped another piece of bread in the dip, dangled it over his face, and then attempted to drop it in his mouth. He missed. The dip-laden bread smacked him in the chin, then went on a rescue mission for the napkin after taking a bypass to the crotch of his khakis.

"How progressive of them." I lifted my tea glass to my lips to keep from laughing and to quell the desperate desire to drown his phone, complete with his endless pictures of plant life, in it.

Retrieving my own phone from my purse, I prayed T-Byrd might've texted to say that my little girl missed me and that I needed to come home immediately, if not sooner. Unfortunately, there were no messages or missed calls.

T had been my husband Chris's best friend and his right-hand man in Special Forces before his death. Clearly, my distress signals weren't getting through. T wasn't rescuing me. Damn him. Of course, he'd need to find a machete strong enough to cut through all of Stevie's botany bullshit.

The truth was, if I'd actually alerted T-Byrd or any of the remaining members of Chris's former Green Beret team to my distress, they would storm the restaurant, beat the fertilizer out of Stevie just for annoying me, and then promptly extract me.

I reminded myself that I didn't need to be rescued. I was a grown woman, who'd willingly agreed to this torturous date, and I was going to have to deal on my own. Welcome to the life of an army widow. The princess always gets to save herself. There are no other options.

At least Olivia was having a ball. Uncle T was her favorite. I'm pretty sure she'd trade me in on him in a heartbeat. Of course, he gives her all of the red and purple Skittles from the bag whenever she wants them and lets her use him as her own personal human jungle gym. What four-year-old could ask for more?

The only men on Earth Chris would ever have felt comfortable leaving our baby girl with were The Sevens, as they affectionately referred to themselves. They would readily throw themselves on a sword before allowing any harm to come to Olivia, which made them ideal babysitters.

"What did you say you did for a living, dear?" Stevie's mother asked. Her lips were puckered into a deep scowl like she'd just given a lemon a blow job. "My boy needs someone who can help him with his botany exercises. Can be quite expensive."

I sank my teeth into the side of my mouth envisioning greenery with their own sweatbands and tiny hand weights. What her boy needed was to grow up, buy a grocery store plant like the rest of us, and get over himself. "I teach second grade at Kimridge," I supplied for no other reason than pushing this car farther down the highway to hell. "Doesn't Stevie have his own job?"

"I do. I'm a part-time compliance supervisor for a local fertilizer factory."

Okay, seriously. Where were the cameras? He's a shit supervisor. That could not be a real job. "Exactly how much *compliance* does fertilizer require?"

"You'd be shocked at the regulatory guidelines involved in fertilizer. I could go on and on for hours with the Nebraska state regulations alone."

"No." I held up my hands as if I could forcibly keep the words from coming out of his mouth. "Please don't."

"But my credit score is well over seven hundred, so it does pay the bills," he insisted. "What would you say your credit score is? Teachers don't make much money. I can't fathom why anyone would choose that for a profession."

Says the man whose job is to make sure shit stinks. I uncrossed and recrossed my legs under the table making sure the toe of my boot collided with his shins on both passes. When he gasped and reached to rub his legs, I couldn't help but grin. "I'm assuming when you say 'pays the bills' you mean the ones you don't have since you live in your mother's basement and don't own a car."

"My work is changing the face of botanical practices across the country."

"How good for us all. I know there are nights I lose sleep over the botanical practices of this country."

"Precisely. Now we're seeing eye to eye. Speaking of eyes, did you know scientists recently discovered that both green and blue algae move towards and away from sources of light? It indicates that, on some level, the entire cyanobacteria acts as a kind of eye or vision source."

"Dear God," I spat under my breath. Mercifully, our food arrived at that moment. On top of having to deal with the King of Cyanobacteria Shit, I'd never eaten lunch. I was half-starved. Stabbing my fork into my broccoli, I shoved it in my mouth. The faster I ate the faster I could leave.

When Steve shuddered, I rolled my eyes. "What? Does eating broccoli negatively impact my credit score as well?"

"Broccoli looks like tiny trees," he whined. "How can you eat that?"

"Artichokes are plants and you just ate an entire dish full of those."

"Yes, but they don't *look* like trees."

"You cannot be serious." I was going to murder Jenn the next time I saw her for forcing me to endure this ridiculous human.

"He's never eaten anything that looks like a plant." His mother sighed. "He's a meat and potatoes man, you see."

"Potatoes are also plants," I pointed out just to be spiteful. Clearly, Stevie and I did not have any kind of future. Relief poured through me, loosening the tight clench of my stomach. I shoveled another stalk of broccoli into my mouth to hide my devious grin. I shouldn't have been excited that my date wasn't going well, but I was. Wasn't the point of dating to find someone you wanted to spend more time with? Hadn't that been the entire reason I'd taken this stupid bet with Jenn and Bianca? The fact that Stevie had exactly zero redeeming qualities secretly delighted me. Besides, I had no idea how to date. I hadn't done it since I was sixteen years old. I wanted to skip all of the getting-to-know-someone phase and go straight to the lounging-around-my-house-with-him-in-sweats-and-me-in-one-of-his-T-shirts portion of a relationship, if I even wanted to have another man in my life. I wasn't entirely certain that I did. Being on my own was something I was quite adept at.

"I don't eat potatoes either, Mother," Stevie huffed.

"Well, now, occasionally I hide them in your soups and you eat them then."

"Yes, but they don't look like potatoes then."

You didn't spend all of your teens and twenties with a soldier and not pick up a few things. It was definitely time for a diversion tactic. "How about that plant over there?" I pointed to the fake greenery stuffed into a half wall near the hostess station. "What are those called?"

Both Stevie and his mother turned and I grabbed my cell phone again. I typed out a quick SOS to T-Byrd.

Stevie scowled at me. "Surely, you are aware those are silk. The woman over there is polishing them. That will lower my score for their Yelp review. The franchisee could afford to have real plant life. It's like I'm always saying, 'every company should employ their own botanist'. Plant life is the wave of the future."

I glared down at my phone. Why hadn't T called? I ground my teeth. My screen lit just then. *Sass?* He'd texted back. Ugh. Stupid autocorrect.

Great. Now I had to create another distraction.

Still starving, I cut a hunk of salmon from my plate, threw it in my mouth, and swallowed quickly. "Excuse me, I just need to use the ladies' room." Before I could execute my escape, Stevie cleared his throat. "You know, dandelions, the taraxacum officinale, are a natural laxative if you're having trouble going. It will strengthen your intestinal fortitude. I like knowing the women I'm with have a hearty intestinal tract."

My mouth fell open. Then shut. Then open again of its own accord. Never before had I been simultaneously horrified while also having the bizarre desire to defend the resiliency of my intestines. Shaking my head, I scooted to the bathroom and locked myself inside the last stall, attempting to put as much space as I possibly could between me and my date.

Not sass. I pressed my fingers against the screen of my phone hard enough to turn them red, half wishing it was Stevie's face. *S.O.S.* I made certain all letters were in their correct order this time before hitting send. Then I quickly added, *Wait thirty seconds, then call me and tell me Olivia needs me to come home.* There. I just had to survive another thirty seconds. Surely, I had the intestinal fortitude for that.

My phone rang just as I was returning to the booth. T really was the best. "Oh, if you'll excuse me. It's my sitter." A grin tempted my lips as I answered.

T chuckled. "That bad, huh?"

Ignoring his question, I went on with my playacting. "Oh, no. My poor baby. Tell her I'll be home in just a minute."

"Seriously, I need to know if this is a person I'm going to want to hunt down because of how he's treating you or if he's just your garden-variety asshole. I've watched you endure Smith and Griff's legendary push-up contests for hours, and you never pled out. If you're leaving, it has to be bad."

"Garden-variety is more applicable than you would ever know. Seriously, you would not believe..." I glanced up to see both Stevie and his mother staring at me. T was far too easy to talk to. He always had been, but I needed to remember my mission. "Uh, how awful that... can be... when you're four," I added quickly.

"You sure you can get out on your own? I can get some camo paint on Livy and we can start her search and rescue training now. She's already in her Rapunzel nightgown, but I can make it work. She's pretty lethal with that princess bow and arrow thing Griff got her."

I choked back a giggle over thoughts of my baby girl taking Stevie and his plant life out with her Merida bow and arrow, complete with black camo paint on her cheeks. Chris would've been so proud.

And there it was. The cold slap of realization, like being submerged in an icy bath fully clothed. The things Chris wasn't here to see, had never been here to see, haunted me. I'd figured out how to pull myself out of the water now, but my clothing remained drenched. Hot tears were often the only way to combat the cold. I keep thinking someday the reality of our lives won't overtake me with brutal blows. It's been four years and still, when I least expect it, it drags me to the ground, rips the air from my lungs, and forces me to feel the gut-wrenching grief all over again. Even if things hadn't been perfect, when you lose the other half of yourself, I'm not sure any amount of time can suture that wound.

"I'm on my way," I assured my knight-in-filthy-combat-boots and his would-be rescue princess.

"See you soon."

I was too thrilled to be escaping to make my face do anything but grin. Before I could offer up my reason for leaving, Stevie leapt. "That wasn't your plant sitter, was it?"

"Plant sitter?" Did he actually hire people to sit with his plants? "Uh, no... wait, yes. Yes, it was my plant sitter. One of my... plants is... drooping. I should go check on it."

"It's the sun. People often think drooping means too little water, but it's usually too little sun."

"You're probably right. I'll see about getting it out more."

2

T-BYRD

"I want to watch anudda one, Uncle T," Olivia yawned through her request. She was curled up beside me on the sofa with her head propped on my leg.

"Pretty sure I'm supposed to put you to bed, Princess Olivia." Who was I kidding? She had me wrapped so tightly around her tiny fingers I'd been in a constant state of cramp for the last four years. I was not going to win this battle of wills, and I knew it.

"But maybe just one more." She held up her index finger and gave me the world's most pitiful one-eyed stare since her good eye was covered with her eye patch. When her bottom lip poked out, I was done for. Surely, even Chris couldn't have turned her down, had he gotten to be around to see his little girl being completely adorable on the regular, that is.

"One more *Sofia the First* and then bed," I negotiated.

"But maybe two more." She beamed up at me.

"Liv." I shook my head.

"Okay, just one. Thank you! I love you muches!" Crawling up on her knees, she threw her arms around my neck. Mayday, if she kept that up, Uncle T was likely to agree to the next — dear God, I glanced at the list of *Sofias* on Netflix — one hundred and two episodes. How many princesses could one girl summon on a Disney show? Clearly, an endless supply.

"You know," I spun her in my lap so she was facing the screen again, "the Cubs are playing tonight. We could watch that."

"Do they have magical amulets?"

"No, but they do have magical baseball bats. Does that count?"

"No." She shook her head. "Do they have princesses?"

"Just ball players."

"Do they even let gurls play?"

I grinned at her pronunciation. "They don't, and that's not fair, is it?"

"Nope. Gurls can play ball even better than boys."

"Agreed."

She settled in as Sofia concluded her intro song about learning to be royalty. "Why do you like this show so much?" I'd been trying to sell her on *Jake and the Neverland Pirates,* but I wasn't getting far. I needed to understand what I was up against.

"Because when my mommy gets married again, I'm going to be like Sofia."

"You think Mommy's going to get married again?" It definitely wasn't going to be with whatever douche nozzle she'd gone out with that night. What kind of loser makes a woman like Maddie Mitchell want to leave? God, she's gorgeous, sweet, brilliant. She does this thing where she wrinkles her nose and bites her lip and I swear.... Those thoughts needed to stop right there before they crossed from G-rated to something far less acceptable. To the kinds of thoughts I'd had too often as of late. Obviously, I was working too much, and it was fucking with my mind or something. Next weekend, I was going to the lake. I decided right then and there. Couple of days staring out at the water, cutting up on the boat, and not thinking about international security deals, or how much I loved talking to Maddie lately, and I'd be back to normal.

"Yes, and then I'll get to be a princess," Olivia informed me. "Now shh." She whipped her head back to show me her finger pressed over her lips.

"Sorry," I mouthed. I'd tried to stop that odd churning that had been battering my internal organs ever since Maddie had asked me to babysit for her date that night. It had been set in motion again with thoughts of her getting married. I told myself it was trying to picture her with someone who wasn't Chris, but honest to God, I knew that wasn't it. That twisted, jaw-clenching, sucker punch of emotion complete with a hot riff of anger felt an awful lot like jealousy, and that was not something I should ever feel about my best friend's wife. Jesus Christ.

I had to get out of my own head and Sofia, as great as she was, just wasn't cutting it. Seriously, how is it always the same bad guy? Can't Sofia's stepdad, King What's-His-Face, pound the creep into the ground and go on about his life?

She'd shot the Cubs game down twice. I needed a new plan. "Hey, you know that Jake show is about pirates. Maybe one of them wears an eye patch, too." In my former life, I was a Green Beret. Pirates were something I understood. Princesses, not so much.

Olivia sprang upwards. "Does he have ret-blasters-oma, too?"

Gutted. Every freaking time she tried to pronounce the word no kid should even have to know existed, it gutted me like a fish. "Retinoblastoma," I gently corrected.

Maddie wanted her to be able to pronounce it correctly in case she ever needed to tell someone about the cancer she'd had in her left retina as a baby. I'd gone with Maddie to hear the diagnosis. Held them both in my arms that day and most of that night.

Once again, Maddie had been the strongest fucking force on the planet. She'd allowed herself one night of tears, and then she'd fought with everything she had left, after losing her husband, to save her daughter's sight and her life. "I don't think he has it, baby girl. We don't have to watch it if you don't want. I could build you another bunker out of the couch cushions."

"We did that already. There was a little boy in my daycare class named Shawn who likes that show and he pulled my hair when Mommy braided it and that isn't nice."

"Did you tell the teacher?" Whoever this Shawn kid was, he

needed to be on high alert because Olivia Ruth Mitchell was not only being raised by her warrior mama. She was also being raised by the remaining members of United States Army Special Forces Team Seven, her father's team, and we were second to none. I don't care if the kid is only four. You come after our girl, we'll make you wish you hadn't.

"I told her. She said it's 'cause he likes me, but if you like someone, why would you hurt their head? I told her if you like someone you're supposed to be nice to them. She told me to sit down."

Oh, it was good she'd be in a new class come September because her old teacher and I needed to have a lengthy conversation about the bullshit she was shoveling.

At the lurch of the garage door, Olivia scrambled out of my lap. "Mommy's home!" She flew to the kitchen and flung open the door. "Mommy!" I made it to her a split-second before she leapt into Maddie's waiting arms.

"Hey, baby girl. Did you have fun with Uncle T?" Maddie carried her inside grinning at me.

"Uncle T wants to be a pirate."

Maddie planted a kiss on Olivia's cheek and then turned to me. "Can't wait to hear about your new life as a pirate. It has to be more interesting than the blind date I just endured. Did you like the soup I made? I should've offered to pick something up for you on my way."

"The soup was great." That was Maddie. No matter what she had going on she was always taking care of everyone else. I attempted to help her with whenever I could. "I think I could pull the pirate thing off. Just need to find a parrot and maybe a sword."

"I have a sword." Olivia wiggled down from her mother's embrace and took off for her bedroom. "Griff?" I guessed at who'd provided her a sword.

"Yes." Maddie giggled. "He's been trying to weaponize her since she was born."

"Weapons Sergeant. It is kind of his gig. Tell me about this loser that took you out tonight." I shouldn't have asked. It was none of my business, but it was gnawing its way through me. None of my emotions made any sense lately. I should not have been both relieved her date had sucked and irritated that some fuckstick had screwed up a chance with her. Maybe I needed a whole week at the lake, not just a weekend.

"Suffice it to say, I am going to kill Jenn for setting me up with him. I should never have agreed to this stupid bet anyway." She sounded so thoroughly disgusted with herself another round of guilt pitched a tent in my gut. I should never have asked.

"What bet?" For some reason, my mouth continued to move despite direct orders from my brain to shut the fuck up about the date.

Before she could explain, Olivia returned wielding a foam sword. It was hard to look too fierce when you couldn't stop yawning, though. I lifted her up into my arms. The sword drooped by her side. "Let's let Mommy relax, and I'll put you to bed. Deal?"

"Deal." Olivia nodded and then buried her face against my shoulder. Yep, definitely had to get my head screwed on straight because my girl needed me to be better than the guy having completely inappropriate thoughts about her mommy.

But then Maddie grinned at me and brushed another kiss on Olivia's cheek. Her breaths teased at my bicep. The soft floral scent of her filled my lungs. The tender swells of her breasts pressed against my forearm as she stood on her tiptoes to access her little girl. I shuddered from the sheer magnitude of the thoughts that slammed back through me with a vengeance.

God, she had beautiful lips. My traitorous gaze dropped to the low-cut black sundress she was wearing. Dancing at her cleavage was the small diamond pendant on the silver chain Chris had given her. She had the most incredible... no. Not going there. What the fuck was wrong with me? Every hair on my arm stood anxious for the weight of her breasts to return.

Definitely needed to get out of town. Pronto. If that didn't work, I could get Smith, another member of Team Seven, to hit me in the face. He was built like a fucking tank on steroids. It'd take weeks to recover, but it might knock some sense into me.

Somewhat appeased that either one of my plans to regain control of my own thoughts would work, I marched Olivia to bed and tucked her in.

"Did she brush her teeth?" Maddie called from the living room.

"Do I look like a newb?" I called back.

Her soft laughter did nothing to quell my current desires. Dammit.

Concentrating on the precious child before me, I helped her slip off her eye patch. I knew she'd be up a dozen more times needing a few more goodnight kisses, to use the bathroom, and to get anywhere from three to one hundred and seven more sips of water, but it was a solid first getting-in-bed effort. I wasn't too bad at this.

"I love you, Uncle T," Olivia whispered as she laid her hand over her eyes to block the fading sunlight outside her windows.

"I love you too, baby girl."

3

MADDIE

Attempting to scale my refrigerator, I accepted my defeat and dragged the step stool from the pantry to rescue the stash of Olivia's Easter candy I'd hidden up there. I'd polished off two marshmallow-stuffed bunnies and was well on my way through a Reese's cup when T returned from her bedroom.

Evidence of my chocolate fix lay in tatters all over the counter and yet that odd fizzy feeling that had been bubbling in my stomach ever since T had arrived to babysit was still there. He gave me his megawatt grin and something in my chest fluttered. What the hell was that? I did not have time for any strange ailments. School started back in a few weeks.

"That's where the Easter candy was." T laughed. He had the best laugh, the kind that filled an entire room with warm sunshine. It always made me smile, even when I was having an epically shitty day. "I swear I looked everywhere but up there and in your underwear drawer."

I feigned shock but ended up joining in his laughter. "I only hide the really good stuff in there."

"Oh, I'm sure you do," he teased. Those gorgeous blue eyes of his sparked with his quip. The harsh angle of his jaw tensed a moment later. I wondered what he was thinking as he stood watching me devour all of my many emotions in the form of chocolate-covered bunnies.

When he dug in his pocket for his keys, my stomach clenched, probably from consuming an entirely chocolate dinner. Disappointment chafed at my chest. I didn't want him to leave. I wanted him to stay, to keep teasing me, and keep making me laugh. I wanted to be with someone who didn't have to ask me any questions about anything because he knew me so well. Someone who'd known Chris. Someone who had no questions as to why I wore my wedding band on my right hand now.

"I'll trade you..." I turned and dug in the Ziploc bag of candy, "three marshmallow bunnies, two packs of jelly beans, and what's left of the Cadbury crunchy egg things if you'll watch *Father of the Bride* with me."

T hadn't just been Chris's friend. He was one of my best friends as well. That was the nature of being married to a Special Forces soldier. The team was family.

"Again?" He cocked his left eyebrow at me, but I knew he was going to give in. I just needed to sweeten the deal a little.

"Okay, I'll give you all of the jelly beans, but we get to watch parts one and two."

I earned myself another one of his killer grins. Seriously, how was he still single? It made no sense. With that grin, those eyelashes, and the muscles that went on for miles, how had no one gotten their claws in him?

"So unfair. You know I can't turn down jelly beans or Martin and Short." He restored his keys back to his pocket. "But I will trade you back two of the three marshmallow bunnies and the Cadbury eggs if you tell me about your bet."

"Ugh, must we delve into my stupidity? Haven't I suffered enough tonight?" I stalked back to the living room to cue up my favorite movie of all time.

I heard the microwave door spring open in the kitchen. "Want me to add more popcorn to your grocery list? This is the last bag," he called.

"Please." I grinned as the distinctive sound of kernels sprang to life in the whirring microwave.

"Done." He took the seat beside me on the couch. "Oh, meant to tell you when you got home. Liv is almost out of her eyedrops."

That was what I'd forgotten. It had been bugging me all day. I knew there was something that hadn't made it on my to-do list. "I'll call for the refill tomorrow. Thanks for taking such good care of us. You really are awesome, you know that?"

"I keep telling people that, but they just don't get it." He laughed.

I was forcing the man to watch a movie he'd already watched with me no fewer than four dozen times. The least I owed him was the answer to his question. "So, the bet." The word itself tasted like regret and battery acid.

"Thank God. I thought I was going to have to hold the popcorn bowl out of your reach until you told me."

My mouth dropped open. "I'm pretty sure that was outlawed in the Geneva Convention or something, Master Sergeant."

He snorted and shook his head. "Let's get back to the bet, Ms. Mitchell."

"So formal."

"You just called me Master Sergeant. I figured I'd return the favor. Besides, teaching second grade should come with combat pay."

"Aww, my kiddos last year were sweethearts except for that one little girl who I swear was demon possessed."

The beep of the microwave summoned both T from the couch and Olivia from her bed. "Your diversion techniques are admirable, but when I get back with the popcorn you're telling me about this bet."

"I want to watch a movie with Uncle T," Olivia pled through another deep yawn.

"To bed, Liv." I pointed back down the hallway. "You already got to stay up late."

"Can I have a sip of water?" She turned those massive green eyes on me and worked the pity angle hard. This kid. I swear, sometimes those looks she gave me were so much like Chris it took my breath away.

"You may get a sip from your bathroom, and then go to bed."

With a distinctive huff and a full-on glare, my four-year-old stomped back to her bed. T waited until she was out of the room to make his reappearance. I knew his game. "You will survive hearing her be scolded and told no."

"I know, but she's so freaking cute, and when she does that lip-poking-out thing, I fold faster than a dollar-store beach chair."

"She is aware of that," I reminded him.

"Yeah, I know." He sighed. "But back to the bet."

Dang, I was hoping he'd give up on that. Not that giving up was even in T's realm of comprehension. "Fine." I sank down on the couch beside him and threw a few pieces of popcorn in my mouth. He handed over a cold beer he must've stuck in the fridge when he arrived. "Jenn and Bianca made this ridiculous bet with me. I should never have agreed. I didn't really think they'd be so adamant about me dating again." The entire situation twisted in my gut, wringing out more awkward discomfort and confusion.

"What was the bet, exactly?"

"That I would go out three times before school starts back or..."

"Or what?"

"Or I have to get rid of half of Chris's stuff in the garage. I know I should be ready to go through it and move on. I just don't want to right now. I don't want to get rid of it yet, even if I'll never use most of it. Anyway, Bianca set me up with this loser from her gym a few days ago. Tonight, I went out with Stevie, the shit supervisor that Jenn knew in high school or something. The whole thing is completely ridiculous. How do I even get myself into these situations?"

Irritation had shadowed T-Byrd's deep-blue eyes. Suddenly, the only thing that mattered was making that irritation disappear. "You're entirely too nice," he informed me. "You agree to things you don't want to do because you want to make everyone happy even at your own expense. If you're not ready to get rid of Chris's stuff, then you're not getting rid of it. There is no time frame in which you have to be ready to do that. There are no rules for grief. I don't care what your friends say. But since you already know I have a thing for saving people, allow me the pleasure. I have a solution to your third date issue."

I adored T for being one of the only people in my life to tell me like it is. He had an uncanny ability to cut through all of my crap, figure out the real reasons for things, and even help me come up with workable solutions that didn't make me cringe. If I hadn't known him for so long, the way he could rumble around comfortably in my brain would've been unnerving.

"I'm listening, but if it involves a guy who has his houseplants on a feeding schedule or one that actually owns the Nebraska state DUDE XL license plate, I am not interested."

"Gym guy?" T guessed.

"Bingo."

He shook his head. "I don't even own any houseplants, and surely you know I'd sooner remove one of my own testicles than ever operate a vehicle with that on the plates."

"Wait. You're going to be my third date?" I could not actually go on a date with T. That would be... wrong. Wouldn't it? He was Chris's best friend. He was several years younger than me. We're just good friends. My brain rattled off a dozen more reasons I could never date T. Oddly, every single reason I could come up with burned along my nerves until I was raw with disappointment. They also felt insubstantial. More excuses than reasons, maybe. Wait. No. I could not go on a date with T-Byrd. There. That was settled. What on earth was wrong with me?

"If you're up for it, yeah. You'd be doing me a huge favor. I have to go to this fancy shindig at the Capitol Winery hosted by Coldwell Harding. I'm supposed to bring a plus one. Full disclosure- it's going to be a shitshow, but if you don't mind hanging with me just long enough for me to make this guy hate me even more, I swear I'll take you out and we'll do something fun afterwards."

"Coldwell Harding? Like the weapons manufacturer? Don't they build the bomber jets or whatever we call them now?"

"They got out of the jet business a decade ago. Set their sights on smaller weapons systems and optics. Hasn't gone well for them, and tomorrow night isn't likely to be any different. Don't worry about it. I can go alone. It was a stupid idea. You'll hate it, and I would hate myself for making you endure it."

So, this wasn't a real date. I could totally go as his plus one. I'd be helping him out, and that delighted me. I owed him for several thousand favors anyway. This wasn't even a big one. "I don't mind going, and I won't hate it. I always have fun with you. Plus, Capitol Winery is beautiful. I've always wanted to attend an event there. I just don't know if I can get a sitter for tomorrow night."

"If you really don't mind going, I'll get Griff and Hannah to babysit. But you have to look me in the eye, put your hand in mine, and swear to me you're not just telling me you want to go because you know it will make me happy."

Making him happy was just a bonus, so I made certain he saw my eye roll before I followed his orders. Going as far as to place my left hand on my heart, I laid my right in his. Some strange spark of electricity centered in my palm at his touch. I stared at our hands. His grip was substantial and comforting. His fingers closed around mine protectively.

Shaking off the peculiar sensation, I stared him down. There was something in his watchful eyes. Something I didn't fully understand. Some distant memory of being on the receiving end of a gaze like that shook loose from my mind. Refusing to acknowledge my own bizarre reactions, I went on with my vow. "I solemnly swear that I do not mind being your plus one even though you did write incredibly lewd instructions to me in permanent marker on my husband's ass when you got him so drunk he passed out that one time back in the day."

That earned me the coveted prize of T-Byrd's hearty laughter. "Dear God, I'd forgotten all about that. I still hold that it was Chris's fault for not being able to hold his liquor. He's the one who passed out after a few shots which meant I got to write *Squeeze me here, honey,* on his sad ass."

I should've come back with something about Chris not being able to hold his liquor due to his squeaky-clean upbringing, which really wasn't his fault, but I was too busy giggling. Somehow remembering with T didn't hurt the way remembering did when I was on my own. The memories could breathe between us instead of stealing the breath from my lungs.

T still had my hand clasped in the strength of his own, and I had no desire for him to release my fingers.

4

T-BYRD

Do not run your fingers through her hair. Jesus Christ, you've done enough inexcusable things. She was your best friend's wife. You are an asswipe of the highest caliber. A few strands of her soft chestnut-brown hair clung to her cheek in her slumber. My fingers itched to ease it away from her face. Brushing a tender kiss on her temple would've been almost required. The desire to taste the dew gathered along her hairline continued to tempt me almost as much as the hunger to devour the slight part of her lips.

I had to get out of there. No amount of me layering my own self-hatred with either guilt or desire was making this situation better. The demon who was currently purchasing property and digging deep roots on my shoulder continued to remind me of the word *was*. It didn't matter that she *was* his wife because I *was* a complete douche for loving the fact that she'd passed out in my lap halfway through the second movie.

Cementing myself as the world's biggest fucker, I'd cuddled her up under a quilt and rubbed her back like she was mine to care for, mine to tend, mine to make certain she slept soundly, safe and warm in my arms - like every single thing that had happened to either of us in the last decade never even existed.

Every fiber of my being wanted to stretch out beside her, coax her up onto my chest, and feel her rhythmic breaths move in time with my own. Oh, there were several other things I wanted to feel, as well. My hands had all kinds of ideas about exotic locales on her body they'd like to explore. My tongue wanted to taste every forbidden inch of her.

As soon as she'd snuggled her sweet little curves up against me, my cock had taken over and had driven any kind of good sense I'd ever managed to possess from my body. Speaking of my cock, damn thing had been hung at half-mast for the last hour. Eager much, buddy? Jesus. I hadn't prayed that someone's hand would slip from its current location and fall to my package since I was in eighth grade. Self-disgust curdled in my bloodstream.

If I'd had any decency or honor left in me at all, I would've gently scooped her up into my arms and carried her to her bed. But, I swear, I didn't trust myself to be able to leave her in tangled sheets alone. I was losing my mind. Exhaustion, stress, work, something had clearly driven me over the edge. Too many people counted on me. The most important two were both asleep under my care. I had to figure out how to get my head straight. I could not be this guy.

Ineffective in my attempt to shake off the ever-growing need to become more than Maddie's friend, I eased out from underneath her and stalked silently to Olivia's bedroom. I tucked her quilt tighter around her and made sure her favorite stuffed bunny, Howie, the one I'd given her when she was a baby, was right beside her. Touching two of my fingers to my lips, I planted the kiss on her forehead. *Uncle T is going to get his shit together, sweetheart. I promise you. I won't let you down like this.* I made the silent vow to my girl before returning to the living room.

Ordering myself to feel nothing at all, I switched off the TV and then the lamps. Since I could bench press twice her weight without much effort, I scooped her up into my arms with ease. That was where the easy part ended. Damn if she didn't wrap her hands gently around my neck, nuzzle her face against my chest, and give me the fucking sweetest, sleepy little sigh I'd ever heard.

No amount of desensitizing myself was going to cut it when it came to Maddie's sexy sounds. I had no weapon that would combat that. Fuck me if the first thing I didn't think was how good she would sound begging for my cock.

Clenching my jaw and trying not to notice her warm weight in my arms, I slipped to her bedroom. She was still in the cute little dress she'd worn on her date, with another man I reminded myself. Oh, but shoulder-demon was quick on the trigger. *A date with another man she hated. A date with another man who will never deserve a woman like her.* There was a sexy-as-sin satin nightshirt on the floor. Damn thing glimmered in the moonlight streaming in the slats of her blinds like it was some kind of siren-inspired sleepwear. There was no way I was going to help her out of what she was wearing and into her pajamas despite shoulder-demon's urging me to do just that. Nope. No way. Not happening.

In an effort to dam every demon housed somewhere in my body, I reminded myself that this was the very bed where she used to sleep with my best friend. Yep, right here. He got to see her naked, got to touch her, got to feel her tremble all for him. He got to hear her tender moans, got to watch her eyes close and her fists clench the sheets in ecstasy, and he got to sink himself deep inside the silky wet heat he surely knew how to draw from her beautiful body. Hell, they'd even made a kid in this bed.

Jealousy latched its sharpened claws into me. I shuddered under the stabbing pain of it. That was not what those thoughts were supposed to elicit. I called myself a douche of whale-sized proportion. What kind of asshole is jealous of his dead best friend?

I eased her under the covers, and that's when all hell broke loose. When I leaned to lay her down, she ran her hands down my pecs and brushed her lips over my neck in what was an unmistakable kiss. I jerked upright and studied her. I half prayed she was still asleep and confused. The other half prayed she was awake and had done that on purpose, that she wanted me to stay even half as badly as I longed to climb in beside her and explore. The conflicting emotions rent me in two.

Her eyes were still shut, moving ever so slightly. She was caught up in a dream and had no idea what she'd done. I hated myself for the tidal wave of disappointment that ripped through me.

Desperation to know what kinds of dreams Maddie Mitchell had fucked with my brain. When she let her guard down, were her dreams as sweet and innocent as she always seemed to be? Or were there a few darkened edges somewhere amongst all of her soft, tender curves? Were there things she longed to explore but kept locked away in the light of day? Did she need someone to free her from the expectations everyone heaped on her as a single mom? Did she ever think of me when she allowed herself a moment to exist unto herself?

Weak against my own craving needs, I squeezed my eyes shut and fumbled with the covers as I eased them up over her. Turning around, I allowed myself sight and ordered my feet to walk out of the room.

"T?" her sleepy whisper reached my ears.

Fuck me sideways. I whirled back around because what else would I ever do if she needed me?

"Yeah?" Do not call her baby. Don't do it. You are not that guy.

"You can stay," she yawned and scooted farther down in her bed. Shoulder-demon rejoiced, and my cock joined in the party.

She absolutely did not mean I could stay with her in her bed. If only I could get my cock to realize that. She meant on the couch. I'd stayed over dozens upon dozens of times since I'd come home without my best friend, without her husband. How fucked up was it that I'd survived and he hadn't? He was the best soldier that had ever walked the face of this fucked-up earth, and I was not.

God, I'd tried though. I'd done every fucking thing I could think of to make the hell she lived day in and day out bearable. I would've taken on Satan himself in a showdown to save her one moment of the pain. I'd held her, cried with her, let her see sides of myself, weaknesses, I'd never let anyone see again. I'd slept on that couch hundreds of times and paced the living room floor even more than that.

Early on, when she'd managed sleep, I'd run bottle duty for Olivia all night long. I'd feed her and tell her every single thing I could remember about Chris. I'd cradled her tiny, perfect little pink form in my arms and hated myself for being able to hold her when he never had. It was my job to make sure she knew him.

Maybe that's where all of this insanity about being attracted to Maddie was coming from. I'd been someone she'd relied on for a long time now. She was so much a part of my existence I could never sever her from my life. My cock had gotten confused about our job here, namely that he had no part in it.

Sanity slowly crept back through me. That had to be it. The exhaustion and stress of work had taken its toll, and my mind had confused itself.

"Go to sleep. I'll lock up on my way out." The words were unnecessary. She'd already passed back out, and she knew I'd take care of everything because that was who I was meant to be for her. Her protector, her friend, the guy she called on no matter what she needed. That and nothing more.

I peeked at Olivia again, dumped the popcorn kernels in the trash along with the candy wrappers from Maddie's earlier raid, and checked the locks on all the doors. Setting the security system I'd had Smith install when she'd purchased this house, I slipped out and wished the incessant whip of the Nebraskan winds would wash me clean of the thoughts that clung to me. Thoughts of being the man who not only got to sleep with Maddie in my arms but the man who woke up beside her every day.

5

T-BYRD

oderately pacified with the idea that I was only having these bizarre feelings about Maddie because my mind was playing tricks on me, I continued to try to rid myself of the emotions. The hot summer winds weren't doing much to whip my filthy thoughts into submission. Maybe a cold shower would work. I swear shoulder-demon actually laughed at the very idea that this could be washed away. Damn him.

For the first time since I'd picked it up three weeks ago, I didn't grin like an idiot opening the door on my so-new-it's-only-obtainable-if-you-know-someone metallic-grey Corvette Z06. That's when I finally had to admit shit was bleak.

I had to get over this, and I had to do it by tomorrow night when I would effectively be taking my best friend's wife out on a date. Because I'd gone and arranged this. Right after I'd made a comment about her underwear drawer and then doubled down with a quip about what she kept in there. Oh, we'd both known I didn't mean the drawer—I meant the panties themselves. She thought I was joking. I'd known I wasn't.

I definitely needed to inquire about that skull punch from Smith.

The low hum of the engine and the scent of expensive leather only slightly boosted my mood. When I'd completed the defensive and evasive driving specialized security courses I'd taken so we could add that to the things Tier Seven offered our clients, I'd told myself I deserved a kickass car. You can't be into cars when everyone you know and love calls you T-Byrd. That's entirely too clichéd. Such is the burden of a fourth generation Thomas Thursten Byrd. Seriously, that name should've died off with my great-grandfather but no, my family just kept it going because we cannot ever let anything go. But God I loved the way my Vette seemed to respond to my very thoughts. I was obsessed with *Knight Rider* as a kid, and I was so living out all my childhood fantasies. I sure as hell couldn't live out my adult ones with Maddie, so why not these? Dammit. Why did she keep popping into my head? I white-knuckled the steering wheel since I couldn't get a grip on my own thoughts.

I tapped the brake to wait on an infuriatingly slow Camaro to back out of one of her neighbor's driveways and drive past. Normally, I'm not a guy who complains about much. I'd seen the worst humanity had to dish up. The mundane shit we dealt with day in and day out wasn't as bad as you might think. But frustration fed the shame mounting in my chest as I was forced to drive my beloved car behind one old enough to have been its parent. "It's a Camaro, dude. It's ancient. I get it, but my God, I could pedal faster," I spat into the ether surrounding me.

An answering shower of exhaust from the Camaro assaulted my car. *Asshole.*

As soon as we pulled out onto the four-lane, I floored it around the relic of a sports car. I had nowhere to be but home. I just needed to get somewhere quickly—somewhere I could think. Logic demanded that I put some space between myself and Maddie, but my gut hated every millimeter I drove away from her house.

Lake water, sleep, and beer was all I needed to get myself squared away. It had to be. Unfortunately, I was jack shit at lying to myself. Switching on the radio, I pressed the accelerator harder, driving faster to nowhere. A male DJ on the alternative station announced that he was signing off and that "Under the Covers with Madeline" would be up next. *Oh, the fuck no.* Jesus, the entire universe was against me. I shut down the radio.

Silence ate at me when I finally pulled into my garage. I knew I'd never be able to sleep, but I went through the motions anyway. I tossed my keys on the kitchen counter, shed my T-shirt and jeans, set my phone on the charger on the nightstand, brushed my teeth—the whole thing only to lie in my cold, empty bed alone.

The absence of her heat and her laughter and, God, that smile continued to taunt my resolve. I squeezed my eyes shut. That was worse. She was there, free to roam, free to grin, to purse her lips, and shake her head at me on the screen of my eyelids. Even the way she slowly blinked in the world around her with those massive doe eyes was sexy as sin. This was a whole lot of fucked up is what it was.

Chris. Think about Chris. Here's the thing with that. I hadn't yet managed to separate the memories. A blade sharp enough to accomplish the task hadn't yet been invented. I had no idea how to sever the good times, the laughter, and the conversations from the final memory. The moment where he'd been clinging to life, fighting with everything he had to keep breathing, and then gone in the next choked out every other memory I had of him. There'd been no more pain in his eyes but also no more life. Not another breath. Just... gone. It was my reality, and I rejected it with every fiber of my being.

I didn't have the capacity to relive the final moment, so I couldn't have all of those that had come before it. They were all mired in blood-drenched sand. I'd been robbed of them as well. Most days I swore there was a fucking hole in my chest. It was a physical space, and every breath stung like I'd been ripped apart. It was a bone deep, ragged burn.

Four years. Same pain. We'd all just learned to exist around the laceration. Never breathe too deeply or more often than we really needed to. If we just existed, never allowing more air in our lungs than the wound could withstand, maybe we'd survive.

I shook off any thoughts of Chris. I wasn't sure I'd ever be strong enough to go there. If going there meant the pain would increase, I wasn't even sure I wanted to make the trip. Maybe I was weak, but I was the one that had to live in my boots.

Flipping over on my stomach, I drove my fist into my pillow and dropped my face into the dent I'd created. My own hot breath into the fabric threatened to suffocate me. Breathing was necessary even if it agitated the mysterious chink in my lungs, so I lifted my face back out of the hole.

There were hundreds of nights when I would've donated an organ to have a bed and a pillow instead of bunking down with spiders the size of your face in sand that would melt your pack. Here I was, lying on some ridiculously high thread count sheets Maddie had picked out for me, hating life. My mind centered on the words *Maddie* and *sheets*.

As it turns out, when you're attempting to decimate feelings about your best friend's wife, guilt is an ineffective weapon.

Feelings? For Maddie? These could not possibly be feelings. I had feelings for my mom's chicken spaghetti. Feelings for my new car. I sure as hell had feelings for my team and the security firm we were pouring our blood, sweat, and brains into every fucking day. But feelings about Maddie? No way.

I had... thoughts. Maybe even normal thoughts. Yeah. They were perfectly normal, healthy, red-blooded, American, male thoughts. Which worked, because I was a perfectly normal, healthy, red-blooded, American male. I loved women, and Maddie was definitely all woman. A brilliant, sweet, sexy... no.

I was her friend and her protector. Nothing more.

Shoulder-demon fell over laughing as images of Maddie tangled in my sheets with me, under me, surrounding me, continued to fill my mind.

Turning back over, the cotton of my boxer briefs slid against the tip of my cock. I swore I'd jacked off more in the last few months trying not to think of Maddie than I had when I'd first figured out how it worked.

Grabbing my phone, I Googled up my favorite porn site and scrolled through the thumbnails on my screen. I wasn't picky. If I were actually man enough to tell myself the truth, I already knew the video clip wasn't going to do a damn thing. A few of my filthier thoughts about Maddie, and I'd be coming like a kid in the back seat of his father's Mustang with the first chick he'd managed to ask out.

Refusing to let myself off the hook, I tapped on a clip of two blondes, with tits bigger than their heads, leaned over some dude in a pool chair. Whatever. I didn't care. I liked blondes, tits, and pools, and I sure as hell loved having my cock sucked. As long as it didn't star some sweet, innocent, brunette, I'd make it work.

A wounded, hitched breath escaped from that damned tear in my chest as the video loaded. The guy's dirty talk was officially cringe-worthy, so I muted it. One of the women leaned in for a long lick. I extended my arm allowing my hand to wander down my abs and crawl into my boxer briefs. The other chick got in on the game, and they met in the middle for a kiss. My cock appreciated the show, but then my eyes closed without my permission. The blondes and the guy receiving enviable head disappeared.

An entirely different X-rated film flickered to life in my mind. I gave a hesitant tug. My abs tensed right along with my bicep. '*I need you,*' she whimpered as she stepped into my arms and rubbed her naked curves against me. '*Please, T.*'

Petite breasts crowned with her rose-petal-pink nipples, diamond hard, pressed against my pecs.

My phone hit the carpet beside my bed. I jerked my underwear farther down and never opened my eyes. The instructions I longed to speak to her when I had her like this began on some kind of teleprompter in my head. '*Show me, baby. Show me where you need me.*'

Her fingers laced with mine as she guided my hand to the swollen folds between her legs. '*Please.*'

A rumbled moan I couldn't quell tore from my throat. Harder. Faster. My cock fucking wept for the situation I was in, making this entirely too easy. I jerked with more ferocity.

The soft skin of her sweet little belly pressed against my cock. Her hungry moans wrapped around me like a vise. She moved gracefully against my solid might. My capable fingers found her drenched and swollen. She needed me. I circled her opening. She shuddered against me and writhed.

My shallow breaths couldn't sustain me. My body seized. Reality and fantasy swirled much too closely together in my mind. I lost all ability to decipher one from the other. My jaw compressed.

I pressed my fingers deep inside of her, reveling in her hungry gasp of my name.

Her eyes, those gorgeous brown eyes, landed on mine. So many questions resided in their depths. Questions I longed to answer. Reassurances I wanted to give her. *'I'll always take care of my baby.'*

My flesh was straining and aching, almost angry at the thing I can never have. She needed me. I dissolved into nothing but the wild need to come. I imagined her tight little pussy pulsing against my cock, and her voice drawn out to nothing more than a breathless plea for more.

The first hot splash of cum on my abdomen pricked the images in my mind, shattering the escape I'd indulged myself in yet again. Shame swept in, slithering over my skin. It always did. My conscience ripped the air from my lungs every single time. Each release ended with a sharp wave of guilt that sliced right through me.

I tried not to hear my own footfalls as I headed towards my bathroom. I tried not to exist at all. In eighteen or so hours, I was picking her up for a date and that little finger-fuck session didn't even come close to some of my longer, filthier fantasies of her.

When I passed by the framed picture of the original Team Seven on my dresser, I forced myself to halt. In the photo, we were leaned up against some tank in the middle of California on a training mission. Potential, determination, and a pride that bordered on arrogance were there on each of our faces. At one time, we were the stuff of military legends. That had all been buried, six feet down at Arlington.

I slammed the frame shut and laid it down. I couldn't stare down a ghost after what I'd just done. I hadn't been able to look in his eyes in months, not since I'd pictured her staring up at me while I sank down deep and dirty inside of her.

I'd spent the entirety of my army career coming up with the best possible plans to combat the worst possible scenarios, and I was damned good at what I did. In fact, I was the best. When we were stuck in Surinam with militia forces fanning to the southwest, a rogue division of the Surinam Army stationed due north, flood waters carrying both human waste and pythons rising towards us from the east, and air thicker than the vines we were using for cover drowning us, our CIA Op informed us that he couldn't come up with a single way to extract us. And yet, I'd delivered eight different ways to get my team out safely. Not just anyone can be Special Forces.

This was the first time in my life where I had no idea what to do.

6

MADDIE

His capable hands scraped up my thighs. I ground against something soft, certainly not him. My own hand's hesitant exploration of his zipper line confirmed that. He thrust against my touch. I was almost embarrassed by the hungry shiver that worked through me. A low male grunt of pleasure sounded in my ear when he found me wet all for him.

My lower body continued to move in rhythm against... a mattress? Confusion swamped my mind. I'd been so certain it was him. He was so warm, ridding me of the icy grip of grief. He was steady and safe and so capable. All I knew was I needed more of *him*.

If I really concentrated, I could remember bits and pieces of being sixteen. I remembered the fizzy sensation in my stomach when Mindy Powell told me in the girls' locker room that Chris Mitchell had asked her if she knew if I was dating anyone. Falling in love for the first time is much like existing with the wind inside of you, ready to lift you off the ground and sweep you away. A constant breathless sensation that you never want to stop. Or maybe that only happens when you fall in love with a man who much preferred flying to being on the ground. I couldn't be sure. For the first six months after Chris died, I would rush out into the sweeping Nebraskan winds to pretend

I could still feel his breath whisper across my face. Try though I might, I couldn't ever seem to recapture the wind deep within my chest, deep within my soul. It existed outside of me. He was gone.

I'd only ever fallen in love once, and I never would again. There would never be another Chris Mitchell in my life. It just wasn't possible. I'd always been Chris's Maddie. I had no idea how to be anyone else.

I remembered waking up thinking of him every morning all through high school, college, and every single day of every single year of our marriage. He was almost never there with me so thoughts of him kept me company.

I know those early morning notions, when the universe allows you to exist between the realms of sleep and consciousness, when you have precious little control over your own desires, should be given the utmost consideration. The universe spoke in early morning moments. It offered its guiding hand then. If only we would listen, it would reveal a path when there was still dew on the grass.

In my sleepy, half-dream state, I extended my hand slowly across the mattress, not certain why I thought he was there. I'd asked him to stay, hadn't I? Or had I only dreamed that? A sudden desperation to crawl up on his chest and have him hold me — maybe even kiss me — had me blinking in the realization that this wasn't the first morning I'd woken up thinking of T-Byrd instead of Chris. Disappointment clogged my throat when I confirmed that I was in bed alone, just like always.

"Mommy, why did you sleep in your pretty dress?"

Jerking upright in the bed, I clutched my chest attempting to keep my heart from pounding an Irish step dance all the way out of my ribcage. "Olivia!" I tried to blink in my little girl, but images of T still played heavily in the fog set over my brain. "Um..." Feeling my way down my chest, I determined that I was indeed still in the dress I'd worn the night before. When had I fallen asleep?

The one distinct memory I had from the evening before was asking T to stay and hoping against hope that he'd strip out of his shirt and crawl into bed with me. Dear God.

That realization washed all remnants of hazy lust from my eyes. *Please, please, please don't let me have said anything like that to him.* I made the quick silent prayer as I took in the situation before me. Olivia was standing at the foot of my bed holding a box of Chex she'd somehow managed to get out of the pantry, and Howie her bunny. "Uh, Livy, is Uncle T on the couch?" I had to know before I made a beeline to the coffee maker with raccoon eyes and a dress that now had more wrinkles than my ninety-year-old grandmother. But why did I care? T had seen me looking much worse than I did at that moment. He'd held my hair back in the early days when I'd cried so hard I would vomit. What was wrong with me?

When Olivia's eyes lit and she raced from my room yelling for Uncle T, I half prayed he was there so she wouldn't be crushed and half hoped he'd gone home because I still had no idea what I might've said to him last night or what I'd say to him now. I couldn't quite remember when my dream about him had slowly morphed into early morning wishes. They'd been much like the sunrise. A glimmer of light, a slight warmth, little by little until the entire sky glowed orange banishing the navy-blue night. Did that mean I wasn't actually dreaming? Was I conscious enough for all of that to have been a fantasy instead?

Bile swirled to a maelstrom in my gut and then took a direct route to my throat loaded down with hot guilt and raw shame. I needed a shower.

The slap, slap, slap of Olivia's little bare feet preceded her return. "He isn't on the couch, or in my room, or in the kitchen, or in the bathroom. Maybe he's hiding. I can find him. Like hide and seek."

The knife of guilt currently lodged in my chest prevented me from achieving my practiced maternal smile. "I bet he went home, baby girl. He was probably tired last night, and he has to go to work today." Crawling out of bed slowly, I let my eyes close as I passed my wedding and honeymoon pictures on my dresser and exited the room. I didn't need to see. I beat a path from my bed to the coffee maker every morning. I could do it from memory.

"But I want Uncle T to play with me," Olivia huffed as she followed after me still carrying her breakfast preference.

The evening before replayed in my mind, but I still couldn't pinpoint when or where I'd fallen asleep.

The date. Holy Mother, I'd agreed to go to the winery that night with T. And there it was. It captured me before I could stop it. Excitement fizzed and bubbled in my belly. That very form of excitement that I hadn't quite experienced since I was sixteen.

Fisting my hands by my side, I refused to allow that to be the case. Clearly, I was having an off morning. That could happen. That didn't explain why I'd been having that same nervous excitement every single time I knew I was going to get to see him for the last few months, but currently, I could only deal with that morning. "You know, I think Uncle Griff and Aunt Hannah are going to come play with you tonight." I rescued the Chex from Olivia's grasp before they ended up all over my kitchen floor and poured her a bowl with organic almond milk. After that, I set a mug under the Keurig spout and pressed the button.

"Are you going on another date?" She wrinkled her nose at the milk. "Uncle T let me have Chex with chocolate milk one time. It was very yummy."

"Did he?" I shook my head.

"Yes, and it was better-er than this kind of milk that I don't like."

"Better not better-er and no chocolate milk this morning."

"Maybe Uncle Griff will bring me chocolate milk. Can I call him?"

"Eat your cereal. You're not calling The Sevens this morning. Remember what happened the last time you took Mommy's phone and called them while I was using the bathroom?"

"They all came to play with me."

"Because you told them you didn't know where I was."

"But you were using the potty for a very long time. I thought maybe you were lost."

I cringed. Only little girl in the world who had four men the size of mountains right in the palm of her hand. Those mountains had invaded my home after I'd had some bad crab dip the evening before.

T had stayed over that night as well. Warmth gathered in my chest, something else I hadn't felt since high school. "Mommy's going to go get a quick shower. Do not call your Uncle Griff. Do you understand me?"

"Yes, but you didn't drink your coffee with me, and you always do that."

Right. Geez, this was serious if I was forgetting coffee. I grabbed my mug and sank down at the table beside my little girl.

"Is your date with a prince?" she asked as she attempted to pick individual Chex squares out of the milk with her spoon.

"What?"

"When Uncle Griff and Aunt Hannah come play with me, are you going on a date with a prince?"

"Oh, I'm not going on a date tonight. I'm going to help Uncle T do something."

She beamed at me. "You're going on a date with Uncle T!" My child practically vibrated in her chair.

My hand landed on my stomach ordering it to feel nothing at all. If only it would take orders from my brain which it did not. In fact, my brain seemed to rather like the idea of me and T on a date. No. Just... no. "I am *not* going on a date with Uncle T. He needs me to help him with something for work and since Uncle T takes such good care of us, I'm going to help him."

Olivia wilted in her booster seat. "I think Uncle T would make a very good prince."

So do I. The thought cemented itself inside my head right beside that fantasy or dream or whatever I'd woken up having. There was no doubt that Master Sergeant Thomas T. Byrd would make someone an excellent prince.

But that someone was not me. And it would never be me. My prince hadn't come home.

7

MADDIE

A jolt of nerves continued to twist up my spine, but I had no idea why. I needed to ask T what to wear tonight. He might've told me it was black tie the night before, and since I couldn't remember everything that happened, I needed to check. A phrase Chris used to tell Team Seven formed in my mind. It chased away my weak excuses. *You can't lie to yourself. You know you're full of bullshit.*

I was. So full of it. I wanted to talk to T. I missed him. I wanted him to answer me and ask how my day was going or to tell me he was excited about tonight.

I worried about Chris's guys. Their security firm was in high demand. Dangerous, high-paying jobs came their way constantly. I required a touchpoint from him. A gnawing sense of unease ate at me. His voice always steadied me, but I sent a text instead of calling.

What are you wearing?

My mouth gaped as I stared at the screen willing Apple to have created some kind of app thing that would suck an already sent text back into the phone. *Tonight. I meant tonight. You know. Tonight. For the thing.* By the third tonight, I assumed I'd made my point so I sent that as well.

That fizzy feeling in my belly returned ten-fold when I saw his texting bubble pop up on my screen. Knowing T, he was going to tease me about asking him the most clichéd opening for phone sex since Alexander Graham Bell had invented the device. Do people even have phone sex anymore? I had no idea. That's how long it had been since I'd been out of the dating game. That's how old I was.

Anticipation zinged through me. I tapped my foot and delight widened my grin as soon as words appeared on my screen. Dear God, what had gotten into me? Where was this coming from? I was acting like a teenager who rushed to tell all of her friends that a boy had texted her.

It lacks originality but I'm thinking my Captain America costume. Might could borrow Griff's Thor suit but then you'd have to go as either Loki or my hammer.

A hysterical giggle erupted from all the bubbles in my stomach. My phone rang a half second later. Thoughts and texts from him were nothing compared to the sheer bliss I felt when I saw his name on my screen. I answered before I could decide just how horrible of a person I really was for even having a momentary, very tiny crush on my best friend, and far more importantly, my husband's best friend.

"Wow, Cap's calling me? You're not still frozen, are you?"

"Come on, we watched that movie together. SHIELD rescued him. He was asleep, not frozen. Nick Fury said so."

"That's right. Please tell me this isn't really a costume party."

"It's not. I just called to hear you laugh." The confession seemed to slip out without his permission.

My mind instantly conjured a tale about him having a teeny-tiny crush on me as well. I mentally called myself an idiot and refused to let that idea take hold. If I didn't get a grip, I'd be doodling his name on my notebooks next.

"Uh..." he cleared his throat, "I'm just wearing a suit. No big deal. I swear we'll go do something fun as soon as I piss off a few people. I'll make this up to you."

"You still haven't told me why you're so certain this thing at the winery is going to be awful."

"Being with you will be great."

I was fairly certain someone lit a sparkler in my chest. My teeth sank into my lip, and I fought not to applaud. Glee danced under the light of that sparkler.

He cleared his throat again. In all of the time I'd known T, I couldn't recall him ever doing that before. "Uh, hey, listen, I need to talk with Smith about... something. I'll explain everything on our way tonight."

"Okay, I'll figure out what to wear."

"Wear that dark red dress you have. You know, the one with the black lace on it. You look *so* sexy in that."

My mouth hung open. Thoughts failed to form in my brain. My lungs forgot how to function. For a moment, I was certain the Nebraskan winds themselves resided in my body. I didn't quite exist on the ground. I was ready to fly. For the second time in my life, I was utterly breathless. "O...kay," I managed. "That's my favorite." Did he know that? Had I told him that? Is that why he wanted me to wear it? Was he just being nice?

"Talk to you later." He ended the call much too quickly.

Whatever was happening in my body right then, I didn't recognize the sensations. It wasn't something I'd ever felt before. Chris had never in all of the years we'd been together ever requested that I wear anything in particular.

Foreign sensations continued to wiggle under my skin. Sexy. He'd said I looked sexy. Not great or good or pretty. He'd definitely said the word sexy.

Chris had died so soon after Olivia's birth, I'd managed to trade in my own femininity and cling only to my new role as a mom. With one dress request and a compliment, T had rushed a part of myself I'd thought long forgotten back to center stage. Captain America might have only been asleep, but I'd been frozen. And the one man who seemed able to melt through the layers of ice I'd submerged myself in was the one man I could not ever have and should not ever want.

Anxious anticipation ignited every nerve ending I possessed. I wanted to dress up for him. A rush of wet heat formed between my legs when I thought of how badly I wanted to please him. I wanted him to tell me I was sexy again. More than anything, I wanted to be sexy for him, wanted to feel the heat of lust sizzle between us, wanted to see the look on his face when he said something like that to me. Shaking my head, I pushed the phone away and stood.

It's just a stupid crush, and he certainly hadn't meant anything by that comment. The way he meant it *sexy* could just have easily been *nice*. My mind had confused our friendship because of that dream I'd had. It was some silly schoolgirl thing. Maybe if your husband dies and you force yourself to only be a mom, you have to go through all of the awkward teen years of dating before you can move on or something.

He was my best friend and nothing more.

There were too many hours between that moment and the time when T would pick me up. I needed something to do, something to occupy my mind. I had to stop replaying him telling me how sexy I looked in my favorite dress over and over in my head. Olivia was seated at the kitchen table practicing cutting with her safety scissors. I retrieved the vacuum from the hall closet.

"I want to bac-uum!" She bolted out of her booster seat. Of course, she did. "I'll help!"

"Okay," I agreed because that's what good mothers should do, right? "We're just doing the stairs up to the room over the garage though." I hoped she'd change her mind. Instead, she grabbed the cord and dragged the vacuum to the steps like it was a pet on a leash. "Careful. Don't break it."

"I won't. I'm a very good helper."

It took entirely too long for me to wedge that child safety thing out of the outlet. I tore one of my already ragged nails in the process. I attempted to suck away the pain while I shoved the plug in and switched on the vacuum. Olivia ducked under the cord and under my feet. Only moms know how to perform feats of balance while vacuuming with four-year-olds.

Pulling the hose from the side, I handed it to Olivia and tried to guide her into vacuuming the dusty edges of the stairs.

"I'm doing it!" she announced over the roar of the vacuum.

"You're doing great." My monotone response and lack of eye contact wasn't sufficient for my girl.

"Mommy, watch me," she urged.

I was trying. I swear. T's comment continued to turn over and over in my mind along with the way his hands on my thighs had felt so real that morning.

I had to get it together before he arrived. I resurrected the well of shame I had at my ready access. That was the most efficient way to drown out this ridiculous crush. I forced myself to imagine telling Chris I had some kind of thing for T-Byrd. He likely would've laughed at me outright. He'd never been the jealous type, but that would definitely be unexpected. Then he would've reminded me why he'd always be the only man for me. Even if he couldn't remind me anymore, we were an entity I had no desire to forget or to erase.

"Careful, baby girl." I leaned in to keep her from falling down the three steps she'd gone up when her toes caught in the cord as she leaned. At that moment, she turned back, tripped, and the vacuum slammed against the bottom step. The hose went flying. I managed to catch it and her just as the sucker part landed squarely on my boob. There was a dust ring on my shirt surrounding my nipple. Wasn't that appropriate? My vag was probably dusty as well. Hell, there were probably a few cobwebs up there.

Managing to loosen the hose currently sucking my nipple, I untangled Olivia and shut down the vacuum. "I think that's enough vacuuming for today." I sank down on a step and tried to wipe away the dust from my shirt. The most action I'd seen in almost five long years was from a Hoover, and that was obviously the explanation I'd been searching for about my feelings for T. I wasn't screwing up my relationship with him because I was horny. How incredibly lame was it that I didn't even recognize this for what it was until I got sucked by a vacuum? Dear God. Maybe I should get a new vibrator or something or at least remember to get batteries for the one I had.

Before I could restore the vacuum to the closet, the house phone rang. Everyone I knew always called my cell phone. Caller ID read

Unknown. Probably one of those spam recordings from Heather or Rachel from account services. I answered anyway, that desperate to burn time.

I swore I could hear someone breathing, but no one spoke. "Hello?" I answered louder the second time. A garbled crackle sounded in my ear and the distant sound of someone speaking. "I'm sorry, what?" Whoever it was hung up. Rolling my eyes, I slammed the phone down. I should just get the stupid thing removed. I'd been meaning to.

My cell phone rang next, and I layered another dose of guilt on top of the shame I was determined to keep in my gut when I prayed it was T calling back. It wasn't him. It was Jenn. Just as well.

"I cannot believe you set me up with that idiot," was my greeting.

"I take it your date with Steve did not go well." She sounded far too knowing.

"He brought his mother with him, and then spent the better part of an hour explaining his plants' feeding schedules to me."

"Well, don't blame me. You picked him."

Gall knotted my stomach and twisted. "What do you mean I picked him? You set me up. That was this whole ridiculous bet you cooked up."

"I did not pick him for you. I gave you a choice of three guys and you chose Steve. I even told you he was about as thrilling as unsalted oatmeal. Now, can we finally delve into *why* you picked Steve?"

I ground my teeth. I was not delving into anything with Jenn. Did she really think Steve was a good match for me? She'd taught with me for years. Insulted didn't even begin to cover it. "I don't have time to be psychoanalyzed right now. I have to get ready for my date."

"Ooh, do tell. Are you going back out with that gym guy Bianca set you up with?"

"Dear God, no. For an accountant who claims to spend six hours a day in a gym his arms were skinnier than mine."

Jenn clicked her tongue. "I will point out once again that you also chose accountant gym rat."

"I have to go."

"Not until you tell me who this date is with."

"It's with... a friend. A good friend." For some nonsensical reason, I just keep talking. "Who is incredibly sexy, and sweet, and kind, and would never bring his mother on a date and also, spends a reasonable amount of time working out but could still be on the cover of one of those Men's Health magazines, so there."

"So, you're finally going out with T-Byrd, I take it?" Her tone bordered on smug.

"What do you mean by that?"

"Oh, I am so not jinxing this by going over all of the reasons we all knew this was coming. I'm just going to say - my work here is done. I'm so freaking proud of you. Have fun tonight. You're right. He is sexy as hell and the kind of guy who deserves you."

"But it's not really a..."

"La, la, la, la, la. Not listening to you tell me this isn't a real date. Nope. I'm ending the call now."

"But Jenn, it's just a favor for him."

Call Ended flashed on my screen.

8

T-BYRD

Hotfooting it across the hall to Smith's office, I ground my teeth but then went on with what I'd come to do. "If I asked you to, would you hit me in the face hard enough to knock me out?" Or knock some sense into me, which was really what I needed.

Smith leaned around his massive bank of computer monitors and gave me two long blinks. "You okay, man?"

I was most certainly not okay. I'd just instructed Maddie Mitchell on which dress I'd like her to wear for me and then informed her that she was sexy in said dress. Fuck me, without lube. I deserved that.

"Is this about the SEALs that were just here? You don't have to hire them." Smith continued on unaware of just how dire this situation was.

Griff ducked inside the office as well. "Thank God. Tell me you're not hiring those pricks. I'm sure they look damned cute in their little sailor suits but come on. If you string them on long enough, I bet you can even get them to cough up their G-Shock watch dealer, but we do not need sea urchins. And what was that bullshit about them leading the raid in Somalia and that safe house in Mogadishu? If there was a safe house out there, we sure as hell didn't know about it."

Griff's bitching ignited my already ragged nerves. "What the fuck is with you and us hiring new people? We have more work than we can do. I want the best of the best. They told us they did that shit because they actually did it. And, of course we didn't know about the safe house. It was a navy safe house. We weren't there to rescue the prisoners. We were there to kill the people who'd ordered them captured, which we did."

"Am I the only one that remembers Kandahar? Seems to me you had plenty to say about the squids that took over our camp."

I should've known that was coming. Dammit, I was so fucking unnerved by my non-date that night I was losing my edge. "Different team. Different time, Griff."

"If it looks like a SEAL and swims like a SEAL, T," he came right back.

"We cannot keep going on every mission we're asked to take. We need some help."

"That was our war. We were there for months before the navy even knew how to spell Afghanistan. But who gets credit for the whole fucking thing? They do."

"Is that it? You want credit. You want some film crew to come in and make a documentary about you and your butt-hurt? They never would've been able to do what they did there if it wasn't for us. Why can't that be enough?"

"It is enough. I just need to make sure before they get their snorkels rammed too far up my ass that they remember who handed them Kabul and Kandahar. Because if they're gonna need someone to toss them a fish whenever they perform tricks, they should get a gig at Sea World."

"Would you like me to explicitly state that in their contract?" I sneered.

Griff's eyes lit with vengeance. "Yeah, I think I would, actually. You might also want to make sure they won't be needing a line item budget for teeth whitener and Gatorz sunglasses."

"You hired Mathis," I raged like a child. I already knew why Mathis was okay and the SEALs were not.

"He's a Ranger."

"Right. I forgot. Army only, right? Because that's how we should run a security firm. Who the hell cares if they're stellar at search and rescue? If they didn't wear a beret, they're worthless."

Voodoo, our own personal medic, with a side of supreme badass, joined us. "Jesus, would you two shut it? Griff, man, you have got to work on your playing-nice-with-other-branches-of-the-military thing. Did you piss Hannah off or something? She make you remove your head from its permanent location between her thighs? Buy her some chocolate. She'll let you back down there."

"My sister," Smith growled. "Can you fuck-offs please remember he is married to my sister?"

Voodoo cringed. "Sorry, man, didn't know that was still a sticking point."

Smith gave him a huff and flipped him off, so he was forgiven.

Voodoo turned on me. "T, what the hell crawled up your ass and lit? You look like shit, by the way."

"Nothing. I'm... fine. Just didn't sleep last night and... I'm hiring the SEALs."

Griff rolled his eyes. I stomped back to my own office. Of course, my entire team followed me. Damn them.

"Am I still babysitting tonight?" Griff asked in a calmer tone.

"Yes."

"You gonna tell me why you wanted me to beat the piss out of you?" Smith inquired.

"No."

I saw the concerned glances shared between them. I didn't care. I had to figure this shit out on my own. "There's a team getting out of MARSOC coming in to interview next week. I should get to talk to one of them at this thing tonight." Stick to work. That was safe.

"Great. Marine Special Forces. Wouldn't want all aquatic life not to be equally represented at Tier Seven," Griff huffed under his breath. I bit my tongue to keep from going after him again. That was decidedly not the way we worked. I'd willingly die for these bastards, even when they were being brats.

"Wait, who are you babysitting tonight?" Voodoo had retrieved a yogurt cup from the fridge and made his return. If Griff wanted to know why we had to hire more people, he should take a look at what it cost to supply snacks for our favorite medic.

"Olivia. Hannah's over the moon about it. She wants to tie-dye with her or something. She's out buying supplies." Just like always, as soon as he thought about his new wife, Griff Haywood was all smiles again. Lucky bastard.

"And you asked T about keeping Olivia because...?"

I was waiting on this. I'd brushed it off with Griff that morning when I'd asked him to babysit, but I had to keep up my game now. If I could make the men who knew me better than they knew the backs of their own hands believe this was just a friendly favor from Maddie, I had a half-decent chance of acting like I wasn't losing my fucking mind when I was with her. "Maddie's going with me to the Coldwell Harding thing tonight." I added a noncommittal shrug for effect. "I needed a date. She said she wouldn't mind." Stop talking, I ordered myself. We'd spent years learning how to find the single lie in a pile of truths. It was always the lies that would get you and your team killed. They knew my tells. They knew every single thing about me. If I fucked this up, there was no out. I was done for. The less I said, the better.

Another quick glance shot around the room. Griff was... grinning. What the hell was that about? Smith managed a nod, but he was trying to conceal a grin as well. What the fuck were they up to?

Voodoo shoved another spoonful of yogurt in his mouth. He smiled around the damned spoon. My God. When he swallowed, he'd regained his composure. "You still thinking Maidlow's gonna make a fool of himself at this thing?"

"He does so at any available opportunity. Can't see him missing a chance tonight, but I'm taking Maddie to Duffy's afterward. Taking Back June is playing. Hopefully, that'll make up for the shit part of our evening." That was decidedly too much information. They stopped even trying to conceal their stupid grins now.

What the hell were their smiles supposed to mean? That they

were okay with me doing whatever I was or was not doing with Maddie? Hello, she used to be our CO's wife. This was the textbook definition of not okay.

Sinking down into my chair, I propped my elbows on my desk and rubbed my hands over my face, wishing I could scrub the erotic images of Maddie from my mind.

When the hell had I decided not to shave? Oh yeah, when I took the extra few minutes to jack off in the shower again that morning.

"Maddie's favorite band. That's cool." Voodoo continued to shovel yogurt into his face.

Smith nodded. "Yeah, she'll have fun. She never gets a break. It's cool you're doing that." He was weighing something in his mind. I knew his tells as well. There was a whole lot he wasn't saying.

"Can you all go find something to do? I need to make a phone call."

"To... Maddie?" Voodoo drew out her name into a dozen syllables like we were all eight and hanging from the monkey bars on the playground.

"No, asswipe. What the fuck is wrong with you all? I need to call the State Department about Ambassador Brido's visit. You know, the one we're providing back up security for in a few weeks or did you all forget that?"

That earned me three sets of eye rolls.

Griff shook his head. "Nah, T, we didn't forget. Call the DOS. We got shit to do." When he shoved Smith and Voodoo out of my office, I officially forgave him for thinking the army was better than any other branch of service. Besides, I didn't necessarily disagree.

9

MADDIE

"Dear God, is that a ...?" I leaned closer to the mirror. The lipstick I'd planned to smear on my lips was propped in my fingers. My mouth dropped open, but it was still there — a tiny wrinkle at the top of my lip on the left side. I tapped it a few times like that would somehow make it disappear. Where had that come from? Wasn't I too young for wrinkles? Why hadn't I listened to that girl at Sephora when she insisted I needed anti-aging moisturizer? I pushed my tongue hard against my upper lip trying to press the slight wrinkle back out of my skin. No dice.

Vowing to myself that I'd somehow find time to go see my dermatologist in the next year, I stepped back and inventoried the rest of myself in case some other bizarre thing had happened to my body while I wasn't paying attention. Despite the wrinkle, I grinned, which did make it go away temporarily at least. The dress showed off all of my best features. The push-up bra wasn't hurting things either. I looked... nice. Not *sexy* no matter what T had said. Just nice and that was all I needed because this was nothing more than a night out with a great friend. I gave myself a single nod like that would make any of that crap the truth.

"Maddie? You ready?" T's voice jolted through me. Can't be a date if the man taking you out already has a key to your house and always lets himself in, I reminded myself.

"Just a sec," I called and then made quick work of the lipstick that perfectly matched the crimson dress. Okay, maybe I looked a little bit sexy... but only a little.

I made it into the living room just in time to hear Olivia explain to Griff that T and I were going on a mo-rantic date.

Griff and Hannah were both trying to hide their laughter.

Ho-ly wow. If someone had taken raw, unfiltered masculinity, stirred in sex appeal, added a shot of rugged good looks, and poured it in an expensive suit they would have recreated T at that moment. My eyes slowly trekked upwards to his face.

Disappointment stabbed through me. He looked horrified at Olivia's announcement. That's what I got for having this stupid crush. In fact, that's what I deserved. He, obviously, would never want to date me. I already knew that.

But then he lifted his head. His mouth opened a half notch, and the horror washed from his features. It was replaced with something far more pleasant. Something that brought the breath back to my lungs and tamped down the shame spiraling through me. Awe, maybe? I wasn't sure, and he didn't speak. I watched his Adam's apple contract with a harsh swallow as he took two steps towards me but then halted. His gaze held a distinctive edge of hunger. I was locked in the force of his contemplative eyes, unable to look away.

Closing my own eyes to break the connection, I forced a deep breath. His masculine wood-fire scent filled my lungs. God help me. "Olivia, we're not going on a date." I didn't sound any more certain when I spoke out loud than I did in my own head.

"But you told the phone that you were going on a date, and you said sexy and then you said sweet."

If someone had taken a branding iron to my face, my cheeks could not possibly have burned any hotter. I was apparently old enough to get wrinkles but also still young enough to blush. Great.

"Uh..." I shook my head but I didn't have a leg to stand on, and I knew it. I had said those things. If I denied it, I would be lying to my child. My head continued to shake back and forth. My mouth hung open stupidly, but I produced no words that could undo what had just happened.

"Well... you two have such a good time," Hannah came to my rescue. "We're going to tie-dye everyone T-shirts and then make Uncle Griff order us lots of pizza," she informed Olivia.

The few brain cells that hadn't died in the raging fire of pure embarrassment blazing through me conjured visions of my four-year-old with unfettered access to fabric dye. I could see the carpet and walls of my home marked with permanent handprints right at Olivia's height. "Please, please be careful with the dyes. Maybe do it in the driveway."

"You got it." Hannah laughed.

"Thank you both for keeping her. Remember, she has to wear her patch for three hours before bed, and you have my cell number if you need it. My parents' and Chris's parents' numbers are on the white-board on the fridge, along with her pediatrician's and her pediatric oncologist's."

"Hey, we got this, right, Short Stuff?" Griff extended his arms to Olivia who propelled herself to him.

"My name is not Short Stuff," she sassed.

"Are you sure?" Griff continued to tease her.

"I'm sure." She giggled.

"We'll take excellent care of her, Maddie. I promise," Hannah vowed.

"Right. I know. Just... a little off, I guess. Have fun, Liv. I'll come kiss you when I get home but you should already be asleep, okay?"

She nodded. "Uncle T, will you come kiss me, too?"

T grinned and tickled her side, making her wiggle in Griff's arms. "You got it, Short Stuff."

He ushered me out the door while Olivia proceeded to dramatically inform everyone that her name was Olivia Ruth Mitchell.

Since melting into the driveway didn't seem to be happening no matter how badly I wished for it to occur, I summoned courage and glanced up at T as he opened the door of his brand-new, fancy Corvette for me. "T, I didn't mean to say... I mean I didn't say... well I did say that, but I didn't mean it like that. Not that you're not sexy. You are. I mean you're completely gorgeous. I was just talking to Jenn, and I didn't know Olivia was listening. That isn't exactly what I..." My brain finally located some form of self-preservation and sealed my lips shut.

A distinctive smirk formed on his features. His incredibly good-looking, angular, ruggedly handsome features. *My God, Maddie. Stop it!*

"Hold that thought for a half second for me," was his instruction as he closed the car door. True to his word, he slid into the driver's seat a half second later. Another harsh swallow contracted his neck. I really needed him to stop doing that. Did I ever think Chris's neck was sexy? I couldn't recall ever having that thought. "You look absolutely, devastatingly beautiful tonight, so if you think I look kinda all right in a suit, that works, right?" And my Green Beret swept in and rescued me, just like he always did, just like he always would.

I grinned. My heart performed that high-flying kick routine once again. "Yeah. That works." *Not* a date. Not. A. Date. Not *a* date. No matter how I said it my brain refused to believe it. This was bad. Very, very, very bad. "And, you look more than kind of all right in a suit." I spoke to the floorboard. "You look amazing."

"You think?" He cranked the car, but I didn't miss the broad grin spreading across his face. I leaned towards him stupidly when he propped his hand on the back of my seat to check the rear windshield. The fresh scent of his aftershave teased at my nostrils.

"Definitely."

"Then let's go show up everyone else at this winery since we have decided that we look sexy tonight."

The event. Yes! We could talk about that and forget all of this extremely awkward, incredibly weird discussion of how we look.

"Tell me why you think I'm going to hate this." There. That was a decent question.

"You sure you want to hear this? It involves a major fuck-up on my part." Regret rode hard in his warning.

My heart fissured. I wanted to help him fix whatever it was he thought he'd screwed up. "Chris used to say you were a better soldier than he was. I doubt you messed anything up that badly."

10

T-BYRD

If I'd been half the soldier Chris had been, he'd be sitting here with Maddie looking good enough to eat off a silver platter instead of me. She shifted and the skirt portion of that dress hiked upwards. I gripped the steering wheel hard enough to leave the indentations of my fingers in the leather. Images of my hands sliding up that skirt and easing her panties to the side filled my mind. The desire to smooth my fingertips over her soft skin ignited deep within me.

Maidlow. Tell her about Maidlow. That's what she asked. "All right, this is kinda long so if you get bored tell me to shut up."

"You are probably the least boring person I know. Tell me the story."

Interesting. So far, I'd learned that she thought I was sexy and sweet. Now, I was decidedly not boring. Bet if I showed her exactly what I'd like to be doing with her, she'd redact that sweet moniker.

The craving that had centered in my chest the moment she walked into the room spiked hard, robbing me of breath.

I cleared my throat and popped a nonexistent crick out of my neck. Nothing helped. The air vents shot her floral, honeyed scent directly to my nostrils. My mouth watered. *Bet she tastes even better.*

Same sweet confection with a shot of musky spice. I sank my teeth into the side of my mouth praying the pain would rid me of my current line of thought.

"T?" She sounded worried. Shit.

"Sorry. Just..." I glanced her way again. I couldn't help myself. God, why did she have to look so fucking beautiful? The loose waves of her hair danced along her shoulders every time she moved. She had to be wearing one of those bras that enhanced everything because her tits were on ripe display. I longed to rip the damn thing off of her. She didn't need it. I only wanted her soft, silky skin, not foam padding and lace.

"You just what?"

I drove my hand through my hair trying to get my brain to re-engage. "Got distracted. Before I was ever selected for Q training, I was stationed down at Fort Bragg. We had this kid, Hayes. He was from a rough family. Great guy. He'd try ten times harder than any of the rest of them, worked ten times harder, too. Used to tell me he'd do anything I asked as long as I never ordered him to go back home. He had this girlfriend that thought he'd hung the moon just for her. She moved out there with him. They had an apartment somewhere off base. Anyway, a few months went by and she turned up pregnant. He came in my office almost in tears. They couldn't afford a kid on his salary."

Devastation cast those beautiful chocolate-brown eyes staring up at me. "Poor thing." Her voice hung with sadness for this kid she'd never met.

"I felt for him. I really did. He wanted to make something of himself. I talked him into going to Officer Candidate School because he had leadership skills somewhere under all of the shit the world had shoveled on him. I helped him with the paperwork, wrote him a recommendation, everything. He was thrilled when he got in, but two weeks before he was set to leave, we were out doing a training mission. I have no idea how it happened but somehow one of the tactical radios came off a drone he was flying and was destroyed."

"I'm guessing tactical radios that go on drones aren't easy to replace."

"The radio cost more than most people's houses."

"Wow."

"Yeah, and our battalion commander wrote the manual on being a hard ass. I knew he'd block him from accepting his appointment at OCS as a punishment."

"Please tell me he didn't get in trouble and got to go to OCS somehow."

I swore a fist latched onto my heart and tangled my vocal cords. She was so fucking sweet, and I was so fucking screwed.

"I refused to let him lose his appointment, but that meant making a deal with the devil."

Her adorable nose wrinkled. "You didn't tell the commander *you* did it, did you?"

"No, but that might've been better. Instead, I went to talk with the Comm Sergeant, Kyle Maidlow." My disdain for Maidlow dripped heavily into my tone.

"I don't know who he is, but I already don't like him," Maddie vowed.

"You're about to get to meet him. Just don't stand too close. You might fall into his cavernous ego. Maidlow made the record of the radio disappear. Changed the serial number and the log book for me. That was ten years ago, and he is still calling in favors every chance he gets."

Her brow knitted. "So, we're going to this thing tonight as a favor to Maidlow?"

"Kind of. He got out of the army and went to work for Coldwell Harding. He thinks he's developed some great, fantastic new comm unit that's really a piece of shit. He desperately wants Tier Seven to put our seal of approval on it before he pitches it to the Department of Defense. Our name attached would likely make for a massive payout and a sizable order he could retire on. Unless he's made some significant improvements to it in the last six months, that isn't going to happen."

"And that's why you keep saying you're going to piss people off tonight?"

"And why we're going to have a shitty time. But after I infuriate Maidlow, I'm taking you downtown to Duffy's. Ask me why," I urged, desperate to see her smile again.

That got me one of her adorable giggles. My ability to survive that night continued to unravel. Her laughter was going to push me right over the edge. "Okay, why are we going to Duffy's?"

"Because Taking Back June is playing."

Like she'd read the script right out of my head, she gasped, "Oh my gosh! I love them! Are you serious? I didn't even know they were in town. 'Stealing Summer' is my all-time favorite song."

"I was aware. I wanted to take you as soon as I heard they were playing Duffy's, but the Coldwell Harding thing came up. I have to at least pretend to give Maidlow what he wants to keep him from alerting the Department of Defense about what I asked him to do back in the day, and anything else he'd like to pin on me, but this is perfect."

"How are you going to keep him from going to the DOD when you refuse to sign off on the comm system?"

"Maidlow has made a career of blaming anyone he can find for his screw-ups. He'd love to take Tier Seven down several notches even with a bogus story, but you know I always have a plan." I winked at her. Dammit. I was flirting like she was mine to flirt with. But there it was, that beaming grin of hers that sucker punched me every fucking time I earned one. Her declaration that she thought I was sexy banished the few precious fragments of good sense I'd managed to cling to.

"Do I get to know this plan or is it some kind of classified strategy that The Sevens all pinky swore on or something?"

Now, I was the one laughing. Another thread on the rapidly fraying tightrope of sanity I was trying to traverse popped and unraveled. She was just so fucking perfect. "Babe, you know we only pinky swear on the truly important stuff. Maidlow isn't worth shit." Babe? Holy fuck. I just called my best friend's wife *babe*, which is approximately one boot length away from *baby*, the thing I'd been dying to call her for far too long. Because I desperately wanted her to be that for me. I longed to care for her in every possible way. I craved her submission, was frantic to prove to her that I'd provide in ways she'd never even fathomed before, and that I would indulge her every fantasy until I drew tears of pure relief from her eyes.

"I see. So, you don't actually have a plan, but you'll come up with one on the fly, right? Remember, I've known you entirely too long, Master Sergeant."

If she didn't stop attaching the Master portion of my formal title to me, I was going to pull the car over and beg her to let me indulge that side of myself. Willing my brain to remain in the head above my shoulders, I forced a chuckle. "Guilty as charged. He could shade my reputation with the DOD, but he's the one that actually made the record of the radio disappear. If he makes up some shit about Tier Seven, the truth will always out. I just like to stay several steps ahead of him, in case I need to nudge the truth along at any point. He likes to think he has me by the short hairs. I play along so I know what he's up to."

The heat of her gaze blistered my jawline. It was good the car practically drove itself because I couldn't keep my eyes off of her. I turned to meet her stare.

"You are an incredibly impressive guy. I should say this more often, but I don't know what I'd do without you. I never would've survived the last few years without your help. Thanks for taking me tonight. I'm excited to see you in action. I'm hoping I can help." Right then, I died ten thousand brutal, bloody deaths because she leaned across the center console of my Vette and brushed a gentle kiss on my cheek. The kind of kiss that meant nothing to her but fed every single one of the demons running rampant in my soul. The kind of kiss she'd likely never remember, and I would never forget.

11

MADDIE

oly mother of all the saints, I just kissed T! Sirens screeched in my head. Bile seared from my stomach to my throat charring my chest. When I started to wonder what he must have thought of that, my internal thermometer dropped to zero and then shot back to somewhere in the general vicinity of the temperature of the sun. I was going to be sick. What had I just done? He probably thought I'd lost my mind. I hadn't died from the humiliation of my daughter announcing to everyone that I thought he was sexy, so the universe had come back for another attempt.

He called you babe. He's never done that before. Some voice of reason I barely recognized as my own internal tone offered me a lifeline. But *babe* is definitely not any big deal. He probably calls Hannah that on occasion and any other female he cares about who isn't his mother. A kiss, even on the cheek, is a thing, isn't it? Maybe not. It *was* just on his cheek.

"Careful with those, sweetheart. You keep doing that, things could get out of hand." His warning sounded rough, almost panicked, and this time he'd called me sweetheart. I could recall no other time in the years of our friendship that he'd ever used a term of endearment for me. What on earth was happening between us? The only thing I understood in that moment was that things getting out of hand sounded far too intriguing.

Digging my nails into my palms, I ordered myself to put the brakes on whatever this was. We were treading into dangerous territory. Besides, he was just being nice. He'd probably wanted to flat out tell me to stop being odd and never to kiss him again. Instead, he'd come to my rescue just like with Olivia telling him I thought he was sexy. I needed to get a grip, then things could go right back to normal.

He switched on the radio to some classic rock station even though I knew he usually listened to alternative. "Jack and Diane" was playing. I forced a small smile. In reality, I hated that song now. I'd been called Diane more than a few times before my life had gone straight to hell by way of a Major knocking on my front door to inform me Chris wasn't coming home. "Do you think Jack and Diane made it?" fell out of my mouth without my permission.

The tension that had set firmly in his jaw from my ridiculous kiss melted when he turned to look at me. His gaze was tender now, laced with concern. "Did people used to call you and Chris that?" he took a guess and somehow hit the bullseye on the first shot. He also switched the radio to the alternative station.

"How did you know that?"

"I know the look when you're remembering something that hurts you. It kills me. I know you just as well as you know me, remember?"

"Whenever I ask other people that question, they look at me like I'm nuts." Why did he have to be so easy to talk to?

"These the same people that used to compare you two to them?"

I nodded.

"That's because people only ever hear what they want to hear. They'd rather look at you like you're crazy than admit they don't know something. In reality, they don't know if Jack and Diane made it. They like to think they're retired in the Midwest somewhere, sitting in rocking chairs on a front porch, and remembering when."

That was true but I still wanted an answer from him. "So, assuming every answer could be wrong, do you think they made it?"

"You really want me to answer that?" He glanced back my way.

"Yes. I really want to know."

"No, I don't think they made it. I think the Heartland swallowed them whole. Can't really build something that'll stand the test of time in the back seat of a car."

"I don't think they did either." I choked out the words that haunted me.

T reached and squeezed my hand. "You and Chris may have been the quintessential all-American couple, but the song wasn't about you. You know that."

I managed a nod. The permanent knot that formed in my throat when I lost my husband began to expand. My mind searched for some comfort. I couldn't go down this road tonight. I didn't even want to. Almost instinctively, I grasped T's hand, before he could return it to the steering wheel, and held on. An audible breath rushed from his lungs.

In all of my pontificating about "Jack and Diane", I hadn't realized we'd pulled through to the gates of the winery.

"You ready for this?" T drove into a parking place near the entrance.

If whatever was going to happen here tonight would distract me from how badly I wanted to keep holding his hand, I was ready for it. "Yep, and I'm pretty good at breaking things to people gently. I do have to survive thirty parent-teacher conferences every year."

"Well, then I'll just let you tell Maidlow his comm system sucks." He slipped his hand from my grasp. The cold air from the vents pricked at my skin. The absence of his heat and his steady reassurances stung. Attempting to breathe in sanity, I closed my eyes while he made the trip around the car to open my door. *Please do not let me do anything else stupid.*

12

T-BYRD

I'd managed to have one sane conversation with her after that kiss, but I swore I could still feel the lush pressure of her lips on my cheek. My mind offered me numerous plans of how to get to feel that same heat and pressure again, each of them more desperate and ridiculous than the one before.

Easing my hand to the small of her back — because who was I kidding that I'd be able to keep my hands off of her in that dress — I guided her through the entrance doors. The winery had originally been a massive corn field. They'd turned the silos and barns into tasting rooms and event locales.

The barn doors opened out onto a field - where tables constructed of wine casks had been set up. We'd made it approximately ten steps outside before the shit started to pour by way of Marcus Finch. Panic seared from the top of my head to the bottom of my entirely-too-tight dress shoes. What the fuck was he doing here? I knew the CIA had ignored the reports Chris had given them back in the day, but I had no idea Finch was working for Coldwell Harding.

Instinctively, I tucked Maddie closer to me. "Senator from Iowa is heading our way with a guy named Marcus Finch," I spoke through my teeth. "He's a fucker of the highest order, and I need for him not to know your last name."

Her eyes goggled momentarily. "Why?"

"Long story."

"There are senators here?" she matched my tone.

"This is going to be a bigger shitfest than I originally pictured." I offered up a smile and accepted the senator's hand. "Senator Kilroy. How are you this evening, sir?"

"I'm fine, Sergeant Byrd. How are you?"

"I'm well, sir. This is... Madeline, a friend of mine."

Maddie accepted his handshake. "Sir."

He pumped her offered hand as only a good politician can. "Lovely to meet you, Madeline. I missed your last name, dear."

"Mitchell, isn't it?" Marcus Finch spent entirely too long taking visual inventory of Maddie. I'd wanted to scorch the ground he walked on before, but now I wanted to turn him inside out and pull his sac out via his throat. "Have we met before, love, or did I only know your husband?"

Maddie's eyes narrowed. "I don't believe we've ever met."

"Marc, I'm going to go speak to Senator Issacs," Senator Kilroy excused himself. Finch never took his eyes off of Maddie's overly enhanced cleavage. The chances of him surviving the night diminished rapidly.

She eased closer to me. Sweet baby. I held her tighter against me.

"How is Captain Mitchell these days?" Finch sneered. My original plans were not brutal enough for him. He knew Chris had been killed. "Still running around with this loser?" He jabbed his finger into my chest, met a wall of muscle, and stepped back. First wise decision he'd ever made as far as I knew.

"Walk away, Finch," I started but Maddie shook her head.

"Chris passed away several years ago."

"Really? God, count yourself lucky. My divorce was a bitch." Finch gave her another once-over and fucking licked his lips like he was staring at a plate of prime rib. Vomit curled in my gut. "I was out there with Team Seven several times, training them on whatever equipment I was working with at the time. Taking excellent care of our boys, of course. They couldn't have done anything without me, right?" He laughed at his own joke. "I remember when I arrived in the Green Zone, Captain Mitchell told me not to die because his team wasn't carrying me out." He downed another long sip of wine before laughing again.

Maddie's mouth gaped in shock, and I officially arrived at the end of my rope. Releasing her from my grasp, I closed the distance between myself and Finch and kept my voice low and menacing. "You left out part of what Chris told you, fucker. He told you we weren't carrying your ass out because you weren't worth it. He wasn't wrong. Turn around and walk away. You come anywhere near her again, my fists will be the last things you see so if you've planned an open casket funeral you might want to rethink that. And so help me, if I catch you so much as glancing her way, I'll let the good senator know how many of those state-of-the-art comm systems you brought to Iraq and how many you actually delivered. You can tell him how much you made selling our equipment in the Iraqi underground."

Fury lit in his yellow eyes. His nostrils flared. I waited. If he wanted a showdown, I'd be happy to oblige. We'd reported his sorry ass in Iraq. Chris had spent months gathering evidence on him. It hadn't gone anywhere. Guy was like Teflon. Nothing stuck to him. "You're still entirely too close to her," I growled. "Walk away."

"If I were you, T, I'd watch my back. Not everyone appreciates your sanctimony. In fact, we're all weary of you wielding Tier Seven's power and your squeaky-clean reputation over everyone else." He shot Maddie one more lascivious glance just to gall me. "Enjoy fucking your friend's wife. Maybe you're finally figuring out something I've always known - everyone has a price." With that last sucker punch, he slithered away.

"T?" Maddie grasped my arm. "Are you okay?"

Taking care of her was all that mattered. I'd deal with my shit later. "I'm fine. I'm so sorry about... that. Let's just go."

"No. We're not leaving. I'm fine too." Her hands wove around my chest. She folded herself into my arms and squeezed. I was a strong motherfucker. My God, I'd survived things most men didn't even see in their worst nightmares. But Maddie hugging me - I wasn't built to have temptation like that in my arms and not respond. I cradled her head in my right hand and snugged her tighter against me. The flare of my nostrils brought her delicate scent to my lungs. I needed more, so much more. Without thought, I dipped my head and planted a kiss on the top of her soft hair and swayed her against me. If I could just keep her there, safe in my arms, clinging to me, this night might be all right.

My cock stirred anxiously. Holding her against me was no longer an option. Every nerve ending in my body protested when I stepped away from her, like I stripped away a life source. "You sure you're okay staying?"

Honestly, she seemed to be handling this whole thing better than I was.

She nodded. "I'm okay. I promise. I will say, no one has ever told me I was lucky that Chris died so there really is a first time for everything."

"That asshole knows Chris was killed. Trust me, they go way back. I should never have asked you to come. I had no idea he would be here."

"You told me the people who work here are jerks." She gave the mingling guests and tasting tables a quick glance. "But why are there senators at this thing for a weapons dealer?"

"Maidlow and the higher-ups at CH must be awfully certain I'm going to give them the recommendation they want. The senators from Iowa, Nebraska, and South Dakota are here to try to encourage CH to build the factory for the new comm systems in their states. I tried repeatedly to tell them this wasn't going to work. Hell, I got Smith to call Maidlow, even though they've never met, to explain why this was a piece of shit. He can't ever hear any voice but his own." I glanced up just in time. "And here he comes." I gestured towards Maidlow and two of his cohorts making a beeline towards us.

Much to my delight, they were cut off by Senator Whilpor from South Dakota. "Saved by the bell," Maddie whispered. Because my gluttony for punishment was reaching masochistic levels, I offered her my arm. With one of those beautiful grins, she accepted.

"We are at a winery. How about a glass of Chardonnay?" I knew that was her favorite.

"Do I have to spit it out?" She wrinkled her adorable nose. "I feel like my grandmother might come back from the grave to scold me if I ever spit anything into a barrel."

Chuckling at that, I shook my head. "That's only at the tasting tables. We can get glasses over here." I escorted her to one of the counters inside the barn. It worked in my favor that it put distance between myself and Maidlow. He'd find me eventually, but I wasn't above putting off the inevitable. Besides, she was on my arm taking it all in, and I didn't want to do anything to change that.

Finch's final comment seared down my chest along with my sip of the wine. He was right. I had made a name for myself and for my company based on stellar ethics and taking the right path even if it was the hardest fucking one to traverse. Sleeping with my best friend's wife did not qualify as either of those things. I had to find a way to decimate my feelings for Maddie. *Feelings.* There was that word again. Dammit.

She brought the wine glass to her beautiful lips. My own mouth watered. I wanted to taste the wine from her, wanted it to meld with her breath, wanted to sate my tongue with the combination of intoxicating flavors.

"Sergeant Byrd?" came from behind me.

I turned and offered Rio Travers my hand. "How goes it?"

He tugged at his collar. My mood lifted as his deep Alabama accent cut through the pretentious air surrounding us. "Shit's a little fancy, ain't it, sir?"

His dress shirt couldn't quite cover the tats on his arms and his suit coat appeared to be two sizes too small for the sheer amount of muscle he'd packed into it. Clearly, he didn't wear a suit often. "Cut the *sir* crap. This is a friend of mine, Maddie Mitchell. Maddie, this is Gunnery Sergeant Riordian Travers, fresh out of the Marine Raiders."

He offered her his hand. "Just call me Rio, ma'am. Nice to meet you."

She gave him a sweet grin. "You, too. How do you and T know each other?"

Rio glanced up at me awaiting my answer.

"I'm interviewing Rio and a few members of his team next week for Tier Seven. We had lunch together last week."

"Oh," she nodded. "Well, good luck. Word of advice, when you meet Sergeant Haywood, ignore like seventy-five percent of what he says. His bark is much worse than his bite."

"She speaks the truth." I laughed.

"I'll do that. I reckon I need to go make appearances." Rio looked like he'd prefer to be traversing a minefield instead of going to enjoy an evening at a winery. Given who was hosting this event, I couldn't say I disagreed with his assessment.

"Coldwell Harding would like Rio and his team to come work for them," I explained.

Maddie did that cute little nose wrinkle thing again but didn't comment. Rio caught it though and chuckled. "If I'm being real honest, I think I'd much rather work for Tier Seven," he assured her.

"That makes two of us."

Maddie nodded. "Three of us."

"You ought to hang onto her, sir. She has great taste." Rio winked at Maddie, took a deep breath, and eased his way towards the outdoor tables.

13

MADDIE

Whatever Rio decided to do, I hoped he didn't take the job with Coldwell Harding. If Maidlow and that Finch guy were the kinds of people who work for them, he'd be better off employed by a snake den. Plus, I could tell T really wanted him to come to Tier Seven.

At least the wine mellowed me some. My ragged nerves mended ever so slightly. I was still clinging to T's arm, which was far more soothing than the Chardonnay. I had no desire to remove my hands from his body. His protectiveness continued to roll off of him in waves. I wanted to wrap it around myself like a warm blanket. I wish I knew what Finch had said to him before he'd walked away. Whatever it was, T looked like he was going to be sick.

We stepped back out into the cool Nebraskan evening air and Maidlow pounced. I braced for impact. "The man of the hour is here." He slapped his hand into T's and spoke so loudly the entire winery heard him.

"Maidlow." T gave him a single nod. My heart picked up pace. T always had a plan for how to handle every situation. I'd never seen him caught off guard. I had no idea how he intended to handle this, but his stance was battle ready and never wavered. I wish I knew some way to help.

Maidlow spared me a quick glance. "Damn man, you always land the beauties, don't you? Where'd you find her and can you go back and get a few for the rest of us? I'll take two," he bellowed. Dear God. Did these creeps all read from the same playbook?

I watched T's jaw clench ominously, but he said nothing. It took three beats of sinister silence for Maidlow to realize he needed to tone it down. He cleared his throat. "Listen, I've got the paperwork in the office here at the winery. I really appreciate Tier Seven's support on this. The headset will be life changing for military personnel across the board. You know that."

"The only thing I know is that you don't need to get ahead of yourself. You don't have Tier Seven's endorsement yet," T warned. Accustomed to him speaking to me with affectionate tones, I noticed the subtle tinge of fury in his voice. I wondered if everyone could hear the disdain.

Maidlow's uncomfortable laughter filled the air. "Hey, I heard you out. I even listened to your Comm guy. We made improvements. I have a meeting with the Department of Defense next Wednesday to show it off."

T shook his head. "What's the battery life on the thing now?" Apparently, small talk was not a part of his plan.

"We're still working on that, but we'll get it up there."

T set his wine on a nearby cask and rubbed his forehead. "What is it right this minute, Kyle?"

"We had some friends out with it last week. Clocked it at an hour and a half on eight batteries."

T gave him a mirthless laugh. "That's twenty minutes shorter than it was the last time we talked using two more batteries. How the hell did you lose time?"

"We added some new functionality that really sets it apart from our competitors."

"Oh yeah, what's that?"

With a pompous smirk, Kyle leaned in like he was going to share some juicy secret that T should be honored to hear. "This is just between us, of course."

"I'm waiting, Maidlow, and patience is not my strong suit."

"We added Bluetooth capabilities. Just think about it, T. Think of what we can do with that."

For the last ten years, I'd wondered what T-Byrd did if something shocked him. He was always so certain about what to do in every situation. I'd never forget the way he handled all of Olivia's doctors and her treatments after her diagnosis. It never threw him. He conquered it just like he conquered everything else.

At the sound of the word Bluetooth, he chewed the side of his mouth, and his eyes goggled for a split second. Apparently, that was his tell, if that's even what you'd call it. "Tell me you're not that stupid," he snarled.

"What the hell is your problem, Byrd?"

Curious onlookers all eased closer. The clatter of glasses and low gurgled splashes of wine being poured were erased from the air around us. "My problem is that anyone, and I mean anyone, can pick up a Bluetooth signal. You know this. How the fuck do you plan to prevent our enemies from hearing our communications or did that never occur to you? And ninety minutes on eight batteries is bullshit."

"We'll work around that."

"How?" T demanded.

"Think about how great it would've been when we were out in the field if our headsets had been wireless. Life changing, like I said."

"My God, how much did you sell your soul for? More batteries mean more weight. More weight means slower soldiers. Slower soldiers mean people die! Don't you get that? A comm unit with a ninety-minute run time is going to get people killed assuming they aren't killed on arrival because currently, ISIS is running one hell of a digital war, so I'm doubting Bluetooth would throw them. You can wrap bullshit up any way you like. It still stinks."

Maidlow rolled his eyes. "I'll have time to improve it before we ship."

"You're solving a nonexistent problem hoping to make bank from the government. You know it, and I sure as hell know it."

Panic broadcast from Maidlow as he realized everyone at the party was now watching him be dressed down. "Man, come on. Calm down. It'll be tested by the army long before it makes it to the field. We'll work out the kinks." He leaned in closer and spoke under his breath. "I just need a down payment to make the improvements. Come on T, you know you owe me. I'd hate to have to let something slip while I'm in D.C. next week."

I barely breathed. I had a pretty good idea what T would have to say to that. "If you need money, I'd suggest cutting the galas at wineries where they're serving five-hundred-dollar bottles of wine. And stop lining the senators' pockets so they'll get on board. I don't owe you anything. You go on and take your system to the DOD. You tell them anything you want. Let me know how fast they throw you out on your ass, because it'll be a cold day in hell when you get Tier Seven's endorsement on anything."

I'd never seen him quite like this. Never seen him so fierce and dominating. A savage edge formed on his features. I'd always known he was an outstanding soldier. I just hadn't realized what his refusal to accept anything but the best from himself looked like in person.

A rush of heat burned in my cheeks and in points below as my body responded to his ferocity. My mouth flooded with saliva and a rush of wet heat coated my lower lips. I'd had the same reaction when he told off Finch. I'd never seen anyone fight so valiantly for what they knew was right. Not even Chris.

Guilt slammed through me ridding me of the lust I'd experienced a moment before.

But still, T was all hard edges and intensity. I wanted to run my hands over the chiseled planes of his body. I wanted to soothe him the way he always did me. More than anything, I wanted to kiss the anger from his lips. Desperation surged through me. I wanted to give him a place to lay the frustration, a place to exist without threats and soul-crushing greed.

"Think about what you're saying." Maidlow gripped T's forearm.

"I'm sure there are a few skeletons in Tier Seven's closets. I'd hate to go looking."

I gulped down a quick breath afraid to even blink. Outrage flashed in T's eyes.

"Get your hand the fuck off of me or I'll remove it from your body." T's tone was steady. The threat was implicit. He could make good on it, and Maidlow seemed aware of this.

"I need this to work," desperation leaked into his voice. "Do this for me."

"You *need* it, Kyle? That's your argument?" T shook his head. He dropped my hand and stepped in front of me. "What you need is a fucking conscience. Go to hell."

With that, T spun on his heels, took my hand, and made his way to the door.

Before we could make an escape, Maidlow caught up to us. "If you walk on this, we'll make you regret it." The threat hung in the air between them.

T laughed in his face. "I learned to live with regret years ago."

"I'm not talking about the tac radio, T. The DOD won't give a shit about that now. I know more than you think I do. Give me a call tomorrow. We're going ahead with this, and we need Tier Seven's endorsement. I intend to get it one way or another." And then, bizarrely, he threw a pointed glance at me. "Hate for Team Seven to suffer any more than they already have."

14

T-BYRD

I'd kill him. I'd kill all of them. I fucking dared Maidlow to try anything with Maddie. Anything at all and I'd scrub this earth of his miserable existence. He didn't deserve to continue to pollute the world with his breath anyway. Not when he was trying to deliver shit like that to the Department of Defense. Why didn't he just hand out weapons to the Islamic State? That would be equally as lethal as his Bluetooth comm system. My God.

I slammed the car door once I'd made certain Maddie was safely inside.

"We don't have to go to the concert," she offered in a heartbroken whisper. Worry plagued her every breath. I searched her features to try and determine if she was afraid because of Maidlow's ridiculous threat or if she made the offer because she thought I didn't want to go. "You don't seem like you're up for it." There was my answer.

Weighing all my options, I knew Maidlow was about as likely to do something as he was to be able to sell that shit comm unit to the DOD, but the very last thing I was going to do was draw him a map to her house. I wasn't taking her home until I was certain he had no plans to follow me. I also knew I was overreacting. She triggered every protective instinct I had.

In reality, I knew he was full of shit. He was the king of bullshit threats and outright blackmail, on occasion. He knew threats of any kind weren't going to work with me. He just wanted to have the last word. Well, he'd gotten it. Now he could crawl back to his cave to lick his wounds. Having the last word didn't get him my seal of approval on his paperwork, now did it?

The shit that had gone down between Chris and Marcus Finch tightened like a screw in my chest. Finch should have already been burning in hell. Chris had just tried to arrange the trip. Nothing wrong with that.

"I want to go. Plus, a few beers might help me chill the fuck out. I'm sorry. That got uglier than I ever thought it would."

"You were pretty impressive back there." She gestured to the tasting room as I laid on the gas, and then pulled her phone from her purse.

The faster I got her away from the likes of Finch and Maidlow the better we'd all be. She glanced down at the phone and laughed. "Hannah's letting Olivia put makeup on Griff." She showed me the picture.

"Save that. Someday that will come in handy." I drew a deep breath. "Maidlow and Finch both make me sick. What the hell won't they do to fatten their bank accounts?"

"I didn't like the way Maidlow looked at me." She traced her fingertips over my knuckles. "Do you think he'd try to hurt you or someone from Team Seven?"

It wasn't my team I was worried about. They could take care of themselves. It was her I was terrified he'd try to use to get to me.

Her every touch managed to swamp my brain with confusion and enliven my cock. Did she want me to hold her hand again? I needed her to be a little more explicit with her signals.

How was I supposed to explain to her that I needed her to stop being so near to me and yet longed to beg her to come closer? I wanted her so close to me I was physically a part of her. No. Fuck. Wait. *She is Chris's wife,* I repeated in my head.

No, she is Chris's widow. Shoulder-demon was back with more ammunition.

My heart continued to pound in my throat. I kept constant watch in my rearview mirror. No one followed us off of the winery's property. His threat was as hollow as his cock. I knew it and still wanted to burn Coldwell Harding to the ground and piss on the ashes. No one would ever lay a hand on Maddie. Not while I continued to draw breath. "Guess I must've made it pretty obvious how much you mean to me. He's not particularly creative. He thought he could use you to get to me. Bastard."

"You don't need to worry about me. I can take care of myself."

"I will always worry about you. Comes with the territory of caring about you." Even if Chris's last words to me hadn't been an order to take care of his girls, I'd still happily spend the rest of my life making sure his girls were well cared for.

Some semblance of calm had tempered my fury by the time we arrived at Duffy's Bar. The place was rocking. Music spilled out the front door along with patrons coming and going. We'd missed the opening band, but Taking Back June hadn't taken the stage yet.

I wrapped my arm over Maddie's slender shoulders and guided her towards one of the open booths. People were lined up on the dance floor so the tables were open. "Want another glass of wine?" I prayed she would. I didn't want to be the only one drinking, and I sure as hell needed some liquid sanity.

"Sure," she nodded. The neon glow of the bar lights shimmered in her eyes as she took it all in. She likely hadn't been in a bar since long before Chris had died. I needed to get her out more. She relegated herself to the singular role of Olivia's mom. Nothing wrong with that, but there were so many other sides to her I wanted her to explore.

"Be right back." I searched every patron I passed between our table and the bartender. I was certain Maidlow was still back at his gala trying to shove his head up any available senator's ass, but with Maddie, I was taking no chances.

Instead of men out to use her to get to me, the bar was loaded with assholes who'd all made note of her appearance. She was on the receiving end of the visual appreciation of at least a dozen men. I shot predatory glares to them all. *She's mine.* Most of them tucked back into the darkened corners of the bar, intimidated and weak. They had no idea she wasn't really mine, and she wouldn't ever be. I was not that guy. I would not give in. I wasn't weak.

"Yeah, a glass of your best Chardonnay and a double bourbon straight up," I ordered as I approached the bartender.

"You got it."

When I returned to the table with our drinks, Maddie beamed up at me. My heart triple-timed its normal rate. I corrected my last thought. I wasn't weak... except when it came to her.

"Do you have any idea how long it's been since I've been to a concert or a bar for that matter? I think it was before I was married. I don't even remember the last time, honestly."

"We need to put a stop to that nonsense. You know The Sevens are up for babysitting anytime you want to get out." Could she hear the hunger running rampant in my tone? Did she have any idea what her sweet smiles and those curious eyes were doing to me?

"I know. It's just," she shrugged, "I never really think about going. Oh, I do remember the last time. I took Olivia to the Disney Jr. Dance Party concert last year." Another one of her intoxicating rounds of laughter made its way to my ears.

"That's just... sad," I teased her.

"I know. I had to dance with Catboy from *PJ Masks* on stage. I spent most of my adolescence praying I'd get pulled up on stage at a New Kids' concert, but instead of Joey McIntyre, I had to dance with a guy who wears cat ears. Seriously, he kept tripping on his own tail."

I shook my head at her. God, she was adorable. I had no idea who Catboy was, but I instantly hated him for getting to dance with her. "I'm making it my personal responsibility to make certain the last person you danced with is not someone who spends an unhealthy amount of time with toddlers."

"Aww, is that your extremely lame attempt at asking me to dance?"

Hell yeah, it was. No. Fuck. I didn't know what it was, but words continued to spew forth from my mouth. "As soon as I finish this," I lifted the tumbler of bourbon, "I'm spinning you around the dance floor, Ms. Mitchell."

"Wow, I've never been on a date where the guy spent an hour telling people off, tried to hire someone for his company, then took me out for drinks and dancing. Dates with you are the most fun I've had in years." She laughed.

Dates. She'd said it. Not me. That's what this was, wasn't it? She'd needed a third date for her bet. I'd offered up myself. And here we were. My resolve slipped several notches and my control followed suit.

She drew a long sip of her wine. I watched the tender skin at her throat contract. Right there, at the hollow on the right side, I longed to suck, to devour.

She continued to study the bar surrounding her like she needed to memorize the experience because she wasn't sure she'd get to have another one.

The slow burn of the bourbon ignited the fiery need expanding in my chest, choking out all other emotions. I leaned closer, needing more of her in any way I could get it. She followed suit. Interesting.

Her teeth sank into her bottom lip as she stared up at me. That's when I saw it. The glowing embers of need right there in her eyes. A hunger that required satisfaction. An indulgence she wasn't certain she was allowed to have. If she wanted that lip bitten, I was more than happy to indulge her, and that would just be the beginning. The things I could teach her tallied in my mind. The way I could make her feel took station in my chest. Thoughts of her sweet little body locked down tight around me surged to my cock.

"Miss Mitchell?"

The appearance of some asswipe at our table shattered the moment between us. This guy had the gall to stand there and speak to her. I turned a hate-fueled glare his direction, but Maddie smiled.

"Oh... uh..." A few quick breaths lifted her breasts, in that ridiculous bra, and drew a map for the asswipe's eyes to her cleavage. "Mr. Kinnick, how's Reese doing?"

Kinnick chuckled. "He's great. Looking forward to third grade. He still talks about you all the time, though. You were his favorite."

Ass kisser. I ground my teeth.

"You're sweet. Reese is a great kid. I enjoyed having him in my class."

"Thanks. Last year was hard on him with the divorce. I really appreciate you being there for him."

Okay, dude, we get it. You're single now. Life sucks and then you die. Move on. I'd officially reached stab-a-motherfucker levels of jealous. Trying to shake off the possessiveness I had no right to feel, I downed most of the bourbon left in my glass.

"Mr. Kinnick, this is a friend of mine, Sergeant Thomas Byrd," Maddie made introductions.

Kinnick nodded, "Nice to meet you."

I begrudgingly shook his hand.

He spared me a split second of his time before he was back in Maddie's face. "Hey, since we're both just out with friends, would you like to dance?"

A storm of rage whipped through me. Who the hell did he think he was? *She's mine.* I gripped the table to keep from beating my fury into his face. My jaw locked tight.

I didn't get to have a say. We were just friends. Indignation roared in my chest. I had no choice but to call it what it was – jealousy, once again, gripped my throat.

Her eyes flickered to mine. Green Berets, the most lethal fighters on the planet, spend years learning to read people. There is no movement I do not notice. A single blink, the smallest sigh, the quick motion of your hand from your shoulder to your face, I register them all. I know what they mean. I understand what's being communicated better than the person who's actually talking. And there, in her eyes, was my redemption call. Her discreet head shake was unnecessary. I didn't require the two millimeters of movement her head made. Her eyes told me everything I needed to know.

She wanted him to go away. She did not want to dance with this fucker who thought he had some claim to her because she'd taught his kid. The honeyed specks in her dark-caramel eyes that had been sparkling moments before had disappeared, chased away by annoyance.

I am aware of my tendency to blur the lines between warrior and savior. I've accepted this about myself. I can't and, more importantly, I won't change who I am. After all, a savior is nothing more than the warrior who wins, isn't he?

"We were just about to dance and... we are not *just* friends. If you'll excuse us." I towered over Kinnick as I stood. Most men with more than three functional brain cells will take a step back when confronted with a Special Forces soldier. He clearly possessed a healthy set of synapses since he scooted away from the table like he was being paid to move.

I offered Maddie my hand. Her brow furrowed. Relief and confusion fought for placement in her gaze as she stared me down. That was better than annoyance. When she placed her hand in my own, I swore the connection point shot from my palm straight to my chest and lodged there, dangerously close to my heart.

15

MADDIE

It's rare for a child who grows up in Nebraska not to know how to ice skate. When I was ten, my father decided I had to get over my fear and learn. He tied my feet into a pair of skates, and set me on the ice. I slipped and slid along for months of lessons, careening into walls and being slapped with the hard sheet of ice every time I tried. My father was patient. One day, he convinced me to let go of the rail. With several cautious motions, knees bent, skates moving the same direction, I managed to skate to him in the center of the rink.

It was that very same few seconds of adrenaline and determination that shot through me when T offered me his hand. The steady hands that would always keep me from falling were right in front of me. All I had to do was let go of the rail. Isn't this exactly what I'd wanted all night long? Isn't this why I hadn't wanted to dance with Reese Kinnick's father? Isn't this what that dream was all about?

I took T's hand and let him lead me out to the dance floor as Taking Back June mounted the stage. He'd just told Mr. Kinnick that we were more than friends. He couldn't possibly have meant that. He'd only said it to make him go away. This was a dance and nothing more.

I could never have this thing, with T, that I wanted more than I wanted to draw my next breath. He meant too much to Olivia. He meant too much to me. I couldn't lose him, and that's ultimately what would come of this, wasn't it? Wouldn't I always play Diane to Chris Mitchell's Jack? I'd been typecast when I was sixteen years old, and there was no way out. Widows don't get cast as lovers.

T folded me safely in his arms. I clung to him, burying my face against his chest, needing those steady hands to keep me upright. I inhaled his wood-smoke scent. I wanted to drown myself in it, wanted this dress that he clearly preferred to hold evidence of his possession of my body.

"I've got you," he whispered in my ear.

He always did.

I'd spent the majority of my marriage not saying things I'd wished I could say. I never begged Chris not to go again, to stop constantly volunteering his team for missions, to find some way to be as happy at home as he was in the field. I knew how to bottle up my feelings and put them on a shelf. That's what I was going to have to do now. Put them away and not think about them.

But with every sway of our bodies back and forth to the beat, my ability to lock away my own desires slipped further from my grasp. I couldn't seem to access my better judgement. Maybe it was the second glass of wine or the way his heat enveloped me. Perhaps it was the way his hardened, army-earned muscles cradled me so gently when I knew the force he had at his ready access.

I'd known from the moment he'd stepped off of that plane four years ago, both of us battered, crushed, and despondent over all we'd lost, that being held in T's arms was one of the only remedies on Earth that really did make me feel better. From the deluge of pain constantly threatening to drown me that day, I'd prayed I might be able to offer him some comfort as well.

On this night, my hopes were similar. I wanted him to find solace and comfort in me.

My need for him continued to wage war with my better judgement. If it hadn't been winning the battle, I never would've tightened my hold on him. When that didn't satisfy, I would never have caressed my hand against his neck so I could be closer to his skin, to his heat. My hips would never have ground against him with desperate greed.

I never would've heard the unmistakable groan of male hunger in my ear or felt the obvious evidence of his steel-hard arousal press against my belly. I wouldn't have met his moan with my own breathless gasp when his hand tracked to my ass and squeezed like that was the very thing he'd been wanting to do all night long.

For the past four years, I'd been dancing with a ghost. This was so very, very real. The hunger was palpable between us, alive with its own pulse and heat. I lifted my head. His eyes were navy-blue pools of desperation. His single blink a lightning strike of warning. There was no coming back from the road we were barreling down. If I wanted to slam on the brakes, I needed to do it now. His nostrils flared as he attempted breath. I knew that feeling all too well. Once the wind swept into your lungs, there was no going back.

"Say it, baby," his graveled tone held the spiked edges of the pure, driven need that existed in the lack of space between us. "If you want me, say the words."

I had never been on the receiving end of a command from Master Sergeant Thomas T. Byrd and I could recall no other time in my life when I had been more aroused. A frantic ache seared through me. My heart pounded out an SOS but I was too far gone. The only cure for the craving need stared down at me, his own hunger apparent in every movement of his body. I followed my orders. "I want you."

His right hand cradled my face. "You have any fucking clue how long I've wanted to hear you say that?" His lips took possession of my mouth. An embarrassingly loud moan escaped from somewhere deep inside of me.

The kiss wasn't the slightest bit sweet. It was a claim of ownership. A flag in the sand that ordered all others to turn and walk away. It issued ultimatums and demands I was desperate to fulfill. This didn't end here, and for the foreseeable future, however long that was, I belonged to him. That message was broadcast loud and clear.

I parted my lips under the insistence of his questing tongue. He tasted like expensive bourbon and forbidden chocolates, placed on the highest shelf, I wasn't allowed to have. I feasted on him, reveled in his hungry groans, and lost myself in the sanctuary of muscle that surrounded me.

Starved for satisfaction for much too long, the dance floor full of people, the bar, the band, and everything else ceased to exist. The spark of electricity between us ignited and my world caught fire. It burned away everything until there was nothing left but me and T.

16

T-BYRD

Holy fuck, I was kissing Maddie. And I wasn't just kissing her. I was signing a freaking deed to her body.

My God, her body. Her tits were swollen and spilling over the low neckline of that dress. My sweet baby kept grinding that needy little place between her thighs against my cock, so hungry for it she was killing me with every pass. I knew precisely how to make it all better. Jesus fuck, I needed to touch her, to taste her sweet heat, to make her sloppy wet all for me. I needed to own her.

I lifted my head to allow her breath. Her eyes were seeking and her lips bruised from my force. "Please, T. Please, I need..." she panted. Her eyes closed shutting away the desperation locked in their depths. "Please don't stop..."

"Sweetheart, I know precisely what you need. I'm gonna take good care of you. Come with me." As I half dragged her to my car, Kinnick's stunned expression, wrought with jealousy, was another accolade to my high-flying ego.

Keeping my hands off of her was some kind of cruel and unusual punishment, but I managed to open the car door for her and scoot her inside. The half hour it would take to get to my house, strategically hidden away in the endless Nebraskan cornfields, was just too fucking long. Clearly, she was thinking the same thing.

As soon as I flung myself into the driver's seat, she was crawling over the center console. God, this had to be some kind of fevered dream. I couldn't be lucky enough for this to be reality.

Her eyes were dark pools of pure hunger lit by the neon lights of the bar. Her honesty in the bar was so raw it was potent. My cock throbbed out its hunger. She continued to chase the breath that eluded her.

We were parked outside the most popular bar in the heart of a college town. No one would think anything of a car with steamed up windows, but I wanted so much more than a quick and dirty session. I needed to lay her out in my bed, to trace my fingers over each and every curve, to suck and nibble and lick the dew from the soft hidden-away places I intended to own. I needed to know which spots made her shiver and which made her moan. I wanted to worship at the altar of her sweet pussy until I'd ruined her thoroughly, until the only recovery was falling fast asleep in my arms. Then I needed to start all over again.

Given the ragged hunger pinned in her eyes, I wondered just how long it had been since anyone had brought her sweet relief. She'd never dated anyone after Chris died. My God, had it really been five years? My own desires could wait. My baby needed some help. It was here that my warrior side and my savior side always united. This was where every single fucked-up thing in this world made sense.

"In my lap, baby doll. Spread your thighs for me. Let me make it feel better." My windows were tinted three shades darker than was legal, perk of working with the Nebraska State PD on occasion. No one would see what was going to belong only to me. "That's it," I urged as she complied. Her thighs split around my waist. The skirt of that dress, that always drove me mad with need, hiked upwards. My cock surged against my zipper like a prisoner at the gates. My blood pounded hot and urgent through my veins.

Letting her desperation drive her, she bucked for me, aligning the wide ridge of my cock with her soaking wet panties. Her tits raked against my chin. Fuck me, this was heaven.

My hands skated up her soft thighs. I brushed my thumbs against her swollen lips restrained behind chaste white cotton. "So wet, honey. Is that all for me?"

A harsh shudder spiked through her. Her eyes closed as I continued to tease with the barest touch, my only answer to her welcoming heat. "Yes." The single word fell from her lips like she was confessing a sin. Sweet baby. I'd show her things there'd be no redemption from.

A low growl of appreciation kicked up from low in my gut. "You should've told me my baby was so needy. I'll always take good care of you."

I centered my knuckles at her slit and pressed. She continued to rock against my hand. On her next pass, her clit rubbed against my index finger, and she erupted in driven hunger, shaking from the effect. It took everything in me not to jerk my pants down low enough to get the job done and impale her on my cock. But it had been years for her, and I owed her so much more than that. "Feels good, doesn't it?" I urged her on. "Feels so good right there."

"Please, T," she whimpered. "More."

My car filled with the perfume of her need. Raw savagery churned through me, but she wasn't even close to being ready for my darker side. No. This was all for her. I'd get mine later. "You sure you're ready for more, honey?" I got a low whimpered hum in response. I'd willingly lay down my own life for her, but selflessness was not something I possessed. Patience, however, I could do.

I ran my fingers under the single scrap of fabric between me and heaven, encountering her drenched curls and delicious heat. I imagined how her pussy would taste against my lips, how she'd smell at the apex of her arousal. Soon, I'd know.

Her tits continued to bounce in my face. She couldn't remain still. She pawed and kneaded at my shoulders like a hungry kitten. Her need fed the demon housed there.

I swept my thumb up to her clit and watched her face contort in ecstasy. Ordering myself to take it easy, which was the very last thing I wanted to do, I hesitantly opened her with one finger. My God, she was so tight. Her sweet pussy latched onto my finger like it was the very thing that would save her. If her hungry little body thought this was good, wait 'til I fed my cock into her hard and fast.

Gently, I added another finger, feeling her stretch to accommodate. Her head shook once, twice, as her body attempted to split the pressure into either pain or pleasure. When I hooked my fingers and began to stroke up and down, she stormed and pitched, out of control at the strength of my knowledgeable hands.

"God, yes. Right there." Her teeth sank into her bottom lip and a cocky smirk formed on mine.

"I know, baby. I know it hurts, so empty without me, isn't it?" With the limited space between us, I managed to rotate my thumb over her clit while she rode my fingers hard and fast. She trembled in my arms — fucking trembled all for me.

"Yes. Please. Oh God, more, please, please more."

My own personal demons howled out their victory and licked their chops knowing this was far from over. When her walls tightened further, milking my fingers, and her sweet, sticky honey free-flowed over my knuckles, I damn near lost my mind. I wanted to fuck her so hard she understood that I am the only one who can take away the ache, the pain, the emptiness. Only me.

She stirred every nerve ending I possessed, whipping them into a frenzy. "Grab me," I demanded.

Her hand skated down my chest and traced over the fierce bulge at my zipper line. The heat from her fingers made my cock fucking weep for her. Then she went further, popping the slide on my pants. Her fingers dove behind the elastic of my boxer briefs. Holy fucking hell.

Her palm centered my crown. I'd fucked dozens of nameless, faceless women, and none of them had ever come close to feeling as good as her hands felt on me.

Another shiver quaked through her as she gasped. She stared down at me in shock. My ego insisted it was awe. "Sweet baby, you knew it was there. You've been grinding against it all night, needing more. It's always there hoping you'll beg for it."

She continued to ride my fingers as I pounded them deep inside of her. Her head fell back and her channel began its rhythmic pulses. "God, yes. I need it."

"And you'll get it." I latched my left hand on her ass, kneading her flesh as she rode, giving her room to work. She hesitantly explored the steel ridges and throbbing veins of my cock. My own need pounded against my skull. Her inquisitive little touches only served to incite the craving greed surging in my bloodstream. I needed to be locked down deep in her pussy, needed her to milk the cum from me, needed to soak down her walls until she understood who she belonged to.

She was right there. I could feel her fighting the tidal wave of pleasure that threatened to tear her apart. "Come on, baby. Let me have it. Let me feel you come on my fingers."

Suddenly, she seized. Her jaw locked tight. Her touches ceased. She came in a series of juicy ripples and frantic gasps of breath. She collapsed against me. I kissed and nipped at her neck as I coaxed her through the climax.

I eased my fingers from her gently and cradled her in my arms. A sweet sigh escaped her mouth as she nuzzled against me one moment and then jerked back the next.

This time it wasn't reality that swept her out of my arms right after the session was over. It was realization.

17

MADDIE

What had I done? I stared down at myself straddled over T's lap. My dress hiked up to my waist was evidence enough. I'd thrown myself at him. Chris would never forgive.... Chris wasn't here to forgive me and that meant.... No. I had done something wrong. Hadn't I? The terror that resided in my stomach spread to my limbs. "T... I'm so sorry. I never meant to...." At the very least, I'd just jeopardized our friendship over... this.

He shook his head. "Baby, please never apologize for that. What's... wrong?" His outright confusion was detailed by the red and green neon lights from the bar advertising Duffy's famous drink, the fishbowl. It only served to highlight where I'd done this. Shame gripped my throat. I couldn't breathe. I had to get away from him. Clearly, I couldn't be trusted around him. I had no self-control, and I had to apologize to... someone. Who, I wasn't certain. Olivia. I had to get back to Olivia. I couldn't have anything like this because I had to be both her mother and her father and nothing else.

Just like always, I allowed the fear and the guilt to consume me.

"I'll just Uber home." I dropped my phone twice before I managed to grip the damn thing and open the app.

"No, you won't." He jerked the phone out of my hand. "Talk to me. You're scared. You're freaked out. You never saw this coming. You aren't prepared to deal with this. I pressured you into it. I'm good with most anything but you running from me."

Since I was the one who'd crawled over the console of his car like I was... the next words were severed from my thoughts with a dull blade. I forced myself to complete the thought. I deserved whatever pain it wrought. I'd crawled over his seat just like I used to do when I was sixteen years old, when it was his best friend's lap I was straddling. Oh God, I had to get out of there. Bile and wine churned in my stomach. Regret clogged my throat. I was going to be sick.

Forcing myself to own up to everything we'd just done, I stared him down. "Please give me my phone," my voice shook harder than my heart that was rattling my rib cage. In the years that I'd known him, I'd seen every imaginable emotion displayed in T's eyes. Horror, humor, devastation, delight, and most every single one in between. But it wasn't until that moment that I saw fear.

Some sick part of me was pleased that he was scared, too. I was somehow less alone but wasn't that the root of this entire problem? I'd leaned too hard on him, asked far too much. I had to stop. I could do everything on my own. I'd been doing it on my own since my wedding day.

He handed over the phone. I flung myself out of the car and raced back in the bar. Reese Kinnick's father was still there bearing witness to my shame. Good. I deserved that, too. Racing into the women's restroom in case T came after me, I requested a ride while Taking Back June sang "Stealing Summer."

He was still in the parking lot when I rushed to the Honda Accord charged with taking me home. I'd had no doubt that he would be. I also knew he'd follow me home to make certain I got there safely. He'd always take care of me, and I'd taken complete advantage. I wasn't certain he'd leave even after I'd made my way inside. I had no idea if he'd face up to Griff who would most certainly give me the third degree over me returning without him.

A cold sweat dewed along my hairline. I needed both of them to leave. They had to stop always fussing over me. I wasn't a child.

Griff and Hannah jerked apart on my sofa when I burst through my own front door. The memory of what I'd just done continued to claw at my skin. Watching them make out wasn't helping. "Uh, thanks for watching her," I managed while blinking back another round of tears.

Griff was staring down at me in two quick steps. "Where's T?"

I attempted to swallow down raw regret to no avail. "He's uh... he had to... go." I tried desperately to remember the lessons Chris had given me on how to effectively tell a lie, a necessary skill for anyone in Special Forces. I'd always been terrible at it.

'My God, you are so bad at this,' he'd chuckled at me affectionately. *'Good thing I'd never let anything happen to you.'* The memory seared against my skull forcing the shame to permeate my brain.

Griff eased closer studying my every movement. "Doesn't sound like T." His soothing tone was practiced. I'd heard that very tone a half-dozen times after Chris's death. He used it whenever I broke down in front of him.

I shook my head. "I... don't know." I didn't know anything. I didn't know how I was supposed to feel. I didn't know if what I'd done was okay. I wanted T and... I needed him and... he wasn't here all because I'd been scared.

Hot tears finally tore from my eyes and rolled down my cheeks. I convulsed.

"Oh, Maddie, are you okay?" Hannah handed me a tissue and wrapped her arms around me. "Back off," she mouthed to her husband.

I forced a ragged nod. "Yes. Can you please just go?"

There was a moment of silent communication between her and Griff. "Why don't you go lie down? I'll make you some tea. You can get some sleep, and we'll stay. That way if Olivia needs anything she won't disturb you," Hannah laid out their agreed upon plan that had required no words. Chris and I had never been able to do that. Why?

It didn't matter now. "No. I'm fine. Just... I need you to go."

"Okay." Hannah eased back and directed her husband to the front door. "If you need anything, call me."

"Thank you." I just had to survive the thirty seconds it would take them to leave. Then I could dissolve. Just like when he died, the pain could take everything good in my life and swallow it whole.

18

T-BYRD

"Holy Mother of God, get your sorry ass out of the bed." An angry growl accompanied the searing pain in my head. I blinked in the too-bright light that had been flipped on in my previously darkened bedroom. Two forms I recognized stomped towards me. The larger of the two jerked my blinds open, worsening the light situation. Damn them.

The dull throb at the base of my skull protested when I tried to sit up, and odd, black flecks floated through my vision courtesy of the sheer amount of booze I'd consumed in the last... wait, what day was it?

"Griff?" Shit. My mouth felt like cotton balls had taken up permanent residence on my tongue. Knots had formed along my spine and neck. Every muscle in my body felt confused. Slapping at the bedside table, I managed to land my hand on another glass bottle. It was mostly empty but what was left would rid my mouth of the cobwebs.

"I don't think so." Smith jerked it out of my hand. "Here." He replaced it with a water bottle instead. Some part of me should've been thankful. My liver most likely. "Drink," he ordered.

I downed half the bottle. "Why are you here?" I forced the four words from my mouth as soon as I could speak.

"Oh, I don't know. It's Tuesday. You haven't been to work in four fucking days, and it was high time somebody did something about it," Griff huffed. "Did you really think we were just going to let you drown in your own fucking misery and..." he lifted another few bottles from the bedside table, "an inordinate amount of shit booze? We're a team. Remember that? We did a pledge. Used to wear hat things that looked similar. Any of this sound familiar to you? We're here to save your ass."

"Griff, come on, save the yelling until we've gotten food into him," Smith commanded. "Then we can remind him what a dumbass he's being." With that he used most of his brute strength to shove me from my own bed. God, what was that smell? I cringed. Apparently, it was me.

Griff sighed. "Yeah, we'll shove your ass in the shower right after we force feed you. Now, there's about fifteen steps down to the kitchen. You good or shall I get Smitty to throw you on his back?"

"I got it." Jesus, did he ever shut up? I couldn't be saved. They should've left me to drown. Gone on without me.

When I stumbled on the stairs though, they both caught me and eased me down. Smith shoved me into one of my kitchen chairs, and Griff served up an inordinate amount of delicious fat and protein courtesy of the Hi-Way Diner, our place. As soon as they'd secured a fork in my hand, I recalled that I'd been starving like two days ago. I wasn't sure I'd ever eaten.

When I'd consumed two omelets and most of the bacon and sausage, and a plate full of potatoes, I started to come around. Fully-formed thoughts danced on the periphery of my mind. Thoughts were precisely why I started drinking. Thoughts were not allowed. Thoughts were bullshit. Even if I could've taken Griff to the ground to get to what was left of my liquor cabinet, there was no way I could get by Smith Hagen. I was stuck here with... thoughts. The food I'd consumed threatened to make a rapid reappearance.

"All right, G, let's debrief shall we?" Smith ordered. "Start with what we know."

"Excellent idea." Griff shook his head at me. "Here's what I know.

After our boy finally worked up the cojones to actually ask Maddie out, I arrived to babysit the cutest kid God ever put on this planet, and I'll take anyone to the mat that wants to argue that."

"Agreed. Go on." Smith encouraged. I rolled my eyes. Damn. That hurt. I went back to the biscuits. Carbs were freaking delicious.

"When I arrived, said cutest kid informed me and my fucking gorgeous wife that her mommy thought our T-Byrd here was sexy. I can also assure you that when our main man saw Maddie all dressed up, he very nearly swallowed his own tongue. Interesting, right?"

"Very. What happened next?"

"Well, see, that's where it gets fuzzy. I'm missing intel on what happened the few hours they were gone, but I can tell you that Maddie came home in tears and when I got out to T's fancy-assed new car and stood in front of it until he rolled down the window, he had her lipstick all over his face and shirt."

I wasn't doing this. I wasn't going back there. I stood far too quickly, swayed, and watched my own kitchen swim through my vision. Smith's massive hand landed on my shoulder and shoved me back down in the chair. He hadn't even had to stand to do it. There was no way out. I was trapped by my own team. How fucked up was that?

"Where's Voodoo?" If I couldn't escape, maybe I could evade this line of questioning.

"Nice try," Griff huffed. "You weren't the only one that needed saving, so we had to divide and conquer. Now, back to what happened Friday night."

"Nothing happened."

They could bring out the waterboards. I wasn't having this conversation willingly.

"Bullshit. Let me take a quick stab at what happened." I'd never seen Griff Haywood look quite so determined. "You and Maddie have been dancing around each other like two dogs in heat for months now."

I scowled.

Smith stood long enough to pull a Gatorade from my fridge and grabbed two Ibuprofen tablets from my cabinet. He handed them over. "You, swallow," he instructed me. "You," he ordered his best friend, "find a better analogy."

"Whatever you want to call it, you two have been into each other but refusing to do anything about it for a while now. I'm guessing things went real well Friday night. So well that you got hot and heavy somewhere and then you both freaked the fuck out. That about cover it?"

I said nothing.

"Maybe that was too many questions. Let's start big and work our way down. Did you sleep with Maddie?"

I remained dedicated to my refusal to even grunt. As hungover as I was, sleeping with Maddie still held vast appeal. How fucked up was that? Hadn't I done enough damage?

Smith fished his phone from his pocket. "T, man, don't make us do this to you."

My brow furrowed. What the hell? I rubbed my temples. My head still protested every movement of my face.

Griff sighed. "We tried to be nice."

"What the hell are you talking about?" I finally demanded.

"This." Smith hit a button on his phone and some god-awful Justin Bieber song assaulted my skull. An ax could not possibly have hurt more. Fucker continually turned up the volume until I wanted to weep from the agony. Just as quickly as he'd turned it on he shut it down. "Now. Did you sleep with Maddie?"

I glared at him with all of the hatred free-flowing through my veins and still said nothing.

"T, we're not dropping this. Team Seven does not back away from a problem, especially if one of our own is at stake. You know this. This fuck nugget has an ungodly number of albums. I downloaded them all just for this purpose. Don't make me use them." Genuine concern riffed in Smith's tone.

I considered all of my options. "No," I finally admitted.

"Was that so hard?" Griff asked.

"Fuck the hell off."

"Yeah, I was waiting on you to get there. We're rapidly making improvements. Next question. Did she freak, or did you, or was it more of a mutual 'holy fuck, we just did this' kind of thing?"

Smith pointed back to his phone with an ominous expression.

"She did." I refused to add that she'd only freaked first because I hadn't gotten around to it yet.

"Oh, but he's clearly handling the whole thing well." Smith pointed to a line of beer bottles on my counter and then to liquor bottles scattered around my living room. I'd switched to the hard stuff when I remembered I'd promised Olivia I'd kiss her goodnight and hadn't gotten to.

"Did you try to call her before you decided to trade places with the worm in the tequila bottle, or did you just go straight for the hard stuff?" was Griff's next inquiry.

"I tried to call all fucking night," I admitted, "and also drank."

"I'm thinking it was a mutual freak-out, wouldn't you agree, Smitty?"

Smith rolled his eyes. "That seemed fairly obvious when we found him in bed at noon on a Tuesday."

Griff's head lowered. "Let's get to the shit none of us wants to say but has to be said. I get that you freaked." He returned his earnest gaze to mine. "Hell, we all get why you both freaked. Chris isn't here anymore, but just because something scares you doesn't mean you turn around and walk away. You're the bravest fucker I know, T. Where's this coming from?" This time his question held no traces of taunting sarcasm.

"He would kill me. I'd let him." I dug deep because I couldn't save myself. I needed their help.

"If he were still alive, there's no way you ever would've made a move for Maddie, man. Come on," Smith scoffed.

"He was my best friend."

"Yeah. We know," Griff choked. "We were there from the beginning. You two were like brothers long before we all actually became brothers. But you also know he wouldn't want her to live the rest of her life alone. He'd want her to move on with the best of the best.

He'd march down from heaven if she got involved with some civilian fuck-toy who'd never deserve her. I don't know a better guy than you. I can't think of anyone more deserving of a woman like Maddie. I heard the last thing he said to you on that chopper. I know he asked you to take care of his girls. That is the very thing you've dedicated your life to doing. Of course, she fell for you. You're the only one who could ever have even come close to competing with Chris. You have two options. You can either stand up and be the man she needs you to be, or you can stay here, scared and stupid, while she finds someone else. No other guy will ever take care of her the way you will. Think about that."

No. I couldn't go there. The scent of burning flesh curdled in my nostrils. I refused the memories. I refused to recall his guttural pleas to me to always be there for his girls. This isn't what he meant.

Smith gripped my shoulder, yanking me back from the cliff, grounding me in the present. "We also know Chris isn't the only reason you've been singing an ode to Jack, Jim Beam, and the good Captain." He stood and held up a half-empty bottle of rum.

Griff nodded. "See, you don't get to plan who you fall for. You can't control this. You don't get to come up with a dozen contingencies and map out every possible issue that might head your way when it comes to her, and that's making you nuts." I went back to my silent game. "I'm taking your lack of response as a yes. Think about it. I am a guy with at least minimal intelligence, right? Do you think I really would've fallen for *his* baby sister if I'd gotten to plan it all out? *Look at him.*" Griff gestured to Smith. He did have a point. "It's not up to you. You just get to hold on with both hands for as long as it works. There's no map. There's no compass. No coordinates. Nothing. It's scary as fuck but it's worth it, man. Just trust me on that."

Air evacuated my lungs in a harsh huff. "That's great, Griff, but she's still freaked the fuck out and it's my fault. She won't even talk to me. I don't get to just decide to date her. She does have a say in it. What if she doesn't want to have anything to do with me now?"

"She does," they both vowed simultaneously.

Griff stood and located a Dr. Pepper from my fridge. He downed a sip before continuing this bizarre intervention. "Do you remember what you said to me when I called busting your ass about getting me to Vegas to be with Hannah?"

I made as much effort as I was capable of in that moment to scrape the memory from my whiskey-logged brain but came up empty. I shook my head. Dear God. That was a bad plan.

"You said, she's worth whatever chaos she brings to our table. Well, guess what, so is Maddie. She's scared. I'm betting you could think of more than a few ways to reassure her that moving on, when she's ready, is normal and healthy. We watched them fold the flag and hand it to her. It sat on her mantel for years, but she did finally put it away. He isn't coming back. On some level, she knows that now, but admitting it has to be scary as fuck. And while she works through it all, I know who she'll want right beside her," Griff eased cautiously. "You've been her rock forever, man. You can't abandon her now even if she's convinced she has to push you away. You have to get through to her."

I stood and managed to remain upright on my own that time. "I need to go see her. I have to fix this."

"No. You need a shower," Smith reminded me. "We sent our favorite medic over to see if he can stitch up a few wounds on your behalf. He's bringing her to Tier Seven in a little while. We're going to get you two squared away."

19

MADDIE

I glared at my phone but didn't really have the energy to see who was calling. It was probably T-Byrd again, and I couldn't talk to him yet. I didn't know what to say to him. He deserved someone who wasn't completely fucked up. I had no idea how to explain to him that I didn't know how to be around him without feeling the rampant attraction between us.

It took me entirely too long to remember that I'd put Olivia down for a nap, and the phone was going to awaken her.

I scowled at the name. Talk about adding insult to injury. Accepting my own fate, I answered Chris's mother's call on the fifth ring. "Hello?" I sounded like I'd gone three rounds with a prize fighter. Since I'd slept a grand total of seven hours in the last four days, I wasn't surprised.

"Maddie? Is that really you?"

I rolled my eyes. She wasn't asking because I didn't sound like myself. That was her greeting for me whenever she'd decided I didn't call to check on her often enough. "Hi, Delores. Sorry. I've been a little busy lately. How are you?"

"It's just difficult, you know. I'd have thought you would've wanted to go to Arlington with us last week but since you didn't, we visited Chris for you. I imagine he found that very hurtful."

Hot rage spilled through my chest. I'd been on the receiving end of guilt trips for the last four years, and I was more than done. "I doubt that," I spat.

I'd spent most of the weekend trying to come up with some way to repair my friendship with T and apologizing to a ghost. Most of Monday was spent in tears because ghosts cannot respond, and I had no clue on how to go back in time so I could correct the mistakes I'd made. Now, I was more despondent than anything else. I had nothing left, nothing that is, except for that hungry ache that still roiled low in my belly whenever I thought of T.

"Yes, well, how is little Olivia?"

"She's fine."

"We wouldn't know since we so rarely get to see her. I'm sure she intended to call us on the eleventh but must've been so busy she couldn't."

"Delores, I've explained this before. Olivia doesn't remember what happened on July 11th. She doesn't remember Chris at all and she certainly isn't old enough to remember to call you on any certain day. I'm sorry." I shut my eyes to her choked whimper wishing it was my ears I could shut instead. "She was only eight weeks old when he was killed. I don't want her to remember the day. I want to spare her that." With that, my mother-in-law burst into tears. I waited, already knowing what would happen next. I couldn't spare her the truth, and I was trying to learn not to allow her to manipulate me anymore. This was how most of our phone calls went. If I'd believed for one moment she was truly struggling with Chris's death, I would've talked with her for as long as she needed me. But this was all for attention. My father-in-law picked up next.

"Hey, Maddie, uh, how are you?" He never knew what to say to me.

"Truthfully, I've been better. How are you?"

"Oh, you know, we're getting by. I miss seeing my girl though.

Maybe Grandpa could come by and take her to play on that McDonald's playground she likes so much."

I managed a small smile. "I'm sure she'd love that."

"You could bring her by the house sometime. That'd make Delores happy. We'd love to have her stay." This was what all of the Mitchell men did. They bent over backwards bowing to Delores's whims. Chris and his brother were no better than their dad.

"I'll see if I can get by soon." I reminded myself that Chris's parents did have the right to see his daughter. A quick knock sounded on my door. I glanced down at my coffee-stained sweatpants and the tie-dyed T-shirt Olivia had made me Friday night. Whoever was at the door was better than this awkward conversation with Chris's parents, even if I did look like hell. "Mr. Mitchell, someone's at my door. I need to run."

"Great. See you soon." He ended the call.

I tiptoed to the door and peeked out. Voodoo stood on my front porch. I'd been expecting the infantry. The medic was an interesting maneuver. I didn't particularly care. I was starved for any news about T, so I flung open the door.

He grinned at me. "Hey there, sweet pea."

"Hey," choked from me. Another well of confusion and fear threatened to overwhelm me. I hated myself for letting my mother-in-law book me yet another one of her guilt trips, but dammit, I should've gone with them to Arlington, shouldn't I?

He held open his arms, and I fell into them. He hugged me tight. I noted that his hugs were nothing like T's. They were friendly and brought me a modicum of ease but just weren't able to put me back together.

"I'm assuming the big hug means I can come in?" He planted a kiss on top of my head before he released me.

"Of course." I stood back. We both watched an old Camaro crawl down my street and turn into the driveway across from mine.

"You get new neighbors?" Voodoo asked.

"I don't think so. That house has been empty for years. The owners won't sell it, but they're never there."

He nodded. "We'll figure that out later. Come on." He sealed me inside my own house and locked the door.

The Camaro only served to tighten the knot of confusion centered in my throat. "Chris used to have a Camaro just like that. His parents bought him one when he turned sixteen."

"Oh yeah?" Voodoo studied me. "He'd moved on to trucks when I met him. He loved that Ram he had back in the day."

I smiled. "Yes, he did. Maybe more than me."

"Nah, not possible." He pointed to my sofa. "You care if we sit for a few?"

"Sure." I settled back in the spot I'd been in for so long I was practically taking root.

He rubbed his hands over his face and then studied me. "I'm just gonna start talking so bear with me. I didn't get all of the training Chris and T got about interrogating people, so I'm not all that good at it. I'm just the guy who puts them back together if we need information out of them, generally after Griff shoots them, but that's not important right now. I'm straight up asking you what happened between you and our fearless leader because he's not doing so great. And, sweet pea, you don't look like you're doing too great either. Seems to me maybe the two of you could make each other feel better."

My cheeks scalded with embarrassment. What on earth was I supposed to say to that? Nothing. There was nothing I could say to Voodoo about any of it. I just shot him a pleading look.

"Okay, then how about this? Griff said it looked like things got pretty hot and heavy Friday night. We've all noticed that you and T tend to kinda like being around each other."

"You have?"

He grinned. "We have. Of course we are trained to notice most everything, so that doesn't mean anyone else noticed."

"I was wondering why I hadn't noticed," I muttered.

Voodoo chuckled. "Now are you sure you didn't notice or was it more like you were scared to admit what was going on?"

The Sevens had known me for years. Clearly, they could tell what

I was thinking even when I couldn't. It was high time I started listening.

"Here's the thing though," he continued, "T hasn't been to work. He didn't come in over the weekend, which is rare for him, and he hasn't been in the past two days. I'm worried about him."

My heart leapt from my chest to my throat. Terror shot up my spine. "Oh God, do you think he's hurt? We have to go find him. He tried to call me. How could I not have answered?" I shook my head letting the guilt pummel me. I'd run away from him and now.... The one thing my subconscious had been trying to force through the barrage of guilt and confusion finally rushed to the forefront of my mind. T was my friend and I was his. No matter where this whole insane thing left us, I could not let him lose another one of his best friends. I had to figure out how to go back to being his friend.

"Hey, hey, deep breaths for me," Voodoo soothed. "He's okay. Griff and Smitty are with him now. I was just wondering if Team Seven could be appallingly selfish and ask if you might save him again. He spends all day every day trying to save us. We all owe him more than we can ever repay."

Again? "I'd do anything in the world for T, but I didn't save him before. He saved me."

Voodoo shook his head at me. "It is so like you to believe that's true but, trust me, that isn't how it went down."

I had no idea what he was talking about, but that wasn't important. "It's just..." I tried to explain the inexplicable.

"It's just you're not too sure how to go from being friends to being more than friends?"

"How did you know I was going to say that? I don't even know if he wants that." It had occurred to me late Friday night that it was possible he was only indulging me on our date. He'd never said no to anything I'd ever asked of him. What if he was just doing everything we did because he knew I wanted to?

"I may not know much about getting people to confess to war crimes, but that doesn't mean I don't know you and T. Trust me, he wants to be with you all kinds of badly. Figuring out how you want to go about that will have to be something the two of you discuss. For what it's worth, God knows it shouldn't have been Chris. It should've been any of us but him."

They'd always said that. It shouldn't have been Chris because of me and Olivia. But I knew Chris wouldn't have had it any other way.

Voodoo squeezed my hand. "But that isn't the way it worked out, and I've watched enough men die to know you can't undo it, no matter how skilled you are. There's no amount of love that can bring them back to life. Everyone knows how much you loved him, sweet pea. No one's doubting that.

"They go on and leave the rest of us to deal with it. I just don't believe anyone gets to make rules on how to deal with losing someone you love the way you did. If you and T-Byrd can help each other heal, you both deserve that. And if anybody has anything to say about it, they can come talk to The Sevens. You and T didn't do anything wrong. Somewhere deep inside, you know that's true. Moving on is something all of us have to do. One step at a time. You've come so far so fast. If T's next on the horizon for you, you couldn't have ever asked for two better men to care about you in this life, and they sure as hell could never have asked for a better girl."

"Thank you." I hugged him again because I knew a few things the world didn't. The United States Army creates so much more than war machines, their elite Special Forces soldiers. They manage to take the best of the best and make them better. It takes some pretty amazing men to do what they do, to fight the way they fight, to come back home shells of their former selves because of their losses, and then to just keep fighting. Sometimes they need someone to hug them, to understand them, to let them be in any format they need to be. I'd always been that for Team Seven. My life was inextricably interwoven with theirs, and I would never have it any other way. "Do you think someday Team Seven might be able to see me as something other than Chris's wife?"

He sat back and grinned. "Do you think you'll ever be able to see yourself as something other than that?"

"I don't know. That's part of the problem."

"I'd say the first step is for you to see yourself differently. Everyone else will follow your lead. As for The Sevens, we're pretty good at adapting. Kind of goes with the beret." He winked at me. As much as I adored Voodoo, I knew I was talking to the wrong Seven. One thing I'd learned when Chris had died - when you run out of weak, there is nothing left but strength. It was time for me to be strong again. T and I had to have some difficult conversations. I had to face the past and the future all at the same time. I had to capture the wind and let it fill me full if that's what it was going to do.

"I need to go see T. I have to apologize to him for running away. God, why was I such a coward?" The need to move, to fix this, to do something had me leaping off the couch. I started to pace. Why wasn't Voodoo moving? I had to wake up Olivia. I had so much to say and do.

"Whoa there, chica. You're hardly a coward. You got a little freaked out. Rightfully so, but all's not lost. Let's get Miss Olivia and head down to Tier Seven. If Griff and Smitty have anything to say about it, Boss Man'll be there when we arrive."

They used to call Chris *Boss Man*. It always made him laugh. They'd moved on. They'd had to. Now, I had to see if I could do the same.

"You're a pretty great guy, Vince 'Voodoo' Grimaldi. How has some woman not snatched you up?"

He laughed. "I am skilled at so many things, sweet pea," he gestured to himself, "it really wouldn't be fair to limit all of this to just one woman."

20

T-BYRD

"Uncle T!" Olivia's shrill voice sliced through my skull just before it took a battering ram to my head.

"Hey, baby girl," I managed without vomiting, which was an accomplishment.

"Why are your eyes so red?" Her little brow furrowed as she latched herself onto my leg.

"Uh," I had no answer for her. There was no acceptable response, and I was far too distracted by Maddie's red-rimmed, swollen eyes that were duplicates of mine. Safe to say, hers had come from tears and mine had come from something far less productive.

"Yeah, Uncle T, why *are* your eyes so red?" Smith shook his head at me. "Hey, Liv, come with me. I'll let you play on my computer."

She considered for a moment. Normally, she loved playing on Smith's massive computer. His monitors were big enough for her to feel like she was inside the Disney Channel website. "Is Uncle T going to be okay?" She grabbed Maddie's hand.

Maddie's gaze hadn't left mine. Devastation, confusion, and something even I didn't quite recognize existed there behind the evidence of her tears. Another round of self-hatred gnawed its way through me.

Voodoo made his way inside the office. He took one look at me and rolled his eyes. "Uncle T is going to be just fine, little one. I'm gonna fix him up right now." My brow furrowed. "Get your ass to the back room, moron," he spoke through his teeth and then shoved me forward.

"That is definitely not helping," I huffed. "And I need to talk to Maddie."

"Yeah, well, you two can have your conversation back here. I'm not the one who decided to see if I could replace all of the water in my body with grain alcohol. Sit your ass down." He shoved me into one of the recliners, dug around in some of his cabinets, and grabbed a massive IV bag full of saline.

"I'll be fine. I don't need that." Not that I could've stopped him in my current condition.

"I'm sorry. Are you arguing with me, the medic?"

Smith bellowed from his office, "I still have Bieber on my phone."

I ground my teeth.

"T, please, let him help you," Maddie pled.

Turning her down had never been an option, and it sure as hell wasn't now, after all I'd done. I offered up my arm. He was an SF medic. He could kill you just as quickly as he could save you. He hung the bag from one of the cabinet knobs, rammed the needle in my arm, and taped it there in record time. "You'll feel human again in just a few. Fair warning, you're gonna have to piss like a racehorse." He smirked. "Either let me help you get the bag to the bathroom or let Maddie."

"Get out," I growled.

"So touchy." He left the door open a few inches as he made his exit.

Maddie dragged one of the other chairs beside mine. "T, I'm... so sorry."

My eyes closed. "Please, stop apologizing. You're killing me."

When her hand landed on mine, I caught it and held on. "I'm not apologizing for what happened. I'm apologizing for the way I acted after it was over. I can't believe I ran away from you. I didn't know what to do with the way you made me feel." I opened my eyes. She shifted her gaze to the floor. "The way you've been making me feel for a long time now."

"Hey." I squeezed her hand. "You're not the only one who's been feeling this way, okay? But if you're scared or just... not ready, I can figure out how to stop feeling this way... somehow. I swear. I can do it." It was the first time in my life I'd ever lied to her. I had no idea how to decimate my feelings for her.

Those red-rimmed eyes found mine, and I got a tiny grin. "I am scared and I'm not ready." My heart somehow both clogged my throat and crash-landed near my feet. I had to figure it out. I couldn't lose her. "But," the single word rushed breath back into my lungs, "I have this ache." She shook her head then stood and started to pace.

"Ache?" I didn't understand. If she was hurting, I'd get Voodoo back in there. I'd fix it, whatever it was.

"Yes. That's the only way I know how to describe it. I have this ache, and it's somewhere deep inside of me. I don't know where exactly. The only thing I understand about it is that you're the only one who can make it go away. It's almost like it calls your name, T. Does that sound crazy?"

"God, no. That's why I started drinking. I couldn't get rid of the pain. No matter how much I drank it was still there. I couldn't even numb it temporarily. I just needed you."

"I was a coward." She stared me down.

"Stop," I demanded. "There's a whole lot of stuff here that we have to work through if we're going to try to be more than friends. None of it makes you a coward. It's just a thing we have to figure out."

With every tremble of her hands, I swore she rocked me to the core. Slowly, she sank back into the chair beside me. I wrapped her hands in one of my own. "Can you just not get up? Please? Can you just sit here... with me?" I was such a weak bastard, but the words escaped without my permission.

"There is nowhere else I want to be. There are two things I need you to agree to before I try to figure out how to be something other than Chris Mitchell's wife."

"Anything." Damn. Whatever it was she needed from me, I was there for it.

"I learned something in the last few days. I learned a lot of things actually." She slowly released a measured breath before she continued. "I learned that I cannot lose you, too. I just can't. So, if we try dating for a little while and... it doesn't work out, you have to promise me that no matter what we'll find some way to go back to being best friends. If we can't do that then..."

"Hey." I traced my thumb back and forth along her palm. I needed to draw her into my chest and hold her, but I only had use of one of my arms because of my own stupidity. "You are a part of me. I'd have to pull the fucking marrow from my bones, drain my own blood, tear myself completely apart to let you go. That's not even an option. You will always be one of the most important parts of my life, no matter what."

She threw her arms around my neck, careful of the IV line. "Thank you for saying that."

"It's the truth."

"I will never deserve you," she vowed.

"Here I was just thinking the same thing." I stared into her eyes for a moment, reluctant to look away. "What was the other promise you needed, sweetheart?"

Her grin at the term of endearment cleared more of the alcohol-soaked cotton balls from my mind. I vowed then and there to call her every pet name I could come up with whenever the opportunity arose. We were doing this. I just had to figure *this* out. In the four long years since his death, I had never needed to talk to Chris more though I had no idea what I'd say to him.

"I need for us to keep this from Olivia for a little while. She loves you so much. She wouldn't understand if we become more than friends and then went back to just being friends."

"Done."

"Really?"

"Really, but now I have one thing I need you to agree to."

"Anything."

"Spend the weekend with me."

She jerked back. Her back went ramrod straight. Her massive eyes somehow enlarged. She stared at me like I'd lost my mind. "The weekend? Isn't that moving... very fast? I mean, I don't know because I don't have the foggiest clue how to do this, but aren't you supposed to not spend the weekend together for a while? Aren't men supposed to be commitment-phobic and not want a woman at their house for a whole weekend?"

I chuckled at that. "First of all, nothing about this frightens me. You running away from me scared the shit out of me. Spending the weekend with you sounds pretty damn close to heaven. You said you didn't want Olivia to know about us yet. We can't go on too many dates before she figures it out. She already knows you think I'm sexy," I teased her. God, that felt good.

Her smacking my chest did not, however. When she giggled, I knew we were on the right path. "Well, you are." Her mouth twisted in consideration. I wanted to kiss those lips. I'd spent four long days seeking the flavors of her, aching to intoxicate myself with her scent and her taste. "Where would we spend this weekend?"

"My house out on Lake Mac. No one will bother us there. We can figure all of this out. The guys can keep Liv."

"Chris's mom has been wanting her to come stay with them. Maybe I could let her do that."

That was certainly an option, but I wasn't sure she was thinking this through. "You think Chris's parents will be okay with you spending the weekend with me?"

Consideration weighted her expression. "Didn't really think of that. Sorry. I haven't slept much."

I mortared another layer of guilt on myself for that. "Clearly, we don't do so well apart."

"I'd say so." She gestured to the needle in my arm. "Promise you'll never do this again."

"You got it."

"Okay." She nodded.

"Okay, you're good with me never drinking this much again or okay, you'll spend the weekend with me?"

"Both." Her teeth sank into her bottom lip, and I had just enough zero-proof fluid in me to need her to stop doing that. "Do you think I'm too old for you?" blurted from her before I could offer to nibble that lip on her behalf.

I laughed. That morning I'd wanted to die. Now I was laughing with her. The world was so fucked up. "You're what, four years older than me?"

She gave me a sheepish nod.

"I've always wanted my own personal cougar," I harassed.

Her mouth fell open, and if there hadn't been a needle in my arm I would've doubled over laughing.

"I will hit you again." It was the cutest threat I'd ever heard.

"I'm aware. And no, I do not think our ages make any difference at all... my little cougar."

"Stop saying that!"

"Yes, ma'am."

"Do not call me ma'am! I even have a wrinkle," she whimpered. Dear God, she was adorable.

I rolled my eyes. "Where?"

"Here." She pointed to her upper lip. I saw nothing but the most beautiful set of lips I'd ever had the pleasure of kissing.

"There?" I smirked. "Bring it closer so I can see."

She giggled and leaned in.

"Little closer. I'm injured."

"I don't think you qualify as injured, Sergeant."

"Maybe not, but I'm milking this for all it's worth. Now hush up. I'm inspecting this nonexistent wrinkle."

When she was millimeters from my face, I sank my lips to hers and let her heal me. I caught her quick little gasp of breath and stole it all for myself. Using my one available hand, I cradled her face and memorized the delicate dips and hollows of her features. I needed more. I needed her in my arms. When she pulled back, I barked, "Voodoo, get this thing out of me. I need to bend my arms."

"You're SF. Improvise."

"Fucker," I muttered under my breath. An eruption of giggles overtook her. Since I hadn't yet gotten to hear her calling out my name in the throes of a climax, that was the sweetest sound in the whole damn world. But I would hear my name called from her hungry lips. I planned to hear it over and over again all weekend. Just as soon as I got it through my head that Chris Mitchell wasn't sitting up in heaven hating me for fucking his wife.

21

MADDIE

I was going to spend the weekend with T-Byrd. I couldn't quite get it to make sense in my head. Yet, that fizzy sensation had begun in my belly again, and the distinctive feeling of wind swirled in the vicinity of my lungs. It hadn't caught me yet, but I was racing headlong into it and I had no desire to stop.

Before I could ask him more questions, my cell phone rang. I retrieved it from my purse. "Why are you calling me?" I held it up for him to see Tier Seven displayed on the screen.

He'd had half the bag of fluids, but still looked a little confused.

It took me far too long to realize what had to be happening. I grinned. "It's Olivia. Calling from Smith's office," I whispered.

T beamed and gestured for the phone. "Go sneak into Smith's office," he instructed.

I headed for the door while he answered her call. "This is Miss Olivia Mitchell's personal assistant. Can I help you?"

I laughed as I spun around the open doorway to Smith's office. But instead of finding my little girl giggling hysterically about her Uncle T being her personal assistant. Instead, she was sitting in Smith's lap pointing to something on the screen that had her enthralled. No one was on the phone.

"You okay?" Smith asked.

I nodded. "Yeah. Keep playing." I checked Voodoo, Griff, and Ryder's offices. They weren't on their phones either. Rushing to the front office, I found Rylee talking into her own personal cell phone. She yanked the phone away from her face.

"You good, Maddie? Need anything?"

"No, I'm fine. Um, sorry to be rude but can I ask who you're talking to? There's something weird with my phone."

"It's the Y. I'm teaching self-defense up there next month. Just trying to work out the schedule."

She was on her own personal phone anyway. That wouldn't have registered as Tier Seven. I rushed back to T. "It wasn't her."

"Yeah, I figured that when someone cursed and ended the call."

"What?"

"Smith," T called.

He appeared, carrying Olivia. "You rang?"

Voodoo came in to check the IV bag. Olivia wiggled down out of Smith's arms and raced to T. "Are you sick?"

"I was." He stared up at me. "But I'm better now. I promise."

She nodded and hesitantly touched the tubing. "I had to have these when my eye got sick."

Voodoo knelt and grinned at her. "Uncle T isn't sick like that. I promise. He won't have to have any more of these because what was wrong with his brain, your mama fixed."

"Mommy is very magical," she vowed. That was when I clutched my chest.

"Yes, she is," T agreed. I needed them to stop.

Voodoo chuckled and offered her his hand. "How 'bout you and me go get a snack?"

"Okay. Then we can read Uncle T a story 'cause he used to read me stories when I had to sit very, very still in the bed at the hops-pital."

All six-foot-six, two hundred seventy-five pounds of pure muscle that comprised Smith Hagen looked ready to weep. "She's killing me."

As soon as Voodoo had Olivia in the break room, T held up my phone. "Any idea how someone phoned Maddie from Tier Seven when none of us made the call?"

Smith jerked my phone from T's grasp. "That's impossible." He studied the missed call list. "I have our lines buried behind so many layers of security no one could spoof the number. Okay, wait, it's our public line. That's a little better. Still weird though. Can I take this for a minute?" he asked me.

"Of course. I do get lots of weird calls on it. I think my number used to belong to a bunch of different people. Bill collectors call all the time and ask for other people's names, and I get all of these calls that say Lincoln, Nebraska but then no one is there."

"Interesting," was his only comment. "I'll bring it right back."

I settled back beside T-Byrd. "Where were we?"

I was the recipient of that megawatt grin. My heart sped and I couldn't quite figure out how to stop smiling. "You were agreeing to be my cougar."

He ducked out of the way when I swatted his good shoulder.

"I can't believe you'd hit a guy with an IV," he continued to tease me. Truthfully, it was so good to be like this with him again, I didn't mind.

"That's what you get for calling me a cougar. I'm lethal. Completely terrifying, really. You shouldn't mess with me."

He laughed at me outright. "Lethal, huh?"

"Definitely."

"I'll keep that in mind, but I thought you wanted me to mess with you."

Pure bliss danced under my skin. *Chris would want me to date someone who cares about me as much as T.* I was going to have to keep telling myself that. "Still scared," I admitted. "But also really excited."

"Same, baby."

"I didn't think Green Berets were scared of anything."

"You know that's not true. We just don't let it stop us."

"Yeah. Guess I forgot that part."

"When he gets this damned thing out of my arm, I'm holding you and I may not ever let you go," he informed me.

"Olivia," I reminded.

"Right. But hey, I'm SF. I'll improvise."

22

T-BYRD

"Mathis!" I bellowed as soon as I'd walked Maddie to her minivan, made certain it was safe without her being aware that's what I was doing, and buckled Liv in her car seat.

"Yes, sir," our newest recruit appeared instantly just like I preferred. He was working out just fine. "Go..."

He held up his hand. "Follow Maddie home without her knowing I'm following her. Then stick around there until you get there tonight. If I see so much as a gnat bother her, call you and kill the gnat."

"You are good. But if something bothers her, kill it first then call me," I ordered.

"You got it and thanks, sir. I'm learning."

"Do not let her see you. I don't want to scare her."

"Hey, I was a Ranger. I can land on the supper table in the middle of Thanksgiving lookin' like a pecan pie. Nobody will know I'm there until I start shooting."

"Good man." Since Griff could blow a gnat off of a cow's hide from three hundred yards away, I'd much prefer it be him who followed her home, but she knew him too well. She'd sense him. Besides, it was really me that wanted to go with her. I could protect her better than any other member of Team Seven, but I'd just vowed to her that I wouldn't let Olivia know about us yet. I had to honor that. I'd figure out some way to spend the night there, but I couldn't show up until after work.

Mathis raced out the front door to his truck.

Smith's fingers flew across the keyboard. He didn't so much as look up when I entered his office.

"How bad is this?" I asked. My gut continued to twist itself into knots. My muscles didn't seem to fully understand how I'd gone from being passed out in my bed to up and moving around. My head was still coming up with every plausible reason someone would spoof our phone number on her phone, all while making plans for every available contingency. My cock, however, was riding high on the fact that we were going to try this being-an-*us*-thing and that she was spending the weekend with me all alone.

"Not sure yet but it's not good."

I worked my jaw and tried to summon patience from the ether while he continued to type. He shook his head and leaned back in his chair. "Someone spoofing the public phone number bothers me a lot less than knowing that whoever spoofed our number knew she was here and when to call."

Rylee joined us behind Smith's desk. "There's a chance it was a coincidence, right?"

I shook my head. "That's a little too coincidental for me."

"Agreed." Smith sighed. "Her number is on every possible sucker list there is."

"What does that mean?"

"Phone spoofing is a relatively new tactic by scammers, but it's not that difficult to override caller ID functionality. People are more likely to answer a call from a local number, thinking it's someone they know or maybe a doctor they don't have in their contact list. Scammers need you on the phone talking to get what they want. Anytime someone answers a call like that, their number is recorded on a sucker list showing it's an active phone and someone answers it regularly. I can attempt to go in and scrub her number off all these lists, but I guarantee you they also exist on local servers I can't get to. It's far more difficult to spoof a specific number, but it can be done as we've just seen. I went into her phone and turned off everything that might let anyone know where she is at any given time. She had the Facebook location tracker off, but her Instagram account is linked to her Facebook account and that was still on. She also has one of those kid tracking apps I'm sure she uses when Liv is at daycare."

I nodded. "Yeah, she does." I recalled her purchasing it when they were staying at the cancer treatment facility. Liv had such a difficult time seeing after her treatments Maddie always wanted to make sure she could find her in the big playrooms or when she was in the different treatment areas.

"Right. That's fine but I'm a little worried someone might be reversing the locater app on her phone. I need to do some more research to even figure out if that's possible so you're going to have to give me a little while. Tumblr is the only social media site that won't let you control their tracking software, but she didn't have the app on her phone so if she has an account there it's on her home computer."

Thoughts of Maddie using Tumblr did wicked things to my libido. An image emblazoned itself in my mind. Her with one hand on her phone and the other between her own legs had me conjuring up all kinds of ways I could have her in my bed long before this weekend. I shook off the images and focused.

Smith shook his head at me. "You okay there, T? Look a little rattled." He laughed.

"Go fuck yourself. Then tell me how panicked I should be - on a scale of 'I go buy her a new phone right now' to 'I call moving trucks and move her into my house tonight'."

"If I had to take a guess, I'd say someone's trying to scare her. She said she's been getting weird phone calls. Could even be some kid she taught who didn't like her. There are a million possibilities. But, if you don't go buy her a new phone, I'm going to. Have her change her passwords on the child tracking app on the new phone. That will put a stop to all of this no matter who's doing it."

I had a pretty good idea who might like to scare Maddie and it wasn't one of her students. "I'm on my way, and do me a favor. Get me a staff list of every single person who works for Coldwell Harding Weapons and Optics, complete with pictures, job title, personal and work phone numbers, car make, model, tag, and color. When you get me a list, forward it to Mathis as well. Tell him if he sees anyone matching their descriptions or their cars to call me."

"You got it." Smith already had their website up on three of his screens. "You really think Maidlow's doing this?"

"The shit-stain all but told me he was going to. Don't worry. I'll put a stop to it."

"No doubt."

23

MADDIE

I swung open my front door just before T's fist connected with it and shook my head at him.

"Surprise," he tried.

"I am not surprised. In fact, I am *so* not surprised, I already set the table for sub sandwiches." I pointed to the two stack in his arms then to my kitchen table stacked with paper plates, a beer for him, a Dr. Pepper for me, and a juice box for Olivia. "But shouldn't we ask Ryder if he'd like some too, since he's been out there for most of the afternoon?" It was sweet but this was ridiculous. "I was married to one of you loons for years. You're all insane." I dropped my voice. "And the most insane one of all is me because I keep falling for you people."

His massive grin got him in the front door. "So, you admit you're already falling for me?"

"Do not make me use all three of your names when I start yelling."

He rolled his eyes. "I'm not going to apologize for keeping you safe. It will always be the most important thing to me. I'll take Mathis a sandwich, but I don't want him hanging out with us."

"T, it was just some stupid phone call. I know it was weird but..."

The truth was it had unnerved me all afternoon, but I refused to be afraid anymore. I'd done that all weekend and it had hurt him.

"Speaking of that." He handed me a sleek white box with Apple's logo on the side.

"Tell me you did not buy me a new phone." But of course he had because he's him, and of course he'd gotten the rose gold one with the amazing camera. Ugh. Why did he have to be so good at spoiling me? I could not let him do this.

"I think the words you're searching for are: The camera on this one is amazing, and it holds ten times the amount of data of my ancient one. I can take an endless number of photos of the cutest kid on the planet. You are the best guy to date ever."

I ground my teeth. "I cannot accept this. It's way too expensive, and I can't afford to pay you for it. I'm a teacher."

"I knew you'd say that so just hear me out. Whoever spoofed Tier Seven's number knew you were there. They had to. It's my fault this is happening. Just let me do this so I can sleep at night. Please."

That wasn't at all what I was expecting to hear. I opened my mouth to protest but none of my prepared arguments worked now. "Wait. How is it your fault they called my phone?"

"Maidlow."

Maidlow's threat at the winery slapped me in the face. Holy crap. "You really think he did this? I thought he was just trying to get to you."

"There is no quicker way to get to me than to scare you, now is there? He's not stupid, and he was one of the best Comm Sergeants in the army. It wouldn't be difficult for him to spoof our number and track your cell. He could probably do it in his sleep. I'm going over there tomorrow to put a stop to this, but please, take the new one. Turn your old one off and toss it. I also need you to change your passwords on a couple of your apps."

I stared down at the box in my hands. "I really wanted one that was rose gold when they came out." I wrinkled my nose.

His chuckle said he knew he'd won. "When I do something, I do it right. Now, let's eat. Where's my girl?"

I closed the door behind him. "Liv, Uncle T brought subs," I called.

She flew out of her room and raced headlong into his leg. "Uncle T! Are you not sick anymore?"

He managed to balance the sandwiches in one hand and hug her with the other. "I feel great, little one. I got you ham and cheese. Want some?"

"Yes, please." Instead of her heading towards the table, she wrapped her arms and legs around his calf and held on.

"This game again?" he laughed. I tried to take the food from his hands, but he shook his head. "I can do it all, baby doll." He took careful steps with Olivia attached to his leg all the way to the kitchen. She giggled the entire time.

"You can tell her no," I reminded him.

"The princess has removed that word from my vocabulary. Plus, it's a killer thigh workout. I just have to make sure she rides each leg equally."

T kept Olivia laughing all through dinner and then helped me give her a bath. It was always great to have him there, but guilt continued to tug at the memories we were creating. He got to do things with her that Chris never would. I wasn't certain I'd ever be able to accept that, but I also couldn't change it.

Now, I was spending the weekend with Chris's best friend. No. I ordered myself to stop calling him that. I was spending the weekend with T.

After he read her *Pinkalicious* and *Purplicious*, her favorites, he tucked her in, and we both kissed her goodnight. "I almost lost my mind when I remembered I hadn't kissed her goodnight like I'd promised the other night," he confessed when we were back on my couch.

"I'm really sorry I pushed you away. I just didn't know what to do. I'm still not sure I know what to do. I just know I don't want to run from you ever again."

"Thank you. I've been through a bunch of shit in this life, and that's the thing that almost did me in."

Before I could apologize again, his lips were on mine. Soft and hungry, perfect pressure, he kissed me like he was starved for it. His tongue explored my mouth like he needed to memorize each individual flavor of our kiss. There was no complacency when we melted against each other. He didn't kiss me with the knowledge that he could do it again whenever he wanted. His touch made me feel cherished. T was an amazing kisser. The thought took hold before I'd meant to allow it. I'd lived with complacent kisses, and I didn't want to compare him to Chris.

"No more apologizing," he ordered.

"No more kissing until Olivia is asleep."

"You're asking a lot."

"I think you'll survive." I wondered if I was using my daughter as an excuse, but I couldn't wade deep enough into that river right then to figure anything out. "What should I pack for the lake house?" There. That was a relatively safe topic, and it had to do with our newly-budding relationship so I wasn't being afraid.

He considered. "If it were up to me, you'd bring a toothbrush and nothing else, but I'm guessing you're going to be dressed more than I'd like for you to be." I have no idea what expression flickered to my face, but he changed tactics fast. "Hey, I'm just teasing you. We don't have to do anything you don't want to do this weekend. I have two bedrooms up there. You can have the master. It's fine. No pressure."

"Thank you for being so great. Most of me doesn't want that, but there are a few parts that are a little timid maybe. I'll work on those before Friday."

"We could work on them together. I still have to get my head straight as well."

At least I wasn't alone in that. "About what specifically?"

"About the way I'm feeling, the things I want to do with you, the ways I want to make you feel."

"With *me* or with Chris's wife?"

"Maybe a little of that."

Relief washed over me like a healing tide. Every breath came easier, but the wind grew ever closer on the horizon. "Thank you for feeling that way, too." I snuggled against him and let myself enjoy his warmth and his scent when he wrapped his arms around me. If I could've stayed in T's arms for the rest of my life, nothing would make me happier, and that scared the crap out of me. I'd thought that about another man, and he'd been ripped from my careful grasp.

"So, this is okay until Liv's asleep but kissing is not?" He cradled me tighter to his chest.

"She's seen me hug you before."

"I know. I'm just getting the rules straight. Did you ask Chris's parents about keeping Olivia?"

"God no. I have a hard and fast rule about talking to Delores more than once a day and she called this morning. I'll call her tomorrow. I'm sure it'll be fine. She'll be beside herself actually. She's been asking for Olivia to stay over there for years."

"Are you sure you'll be okay with it?" That was fair. I'd never left her overnight. She'd been the only thing I lived for after Chris had died.

"No." I grinned at him. "I put the parts of myself that I need to be able to focus on spending the weekend with you away for such a long time. I think they might've started to come back two years ago, but then she got sick and they went right back into hiding. When you kiss me, or we do things like we did in your car, it feels so good but so foreign. I have to get to know that part of myself again. This is something I want to do, and Chris's parents deserve to see his daughter, right?"

"That's entirely up to you, baby. Never forget that. Don't let them guilt you into this. It doesn't sound like you get along with his mom. I don't remember Chris ever saying too much about his family, but I got the impression he didn't care for her either."

My stomach clenched. Chris could say he didn't like her, but if I said that, it made him angry. "He used to say he loved them but he didn't like them very much. He fought with his brother all the time, just typical sibling stuff." I shrugged. "His brother wanted everything to be a competition. Chris hated that even though most of the time he won whatever it was. His mom should be a travel agent for guilt trips. His dad is nice but is incapable of telling his mother no. Whatever Delores wants all of the Mitchell men do so they can avoid her drama."

"And you're sure you want Olivia staying over there?"

"They love her very much and no one is perfect. I want her to know his family. I can't stand to be around them for extended periods of time, but that doesn't mean Olivia can't have fun over there. My parents made me spend a week with my grandparents every summer. At first I hated it, but it came to be one of my very favorite weeks of the whole year."

T fished his phone out of his pocket when it vibrated. His eyes narrowed and a cool darkness shadowed his features.

"What's wrong?"

He showed me the text from Ryder.

Black Audi Roadster matching description for Maidlow's car just drove down her street. Turned East on Piedmont. Couldn't make out plates. Want me to follow?

T touched Ryder's name and had the phone to his ear before I could ask what we should do. "Don't follow him. Come stay with her. I've got this."

"T, no," I pled when he ended the call. "This guy is crazy. He has it out for you, and I do not need a babysitter." Truthfully, I had no concern over myself. It was him I couldn't bear to think about being in harm's way. You'd think after being married to an SF officer for years I'd have gotten used to them leaving to do terrifying things, but I never did.

"I'll be fine, baby. If you don't want Mathis to be here for you, let him be here for Liv. I'll be right back."

I watched him storm past Ryder as soon as he arrived. "Anything happens to them while I'm gone, I'll kill you." He was in his Vette and gone in the next second.

"He'll be okay, right?" I asked the Ranger they'd hired a few weeks ago. I didn't know him well yet. He didn't seem terribly concerned about T's threat.

In fact, he grinned at me. "Ah, he's just showing off for you, I 'spect."

"I don't think that's it."

"Even if it isn't, he was Special Forces. They're the best of the best. You can't bring them down."

I managed to nod out my lie. You could bring them down. I knew only too well.

24

T-BYRD

Rage shot through my veins as I whipped around an Accord three cars behind Maidlow. I burned with it. It pissed me the fuck off that he knew which buttons to push, knew precisely how to exploit me. But that was nothing compared to the fury I felt for anyone who thought they could scare her. He'd better pray his precious comm system can reach someone who gives a fuck when I bury him alive.

The car directly behind Maidlow's Audi slowed to make a right-hand turn. I floored my Vette, crossed the double yellow lines, and matched the speed of the car in front of me. Then I made my move it. I whipped behind his Audi when the Camry made the turn. Horns blared behind me. One guy started yelling. He'd live.

Maidlow had a factory tint job on his rear windshield. I couldn't make out his features, but I saw his shadowy figure glance in the rearview. "That's right, fucker. You're done for."

I edged closer. He sped up. I laughed. "Run, asshole. Let's see how well that ends for you."

The road ahead of him was wide open. He approached ninety and held. Coward. I could run my Z06 on two cylinders and do a hundred. German engineering my ass. I was back on his tail in a half second.

Maidlow was spending entirely too much time staring in his rearview. I saw it long before he hit the brakes. A farm truck carrying several dozen bales of hay was crossing in the distance. I'd already eased up when he finally slammed on the brakes. I chuckled when he spun out in a corn field.

Leaping out of my Vette, I raced to his car. Vengeance hammered hard in my chest. I jerked the door open and yanked him out of the front seat.

Only... it wasn't Maidlow. Dude stared at me like I was Satan coming for his soul. He held up his hands. "Take the car. My wallet's in my pocket, phone's on the charger, just please don't hurt me. I have kids, man."

Fuck. I let him go. "Sorry, thought you were someone else. Uh, here." I dug two hundred dollars out of my wallet and slapped it into his hand. "Get the car detailed on me. I'm really sorry."

Dude was shaking. "Who did you think I was?" he finally asked.

"No one. Just... don't worry about it."

He managed a few slow nods. I made my way back to my car and waited to make sure he could get out of the corn field before I made a return trip to Maddie's. It didn't matter. I knew where Maidlow would be bright and early tomorrow morning. I'd be in his office long before he arrived.

"You get him?" Mathis inquired when I let myself back in.

"I caught someone who wasn't him." I cringed.

"Are you okay?" Maddie was in my arms and suddenly making a fool of myself didn't matter quite as much anymore.

"I'm fine, baby. Might've given some poor guy a slight heart attack, but I'm good."

"T, this is ridiculous. You don't know for certain that Maidlow is the one who called my phone today."

Mathis cleared his throat. "Uh, I'm just gonna let you two hash that out. You want me to keep circling out there, sir?"

Maddie leapt before I could answer. "No, Ryder. Thank you for all you've done, but I'll be fine. You go home and relax."

"I'm staying tonight," I informed him. "You go on."

"No, you're not," Maddie countered.

Mathis chuckled as he made his way out her front door.

"Why not?"

"Because Olivia cannot get used to you staying here with us... yet."

Okay, I could deal as long as there was a yet. "I'll sleep on the couch. I've stayed over dozens of times. You told me to stay when I put you to bed the last time I was here."

For some reason, she suddenly looked like she'd held her cheeks to a flame. What was that about? Was she embarrassed I'd put her to bed? Surely not. "I thought I'd dreamed that," she whispered.

My eyebrow arched in intrigue. "Do you frequently dream about me, baby doll?" I edged closer like she was the very center of my gravity.

She took a step back. That was decidedly not what I was going for. "Sometimes," she confessed in a slight choke.

"And that bothers you."

"No. Well, it did, but not so much now. I didn't know if I was the only one who felt this... thing between us. Did I do anything else besides ask you to stay?" Embarrassment played cruelly in her eyes.

Sweet baby needed to be reassured she wasn't alone in all of this. "You kissed me, right about here." I ran a finger over the precise spot on my neck where her lips had been. "I have a question for you. Do you have any idea how many times I've jerked off thinking about you lately?" Okay, maybe that was a little crude, but I couldn't have her thinking I didn't want her every fucking moment of every fucking day.

Another one of her harsh swallows drew my gaze to the hollow at her throat. She eased closer. Perfection. Her quick, shallow breaths brought my gaze lower to the rise and fall of her breasts. My mouth watered. "I think... I'd really like to watch you do that sometime." She bit her lips together preventing any more confessions. Heat poured down from her face in streaks. Her neck and chest glowed red now, too. She refused to look at me, staring instead at the floor.

"Would you, baby?" I drew her into me. If she wanted to hide from her own needs, I'd allow it as long as she hid in me.

"That's weird, right?" She buried her face against my chest. I kissed the top of her head.

"Fuck, no. Not at all. I want to hear every single thing you've ever dreamt about me and every single fantasy you've ever had. They're going to belong to me. I'm going to own each and every one. I'm going to make them come true. And I'll tell you this, I'll let you watch me jack off to your gorgeous body sometime, but the next several times I come it'll be deep inside of you."

I captured her breathless, craving moan with my lips. Her fists knotted my T-shirt. Her hips made a gentle thrust against me. Her sweet little body knew how to beg for what she needed even if she was afraid of it. I'd deal. I'd get her there. I'd be anything in the world she needed me to be, but I was going to own her thoroughly.

25

T-BYRD

By zero six fifty-five the next morning, the Coldwell Harding parking garage was full. I'd pulled in three hours before, as soon as Smith had taken over watch of Maddie's house. Neither Maidlow nor his Audi had appeared... yet.

By zero eight hundred I was tired of waiting. Hurling myself out of my car, I stormed past the security guard. I'd eat my left big toe if the kid weighed a hundred pounds soaking wet, and he was more than distracted by some gaming site he was studying on his computer screen.

"Uh, hey man, you can't just go up there." When he finally noticed me, he leapt up from his desk as if he thought that would be more intimidating. "Who are you, anyway?"

"I didn't ask your permission. Everyone in this building except for you and the guy hawking bagels from that counter over there knows who I am. I'm certain they're expecting me."

"Who are you here to see?"

I ground my teeth. "Maidlow."

"Captain Maidlow?"

"Do you have more than one?"

"No, sir."

"Then that's the one."

"Are you armed?" The kid looked decidedly hopeful. Either he played entirely too many video games, his job was about as thrilling as watching paint dry, or he hated Maidlow almost as much as I did.

"Generally."

"But you're not gonna hurt him, right? I can't let you up there if you're going to hurt anybody."

"And we're back to I wasn't asking for permission." I turned to stalk towards the elevators. Coldwell Harding's office building was just as pretentious as most of their employees. A pair of sleek bronzed elevator doors distorted the fury etched on my face.

"Sir, I have to open the doors," security boy informed me.

"Then do it," I seethed.

He spluttered for several seconds and then came up with, "I should probably at least tell them you're on your way up."

"No one's stopping you."

"I don't know who you are."

"Call Captain Fuckoff and tell him T is here. He'll know precisely who you're talking about." While he was trying to remember how to use a telephone, I made it back to him in three steps, reached behind the counter, and hit the button.

My fury climbed right along with the elevator after I stepped on. The doors parted on what could've been an office scene from Mad Men. Evolution had somehow forgotten all about Coldwell Harding. I rolled my eyes and headed towards Maidlow's office. I was Special fucking Forces. Finding people who didn't want to be found was one of my specialties. It had taken me less than five minutes to find Maidlow's office number.

"Um, sir, can I help you?" An admin assistant chirped from behind me.

"Need to talk to Captain Maidlow."

"He isn't here." She shook her head.

"Right."

"He's in D.C., sir." She pointed to a television set hung on a wall in a conference room. Okay, so maybe they had evolved some. There on the screen was Maidlow. It was a live telecast of his presentation to the DOD that was apparently taking place that morning. Damn, he'd told me this. That didn't mean he wasn't trying to scare Maddie, even if he was just trying to piss me off. But they'd gone to D.C. without my signature. Pissing me off didn't seem like enough motive to have rigged up the phone spoof. According to Smith, that would've taken several hours' worth of work. The telecast left me with more questions, but it did narrow down my suspects.

"Where's Finch?" I demanded.

"Marcus Finch, sir?"

I rolled my eyes. "Yes, Marc Finch."

"His office is there." She pointed to a darkened office with the door open. The desk plate did indeed say Marcus Finch. "But he left for South Korea last night."

Shit. "Guy's always ahead of the game, isn't he?" I ground out.

"I'm sorry, sir?" She looked utterly confused. Clearly, she was unaware of Finch's side businesses.

"Nothing." I headed back towards the elevators.

"Would you like me to tell either Captain Maidlow or Mr. Finch that you came by?"

"No. I'll take care of it."

"Yes, sir."

I stomped into my own office a half hour later and flung my keys on my desk. Griff and Voodoo were at my desk before I could sit down.

"No, you're supposed to be happy T-Byrd now," Voodoo huffed. "You get a chance with Maddie. You've had a hard-on for her forever. Why are you still pissy?"

"Maidlow's in D.C."

Griff narrowed his eyes. "Doesn't mean he didn't set that phone thing up before he left."

"Maybe, but whoever called knew where she was. She hadn't been here fifteen minutes before the call came through. Someone is watching her."

"Maybe he did it before he left."

Voodoo rubbed his chin thoughtfully. "Or maybe he's got some weapons dealer lackey doing this for him while he's gone."

"Maybe, but why? What's his motive? He went to the DOD without our sign off. What's it gonna get him now? Maidlow doesn't do anything unless he gets something out of it."

"What about that other guy from Coldwell?" Griff wondered. "The king of the Iraqi black market back in the day? Doesn't he work for them now?"

"Marc Finch. Yeah, he's working there. He left for South Korea last night."

Griff rolled his eyes. "Setting up shop early, I see. Fucker."

Voodoo screwed his face into his look of thoughtful consideration. "If he didn't leave until last night, he could've followed Maddie and called when she got here yesterday afternoon. Of course, I was right behind her on her way here, and no one was following us. If they had been, I would've shown all of my supreme I-will-kick-your-ass-and-withhold-pain-killers-later skills."

"So, maybe he was watching Tier Seven and not Maddie," Griff suggested.

"But why?" I asked again. "What's he get out of that?"

Griff shook his head at me. "You are such a fucking idiot when it comes to her. Maybe he was only playing nice because Maidlow told him they needed your signature. He knows Chris went to the CIA and reported his black market shopkeeping. You didn't sign off on their comm system. Anyone who's ever been in the general vicinity of the two of you knows you've got it bad for Chris's wife. He's likely been out for revenge ever since Chris went after him, but he didn't act until he was sure you weren't going to give them what they wanted."

Chris's wife. The two words that haunted my dreams sliced through me and sank deep in my chest.

Griff cringed. "Fuck, man. I'm sorry. I didn't mean it like that. I just meant..."

"I know what you meant."

He continued to backpedal. "Seriously, T, I'm sorry. I'm happy for you two. You both deserve for this to be good."

I managed a haggard nod. "Thanks. Can you both just go? I need to think."

"You got it, Boss Man," Voodoo towed Griff out of my office and sealed the door shut. *Boss Man. Damn. I really was just stepping into all of his roles, wasn't I? Some best friend I turned out to be.* Nausea thundered through my gut. Bile seared from my stomach to my throat. I'd breathed too deeply. She'd given me that, but now, the wound in my chest enlarged.

I had to keep her safe. That was all that mattered. I lifted my cell to my ear and listened to it ring. "Go for Rio," he answered.

"Hey, it's T."

He cleared his throat. "Oh, uh, yes sir."

I rolled my eyes. He had to cut that shit out, but he'd been out of the Corps less than two weeks so I decided to cut him some slack. "Can I ask you something about Friday night?"

"Sure." Intrigue dipped into his tone. Good. I needed him curious and ever ready.

"When I left, was anything said about me or the woman I was with? Anything at all."

"That Finch guy had plenty to say about her, but I'd rather not repeat it."

"Can you give me the shorthand version?"

An audible breath from Rio reached my ears. "Do I have to?"

"Are you asking me if this is an order?"

"Kind of."

"Then yeah, it's an order."

"He said something about her... you know... being passed around Tier Seven and all the names that go with that. Said he'd like to get in on it. He kept running his mouth about literally screwing you over, which he thought was hilarious. For the record, when he said it I let him know what I thought about talking about women that way. After that, I left."

It would take me a day to get to Seoul, a few hours to find Finch, maybe a half hour to impale his ass on the Namsan Tower, and then a day to get back. I could get it all done by this weekend. Not a problem.

"Thank you for whatever you said to him."

"No problem. Maidlow was pissed you'd left, but he was making nice for the senators. Didn't say too much but I could tell he was ticked."

"Hey, Rio," I went with my gut. It had only let me down once and this felt right. Of course, the one time it had let me down my best friend had gotten killed.

"Yes, sir?"

"You're hired."

"Just me or Kingston and Garrison, too?"

"All of you. Meet me up here Monday morning. You can sign the paperwork."

"Thanks, sir. We won't let you down."

"Good. I'll see you next week." I ended the call.

26

MADDIE

Olivia recounted the plans while I drove her towards my in-laws' home Friday. "I am going to stay with Nana and Pops for tonight and for tomorrow night and then you will come and get me on the next day."

I was driving five miles under the speed limit. Life was spinning plenty fast enough lately. Slowing it down held great appeal.

"Right," I confirmed, "and you can call Mommy anytime you want." My right hand caught my gaze as I turned the steering wheel. I'd worn my wedding band on that hand for years, but I'd decided to take it off that morning. My fingers looked naked without it. It was safe at home in my dresser, and I didn't miss the weight on my hand like I'd been convinced I would. Maybe, I was more ready for this new relationship than I'd originally thought.

"And Nana is making me cookies."

"She told me she already made some and saved some for you to make with her tomorrow." Delores could be kind, as long as she was getting her way.

I glanced in the rearview mirror. Olivia didn't look worried, but she was rubbing Howie's ears. It took everything in me not to turn the car around and cancel the entire weekend. *You are not a coward.*

Besides, you want to do this. And I did. I wanted to have T all to myself for forty-eight whole hours where we could talk and laugh and share and do... other things. My stomach seized on the *other things.* My breaths disintegrated into quick staccato intakes, but I was determined.

"Will Uncle T come with you to pick me up on the next day?"

I bit the inside of my mouth to keep from grinning. She had no idea I was going on this trip with T. I'd lied to my own child about where I was going, but it was for her own good, kind of like Santa and the Easter Bunny. "I don't know. Probably not."

"But maybe he will," she insisted.

"Okay, maybe he will."

"Does Uncle T have kneecaps?"

I giggled under my breath. Four-year-olds. Who knew what was going on in their brains at any given point? "Yes, Uncle T has kneecaps."

"But he's a boy."

Doc McStuffins hadn't quite gotten her message through this morning, clearly. "Boys have kneecaps too, baby."

"No, they don't, Mommy," she huffed like I did not have a brain in my head.

"Yes, they do. Boys and girls both have kneecaps. They help us walk."

"Have you *seen* Uncle T's kneecaps?" she demanded.

Weren't we sassy today. "Yes, Liv, I've seen Uncle T's kneecaps."

"You have!" she gasped.

"Yes, I have."

"But they're private!"

"No, baby. They're not. You can see them when he wears shorts. Wait, where do you think kneecaps are?"

"On girls' legs." That didn't necessarily mean she had them in the correct location. "Boys don't have kneecaps because boys and girls have different parts."

"Uh, well yes, but the kneecap parts are not the different ones."

"What are the different ones?"

I nudged the gas pedal a little harder on my in-laws' street. I wasn't above letting her pre-K teacher work through the kneecap issue. "Let's talk about that after Mommy gets home. Look, we're here."

"Is this where my Daddy lived when he was a little boy?"

"No. We used to live in Omaha. They moved here after Daddy joined the army." The gold star flag still hung prominently in the window. Delores hadn't spoken to me for three months when I'd refused to put one in my own window. I just couldn't. Back then, I could barely breathe much less talk with random people about my husband's death. The flag on her home still pricked at my vocal cords.

"Are we near Gramps and Grans?" Olivia wiggled out of her seat when I popped the seat belt.

"Yes. Very close and they know you're here. If you need them while I'm gone, they'll come get you." My parents were the best. My mom had even encouraged this trip with T. She'd spent a solid half hour singing his praises. Of course, the first time she'd met him had been in the pediatric cancer treatment facility. He'd been holding a sobbing baby Olivia, walking her back and forth to calm her down, while I had to sign paperwork promising not to sue the hospital if my child didn't make it through surgery.

"O-livia," Delores sang when she opened the door. "Do you even remember your dear Nana?"

O-gag me. I fought my eye roll. We'd come over for dinner a couple of weeks ago. Or maybe it was months, but whatever, it hadn't been that long.

"Hi, Nana. Do you have my cookies?" Olivia grinned.

"Liv, that isn't polite," I ground through my teeth.

"Give Nana a hug," Delores insisted.

Olivia begrudgingly complied and then pressed on towards the kitchen. The house had been constructed in the early nineties which worked well because my mother-in-law's taste in decor hadn't changed since then either.

The built-in oak bookshelves in the living room paid homage to mine and Chris's relationship. Prom photos, wedding photos, dating photos — each year was represented in all its glory.

Every single thing in the kitchen was heart-shaped including the pink and teal rugs at the sink and stove. The pink hearts on the wallpaper border were the size of my head.

Chris's father, Cad, stood from the ancient computer stuffed in a corner of the kitchen. "Hey there, Livy-Lou. Come see your grandpa."

"May I please have a cookie, please?" she pled. Clearly the two pleases were how she intended to correct her lack of manners a few seconds before.

"Of course," he whisked one off of a heart-shaped plate on the counter and presented it to her.

"Thank you very much."

"Cad, she needs to give you a hug before you give her a cookie," Delores smarted.

"Oh now, she can hug me later. We're just happy she's here," he reminded her.

A knock sounded on the door from the garage into the kitchen. Cad opened it for his youngest son, Carl. I forced a smile. Since Delores had dictated that Carl purchase the home across the street from hers, he was over a fair amount. Poor guy.

"Hey, Carl, how are you?" My eyes searched for anywhere else to look but at his face. The countertops worked.

"I'm good. How are you?"

"Great," I lied. He looked so much like Chris it was like staring down a ghost. A cold chill reached through my bones when he gave me a quick hug.

"Can Howie have a cookie, too?" Olivia held up the bunny. She was good. I had to give her that.

"I don't think Howie or Olivia needs two cookies," I informed her.

"Is that the thing Chris's little friend gave her?" Delores asked with her customary forced choke over his name. She followed the question with a, "God rest his precious soul," and the sign of the cross.

His little friend. I ground my teeth. Because no one could ever be bigger than Chris, of course. T was actually several inches taller, but that would never matter.

"T-Byrd and yes. It's her favorite."

"Uncle T stays at my house lots of nights. He reads very many stories and does voices," Olivia reported when she finished the last few morsels of her cookie.

All of the blood that had formerly been in my head made a direct flight to my feet. Every eye in the room turned to stare me down, but they all swam in my vision. "Uh, she doesn't mean like that. She just means... well when she was sick... and now sometimes ...but it's not what you think." My mother-in-law's chin trembled. She grabbed a dishrag and started to dab her eyes.

My daughter had inadvertently handed her gold. Delores would go to bed for weeks over this. She'd have Cad and Carl doing her bidding constantly when she wasn't calling me to sob into the phone about how I'd betrayed her son. "We're just friends. Nothing more," I vowed.

She put the dishrag down. "I see."

How did people do this? Back at Fort Carson, countless army wives had stopped by to bring me dinner, rock Olivia, and attempt to help me with my grief, but they'd never explained to me how I was supposed to tell his parents I was trying to move on. Even the grief counseling the army had offered up never went over this part.

Carl gave an uncomfortable chuckle. "Um... Olivia." His eyes roamed the room until they fell on her. "Want Uncle Carl to take you to the park?"

"You're not my uncle."

Fuck me now. "Yes he is, Liv."

"But not like Uncle T and Uncle Smith and Uncle Griff and Uncle Voo-doo." She wiggled her rear end back and forth as she said Voodoo's nickname.

"Not like them, but still your uncle," I insisted.

"Uncle Carl is your *real* uncle," Delores huffed.

"But maybe not." Olivia shook her head.

I searched for a brick wall to beat my head against but came up short. "I'll get her bags and car seat." I sped back outside the house. Air rushed back into my lungs. Dear God, what would she say while I was gone? Did other parents occasionally regret teaching their children to speak, or was I just the worst mom in the entire world?

Carl appeared beside me as I grabbed her duffle bag from the back of the van. I screamed and then cringed. "Sorry. You startled me. I didn't see you coming."

He stared at me like another head had just grown out of my stomach or something. "Sorry," he offered. "Just thought I'd help." He unstrapped the car seat rather expertly for a guy with no kids.

"Thanks."

"Hey, Maddie." He stopped me as we made our way back into the house. "Don't let Mom get to you. In her head, she has this picture of how everything's supposed to be – she always has. She wants everyone to comply with her picture, but life doesn't always work the Delores Mitchell way. That's not your fault."

"Thanks for saying that. Guess I needed to hear it." He was the one who'd moved across the street at his mother's insistence, but who was I to remind him of that?

"We all need to hear it," he admitted. "Have a nice weekend. Some kind of teachers' trip or something, Mom said?" His eyes narrowed like he was trying to determine if I was lying.

"Yeah. Uh... it's a conference." I'd been a teacher for seventeen years and had never even heard of an overnight teachers' conference in the middle of summer, but that was my story and I was sticking to it.

"Right." He nodded. "Well, have fun. I'll make sure Mom doesn't get on a crying jag and force Olivia to sit and watch every baby video they made of Chris."

"Thank you."

"No problem. I'm here if you ever need anything. You know that, right? I was his brother. I could help out more."

"You're sweet, but Liv and I are good. I promise." I followed him back inside the house. "All right, I need to get on the road. Remember she has to wear her eye patch for three hours every night and let me give you my new cell number."

After lots of hugs and promises that I'd bring Uncle T with me to pick her up, I made it out the door. I could do this. I could definitely do this.

27

T-BYRD

I had no idea what state Maddie would be in when she got back from Chris's parents. I wasn't stupid enough to hope for excited. I was forcing her to leave her little girl with people it sounded like she endured but didn't like.

All of The Sevens had offered to spend the weekend with Olivia at the house. She'd turned them all down. Still feeling guilty over his *Chris's wife* slip up, Griff had even offered up his and Hannah's home for the weekend, but she'd been relentless. Chris's parents deserved to get to do this. I was fairly certain his mother was playing her like a fiddle, but we weren't far enough into this for me to determine that yet.

I was SF. Preparing for the worst was how we did things because life would inevitably punch you in the face. Worst case, she came home bawling. I could deal with that. Best case would involve her wanting to make use of her bed before we headed to the lake. I batted that idea off because hope was a cruel motherfucker that would knock the breath right out of you at every available opportunity.

Sprinting to the garage when I heard the lurch of the door and chug of her motor, I prayed for minimal tears. Relief washed through me when I opened her door for her and found her trying to smile. Annoyance played cruelly in her eyes as well though.

"Anxious much?" She climbed out of the van and into my arms. Couldn't ask for more than that. The flutter of fabric from her short sundress against my arm quickened my pulse. In my opinion, nothing goes better with a long drive than a short skirt.

"I won't even try to deny that. Did Liv do okay?"

"Do you mean other than telling my mother-in-law that Uncle T stays at her house lots of nights?"

I cringed. "I'm guessing Chris's parents would not approve of me staying over in the more traditional way?"

That got me something between a laugh and a huff. "The only way I would ever be allowed to have sex again would be if there was a second resurrection, and it involved my husband. Do not make a joke about a second coming," she commanded.

"Hadn't planned to. There were no tears, right? If you tell me she cried when you left, I'm probably going to go back over there and get her, fair warning."

There was my beautiful smile. A glimmer of possibility glowed in her eyes. I could definitely deal with that. "No tears, just lots of rubbing Howie's ears."

"Ear rubbing I can probably deal with... maybe."

"Oh, if she asks you about your kneecaps, I don't think she's talking about your actual kneecaps. I think she might think kneecaps are something else."

I set her down in the kitchen and grabbed the three suitcases she'd packed for one weekend at the lake house. What in God's name she had in there I had no idea, but if it made this less awkward for her I was more than happy to become her own personal pack mule. "What does she think kneecaps are exactly?"

"Not sure yet. Just thought I'd warn you."

"Kneecap warning has been noted. Now, are we ready for this?" My traitorous eyes tracked to her bedroom. We were deliciously alone. I called myself an ass for good measure.

"I guess so." Her eyes also scanned the house only she glanced around like she might never see it again. Fuck.

"Baby, we don't have to do this."

"I know. Let's just go. When I rehearsed everything I have to say to you, I saw us having the conversation in your truck."

What the hell did that mean? See, hope, it would never fail to let you down. "Lead the way."

I set her alarm, locked up, and followed her out to my Silverado. Pulling my Mastercraft X25 with the Vette wasn't really an option. The couple who'd sold me the lake house had been looking to unload the boat as well. I made them an offer on both, and we'd all left the table happy. I kept the boat at my house on the off chance that I could get out to nearby Lake Wanahoo for a few hours on a Saturday when I couldn't get all the way to Lake Mac for a weekend.

But Lake Mac was one of my favorite places on Earth and spending the weekend with her there had been what had kept me going for the last couple of days. Since Finch was still out of the country, she hadn't gotten any more fake phone calls from Tier Seven. Of course, she hadn't been back up there, and she had a new phone.

I cranked the truck and eased it forward checking the trailer and the boat as we left. "What was all that about what you rehearsed or whatever? You know you don't have to practice saying things to me. You can just say them."

She grinned and laced her fingers through mine. Was she holding my hand to try to let me down kindly or because she wanted to be in contact with me as badly as I wanted to hold her? "I do know that. I'm just nervous."

"About me?" That seemed crazy. We'd been friends forever. If she just wanted this to be a friendly weekend where we share the coffee maker but not a bed, I'd learn to deal eventually.

"No. About this." She used the hand not currently occupied with mine to gesture to the air around us.

"This?"

"Yes, this. I have absolutely no idea how to do any of this, and that's what I had to tell you before we get there."

"Still need you to be more specific. I could get a better idea if I could watch you talk, but wrecking my boat and my truck would suck."

She laughed. "I don't know how to date you. I don't know how to date anyone that isn't Chris. He's the only person I ever dated. We were an entity for most of my life. So, as much as I wish I knew what I was doing, I just don't."

I was skilled at withholding reactions. Nothing displayed on my face. I squeezed her hand. "Hey, you don't have to know how to do anything at all, sweetheart. We can figure it out together." The realization rocked me to the core. He was the only guy she'd ever slept with. In concept, I'd known they'd started dating when they were sixteen, but it hadn't ever fully cemented that he was her one and only. I had no doubt in my skill to impress in the bedroom, but I also did not relish the idea that she'd be comparing me to my best friend.

Before I could say more, she plowed on. "I have no idea what your preferences are. No idea what I'm supposed to do, or to initiate, or not initiate, or when to initiate it. I don't know if I'm going to freak out at some point or what memories all of this might bring back. I don't know anything."

"My main preference is you, baby. Just you. In any format you need to exist at any point. I'm there for it. Just don't shut me out, and I'll make it work. If you freak out, tell me. We can freak out together. If I do something you don't like, tell me you're not into it. If there's something you want us to do, tell me that, too. Just talk to me."

She gave me a nod and kept fidgeting with the hem of that dress that showed off her short legs to perfection. "So, I'm just supposed to tell you whatever I'm thinking."

"That works for me."

"That might be even more intimidating than thinking about sleeping with you."

"Have I ever let you down? Ever? One single time?"

"Never," she vowed readily.

"I have no intention of starting now. So, yeah, tell me everything, even the random shit you think is stupid. I want to hear it."

"What if it isn't random or stupid, but it is about Chris?" The quiver of her voice shook through my soul. "What if I can't stop wondering what he's thinking about this, not that he's necessarily thinking anything. I mean... I don't know what heaven is like."

Clearly, we were going out into deep waters sooner than later. "Here's what I decided last night when I was hating myself for being involved with you. I don't want to replace him. I've never wanted that. I want you and Olivia and hell, even me, to always love him. I get that he's going to be a part of this relationship, and I'm fine with that." I was fairly certain that wasn't entirely true, but it's what I was supposed to feel so I went on with the one thing that was one hundred percent truth without margins. "He loved you so fucking much, and I never want you not to have that, even if he isn't here to show you anymore."

"Wow." She turned those beautiful doe eyes on me. "That was... perfect. I wish I could say stuff like that."

"You aren't the only one who rehearsed what they were going to say today." I winked at her.

We flew past the Lincoln city limits and headed out into the endless cornfields.

She stared out at the corn like she was viewing headstones. "Can I tell you something else? I feel so guilty about this I'm afraid it could ruin this entire thing."

"Nothing is going to ruin this, sweetheart, but yes, tell me."

"The other night in your car...." Her teeth locked down hard on her bottom lip preventing the rest of the confession.

"I'm guessing it's been a long time since you felt that way." I took a stab, but had no idea if that's what she'd been planning to say.

She nodded. "Not just a long time, though." She squeezed her eyes shut like she couldn't be in the presence of whatever she was going to say. "I don't remember ever feeling like that."

Damn. *Okay, Byrd, what are you going to do with that?* I fished around in my head and ultimately went with the first thing that popped in there. "Honey, you were sixteen when you and Chris started dating. I'm doubting either of you had much experience at that point. It has to be different to start something new in your thirties."

"I guess. I don't remember dating. I mean, we must've done stuff in high school besides just prom and football games or whatever. When he was at West Point, I only saw him a few times a year. After he graduated, he went straight into the 82nd and then straight to Afghanistan. It never stopped. When he was selected for Q, there were days I wasn't sure if I'd recognize him if I saw him on a street corner he was gone so much. It's hard to do much exploring when you're never together. At least that's what I keep telling myself."

"Well, you should listen to yourself because you're right. Something like eighty-five percent of SF soldiers end up divorced. It wasn't just the two of you who struggled. It's everyone. It demands everything from you and not giving it your all will get you or your team killed. It's hell on everyone involved."

"A hell he kept choosing," escaped her mouth before she locked it up tight again.

It was true. We all knew it. Chris Mitchell didn't know how to be at home for any length of time. It made him crazy thinking other teams were out in the field when we weren't. The entire team used to get late-night phone calls from him itching to get back, telling us he was volunteering us for another deployment, urging us to get ready to go even when we had no orders. I just never realized she blamed herself for it. "You know Chris wanted to save the world, baby. I know it may not have always seemed like it but, I swear, everything he did, he did for you and Olivia. He wanted to make it safer for his little girl. He may not have always gone about it the right way, but know that."

28

MADDIE

I did know that, or at least, I told myself I did. When you're the choice that is never selected, it gets to you. There was one other thing I wished I could ask T about, but I just couldn't. Maybe someday but not anytime soon. I needed a new topic. Since everything before me was new, that wasn't hard to find.

"I didn't know what kind of lingerie you like," leapt from my mouth. "And shopping for lingerie with your four-year-old is impossible. Also, I couldn't stand the thought of Smith or Ryder following me to the mall since I know you've had them keeping an eye on me so... I don't have any." I could literally have picked anything to talk about, and that is what I'd stumbled upon. Clearly, my daughter got her penchant for saying cringeworthy things from me. But I loved the flash fire of hunger that burned in T's eyes. The way his jaw flexed when my words registered in his mind and - I glanced a peek at his jeans - points below. Being desired was a heady thing. I didn't know the last time I'd felt that way. "What are you thinking?" If he wanted me to tell him everything on my mind, he needed to be open and honest with me as well.

"That as much as I love the idea of you dressing up for me,

lingerie isn't what this weekend is about, and you're fucking gorgeous no matter what you're wearing."

"What is this weekend about to you, exactly?" There. That was a decent question.

"Connecting with you in a way we haven't yet. Letting you know a few of those preferences you were talking about. Discovering yours. Talking. Showing you my favorite places. Holding you in my arms. Touching you. Hearing you laugh. Being with you in ways we can't until we're ready to tell Olivia about us."

"I don't think I have any preferences," I blurted. If I did, it had been so long since I'd had sex, I'd forgotten them.

"You have them, honey. Maybe you need someone to help you figure out what they are. I intend to be that someone."

My nerves twisted until a trill of excitement lit through me. "How long does it take to get there?"

A low chuckle scraped from his chest. "Anxious, baby?"

"I won't even try to deny that," I quoted what he'd said to me back in my garage.

"Takes a little over four hours pulling the boat, and we have to go by the grocery. We'll need sustenance. You know, so you can keep up your strength."

I knew T-Byrd better than I knew most anyone else. He'd had to force that last comment. I wasn't the only one who'd decided to fake it until we made it. That realization soothed me above all others.

With every mile we progressed my nerves tied themselves into a tangle of anticipation and outright anxiousness. I could do this. I *wanted* to do this. Just needed not to think about Chris. Yeah, like that was going to happen.

The drive all the way to the other side of Nebraska reminded me of the last few hours before Chris would come home from deployment. The days were unending when he was gone. At the two-week mark, they would somehow slow even more. The last few hours felt like they went on for months. I was fairly certain the four-hour drive to Lake Mac actually lasted a week.

"Do you have to pee, honey?" He studied me.

"No." Why on earth would he ask me that?

"Then why are you wiggling? We could probably find you a hay bale to hide behind, but there's not much else before we get to Ogallala."

I laughed. "I'm a teacher. I can hold it for days if I have to. I don't know why I'm wiggling. I wasn't really aware I was doing it."

"Nervous or excited or some combo of both, maybe?"

"Definitely both."

"Good. We're on the same page."

Finally, he pulled the truck into a parking space near the back of the Safeway.

I watched him pile three packages of steak, two packs of hamburger meat, and a half-dozen chicken breasts in the cart all before he moved onto the sandwich meats.

"You know we're coming back Sunday, right?"

He laughed. "You know I like to eat, right? Plus, I'm going to impress you with my grill-skill."

I beamed at him. "You are supremely impressive."

He waggled his eyebrows. "In all things, really."

"And always so humble," I teased.

"Always." He loaded in a five-pound bag of baking potatoes, a few other vegetables, and half and half for my coffee. I watched other people watch him. Special Forces soldiers out in the wild were rather intimidating. They carried themselves with the knowledge that they could destroy anything that got in their way. I'd forgotten how cautious and intrigued women were with them. The way they stared at his ass, wrapped up in worn shorts, when they thought they wouldn't get caught. The way the shadow of his angular chin reflected on the white T-shirt that was stretched across the impressive expanse of his chest. A tinge of jealousy resurrected several old memories I didn't want to recall but, just like Chris always had, T only had eyes for me. It was beyond me how that was possible. One of the girls checking out T couldn't have been more than twenty-one. A busty blonde with perfect teeth. He'd surely noticed her. Special Forces notice everything, but he paid her no regard.

To my knowledge, T would date women a few times and then lose interest. My confidence continued to spiral downward. I wondered how many women he'd slept with. I wondered if any of them had kids. The jealousy increased tenfold with that thought. It was a fact that children were not particularly kind to your body. I had saggy boobs from nursing Olivia, and my stomach just didn't look the way it had before her. No one had to look at me without clothing but me, until now.

He steered the cart into the checkout and then wrapped his arms around my waist from behind me. He nuzzled his face in my hair until he accessed my ear. "Whatever you're thinking, stop right now," he commanded.

The throaty rumble of his voice replaced a little of my self-consciousness with unadulterated lust. How did anyone ever turn him down for anything with that voice and that body? My back melded against the wall of solid muscle of his chest.

"I'm allowed to have thoughts, T." I had years of arguing with a Green Beret to draw on otherwise, I would've been lost in his order.

"Not those thoughts – the lies that make you think you'll never measure up to whatever it is going on in your head."

"How do you do that?"

His chuckle shook through me. "I'm just that good at you."

He was good at me, and I was going to have to remember that.

THE DESCENDING SUN was chasing the corn fields we'd passed on our way when he expertly put the boat in the water down by his dock. His house was tucked away along the shoreline in a discreet alcove. The last house we'd passed on our way in had been a half mile back. The fading rays of the sun skipped along the lapping water. A faint scent of sunscreen, no more than a memory, played in the air. We were truly, entirely alone.

When you lose someone you love, you cherish every memory you have of them. I'd even tried to write down a few of the most impor-tant ones about Chris, so time wouldn't rob a single detail from me. It was the first time since his death that I wanted to push the memories away. I wanted to be able to place them on a shelf the way I used to set aside my anger and my hurt at his inability to be happy at home with me. I'd always want to be able to take them down and visit them, but right then, I wished I could put them away.

My wishes were denied. All I could think was how Chris would've loved it here. Maybe he could've finally relaxed. Been happy for a moment. Maybe not. I'd never know.

The sun caught T's long eyelashes and highlighted the dots of water that permeated his T-shirt when he'd gotten in the water to release the winch line. The Master Sergeant at the helm of his boat was a sight to behold. He moved succinctly, knew precisely what to do. The square set of his shoulders said he had no doubts in his ability. For as long as I'd known him, he'd always been that way. I wasn't aware of how utterly appealing that was until now. Or maybe I was and denied it so thoroughly I'd managed to convince myself.

I glanced back up to the house. From where I was standing, it appeared to be all decks and windows. I wanted to see it from the inside out. The views had to be stunning.

"Do you need any help?" I finally remembered to offer.

"Like I'd let you drive my truck," he harassed.

I shot him a rueful glare. "Do you think I can't?"

"I was teasing you. I have no doubts about you doing most anything, but this weekend I'm taking care of you. You just relax." He hopped out of the boat and climbed back in the truck to pull the trailer from the water.

29

MADDIE

"So, this is the living room, obviously," T gestured around the expansive room. It had a massive fireplace and was filled with overstuffed couches that looked perfect for taking a nap. An equally large television was hung over the mantel, of course. Special Forces often live with the barest of necessities, so when they were home, they were the guys who took blowup mattresses and sheets to the field for training. Everyone else in the army was afraid of them, so no one ever said anything about it.

They took their comforts where they could get them. I wasn't surprised that T's lake house had a few of the finer things life had to offer. The windows I'd seen from the dock took up an entire wall. And the views out to the water were indeed stunning. "Kitchen is this way," he continued his tour. A large deck with chairs was off of the kitchen and den.

He was gnawing on the inside of his mouth and working his jaw when he wasn't speaking. His tell. The house was gorgeous, but I was far more intrigued with the guy showing me around. His nervousness touched some place deep in the well of my soul. It prodded at it tenderly, almost seeing if I could bring it back to life. He wanted me to like the house.

"T, this is amazing. It's beautiful." I gestured to the indigo sky swallowing up the orange rays of the sun in the distance.

"You like it?" The way he sought my approval was a set of defib paddles to that place in my soul. Miraculously, it seemed to stretch its legs and start to breathe again.

"I love it."

That got me his megawatt grin. He took my hand. "Bathroom here." He pointed to a bath in the hallway. "Guest bedroom," was next on the tour. "If you ever want to bring Livy out here with us, she has her own room."

I'd been trying not to think about her. I hoped she was having fun and that I hadn't made a huge mistake leaving her with Chris's parents instead of The Sevens. When he pointed out the room, I wondered momentarily if he'd always thought of it as hers.

"Master bedroom is this way." He guided me to an expansive room at the end of the short hall.

"Wow," I gasped. The view from here was even better. I watched the boat bob in the water as the last fingers of the sun caressed the dock.

"Don't wow yet," he challenged.

"Okay, when should I wow?"

"Come with me." He eased me into a huge and distinctly masculine master bathroom done in shades of tan and brown. The shower had two heads but there was only one sink. It was very T-Byrd.

"Do I wow now?" I teased.

"Not yet, and we can make this girlier if you want to."

I giggled. "How would we do that?"

"I don't know. Tampons maybe?"

"I'm still waiting to wow."

"I'm getting there. My cougar is so impatient."

I pinched his chest rather hard.

"Damn, woman. That's going to leave a mark." He rubbed his hand over the spot on his pecs where I'd attacked.

"Which you totally deserve."

"Would you just come here?" Taking my hand again he led me to the deck off of the master bedroom. It was shaded from the water by a few massive cottonwood trees and a low roof constructed of rough-hewn timbers. Steps led from the deck down to the dock on one side but on the other was a hot tub. It was tucked away from the water's view, safe from prying eyes. "Now, you can wow."

"How many women have you brought out here?" I asked though I probably shouldn't have.

He drew me into his chest and wrapped his arms around me. "I've never brought anyone else out here."

"Wow." He was sharing this with me, this place that was truly a sanctuary from all the world had dealt him. My vocal cords tangled. I had no idea how to express my thanks, so I lifted my head. His right hand cradled my face and his lips met mine with that hungry intensity I'd come to expect but would never forget to relish.

A quiet moan slipped from my mouth into his when I opened for his exploring tongue. I gripped his T-shirt, desperate for something to cling to, when I felt like he might lift me so high I flew away. At that moment, on that deck, the winds rushed into my lungs, and I lost all ability to breathe.

I let my head fall back trying to catch my breath, but it was gone. Once the winds worked their way inside, it was all over. There'd be no coming back, so I had to figure out how to do this.

He moved his kisses to my neck. "Do you have any fucking clue how hard it was for me to keep my hands to myself with you in my truck, in this little dress, with your feet propped up on my dash?" His questing fingers rasped under the dress, explored my hips, and gripped my ass. He ground my pelvis against his rapidly stiffening cock.

A few breathy sounds of encouragement were all I could manage. Nothing sensical would come out. God, that just felt so good. "I need a fix, baby." I had no idea what that meant exactly, but I was on board with most anything. "I want a do-over. You're going to come so hard on my fingers again, but this time you're not running away from me," he growled.

"Please," I gasped. There. That's what I'd been meaning to say.

"I love you begging for me. I'm gonna teach you to do that every single time I have you."

His demands were subverted by the craving need roaring in my ears as his talented fingers dipped under the crotch of my panties. My hands slid to his shoulders, needing something far more substantial than his shirt to cling to. I gasped as I was lifted into his arms. For a half second, I thought I was actually flying but then he gently laid me on a low-slung lounge.

He eased the dress up to my waist and stared at the white lacy panties I'd selected for this day in particular. It was one of the only pairs I owned that also had a matching bra. "So fucking beautiful." His vow held reverence laced with greed.

My body rolled against the thick cushion on the chair. I needed him. Needed his touch. Needed his scent to engulf me. Needed to show him how much I wanted to be right where I was. I needed to not think. His fingers hooked into the top of the panties and slid them slowly down my legs. When he had them off, he shoved them in his pocket. Ownership indeed.

The heat of his mouth caressed my pussy, easing the dampness that resided there. "You have no idea how many nights I've dreamed of tasting you, do you, sweet baby? The torture I endured imagining having you like this but never getting to actually live it." He lapped his tongue up my slit and moaned. "So fucking sweet."

When T set his mind to something, he went all in. The feather-light teases of his tongue rendered me mindless. He provided the very thing I'd needed most.

He eased me apart with his thumbs and cleaned me of the creamy need that had been building for days. "So fucking good."

He continued his rapt adoration, and in that moment I hung everything I was on his pleasure. When his tongue spun up to my clit to tease, the world itself seemed to float away from us. We existed on some other plane. One without all of the pain we'd endured. A harsh moan vaulted from low in my belly. "You like that, honey?" Did I like it? Like didn't even begin to cover it. It was otherworldly perfection.

Another slow pass with his tongue made me whimper. I trembled. My body begged. "Feels good, doesn't it?" He drew my clit into his mouth and began to suck. Digging my heels into the chair, I lifted upwards towards his mouth desperate for more. I should've been ashamed but shame was on that other plane. Not here. Never here. My fingers wove through his short, brown hair. I wanted to hold him against me. Pure satisfaction sizzled down my spine. My mind centered on his hungry moans. "You ready to come for me, baby?"

That wasn't really a question so much as it was a declaration of his intentions. And his intentions worked just fine for me. Just like he had the other night, one of his fingers slowly dipped deep inside of me. I groaned out my desperation for more. He complied, easing a second finger inside and stroking slowly. "My God, you are so tight. You're going to feel incredible on my cock."

When he leaned his head down to suckle at my clit again, I had no capacity with which to consider his accolades. My body was capable of nothing but feeling the way he expertly orchestrated my impending climax. My eyes closed. My head shook back and forth. My jaw tensed. My channel began its telltale spasms. I couldn't stop it. I wasn't certain why I wanted to.

"That's it, baby. It's right there," he urged before he returned to my clit, "just let it go for me. It's all mine."

The bundle of nerves pulsing behind my mound unfurled. I choked out a sob and gripped his shoulder as the orgasm barreled through me.

"Damn, you taste good," he urged as he cleaned the release from me with his tongue.

Still lost in the aftershocks, I was barely aware that he'd lifted me back into his arms, had taken the lounge himself, and cradled me in his lap. "This is how it's supposed to end," he reminded me. I couldn't yet speak. Because the way it always ended for me was with the heavy hand of confusion slapping me in the face.

30

T-BYRD

I could find a single man, buried deep in the jungle, with nothing more than a compass and a protein bar, but I couldn't navigate the recesses of her mind to figure out where she'd disappeared to. I had a pretty good idea, but since I was lost in my own guilt I wasn't certain how to reassure her. She continued to hide her face in my chest this time so we were making progress. I tried to cling to that knowledge.

"You okay?" I whispered as the automatic outdoor lights flickered on.

"Yeah," she squeaked.

"Please don't lie to me."

"Okay, no."

"Yeah, me either."

She lifted her head. "Why?"

"Being with you..." I started but that wasn't quite right. I'd been in her presence almost daily for years. "Touching you. Making you come. God, Maddie, it's incredible. You're incredible. But there are days I can still hear him." I let my eyes close and forced Chris's wiry form to my mind. "Still hear him telling me the best way to do things. Teaching me how to be an effective leader and a kickass soldier. I still fucking see him sometimes. Like his ghost walks the halls of Tier Seven. He should've been there. We shouldn't be doing this without him, but the universe doesn't frequently ask my opinion of things so here we are. I want this relationship more than I've ever wanted anything in the world but sometimes it feels like I'm..."

"Replacing him," she choked.

I managed a haggard nod. "I don't want to replace him." Except when I had her like that, but if I said it enough, maybe I could convince myself, so I went on. "I want him to be a part of this relationship as fucked up as that probably sounds. I'm hoping you know what I mean."

She brushed a tender kiss on my jawline. "I do know what you mean, and I don't think I could ever be with someone who didn't want that. I like that figuring-this-out-together thing you keep talking about."

"Yeah. I think that's the only way through this. I need you to know that no amount of guilt could keep me from you. You're a part of me, like I said." That wasn't quite what I'd meant to say so I went on. "I need you to know I refuse to choose my memories of Chris over you." I longed for her to make the same vow, but I would never voice that request.

She gave me that same broken smile she wore for the first year after he was gone. "I think we just have to let each other feel however we're going to feel. I don't think we get to decide not to feel guilty." Once again, hope got in a sucker punch. That wasn't at all what I'd wanted to hear.

"Let's try," I begged. "Can't we fucking try?"

"Yeah, we can try." She nuzzled her head under my neck. "But it isn't going to work."

Telling me it wouldn't work was the quickest way to get me to double down on my determination. We could do this. He was gone. We were left behind. If we found comfort in each other, there was nothing wrong with that. We had nothing to feel guilty over. I refocused on her. I wanted this to be a weekend that made her wet all over again whenever she thought about it.

"Put your arms around my neck," I instructed.

With a genuine grin, she complied. My cock all kinds of liked her doing as she was told. I stood with her in my arms. When she tried to get down, I halted her progress. "Where do you think you're going?"

"You are not carrying me all over the house," she informed me. One thing was for certain, Olivia Mitchell got her sass from her mama. She forced the issue, and I stood her on her feet.

"Why not?"

"Because I have two perfectly good feet I can stand on." With the lift of her eyebrow, she shot the message right at my chest. She could take care of herself. Yeah, I got that. But I was also a warrior, and I'd never allow her to fight another battle alone.

"I hold Olivia while I cook at your house. Why can't I hold you while I cook here?"

She rolled her eyes. "Because I am not a child, and I weigh significantly more than my little girl."

"You think I can't hold you up?" I huffed.

"Dear God. Men. I swear. Take the ego down a notch or twelve, honey. I'll let you cook for me, but not while you're holding me."

"Kinda like it when you call me honey," I teased.

"That is literally the only thing you heard in all of that, isn't it?"

"No. I heard you. I didn't like it, but I heard you. Who knew cougars could be so stubborn?" I ducked out of the way when she grabbed one of the outdoor throw pillows from a nearby chaise and hurled it at my head.

She made a grab at my jeans when she chased me into the house. I caught her hand. "Handsy, too."

"You failed to return my panties, Sergeant."

"I'm aware of that."

"Give them back."

"No." I couldn't choke back my laughter.

"T!"

"That is my name." I leaned down to pull two steaks from the fridge along with a couple of beers. She swatted my ass. "Mmm, getting dirty already. I like it."

Her jaw cocked to the side. She tried to look threatening, which was genuinely comical. A full minute into our staring contest, she conceded. "Fine."

I gloated as I seasoned the steaks. She started making a salad. "Ouch! Dammit!" She jerked her hand away from the bowl. When I spun, she had her index finger in her mouth. She was cringing. My heart rode on the panic surging through me and landed in my throat. I rushed to her.

"What happened?" I reached over her head to grab the first aid kit from the cabinet, while I wrapped her up in my arms.

"Ha!" She yanked the panties out of my pocket triumphantly and then shimmied them up her legs. I appreciated the show and her delight that she'd gotten them away from me more than anything else.

"That was low down," I scolded. "You'll pay for that, my sexy little minx."

"Exercise extreme caution when approaching a wounded enemy soldier. Don't they teach that in Basic? Come on. Thought you were a Green Beret," she sassed.

"Keep talking like that, honey. I'll fill your mouth so full you'll learn a whole new definition for trench warfare." I watched closely to see what she'd make of that.

"Fill it with what?" she cooed and batted those eyelashes at me.

I shook my head at her. This was going to be a weekend neither of us would ever forget.

SHE RAVED ABOUT DINNER. I do make an excellent steak if I say so myself, but it was nothing compared to the sinful spice of her sweet heat on my tongue. I needed another fix. This time I needed more than to bury my face between her warm, willing thighs. I needed to bury my cock deep inside of her.

Rushing her was not an option. I wasn't that guy, but, my God, I was starved for her. I walked a knife's edge of arousal fed by the endless fantasies I had about her and the nights I'd willingly slept on the couch at her house so Olivia wouldn't know about my new role.

She reclined against me on the chaise we'd made use of earlier and sipped another beer. I'd gone from measuring time in breaths to measuring it in heartbeats. Damn, I needed her.

"It's getting late," she whispered.

Was it? I hadn't noticed. The entirety of my focus was on the way her lush asscheeks cradled my cock when she laid back against me. The memory of her body milking my fingers drummed in my head. Needed her. Now.

"Let's go to bed, baby." My voice was the consistency of gravel. Nonchalance wasn't something I could feign any longer.

She sat forward and stared up at me. "What happens when we go to bed?"

"That is entirely up to you."

That got me a few mechanical nods. "What if I just wanted to go to sleep?"

That isn't what she wanted, but she needed to be reassured that she always had an out. I would always provide everything she needed. "Then I'll open the windows." I tucked a few loosened strands of her hair behind her ear and stroked her cheek. Her eyes closed as she reveled in my caress. Her body made an effort to communicate its needs on her behalf.

"Why would you open the windows?"

"Because if you just want to sleep then that's exactly what we'll do. But I'm going to tuck you close to me, under the blankets on my bed, and hold you all night long. If the house is chilly, you'll scoot closer, let me keep you warm." Dammit, I needed to be her choice.

She grinned. Her own hunger reflected off the moonlight in her eyes. "I don't just want to sleep."

"I know." I drew her back to me, cradling her in my arms. "I know what you need and what you're afraid to want. Let me worship you tonight, baby. You have always deserved that. Let me show you how good we can be together."

"See, you don't get it." Her hand splayed over my chest. The heat amped the electricity flowing readily between us.

"I don't get what?" That was a direct hit to both my savior and my warrior sides. What the hell did she think I failed to understand? I understood every single thing.

"I already know how good we'll be together. That's what scares me most of all."

She was wrong. I did get that. I just didn't know what to do about it. We were so hot we were combustible. There was an undeniable magnetism between us. That was why I'd had no qualms about bringing her to the lake house, sharing my sacred ground with her. She fit. Like the puzzle piece that had been missing for years, she slipped into place, going from best friend to lover to something more, something undefinable. I had no idea how to explain that, but I was also tired of fighting the tide. I hadn't yet staked my claim. After that, then we could put the rest together piece by broken piece.

31

MADDIE

I envied women who'd slept with multiple partners. They likely couldn't pinpoint the precise place where they'd obtained the knowledge they had. Everything I knew about men and sex all came from Chris.

This would be different, but I was ready for the differences. It was the similarities that had me worried. I didn't want to be reminded. I wanted to forget.

Still, I pressed onward determined to show T how much he meant to me and how badly I wanted this relationship to work. With his hand clasped in my own, I led him back to the master bedroom. The sliver of moonlight danced over the lapping waters of Lake Mac, but I had no capacity to consider anything besides how intoxicatingly gorgeous T-Byrd was. He was trying to tame the dark fire in his eyes loaded with carnality. His hungry gaze scorched a few of the nerves I carried.

He jerked me to a stop near the footboard. "Maddie, baby, I..." he searched for words that didn't exist. There was no right thing to say in this moment. Nothing that would free us from bondage because our own guilt was the only warden. "Once we do this..." he tried again and came up empty. Once we did this, everything changed. I knew that, too. But if we fell apart, we already knew how to put each other back together. We'd already lived that. By now, we were experts, so I pushed that fear away as well. Everything would change between us, but wasn't that precisely why we'd done this? Isn't that the very thing we both wanted?

"I know," I assured him. "I want this more than I can ever tell you. I've wanted it so much longer than I even allowed myself to realize."

His eyes flared with my vow. "I need you to be certain. I'm too far gone. I've needed this for too long. Once I start, I'll never stop needing you. I'll never be satisfied. I'll crave you constantly. If that's too much for you, I get that, but I need you to speak up now."

Being craved by him was the closest thing to heaven I could imagine. I stepped closer, anxious for his heat, for his weight on me. His breaths caressed the top of my head.

Staring up at him, I managed a timid smile. "My bra and panties match." I rather enjoyed the way his brow furrowed.

"I want them off of you."

If I had been attempting to do this with any other man, I never would've been comfortable enough to smirk but, somehow, I did. "Don't you know, Sergeant? If her bra and panties match, you're not the one who decided to have sex."

His nostrils flared right along with his eyes. His jaw tensed for one heartbeat. "Show me," he commanded.

There it was again. The flood of arousal that filled me when he gave me an order, but I had no idea how to strip for a man. My plan had been to manage seductive without actually allowing him to see much of me. My hands instinctively covered the stretched skin on my lower abdomen from carrying Olivia.

"Now, honey. I've been patient for days, months, maybe even years, but I'm all out. Take that little dress off nice and slow for me. Show me what belongs to me now."

He settled on the bed, giving himself a front row view of the show. His eyes consumed me with a hunger that bordered on possession. A raw, almost primal need unhinged deep inside of me at his order. With shaking hands, I popped the first button on the dress. Then the second. His jaw worked constantly. "Keep going, sweetheart. So fucking beautiful. Show me."

A full-body shiver overtook me. I'd never stripped for Chris. Perhaps that was the point. Maybe he somehow knew that and was trying to make sure nothing reminded me of him. Something about the glimmering warning in his eyes said that wasn't it.

My nerves continued to knot along their ragged endings. Two lamps in the room glowed brightly. Wouldn't he prefer it if we did this in the dark? The intensity of his fixed gaze said there was not a chance in hell he'd allow me to turn them off.

Another button. My stomach clenched at the next. I gnawed on my lip. He did something else I hadn't expected, something that surged a hearty dose of sexual confidence through my veins. He popped the snap on his shorts. His cock was pressed to his abs by his boxer briefs but had swollen to the top of the elastic band. Tugging the shorts further open, like he was being strangled, he stroked himself over the cotton once, twice. I watched every movement of his hand. "So fucking hard for you." He kept his darkened gaze locked on mine.

I'd wanted to taste his salty musk ever since that night in his car. My mouth watered at the thought. I licked my lips instinctively.

"Sweet baby, I'm going to give you a taste as soon as you get rid of the damned dress." That drove me onward. The coaxing rumble of his voice raced through me, setting me on fire. I completed the last two buttons.

He was on his feet before me, rescuing me because that's what he always did. His capable hands splayed on my chest just above my bra. "My God, Maddie, baby, you are gorgeous." He slid the flowy fabric off my shoulders. "Relax and let me see you." At his command, I let my hands fall to my side. The dress whispered over my highly sensitized skin, igniting every nerve ending in its path. My breaths stuttered as they left my lungs.

His eyes tracked downward. His fingertips followed the course they'd taken until he traced over the wet heat gathered in my panties. "I don't fucking deserve this," he ground out. His eyes closed as he continued to explore. No one had ever said anything like that to me before, and I had never felt more beautiful.

I shivered against his tender caresses and longed for more of him to touch me. Working his shirt upwards, I stood on my tiptoes but still wasn't tall enough to rid him of it. He chuckled. "Need some help?"

"Please," I whispered.

"Do you have any idea how sweet you sound begging?" He popped the T-shirt up over his elbows, eased it over his head, and tossed it on the floor. My eyes feasted on every magnificent rope of muscle, every timeworn scar, and the shield and map tattoo that covered his chest, his right pec, and shoulder.

I slid my hands slowly over his chest. They memorized every dip and harsh angle, the heat that resided there. I ran my finger over a jagged white marking just above his collarbone. It was from the attack that had killed Chris. I knew. He was the one who'd radioed for help. They'd held a knife to his neck. No one knew why they hadn't killed him, too. For some reason, they wanted him to watch.

T was an expert in hand-to-hand combat. He'd gotten away and had made the call. The man who'd attempted to hold him had ended up with the knife in his own chest. If T hadn't gotten the call off, none of them would've come home.

I refused the memories and sought only to soothe his wounds both visible and invisible. His eyes closed again as I trailed my hands over the smattering of hair covering his upper chest, roughening his already impressive edges. I continued to explore, trailing my fingertips down past his navel to the dark trail of hair that beckoned. I admired the fluid flex of his abs under my touch.

Dipping my fingers behind that elastic banding, I let the heat spilling off of him be my guide as I wrapped my hand around his thick length. A low curse slipped from his lips. It stoked the fire already blazing through me.

I wanted to see him fully, to touch him and watch him throb. My fingers barely met as I attempted to circle them around his erection. With no conscious memory of deciding to do it, my tongue licked at his chest as I consumed the salty taste of him mixed with the vague citrus scent of his soap. He allowed me this until the need ignited in my chest, and I gripped with more need and sucked with more fervor.

I should've told him about my tattoo, but speech would've robbed me of his flavors filling my mouth.

32

T-BYRD

Jesus Christ, she was killing me. I wanted to pin those inquisitive little hands over her head while I took her so fucking hard the only thing keeping her sane was my next thrust. Tonight, I couldn't have that. Someday soon, I would. Tonight, I had to take this agonizingly slowly, or she would fall right back into the riptide of guilt she didn't think we could outswim. I knew better. I just had to prove it to her.

Her index fingers circled my nipples, and I damn near lost my mind. I jerked her forward, trapping her against me. That's when I saw it. There was a marking there at the top of her right asscheek. I gripped the globe and tried to study it from over her shoulder.

Her head lifted. Panic flared in her eyes.

"Let me see it," I ordered.

"It was this stupid thing I did trying to get his attention when he was at West Point." Her jaw clamped. I turned her slowly. There, on her sexy little ass, was a tat of a slightly altered West Point crest. Chris's initials were in the helmet. I covered it with my hand and began to knead. I couldn't go there right now.

Slow wasn't going to cut it, either. *Mine.* It was the only word my mind could form. Stepping back around her, I cradled her face in my hands. "Be right here with me, baby." That was key. I'd made promises to several lovers that I'd fuck their exes right out of their systems, because I'm a guy and we say bullshit like that. I shouldn't even want that this time, but I did, and I had no idea what to do with that. She was Chris's before. Now, things were different.

"I am," she whispered.

"Good." My mouth crashed down over hers starved for her flavors. I drew her tongue into my own mouth and sucked the soft seduction from her lips. I was a man of many talents. Special Forces meant I excelled at multitasking, so I wasted no time popping the clasp of that innocent little white bra. Her nipples were drawn to stiff peaks, dark and needy and trapped in lace, taunting me. No more. I jerked my head away allowing her breath, allowing myself to see her.

My thumbs circled the stiff peaks of her petite breasts. "My God, honey, so pretty." Touch wasn't enough. I needed to taste the dew gathered between her tits, needed to draw her into my mouth, nibble and suck, and see what she made of that. I needed more. I needed days, weeks, maybe years of making her come, making her mine.

She swayed before me as I drew her lush tits together and bathed them with my tongue. A quick gasp preceded her ragged groan. I released her breasts and drew her right nipple deep into the heat of my mouth.

"Oh...mmm...yes," whimpered from her as I sucked. Rolling her left nipple between my fingers, I continued my ministrations. "Please, T, more," finally tore from her lungs. I lifted her into my arms and half tossed her onto the bed. She propped up on her elbows while I made quick work of my shorts and boxers. I allowed myself a quick second of ego stroking while she stared at my body with enough appreciation to keep me going for years.

The scars marring my skin didn't throw her. She knew how I'd earned most of them. Her eyes took them in until she reached for me. "One second, baby," I soothed. Hooking my fingers back in those panties she'd stolen from me, I slipped them down her legs once more. "You're not getting them back this time." I brought them to my face and inhaled the delectable feminine musk of Maddie aroused. A wet patch in the cotton assured me she wanted this just as bad as I did.

I took my time now, taking her all in. She was stunning. Her expression eager for me to bring her satisfaction. Her breasts were mounds of pure need, crowned with her cherry-red nipples, hungry for my mouth. Her soft stomach was pulled taut, from nerves I suspected, but I'd deal with that later. The sweet little pouch where Olivia had resided inside of her rendered me weak from the craving need that consumed me. Desperation clawed deep into my chest. I allowed the image to take hold for one breath. Her stomach stretched tightly over my baby, residing there in her womb safe and nurtured. I imagined my lips on the swell. I shook off the images from an entirely uncertain future. Never before, never with any other woman, had those thoughts intruded on sex. This was so much more, and we both knew it.

I forced my hungry gaze to travel on to the warm wet heaven between her thighs. I was going to sink myself so deep inside of her she would ache from the emptiness when I was finished. I had to keep my focus right there, right where she needed me to be.

Another craving moan escaped her lips. I crawled up her body, letting her feel my friction against her skin. She bucked against me pushing me ever closer to the brink of insanity. "Believe my sweet baby had a request I intend to indulge." I cupped her breasts and plied them until her head shook back and forth against the pillows. I lowered my mouth to her left this time and suckled until she ground her sweet little pussy against my thigh, that desperate for relief. Her breaths shattered into quick, shallow pants. I punished and forgave each nipple in turn until they were raw from my hunger.

Her fingernails bit at my back as she began her begging. "Please, T, please."

Hearing my name on her lips when I had her like this was the climax of a thousand wet dreams. "Please what, baby?"

I switched breasts. My right hand followed a trail of heat to her thighs.

"Take me." She gulped in a quick breath. Take her indeed.

"Let's see if you're wet enough for what you're claiming you want, sweetheart."

"Please," she clawed against my back now, unaware. The pain registered instantly as pure, unadulterated pleasure. It sizzled along my spine and rid me of my guarded caution. Dipping two fingers deep within her drenched tissues, hard and fast, greed flooded through me. She was more than ready. Thank God.

I sat back to retrieve a condom from my wallet and she followed after me. As I leaned back, her tongue danced up my cock. "I promised you a taste, didn't I?" ground from my mouth. It was unexpected but magnificent.

Her fingers pressed against my ass. She brought me closer and drew me into the velvet sanctuary of her mouth. So fucking good. I intended to tell her that, but words eluded me. Hell, the room, the house, the lake, the entire earth itself eluded me. My mind spun. She was writing some kind of erotic poetry on my shaft with her tongue, and I sure as hell didn't want to interrupt.

"You taste so good," she gasped as she pulled back for breath but kept me going with her hand. Dammit, no matter how hard I tried I couldn't help but wonder if she used to tell him that as well. I ordered the thoughts away. "I always knew you would," she moaned. Always certainly did not mean *always* but it did wicked good things to my ego to hear that. My brain managed to reengage long enough for me to thread my fingers through her soft brown hair when she leaned in for another long suck.

"You like that, honey? Good, because I'm about to fill you full of it," I rasped. Her cheeks hollowed, and I had to stop her. It was all too much. I had to take her. Now.

Guiding her face away, I laid her back down in the bed, rolled on the condom, and pressed myself inside of her an inch, maybe two, but no more. Her sweet little channel nursed at my head. I gripped the sheets refusing the pleasure I required to survive. I had no fucking clue how she had a kid because I'd never felt anything so exquisitely tight in all my life. "Can you take more for me, honey?" I pressed as gently as I was able.

A frantic moan accompanied a tremble. She tried to adjust for my size but struggled. It really had been so long. "Please," she begged. Her pussy continued to flex trying desperately to pull me deeper. "I want all of you."

Jesus Christ. So tight. "I don't want you to hurt. Nice and slow, okay? Take a little more for me." I managed another few inches.

"T, please," frustration mounted in her voice. I gave her two quick, easy thrusts feeling her stretch around me. Holy fuck that was incredible. "Now."

With one fluid movement, I caught her hands, pinned them over her head, and sank myself to my hilt. She melted around me.

That was when my entire world tipped off of its axis. I released her hands so I could cradle her head. Desperately, I tried to shield the entirety of her body with my own. She would only ever be vulnerable to me.

I retreated and on my next thrust her eyes blinked open, frantic and timid. "T?"

"I'm right here, baby."

"It's...mmm." Her teeth sank into her bottom lip sealing off whatever she'd been about to say. "Amazing," finally escaped the trap of her lips.

"You're incredible, sweetheart. It's all you," I panted. I picked up pace, pounding into her, burying every mistake I'd ever made deep within her. She washed me clean. She sang out my name like a hymn, the only one she'd ever known. The savior within me fell to his knees in reverent worship of the angel before him.

This was more. This was us. This was everything. This was the answering supplication for everything the world had robbed from us.

She trembled. Her body rose against my every thrust. Her pussy milked every twitch of my cock. Perfection. Heaven held nothing on her, on us together. She broke on a wail of my name, and I collapsed against her. Every inch of her skin was a holy grail where I heaved my body in sacrifice. She silenced the constant chaos that ruined me every single day since I'd lost half of our team. I buried myself in the balancing force.

The hungry pulses of her pussy tore the mended edges of my sanity. Her eager lips seized around me. I lost all ability to delay my own climax. Her aftershocks drove me over. "Maddie," groaned from my lungs as everything I'd ever be filled the condom. *I love you* danced on my tongue. I managed to keep that truth from her. Her name would have to do.

I pulled her up onto my chest and traced my fingertips up and down her back, half expecting tears. I had no hope of keeping up with the parade of emotions marching through her eyes. She was distinctly quiet. Processing maybe. "That was incredible," I readily told her.

She nodded but still no words. For tonight, I supposed I'd have to allow that. I wondered if she was this quiet after she and Chris were together. Did it feel like that to him? It couldn't have. If it had, he never would've wanted to leave her. It killed me that most of the time that's precisely what he did.

I stayed awake while she slept, contemplating, questioning, unease rubbing me raw. She'd fallen asleep in my arms without saying one single word to me after all of that. Nothing. But then, in the middle of the night, when she was still mostly asleep, she crawled up on my chest, and whispered two sweet, sleepy words that ultimately brought me peace. "Thank you."

The next morning, I awoke to an empty bed. Panic spiked hard in my gut. I scrambled into a pair of sweatpants and searched. I didn't have to go far. She was there, out on the back deck, sitting on the chaise, staring out at the lake. Her legs were drawn to her chest. Her arms wrapped tightly around her like she wasn't allowed to take up any earthly space.

My heart ached until I saw that she was wearing the T-shirt I'd worn the day before. It was like a flag on a conquered fortress, and I knew whatever had driven her outside before sunrise could be conquered as well.

33

MADDIE

Silent tears I'd fought for years tracked slowly down my face. The wind refused to blow. It wouldn't dry them. I was in the middle of Nebraska on a lake, and there was no wind. How could that be?

These weren't tears of grief. I'd cried an ocean full of those. These were different. Tears of crushing disappointment, of confusion, of shame. Tears of the truths I wasn't sure how long I'd been running from.

"Maddie?" T's voice shook through me. Concern rode hard in his rough morning tone. I turned to stare him down. I certainly couldn't hide from a Green Beret in his own home though that's precisely what I wanted to do. "What's wrong, baby?" He was on the deck in nothing but a pair of grey sweatpants with rumpled morning hair and that voice of his. I could recall no other time in my life when I'd ever witnessed something so incredibly strong and sexy, and that only brought on more shame.

He settled on the end of the chaise. Confusion was pinned in his deep-blue eyes like a storm brewing over the waters. "Come here." He tried to gather me into his arms, but I shook my head. I didn't deserve his comforts. The confusion in his eyes turned quickly to devastation. "Why can't I hold you?"

I could only manage another head shake. He'd never understand the answer anyway. I could never tell anyone how awful I'd been, what a wretched person I really was.

"No." He finally huffed. "I let you shut me out last night, but that ends now. I shouldn't have allowed it then. I was trying to give you some time, but I won't let you fall back into that well you kept yourself in for years. Tell me what you're thinking."

"I can't." A sob convulsed from me with those two words.

He scooted closer. The hurt in his eyes almost drew the confession from me. Almost. But what I would say would hurt him more than my silence. He wiped the tears from my eyes with his thumbs. They were quickly replaced with more. "Come on, baby. It's me. You can say anything to me. Did I do something last night that scared you?"

Another violent head shake flung the tears away from my face. He had, but not in the way he thought. The entire experience had been rapturous. I'd never felt anything like it, never felt so worshipped and adored, had never felt so deliciously wrung and sated. That was part of the problem.

"Then what is it? Did Olivia call? Was she upset?"

"I haven't talked to her since last night," the haunted whisper scraped from the ashes in my throat.

He nodded. I saw him gnaw on the side of his mouth as he tried to figure out what to do with me. I didn't know myself so I was of no help. "Why won't the wind blow?" exploded from my mouth.

T caught my chin in his hand and wouldn't let me look away from his terrified face. "Tell me what got to you. Please. I'm begging here. I won't let this go. I'm not going inside. I am not leaving this chair until you tell me what it was that drove you out of my arms." SF soldier through and through. There is no white flag. There is no retreating. There is only forward motion towards the goal, even if the goal means tearing yourself apart piece by piece to save your team. "Talk to me," he whispered. The quiver of his voice served as a reactant, drawing the words I refused from my lips.

"I was so angry," took flight from the shattered fragments of my heart and vaulted from my lips. I clenched my teeth to dam back any more. No one could know. They'd never forgive me. *He* would never forgive me. It would hurt him. I could never hurt T more than I already had by running from him.

"When Chris died?" He wrapped his arms around me despite my refusal to allow myself the comfort. I nodded against him. "All right, you were angry. There's nothing wrong with that. I'm still angry. I don't think that's going to change anytime soon." He didn't understand. I wasn't just angry at the universe for taking him away. I said nothing, just shook with my own self-disgust. "Being angry is a part of the process. You know that."

Still, I remained silent. I had to bury this right along with my husband six feet down in Arlington.

"Wait." He leaned back and lifted my head again. Realization softened his gorgeous blue eyes. "Were you angry at me?" he missed the nail ever so slightly.

"No," erupted from me along with another deluge of tears. That was the problem. I was never angry at him. There were four agonizingly long days before they flew T and Voodoo home from Germany. Griff and Smith's injuries were much worse, and they had to stay in the hospital longer. In those days where grief filled every crevice of my body until I couldn't breathe, when people buzzed around talking at me because they were too afraid to talk to me and no one knew what to say anyway, I'd longed for T.

Everyone thought I was insane. I had an eight-week-old baby, but I was determined to meet him at Walter Reed. Smith's father, General Hagen, was the head of the Fourth Infantry at Fort Carson. I showed up at his house, with Olivia in tow, and begged him to get me to D.C. when they landed. Probably terrified of a crying woman, the only thing that could possibly scare a Four Star General, he'd agreed.

"Okay," T nodded. "I'm only so good at reading your mind, and you're scaring me to death. Please talk to me."

The words I wanted to set fire to erupted from my chest. "I hated them."

"Them?"

I nodded. "Yes, all of them. Even Griff and he was hurt so badly, and I still hated him for coming home. I can't believe I..." I shook my head and let the emotion saw through me once again.

When I could draw another breath, I went on with the rest of the confession. "I was so angry and hateful. I was awful. I had awful thoughts. I'm so ashamed. I'm so sorry. But I was never angry at you. I hated all of the rest of them. How could I ever have hated the people who mean the most to me in the entire world? God, how can you ever care about someone that does that? I'm a monster. And the worst part of all is that I never hated you." My fists clenched at my sides so I could pound out my confusion on the chair. "Why wasn't I angry at you, too? Why...?" Because I was a wretched person. That's why.

Suddenly, the sanctuary of his arms wrapped tight around me. "Because that would've killed me, and you knew it." I eased back and rubbed my hands over my eyes. My confusion must've been apparent even through my tears. "After everything that happened, all we'd endured, if you'd been mad at me even for a few seconds that would've been what ended it all," he readily confessed.

"I don't..." 'Understand' didn't feel like the right word, but nothing better came to my addled mind.

"Don't you get it, sweetheart? You saved me."

How was that possible? He was the one who'd put me back together. "I didn't. You were the one that stayed with me all those weeks and helped me take care of Olivia. Then you took care of us again when she got sick. It was all you. You're my hero, T. You always have been."

"It looks like I did a great job of making it seem like it was you who needed me. But that couldn't be farther from the truth. You were the reason I got out of bed. You were how I managed to breathe. Those first few months... you were the reason I existed. A little while after that, you were the reason I started Tier Seven. Now, you're the reason I started living again. That night in my car, it was the first time since we lost him that I could think about him without his last day twisting every other memory. I swear, when you sat beside me and agreed to date me, that was the first time in four years I could take a breath without it burning through my lungs. I told myself, hell, I told everyone, you needed me. That was never true. But I needed you. I needed you to need me. I couldn't do jack shit without you, Maddie. So never, for one second, let yourself think that you were the weak one, because that's just not true. You were so fucking strong. You still are. You stared down death and being a widow at thirty-five with a newborn. You took on Olivia's cancer and everything else life has heaped on you with a defiance and a determination that boggles my mind. On top of all of that, you put me back together, too. I could never have done it without you. If I'd gotten off of that plane and sensed, even for a second, that you were angry at me, I would've just let the pain take me. I never would've fought it, never would've made myself go on."

"You're just saying that." He wasn't. I recognized the fervor in his tone, but none of his vows made any sense to me.

"No. I'm not. You were mad at them. Okay. You had every right to be angry at everyone. They could take it, and you knew that. Griff, and Smith, Voodoo, Aaron, all of them. They were so much stronger than I was. What happened to us... it was all my fault, and I won't ever forget that. They could take your anger. I couldn't have. It would've ended me."

This time it was me who cradled him close. "You're the strongest man I know, T. None of that was your fault. Surely you know that. None of it."

"But it was. I knew something was up. Aaron kept telling us they were going to turn. He just didn't have the proof yet and..."

"Chris wouldn't listen." I already knew that's what had happened. He refused to acknowledge the truth. "He thought we had more time to catch them, thought we could get more on them before we turned them over. But I knew. I should've followed them more closely when they left the camp. I should've done something."

"It was no one's fault, T. It was a horrible thing that happened because there is so much fear and hatred in this world, but that isn't your fault either. Even if you'd done everything differently, run one of the million scenarios I know you obsess over in your mind, that doesn't necessarily mean things would've ended any differently."

"See that," he choked as he wiped away the last of my tears. "You're still the only one who can ever put me back together when I fall apart. You not being mad at me back then had nothing to do with you feeling some way about me you shouldn't have felt and everything to do with the fact that you knew how badly I needed you."

"I love you," I finally admitted the thing that had driven me from the bed that morning. "I think I always have. I don't know when it went from a friend kind of love to what I keep telling myself I don't feel, even though I do. I need to stop running timelines through my head. You don't have to say it back though. I just wanted you to know. You mean the world to me."

His broken smile shattered the remnants of my heart. "I wanted to tell you last night, but I was afraid I was pushing too far, too fast. I love you too, sweetheart. So fucking much."

"I came out here because sometimes the wind reminds me of Chris. I know that sounds insane. I thought I should tell you so you know I'm probably crazier than you originally thought."

He shook his head at me, like I was adorable, which I was decidedly not at that moment. "You're talking to a guy who used to fling himself out of airplanes for a living. The wind is the only thing that makes any sense to me most days. I can feel them all in it. It takes my breath away, and like I said, breathing for the last few years has been excruciating. I get your kind of crazy, baby. If you need some wind, come with me."

34

MADDIE

I let my hand dangle over the side, allowing the spray of water to tend my internal wounds, while T's boat sliced through the quiet lake. I faced the rising sun, letting it rid me of the freezing cold I hadn't been able to escape. The wind created by the speed of the boat was so forceful I had to close my eyes. It allowed the memories I'd wanted to put away the night before to replay once again in my head.

I could still see him standing in uniform searching for us. I'd gone with his parents to visit him during Plebe-Parent weekend his first year at West Point. I'd spent most of my freshman year envious of my friends at Creighton who actually got to see their boyfriends on occasion. Of course, none of them were dating a West Point cadet. I'd known from our first date that Chris's ultimate goal was Special Forces. I just never knew how much that would cost us, or what he'd be willing to sacrifice to get there.

His mother had been whining about not being able to find him and how he should've arranged to meet us somewhere specific. Her incessant bitching was drowned by the wind coming off the Hudson as soon as I spotted him. I cherished the moment, not pointing him out to her, just letting him exist all to myself for a moment.

He'd rushed to me, his eyes alight, his cheeks ruddy with excitement and hugged me like I was the only other person on Earth. His mother refused to speak to me for the rest of the trip, because it was a full five minutes before he even acknowledged his parents. Chris and I had spent the next few days trying to remember who we'd been when he'd left and why we were so certain we wanted to endure this.

That was the first time I'd understood how awkward my life was going to be. Being thrilled to see someone but accustomed to them being gone meant having to constantly rediscover each other all while preparing for them to be erased from your life again. It was how I'd spent the entirety of our marriage.

In the early days, we'd spend most of his leave in bed. It was heavenly, but eventually sex wouldn't subdue his cravings to return to the field. Some soldiers fight so they can come back home. Chris came home so he could go back and fight. There was always more that needed to be done, and he was so certain he was the only person capable of accomplishing it.

I'd made myself believe Olivia would quell his thirst better than I was ever able to. I never got to find out.

Gripping a handrail, I eased towards T as he leaned back against the seat at the helm. "Careful, baby." Gently, he eased the speed on the boat so I wouldn't fall, this man who could create wind so I could remember and so I could forget. His arm wrapped around my waist. He pulled me down into his lap, right where I'd wanted to be.

"Thank you for doing this," I shouted over the motor as he accelerated again.

He winked at me. "There was a reason I bought a boat. Life doesn't always give me the wind I need. Sometimes, I have to make my own."

I hugged him tight as the wind we sought whipped my hair against his chest. I smiled as I recalled Jenn and Bianca's determination that I start dating again. I'd been proposed to at the train station at West Point and was married at the West Point chapel. The army had dictated every facet of my life for years. I'd adamantly refused to even consider a date with anyone in the military, and here I was already in love with another Green Beret.

The way our friends had reacted to our first date made me grin. No one else ever stood a chance, and they'd all known it.

My marriage had been constructed on the rocks, and yet, neither of us was ever willing to walk away. I never wanted out. I just wanted him. It had been four long years and that boat ride, clinging to T, was when I'd finally admitted that to myself. I could miss him like crazy even though things were never perfect.

I squeezed T tighter. The internal wind I'd sensed in the last few days was still locked in my lungs.

I GIGGLED that evening when he crawled over me yet again out on the deck to kiss and nuzzle my neck. "I'm going to have really weird tan lines."

"You smell so good right here." He proceeded to lick the hollow just above my collarbone making me squirm. "Sitting out on my deck with your sun-warmed skin and your gorgeousness. It's entirely your fault I'm addicted to having sex with you." He was indeed stiffening again as he ground against my bathing suit. I wondered if that was something they taught them in the Q course or if it was just that the testosterone required to do what they do had rather nice side effects. Either way, I'd genuinely smiled enough that day to make up for the years when every smile had been fake.

His lips trailed to my own. He tasted like beer and sunshine and wind. I smiled against his kiss. He chuckled and dragged down the straps of my suit until my breasts were exposed to the fading sunlight. My back arched. I loved the hungry growl that elicited from him. Wiggling to the side, I managed to slip my hand between us so I could feel the response his body had to my own. A heady sense of power surged through me.

"You needing that again?" He thrust against my hand.

"You are extremely impressive," I whispered.

That got me one of his wicked grins. "Only the best and biggest for my baby."

"Very funny."

"I need you to never say that in reference to my cock ever again."

That did it. I giggled hysterically.

"Also, laughing does not do much for my ego."

"I was laughing at your obvious infatuation with yourself."

"Well, you have seen me. Can't really be helped, right?" He waggled his eyebrows.

I shook my head at him. "You are incorrigible."

"You're not the first person to tell me that."

"That doesn't surprise me."

My cell phone rang from the nearby table. I sighed. Frustration mounted in his eyes though he did hand it over before he went back to kissing my chest.

"Stop. It's Chris's mom."

He sat up. "If nothing is wrong with my girl, I'm going right back to your tits, but I'll keep quiet."

Rolling my eyes, I answered Delores's call.

"You do not care about Chris at all? You never did," she declared.

My heart pounded frantically. Sitting up, I searched the empty shoreline and deck as if someone could've been spying on us. "What is wrong, Delores?"

T stood. "Do I need to pack?" He mouthed. I shook my head. I was not caving to her lunacy... yet.

"All Olivia talks about is 'Uncle T this' and 'Uncle Griff that'. You've never even told her about my Chris. She doesn't even know him. How dare you?" Cue the sobs which I doubted contained any real tears since I wasn't there to see them.

The knife lodged in my chest turned a half notch with every word she spoke, though. "That isn't true."

"It is true. Carl said she talked about nothing but them the entire time she was with him today." Carl also never missed an opportunity to say the things he knew his mother wanted to hear. I shook my head. The past would always be there to yank me back in time. There would be no escape until I severed the cords. "T and Griff and all of The Sevens help me keep his memory alive for her. How dare you call me and say something like that?"

T barely blinked. To my knowledge, Chris and Carl had never stood up to their mother. I wondered what she'd make of my question. If only my voice would stop shaking.

"I will never speak to you again for this."

I rolled my eyes. If I counted up all of the times she'd sworn she'd never speak to me again, it was almost comical. "Well, since you're not going to talk to me, let me speak to Olivia," I demanded.

A few seconds later, Olivia was on the phone. "Hi, Mommy."

"Hey, baby girl. How's it going at Nana's?"

"Carl took me to the park, and Howie liked the swings but not too high. Nana won't let me watch tele-blision, but we made cookies, and I told her about the time we baked Uncle T a big, huge, humongous cookie with cake for his birthday and how about when he put icing on my nose, and how when he lets me have the biggest pieces."

That's when the trouble had started. I was sure. "That was fun when we baked Uncle T his cookie cake wasn't it?"

T grinned and settled back down at my feet. He rubbed my leg consolingly.

"Yes. And maybe we could make him annuda one even though it's not his birthday again yet."

"I bet we could do that. What else did you do today?"

"Nana takes lots of naps even though she's a big girl, so Pops took me to the toy store, and he got me a princess tent with sparkle stars, and he builded it for me."

I grinned at her exuberance. "Wow! It sounds like you had lots of fun today."

"Yes, and Uncle T is going to come pick me up on the next day," she reminded me.

I glanced at T. He was her hero, too. I couldn't blame her. She had great taste. "I bet I can talk Uncle T into coming with me to pick you up tomorrow."

"Was already going to." T whispered.

Of course he was. "Hey, Liv, let me talk to Pops real quick."

"Okay, bye, Mommy. Love you much!"

"Love you much, too, baby."

"Hey, Maddie, uh… how are you?" My poor father-in-law. Maybe someday he'd know what to do with me.

"Hey, Cad, is Delores okay? She sounded upset. I didn't know if I should come get Olivia."

"Oh, I wouldn't do that. She's having a good time. You know how Delores is. She just gets tired. It's a lot to deal with." Oh, yes, I knew precisely how Delores was.

"Well, if Delores is too upset to handle Olivia, I'll come get her."

"I can let you know. I think Carl was hoping to take her out to breakfast tomorrow morning. She'll like that."

"I'm sure she'll love it, but I won't have Delores's mood scaring her." I'd take a fair amount of crap from people, but when it came to my little girl, I became a mother shark. If you messed with my kid, I'd remove your limbs.

"I'll talk to Delores," Cad sounded like I'd ordered him to walk across hot coals.

"I appreciate it. Call me if you need me."

35

T-BYRD

I sure as hell was going with her to pick up Olivia. I'd met Chris's parents a few times back in the day when they'd show up at Fort Carson. The first time they'd come to Chris and Maddie's house to meet the team, Chris had whispered, "My mother is a manipulative bitch, so watch what you say." That's the only time I recalled Chris Mitchell speaking negatively of anyone that wasn't shooting at us. Maddie was blinded by her own guilt. I wanted to make sure it was healthy for Olivia to have a relationship with these people. Not that I really got a say. That fact continued to agitate my nerves.

"When do you want to tell Liv about us?" I asked as soon as Maddie ended the call.

Shock widened her eyes. Since I'd just been trying to coax her back into bed with me before her phone call, my question was probably unexpected. "Soon, but it's really only been a few days."

Actually, it had been a few years but whatever. "What was that all about?" I gestured to her phone.

If she'd rolled her eyes any harder, they would have lodged in her skull. "Chris's mother is insane."

"Did she upset Olivia?" Because I'd have plenty to say about that right after I stormed in and got my girl.

"No. Liv doesn't even seem aware Delores is upset. She's having a big time."

"What did Delores say to you?"

The air compressed from Maddie's lungs. She deflated before my eyes. "Oh, you know, the usual. She's never speaking to me again because Olivia was talking about you and The Sevens. According to her, she doesn't even know Chris, which isn't true but she's four. She knows *of* him but...." Her shrug carried the weight of a thousand nights of grief, and here I was interrogating her.

"That isn't your fault."

She stared back at me with defiance alight in those gorgeous eyes. "What happened in Iraq isn't your fault either, but you still blame yourself."

She had me there. "How about both of us work on not blaming ourselves for everything that resulted from July 11th?"

Her gaze softened. She squeezed my hand. "You let me know when you work on it, and I'll do the same."

"Let's go get her." I went on with my original plan.

"No. She's having fun, and it wouldn't help for you to storm in there early and take her home. My father-in-law or brother-in-law will let me know if Olivia gets upset. Delores wants attention. She gets some kind of sick thrill off making people miserable on her behalf. I don't want to give in to that." Before I could respond, she went on with words that sounded like they'd been brewing under the surface for years. She could no longer hold them back. "Chris was her golden child. Everything he did was perfect. I mean, you know how he was. Straight A's, football quarterback, West Point. When Jennifer Hanson was prom queen to his king, his mother tried to talk him into dumping me. According to her, Jennifer would make prettier grand-children and she was obviously more popular. Delores was awful before he died. Now, she's impossible. Whenever she feels like she isn't getting enough attention, she threatens to go to bed or to stop speaking, so Cad and Carl will cater to her endlessly. It's just so ridiculous. When they presented me with his Silver Star instead of her, she refused to eat for three days. She still tells everyone in her general vicinity that her son was killed in Iraq. It's like she feeds on pity. I can't stand her, but Chris would've wanted Olivia to know his family, don't you think?"

I considered everything I knew about my best friend. He'd never want his little girl to be in any situation that made her uncomfortable or frightened her. What father would? He did endure his mother on occasion though, so maybe Maddie was right. All I knew was that I hated the woman for making my girl feel like she was less than, even if she was only eighteen at the time. "He'd want her to be safe and happy, sweetheart, just like we all do."

"For the moment, she is safe and happy. I need to swallow my own irritation and let her get to know them without my interference. Just because I don't like them doesn't mean she shouldn't. She's her own little human with her own feelings."

My own phone buzzed in my pocket. I tried to nonchalantly ease away from Maddie while I answered Smith's call. "What's up?"

"You're in a good mood."

"Kinda pissed at the moment actually," I corrected him, but in general, yeah, life had gotten pretty damn great in the last few days.

"You sound better than you have in a while. Why are you pissed?"

"Nothing I can fix. What did you need?"

"Everything still the way it's supposed to be with you and Maddie?" Concern etched his tone. That was Smith Hagen speak for 'don't fuck this up, man'.

"We're perfect."

"Good. But listen, Finch just landed at Dover. A plane bound for Lincoln leaves with him on it in fifteen minutes."

"How the hell did he get to land at Dover?" The air force base hosted foreign diplomats, the president, congressmen, and military bigwigs. Not low-level supply contractors from weapons development companies.

"You know I'm all over it, T," Smith reminded me. "I called Hughes after I caught the flight plan from Seoul. He let me know when Finch landed. He was just as baffled as we are as to why the hell a pantywaist like Finch got air privileges at Dover, but he's looking into it for us." Matt Hughes was stationed out at Dover and occasionally helped Tier Seven out with contract work.

"Let me know what he finds. Finch has no idea where she is right now so I'm not too worried."

"Agreed. If anyone can keep her safe, it's us."

I grinned at that. "Thanks, man."

"Get back to Maddie."

"I intend to do just that." On the agenda for that evening was another boat ride since they seemed to delight her, dinner, wine, and the hot tub. After that, I'd indulge in her yet again. God knew I'd never get enough.

36

T-BYRD

Exhaustion tugged at my eyelids, but I fought sleep. It was nearing zero one hundred, but it was the last night I'd get to lie in bed holding her in my arms for a while. Like a sap, I'd been memorizing the warmth of her body naked against me, her soft breaths on my chest, and her leg slung between mine. If I got to do this every night for the rest of my life, I'd die a happy man.

There was more keeping me awake than the tranquility of my current situation. Something was off. I could feel it, and I needed a plan. I just didn't know what I was planning for yet. It set me on edge.

Driving the heel of my palm into one eye and then the other, I ordered myself to sleep. I was going to be shit the next day if I stayed up all night. I'd managed to doze for a few minutes when I heard it. Maddie may not have been army trained but she was a mother so she heard all sounds at all times.

Gasping, she sprang up in bed. "What was that?"

I shook my head and eased my feet silently to the floor. The motion sensor outdoor lights flickered on. Listening intently, I heard a second car door close. I was outnumbered. Not a problem. Sliding my bedside table drawer open, I lifted my Glock and made quick work of the pair of sweats I'd worn that morning.

Maddie slid out of the bed as well. Had I not been standing right beside her, I would never have heard her. She heel-toed it like a pro to her suitcase without a single sound. Woman was impressive as hell, but I already knew that. A slight tremble betrayed her nerves when she slipped on my T-shirt and a pair of her pajama shorts. She eased her hand into a back compartment of her bag and produced Chris's M&P.

She was badass through and through. Chris had taught her to shoot so no doubt she'd hit her mark, but her wielding a handgun scared the shit out of me. It's one thing to have knowledge of how to take aim and pull a trigger, and a whole other to actually stare down and shoot a person. A twig snapped under the weight of a boot much too close to the house. The bottom step on the deck off the living room gave its customary creak. I pointed for her to hide in the master bathroom.

She shook her head.

"We're going to end up shooting each other," I mouthed as quietly as I could.

The lights on the deck illuminated her scowl. She pointed to herself and then to the interior bedroom door. Then she pointed to me and to the exterior exit. I shook my head. "There are two of them," I hissed.

"There are two of us!" she came right back. Grabbing her phone off of the bedside table, I turned it to her favorites page where all of The Sevens were listed, and thrust it into her hands.

The thought that I was being lured away from her welled in my mind, making me sick. Before either of us went anywhere, I hit every light switch beside the doors to the deck. Light pierced the hooded darkness, illuminating everything from the house to the dock. The sound of heavy footfalls raced away.

We both sprinted for the door to the deck. "Stay behind me," I ordered. I cleared the deck before hotfooting it to the stairs. Maddie managed to cover me while searching out every darkened corner.

A car up on the main road roared to life. The lights had given them too much of a head start. We headed that way. Dust from the spinning back wheels assaulted the air. By the time I reached the road, I couldn't make much out. Definitely a small car, dark in color as it blended in with the night. The exhaust said it was an older model, but it was too dark to have ever hoped to see the plates or the make.

"Should we go after them in the truck?" Maddie panted for breath from our sprint.

"I'd never catch them with the trailer on it. Come on. I need to think."

When we'd made it back to the house, her cell phone rang. She pulled it from her pocket. Her face was ashen as she turned the screen for me to see that she had an incoming call from my cell. Keeping my gun up and my eyes wide open, I guided her to the deck off of the living room. If someone was inside my house using my cell, I'd rain hellfire down on them, but somehow I knew that wasn't it. My phone sat on the charger beside the couch right where I'd left it. It wasn't even on.

I jerked her phone from her grasp and answered it. "I hope your little game is worth it, Finch. I really do. Chris may not have been able to bury you under your own shit, but I will. Mark my words." The call ended.

"What is that?" Maddie pointed to a wad of paper shoved between the door and the jamb. I slid it free and made certain it was nothing more than paper before I unfolded it.

"Oh my God!" One hand flew to her mouth while the other clung to the M&P. I stared down at a black and white image of Chris in his blues. I didn't need to read the words that accompanied the picture. I'd seen the death announcement in the paper far too many times. "Who would do this?" Maddie demanded.

"I have a pretty good idea, but this is sick even for him."

"Who keeps a paper for four years?"

I knew she still had a copy somewhere. I just had no idea why Finch would have one or what message he was trying to send.

With that same fierce defiance that got her through life, Maddie stomped back to the bedroom deck and flung open the door. I raced after her. She marched to my phone, turned it on, and touched my call list. Her number was on there a dozen times but there was no record of the call that had just come through her cell. "Can we do that triangulate thing they do on TV?"

"It's not quite as easy as they make it look. Smith would have to know when a call is coming in and have the equipment set up. We'd have to keep them on the phone long enough to find them."

"Every time this has happened, you've answered the call. Maybe whoever this is wants to talk to me. If I answered, maybe they'd talk."

I despised the idea of allowing her to talk to whoever was arranging the calls. "Maybe, but we have no idea when this will happen again."

"What was that you were saying about Chris not being able to bury someone? Explain that to me."

I eased the pistol from her grasp and set it on the table with my own. Our would-be intruders had surely disappeared back into Ogallala by now. It was a small town but plenty big enough to hide in plain sight. I could've hunted them down, but I couldn't shake the feeling that someone wanted me away from Maddie. They wanted her frightened and alone. I'd sooner set myself on fire than ever allow that to happen.

Sinking down on the sofa where I could see the expanse of my backyard and the lake front, I tried to determine how much to tell her. "You remember Marcus Finch? The first guy you met at the winery the other night?"

She nodded. "The one who said something that bothered you so much you looked like he'd stabbed you."

"Yeah, him. For what it's worth, he told me to have fun fucking my best friend's wife." The words tasted like gunpowder on my tongue.

Her mouth hung open. "That's... awful."

"Yeah, well, so is he. He's worked for different weapons dealers for years. Loves the game. He gets in good with the top dogs, gets extra product to 'deliver,'" I made liberal use of finger quotes, "and then sells the extra to the highest bidder on the black market. Most often they go to our enemies. He loves to fuck with people, mainly for profit. There must be something he wants from me for him to be doing this."

"How is he not in prison?"

"Guy's got way too many friends in way too many high places. In Iraq, about six months before shit went to hell, Chris decided Team Seven was going to take him down. He spent months gathering evidence, taking pictures, even talking to the buyers that he could get to. He turned it all over to the CIA a couple of days before we were attacked. Nothing ever came of it."

"So, you think he's coming after me because of what Chris did? That doesn't make any sense. It was a long time ago."

Defeat sucker punched me. I couldn't believe I'd allowed her to become a pawn in this game between Tier Seven and Coldwell Harding. This was entirely my fault. "The timeline does fit. Coldwell Harding almost lost their shirts six years ago when they were caught by NCIS for billing the U.S. Navy for things that were never delivered. Then they developed a new scope that turned out to be shit. When a few SF teams were asked to try it out, Griff told Clint Tucker, the president of the company, that it wasn't fit for Red Rider BB Guns, much less military weaponry. Maidlow and Tucker used their own personal money to keep the company afloat after that. This comm unit was supposed to be what drove them back into the black. They've been working on it for years. I'm sure to them it seems that Team Seven is always who's standing in their way. Finch was holding off on his revenge against us in hopes I'd give them the coveted Tier Seven sign off. This all started right after I walked. You're an extremely appealing pawn to them. You're the way to get to me, to the team, and even to get back at Chris, if that's possible. Believe me, Finch is low enough to want revenge on the dead."

37

MADDIE

G uilt shadowed T's handsome features, swallowing him whole. I couldn't stand it. "Hey, look at me." I settled on the sofa beside him. "None of this is your fault."

"Then whose fault is it?" Skepticism played harshly in his tone.

"I'm going to go with the people who are doing it."

"They wouldn't be doing it if I hadn't ever taken you to that gala."

"If you hadn't taken me to the winery, we'd still be dancing around each other, too afraid to admit our attraction to each other. Personally, I think what we're working on here is more than worth whatever these idiots are doing. Besides," I eased closer and wrapped my arms around him, "I happen to be dating the president of Tier Seven Security. He's this amazing man who loves with his whole heart and fights to protect the people he cares about just as hard. I know he'll catch this Finch guy or whoever is doing this. I'd really like to help him."

I prayed T's deep breath washed some of the guilt from his soul. He tightened his arms around me. "You know I'd die before I ever let anyone hurt you, right?"

"I do know that." I knew it, but I also knew I could not survive this life without him, so we weren't even going there. The crumpled copy of Chris's death announcement in the Omaha World-Herald stared back at me, mocking and cruel. "I wonder if his intention was to shove that in the door and nothing else. I bet he wasn't counting on us waking up. He wanted us to find it in the morning."

"What makes you think that?" T quizzed.

"Because it's straight out of some kind of corny horror flick. I mean, come on. It's creepy. It makes sure we remember who pissed him off, but it's not terribly threatening. If he's still so angry about Chris turning over that information on him, maybe it's some kind of lame veiled threat or something. It's certainly not very specific. We both know he died. You were there."

"Maybe." I watched T gnaw the inside of his mouth as he considered. A full minute later he shook his head. "I want to know who the other person was. Two car doors closed. They weren't even all that quiet about it. Finch knows I'm extensively trained. He went up against a Green Beret and a mom, the two most vicious fighting forces on the planet. It was almost like he wanted to get caught. I definitely think it's Finch but I'm not ruling out any possibilities."

"If they'd wanted to be caught, they sure got out of here quickly."

"None of it makes any sense."

I recognized the hard-lined expression on T's face. "Maybe Finch is just really bad at being quiet. Maybe he thought he'd be able to get up on the deck without us knowing. What aren't you telling me?" Until that moment, I'd had no fear, but whatever had him unnerved was pricking at my determination to appear unaffected by all of this.

He shook his head.

"Tell me. I'm the one this guy is trying to scare. That's my husband's death announcement he shoved in the door. I deserve to know all parts of this."

He cradled the back of my head in his hand and guided me to his shoulder. "How did he know you were here, and how the hell did he know how to call you on a brand-new phone?"

Okay, I hadn't gotten there yet. My heart triple-timed its normal beat. How had he done that? I had no logical answers to offer up. It made no sense to me that someone who'd been reported but clearly hadn't gotten into any trouble would care enough to come after me. "I don't know," I finally admitted.

"Yeah, me either, but I intend to find out."

"I know you'll catch whoever this is. I have no doubt."

"I plan to call in a few favors tomorrow morning. I need more to go on, but I plan to start at the top and work my way down."

"I want to help you." He had to let me. If Chris had anything to do with this, I had the right to help.

"I know you do, sweetheart. I don't even have a plan yet, so there's nothing for you to help with. I won't keep anything from you. I just don't have any answers yet."

"Just promise not to be some kind of martyr and decide I'm better off without you, please." I could see those very thoughts hovering on the horizon. Shame was fighting for placement in his eyes.

"Probably should've figured that out before the Coldwell Harding event."

"T!"

He shook his head. "I told you, you're a part of me. I'd have to strip sinew from bone for you not to be a part of my life, baby. I would never let anyone hurt you. It pisses me off that they successfully scared you. I'm going to figure this out and then we're going to go on and be together just the way we want."

Here's the thing about the men in Special Forces. They know how to lie so well they occasionally even believe themselves. On top of figuring out who was doing this, I had to convince him that life didn't always go according to plan, but that doesn't mean you stop living it.

I'd had to convince him of that once before. He was right. We'd saved each other.

38

T-BYRD

I finally managed to get Maddie back to sleep in my lap on the couch. She'd checked that app thing that assured her Olivia was right where she was supposed to be a dozen times. She was asleep at her grandparents' house, safe and sound. My sweet baby was a sucker for me running my fingers through her hair while she cuddled under a blanket, so I'd made liberal use of that tactic. I'd finally gotten her to put the phone down and go to sleep. She was out like a light, but I had no intentions of following her into slumber. I had to keep her safe. It was my fault she was caught in their web.

Easing my phone off of the table, I checked the time. Smith would have to get over the late hour. I touched his name.

"I fucking hate you so fucking much," groaned out of his mouth in some kind of odd mumble.

"I love you, too," I whispered.

"Why the hell are you calling me at...zero three thirty?"

"We had some late-night guests up here at my fucking lake house. You know the house approximately five other people on this planet know I own. One of them is the woman sleeping in my lap." That got his attention.

"Holy shit, Finch showed up at Lake Mac."

"I didn't ID him, but he shoved one of the newspapers about Chris's death in my sliding glass door. He used to pull shit like that all the time back in the day."

"Sick bastard. Did Maddie see it?"

"Yeah. She handled it better than I did honestly." I kept my voice to a low whisper.

"He's just fucking with you, T. Same way he did with Chris. This is his sick game."

"Yeah, I know, but how the hell did he know where we were? After he left, Maddie got another spoofed call on her new phone. This one said it was me calling from my personal cell."

"How the hell?" Smith gasped.

"That's what I want to know."

"Maybe he's getting to her through you."

"Explain that," I ordered.

"He could have your phone tagged someway and have gotten her new number through your phone. Takes some pretty high tech fuckery to do that, though."

"But that is a possibility?"

"Kind of. Maybe. I need to research. Let me make some coffee and get to the office. I'll see what I can dig up. I'll call you as soon as I know something."

"Thanks, man."

"I'd say 'anytime,' but if we could avoid the middle of the damned night, I'd really appreciate it."

"I'll do my best."

"You go take care of our girl. I'll call you later." *My girl.* I mentally corrected him. My girl and my fault. How could I have been so fucking stupid? I'd spent all of my brainpower coming up with contingency plans for Maidlow and had forgotten all about Finch's dealings with Chris. There was one more call I needed to make, one that might explain all of this. But I wasn't CIA Op Roman Becker's boss, not that I hadn't tried to hire him a half-dozen times. Calling him in the middle of the night was a no go.

If someone had informed me a year ago, or hell a month ago, that the CIA had finally decided to go after Finch, I'd have been delighted. I would've flown to D.C. for the trial on my own dime just to see him burn. But not now. Not if it meant Maddie was the insurance policy he planned to use to get out of his shit dealings. I had no idea how he'd skated through Chris's endless evidence last time. Bribery and threats were the only thing that made any sense at all. I stared down at her fast asleep in my arms. It was the first time in my life that I had something I'd willingly choose over watching a rat bastard burn in the hell he deserved. It was the first time I had something I simply wasn't willing to lose.

Maddie woke up a little after five. She'd been irritated that she'd slept and I hadn't. I poured some coffee down her and she came around. I wasn't trying to cut her out of this shitstorm we were standing in. I also wasn't in the habit of letting someone else clean up the mess I'd created.

We'd planned to stay through lunch and then head back to pick up Olivia, but the only place I'd ever found any peace had been violated. Until I got my hands on the asshole that did it, I'd have no rest. As soon as Maddie stepped into the shower, I called Roman.

"If it's not the mighty king of Tier Seven Security, the hottest new firm to frighten the D.C. elite in quite some time. How are you, your highness?" he chuckled. I had to give it to the guy. He was infuriatingly charming.

"Been better."

"Anything I can do to help?" Roman was smoother than the barrel on a sniper's long gun and twice as lethal. He's the kind of guy who makes you glad he's working for us instead of them.

"Maybe. Has the name Marcus Finch made the rounds up there recently?"

"Come on, T. If it has, I can't tell you that. If it hasn't, I can't tell you that either." Every single time I'd ever discussed Finch with Roman, his voice sharpened with what sounded like fury. I wondered what Finch had done and what he'd ultimately pay for.

"What can you tell me?" I'd play the game if I had to.

"I could perhaps mention that the Director of Central Intelligence and the National Security Advisor are both extremely interested in what we frequently refer to as revenue loss."

Shit. So, they weren't going after Finch for treason. They were going after the money the DOD was losing in misappropriated equipment, which would obviously lead right back to Finch.

"I'm guessing you're already aware he's been in Seoul. I assume he's setting up shop."

Roman gave me a mirthless chuckle. "Has he?"

Knowing him, whoever Finch thought he was meeting with in Korea was actually an undercover CIA Op. *Dumbass.*

"Would my name be on the list of witnesses in this revenue loss case?"

"What do you think?"

Every curse word I knew marched through my head. "Listen, do you remember Chris's wife, Maddie?"

"Madeline Lewis Mitchell, age thirty-nine, second grade teacher at Kimridge Elementary, mother to Olivia Ruth Mitchell, age four. I might've heard of her."

"That's fucked up. You know that, right?"

That got me genuine laughter. "I leave no stone unturned. You know *that*, right?"

"Yeah, well, Finch is trying to scare her. I'm sure he's still worried about all of the information Chris handed you guys. He's after her."

"Congratulations, T," Roman's smile was evident in his tone.

"What the hell are you congratulating me for?"

"Falling in love. I expect an invite to the wedding. I take it you're calling me because of your concern that Marcus might use her to keep you from... performing duties that are best for the interests of the United States. Why don't you just enjoy Maddie and let me do what I do? Leave Finch to me." There it was again. Roman's tone dripped with something akin to vengeance.

"As long as he's after her, I'm not backing down. What the hell are you going to do from D.C.?"

"Who said anything about me being in D.C.?"

39

MADDIE

"You called the CIA while I was in the shower?" I tried to recall exactly how this had become my life. I also tried to remember if Chris had ever phoned anyone at the CIA while we'd been married. If he had, I didn't know about it. T was much more forthcoming with information than Chris had ever been. T had promised to tell me everything. So far, it seemed like he intended to do just that.

"I did." T ground his teeth. The interstate outside of Ogallala had turned into a parking lot for some reason.

I leaned up in my seat. "I see flashing lights up ahead, but I can't tell what happened."

"Probably too much to hope that a manure truck overturned on Finch's car while he was making his escape."

I grinned. "I'm not that lucky. He deserves it though."

"I did promise to bury him in shit." A harsh breath escaped T's lungs.

Beaming at that, I laced our fingers together. It had been such a long time since I'd held anyone's hand while they drove. There was certainly no wind in T-Byrd's truck save the air conditioner, but I still couldn't quite catch my breath. We needed to hurry up and find this

Finch guy so we could enjoy this. T might've been hoping for overturned cow shit on our enemies, but I was crossing my fingers that maybe this time I could capture the wind and keep it. "Well, what did the CIA say?"

T chuckled. "I called Roman Becker. I didn't get to talk to the entire agency or anything. Roman never says much and always says enough. That's one of the reasons I'm determined to get him to leave D.C. and come to Tier Seven."

"Roman Becker. That's such a CIA kind of name. I wonder if his parents knew he'd end up working for them when they named him." I was running out of things to say. My brain was filled to max capacity with how this Finch person knew where I was, knew how to call me, didn't seem afraid of T, and what he might do next.

T rolled his eyes. "See, women even think his *name* is sexy." He shook his head. "Maybe I should rethink hiring him."

That yanked me out of my reverie. "Aww, honey, don't be jealous. I'm much more of a Special Forces kind of girl." I leaned across the truck and brushed a kiss on his cheek. My lips tingled from the connection. Definitely needed to remember that in case it went away when I became accustomed to it.

Finally, I got one of his full-on grins. "Oh yeah?"

"Definitely. What is it you all used to say about being a Green Beret?"

His hearty laughter filled the cab of the truck. The tension locked in my stomach subsided at that sound. "We penetrate deeper, last longer, recover faster, and carry a heavier payload," he quoted back to me complete with an eyebrow waggle.

"That's it." I shook my head. "Did Chris come up with that?" I'd never thought to ask.

Since we hadn't moved in ten minutes, he put the truck in park. "You kidding me? Chris was way too Eagle Scout to ever say shit like that except maybe to you. That was all Voodoo's work."

I giggled. "Should've guessed that." Disappointment continued to tug at my heart though. This wasn't how our weekend was supposed to end. "Thank you for taking me to the lake. It was amazing. I hate we had to leave early." That's what I'd been trying to tell him for the last hour.

He squeezed my hand. "I loved you being up there with me. I'll bring you back as soon as I've turned Finch inside out and fed him his own sac."

"That's quite the image."

"I just wish the CIA would move in on him before he pulls something else."

"Why won't they? I mean if Chris gave them all of that evidence and they're going to finally use it, why don't they just arrest him?"

"I don't have a security clearance high enough to get to know that. Roman's waiting on something. I could tell that, but I have no idea what. He's wanted Finch for a long time."

"That is supremely frustrating, but I'm tired of talking about him. When we were on the boat last night, I kept thinking that you're like summer." That breathless sensation continued to make me grin.

"I'm like summer?" His brow furrowed.

Occasionally, it was fun to confuse Special Forces. "Yeah."

"Summer means what exactly?"

"Since I became a teacher, I still live for that excitement about summer each year, just like kids do. I love my job, but every year, right around April, I still get spring fever. I think it's because in summer you can be you. You can exist outside of everyone's expectations, you know? I don't have to be Ms. Mitchell the teacher. I can just be Maddie. You always make me feel that way. I can just be me when I'm with you. I love that."

I watched his chest expand with a deep breath. I wondered if it still hurt him to breathe or if maybe I was easing that a little. "I spent years becoming whatever I needed to be in order to get a mission accomplished. Culture training, languages, studying to assume another identity. We did it so often for so long I used to worry I wouldn't recognize the man I actually was if he throat punched me. You have to have a lot of constants in your life, permanent points on your own map, to get you back to where you were. You've always been that for me, baby. I get what you're saying. This being in love thing is pretty cool."

"Wow. Do you just always know the perfect things to say?"

"Nah. I just love you. I think that helps me say good things."

He kept saying that, too. I assumed that came from being friends with someone for years and years before you fall in love with them, but I swore every time he made the vow it flowed through my body, found the places I was most ruined, and healed me there. "It's very cool." Even for the second time.

"Finally," he huffed as we were allowed to move ahead approximately a hundred feet. His phone rang in the center console. Smith's name flashed on the screen. "'Bout damn time," he mumbled before he answered the call on speaker. I knew it was such a stupid thing to be excited about, but I was genuinely touched that he was really going to let me know all of the details about this Finch thing. "Do you think he's getting her number through my phone because I can pitch it right now," he demanded.

"Listen, T, we have bigger issues," Smith sounded grave. My stomach turned and bile slithered to my throat.

"Are you okay?" I leapt into the conversation. "Did Finch hurt one of you?"

"Uh, hey, Maddie. I'm... okay. We're all... okay. T, man, I need you to take me off speaker."

40

T-BYRD

That was not a good sign. I brought the phone to my ear. "All right, it's just me. What the hell happened?"

"Where are you?" Smith demanded. Fuck. This was getting worse.

"Just made it through Ogallala. Traffic was at a standstill for a while."

"Damn, that is not what I wanted to hear."

"Just tell me what the hell happened."

"I got the notification that the alarm at Maddie's house had been tripped. We all got out here in under twenty minutes and the police beat us here." A hurricane of vomit swirled in my gut. I'd kill him. Whatever the CIA had planned for him, it wasn't enough. I wanted a go at Finch before they ever got their hands on him.

Like any good SF soldier, Smith marched on. "But the house is a disaster. Everything has been gone through. If anything is missing, one of you is going to have to tell the cops that, because it looks like it's all here just not in the location she normally keeps it. Even her jewelry is on her dresser, but the jewelry drawers themselves are empty. Her laptop is open on her coffee table. Who doesn't take the laptop? That's the thing. He had to have been in here for hours to have done this. I can't figure out the timeline. Maybe he figured out her code, got in, went through shit, left, and then decided to come back in but didn't get the code entered in time or something. It doesn't make any sense. How do you get in once, but then get tripped up by the alarm?"

"If the alarm went off twenty minutes ago, he has to be close. Get off the phone with me and go find him," I seethed.

"T, come on, give us a little credit. Griff, Voodoo, and Ryder are all over it. So are the police. Griff even admitted we need to hire more people, so you know, small win for the day. They tried to get a print off the door, by the way. He wore gloves, but we'll find him. Besides, I have something he's probably going to want. In fact, I'm hoping now that the cops are gone he might come back for it. I'd love to watch him attempt to get it from me. I think I'd pay good money to see him try."

"What do you have?" Maybe we'd actually get a break on this.

"In his hurry to get out, he dropped a flash drive by the front door. A flash drive from Blackman Tac Gear, which, as I recall, was where Finch was working a year or so before he met us in Iraq." Smith sounded like the cat that caught the canary. "I wanted to make sure it wasn't Maddie's before I dig into it. That's part of why I was hoping you all were closer."

"Why the hell would she have a flash drive from Blackman?"

Maddie had been staring at me the entire time I was on the phone. Something I'd just said seemed to jog a memory. Her eyes glazed for a moment, and she stared through me instead of at me.

"It's in her house, man. I'm not just going to start going through shit." I supposed I should be thankful for that.

"Whatever is on it Roman's going to want to see it." It wasn't too often that Tier Seven had something the CIA didn't.

"Well, Roman can wait. I found it. It's mine."

I was a coward for not wanting to get off the phone with Smith. I had no idea how to tell my baby that her home had been overturned. We'd all watched her methodically construct her own little nest in that house. She'd agonized over every detail. Over the years, the boxes of Chris's stuff had moved from her bedroom, to the living room, and then eventually to the garage, close by but no longer a permanent fixture.

"I'll get her there as fast as I can," I vowed.

"If I can figure out where any of this stuff goes, I'll try to put it back as best as I can. I'll let you know when we have our hands on Finch. My money's on Griff. All of his pent-up rage has a target. I almost feel bad for Finch if he finds him without witnesses. Almost."

"Yeah." I couldn't even look at her. How the hell was I supposed to tell her this?

"You do know you're going to have to get off the phone with me and tell her, right?" Smith called me on it outright.

"Easier said than done."

"When Griff has to tell Hannah something he knows she doesn't want to hear, he does this thing where he warns her that it's going to piss her off, and then he promises to be even angrier at whatever it is than she is. If applicable, he tells her he'll destroy whatever it is and let her light the match. Then he takes her to the gun range. Maybe that would work for Maddie, too. Maybe not. My sister's weird."

"I'll figure something out."

"I'll be here when you get here. Hopefully, I'll have Finch strung up by his ankles. Think I'll make him recite the Pledge of Allegiance over and over again."

"And I'd pay good money to see that."

"I'm ending the call now. You have to talk to her."

"Yeah, I know." I tossed the phone down.

"What's wrong?" she demanded.

I had nothing. No ideas. No plan. Nothing that would keep her from realizing that she'd been better off before I was her boyfriend. My brain latched onto the only plan I had ready access to - Griff's. "First off, I am so sorry about all of this, and I am so fucking pissed about it. However furious you're about to be multiply it infinitely, and that's still not even close to where I am right now."

"T," she put my hand in both of hers. "Whatever it is, we'll get through it."

Interesting. I nodded. "Finch broke into your house, baby. He must've been looking for something. Smith says nothing is missing that he can tell, but everything has been gone through. I swear to you, when I find him, I will tear him limb from limb. Actually, I'm going to hold him down and let you have a go at him with a metal baseball bat before I take over. If I let him live long enough to get to the hospital, he'll have to go in multiple ambulances."

She sat motionless for so long, I was momentarily concerned she'd actually turned to stone. "Okay," she finally said. "It's just things though, right? And nothing's even gone. I don't want you destroying anyone. I don't even want to think about you being close enough to this creep *to* destroy him. I'll figure out what to do once we get back."

"Do you want me to take you to a gun range?"

Her face contorted in confusion. "Why would I want to do that? I just told you I don't want to hurt him. I just want him caught and locked up."

Okay, so that part was specific only to Hannah. I could work with that. "You're handling this remarkably well."

She rolled her eyes. "I'm a pro at bad news. Do you have any idea how many times someone called to tell me Chris was hurt before they showed up to tell me he'd died? Do you have any idea what it's like to be all by yourself when they come to your house? Or when someone calls to tell you that your child has cancer? As pissed as I am about this, it helps so much to know you're even angrier. I finally feel like someone's right beside me no matter what happens."

It was then that I had to admit to myself that Griff Haywood was a fucking genius. But I didn't want her to have to endure any more bad news. Jesus, the universe needed to find someone else to pick on. I wanted to make everything in her world good.

41

MADDIE

It could have been a fire or something much worse. My little girl is safe. I have T. That's all I really need. I even have The Sevens. We are all healthy. I can get through this. Trying to think of worst-case scenarios always helped me deal. I'd been doing it for years. I tried to envision what my house must look like. *My house!* No, I would not even whimper. It could be so much worse, but maybe I wouldn't mind T holding this guy down and letting me take a few swings when they found him.

Like he was driving me to my end, T crawled down my street stopping entirely too long at each intersection. That wasn't helping. "Let's just get this over with," I urged.

He gave me a begrudged nod and pulled up in front of my house. The garage door was open and all of The Sevens' cars were parked along the street, but other than that nothing looked different than when I'd left. Except... I dug back through my memories of the garage. Hopping out of T's truck, I raced inside. T followed after me.

"There were more boxes," I announced as Smith, Voodoo, Griff, and Hannah spilled out of my kitchen door.

"There were?" Smith sounded intrigued.

"Yes." I'd stacked them one at a time into a four by four mountain in my garage. They were the boxes of Chris's things the army had packed when I'd moved from our home at Fort Carson. I'd never gone through them. I just liked having them in case I ever wanted to. "There were sixteen of them. Now, there are only twelve."

"Do you remember what was in them, honey?" T wrapped his arm around me.

"I have no idea. I never opened them. They were from Chris's office and the stuff he had on him when... you were attacked." A knowing glance spread like wildfire through all of The Sevens' eyes. "But you seem like you know so tell me," I demanded from T. I hadn't freaked out and I wasn't going to, but he needed to keep telling me everything so I could remain sane.

"I'm betting Finch is looking for copies of the evidence Chris provided the CIA," T eased softly.

"It would help his lawyer build his defense, sweet pea," Voodoo explained. "That must've been what he was looking for inside."

"Since all of you are out here, I'm assuming we don't actually have Finch. Why?" T growled.

Griff shook his head. "We combed every fucking inch of Lincoln. You know we did. We went all the way to Omaha and over the state lines. Ryder's stationed out near his house. He hasn't been home. It's like he fucking vanished into thin air."

Smith held up a light brown flash drive I knew only too well. "Hey, Maddie, this might have something on it that would make Roman move in and get Finch. I just wanted to make sure it wasn't yours before I dug through whatever's on it. He dropped it by the front door."

Heat scalded my cheeks when I considered Smith Hagen seeing what was on that drive. I snatched it out of his hand. "That's mine. Not his. It's the... well... it's the video my mom took of Olivia's birth."

Smith looked physically ill. "Thank God I did not open that."

"You put Liv's birth on a Blackman flash drive?" Griff asked. Hannah elbowed him.

T sighed. "It was from that gear expo they did at Fort Carson back in the day, right?"

I nodded. "I used to send videos to Chris on them in care packages. He'd always grab me tons of flash drives at those expo things since they gave them away for free. I don't know if he ever got to see this one. It was in the box that was sent back to me along with his effects." Just when I was beginning to consider a complete breakdown, T's arms wrapped tightly around me. I squeezed my eyes shut and buried my face in his chest. Apparently, my breaking point was some gross, disgusting person, who was a traitor to the country my husband died to protect, watching me give birth.

T whispered sweet, soothing things in my ear. He told me that he had me, that he was right there, how much he loved me, and then because it was the perfect thing to say, he whispered how much Chris had loved me. I heard the squeak of boots as everyone else went inside leaving me there with him. I let him sway me back and forth. "I will find him and I will end him, baby. I swear to you."

"I don't want you to do that." Clearly, there was no boundary Finch wasn't willing to cross to get what he wanted. The thought of T being anywhere near him made me want to vomit. "I don't understand why he'd want that flash drive. There isn't any evidence on it."

T strengthened his hold of me. "I doubt he knew what was on it, sweetheart. He just grabbed it. Thank God he dropped that one."

"Are you saying that because you don't want anyone to see me like that or because it's Olivia's birth?"

"Both. The thought of him seeing my girls in... uh... a rather vulnerable state makes me want to gag him with his sac while it's still attached between his legs."

"That is a very specific threat."

"I had hours to come up with things I'd like to do with him while we drove."

I grinned at that. He actually made me grin after my home had been broken into. "I guess we should go see how the inside looks." I tried to steel myself as best as I was able.

"I will be right beside you the entire time." He kept me tucked near him while we went inside.

It wasn't as bad as I'd been envisioning. It was a disaster but not necessarily more so than when I'd moved in. "We have to get all of this put back just like it was before we get Olivia."

Confusion cast every face staring back at me.

"This is going to take a while to clean up," Smith eased cautiously.

"No, it won't. We don't have a while. I do not want her to know anything about this. I will not let her world be rocked by Finch or whoever did this. Didn't you all used to set up camp in under five minutes or something? Start setting up camp," I ordered.

"You heard the lady," Hannah jumped on board and started stacking photo albums in the living room and restoring them to the cabinets.

"Baby, I really think it would be safer for you and Olivia if you came to stay with me, just until we find this guy," T stated like that was even some kind of viable option. Only a man would think that way.

"No." I restored all of my bills into my bill holder and rehung it on the wall by the door to my garage.

"Yes."

Oh, he did not just say that to me. I narrowed my eyes. "No."

"T." Griff shook his head adamantly. "Sarajevo."

I had no idea what Sarajevo had to do with my house, but I was not going to stay with T. This was my home. This was the only home my daughter had ever known. No asshole from Coldwell Harding was going to drive me from it.

"Oh, Maddie, it looks like some pictures are missing from your wedding album. Do you have copies somewhere? I can reprint them for you and get them back in here." Hannah sounded devastated.

"Some of them fell out in one of our moves." I went to inspect. I couldn't exactly remember which had been there before Finch had decided to go through my home, but it did seem like more of them were gone. "I have copies of most of them somewhere. I'll redo it sometime. Right now, let's just get this looking the way it did before Olivia left."

T was still standing in my kitchen looking utterly confused. I whipped by him as I headed towards my bedroom, hoping the slight breeze I created would set him in motion. We didn't have time to stand around pouting because I'd told him no.

"Sarajevo?" I heard him ask Griff.

"Oh, man, worse. So much worse," Griff vowed.

Eventually, he joined me in my bedroom, refolded my clothes, and shoved them back in my dresser drawers. "What was in this frame?" He pointed to a now empty picture frame.

What was up with this sicko? "The wedding picture of us outside the chapel," I huffed. "Why would he want that?"

T shook his head. "He came here for copies of evidence, which I'm betting he got, but remember his goal is to scare you. He's a sick fucking bastard."

I shook my head. I had a dozen copies of the picture, and my mother had several, too. It wasn't like it couldn't be replaced. It was just such a bizarre thing for him to take. I began putting my jewelry back in the top drawers of my dresser. The diamond pendant Chris had given me on our tenth anniversary was around my neck but there was one piece missing. I dug my nails into my palms. "My wedding band is gone."

"Are you sure?" He searched the room high and low. "I swear to you I will find him and I will find it."

I was certain he'd find Finch, but I doubted the ring would still be on him. Some piece of me was missing, some internal organ had been stolen with that ring. Acid swirled in the emptiness that had at one time been my stomach.

In four hours, I'd largely regained my cool, and we had my home back to the way it had looked Friday before my world had been turned upside down. "Okay, if you won't come stay with me then I'm staying here until Finch is either behind bars or in the ground. I honestly don't care which. You and Olivia will have twenty-four, seven security detail from Tier Seven and you will not complain about it."

"Fine," I readily agreed. I was thrilled he was going to stay. My brave face only went so far.

"Can we tell Liv about us now? I'd much rather sleep in the bed with you instead of on the couch." He was still pouting about me not staying with him, but he'd get over it.

Griff and Voodoo both shook their heads this time.

"I don't know." I cringed. I hated disappointing him, but I had to put my daughter first always. He knew that. In fact, he always put her first as well. "I'll think about it. Let's see how her weekend went first."

When he huffed, Griff held up his hands. "Valdivia. So fucking much Valdivia!"

"Can we just go get her?" I grabbed my keys.

"I'm going with you two," Griff informed us. "I'll be your security detail for this trip."

"Pretty sure I can handle it, asswipe," T ground out.

Griff laughed at him outright. "Bro, I am not going to keep her safe from Finch. I'm keeping you and your dumbass mouth safe from her."

"What do Sarajevo and Valdivia mean exactly?" I finally asked when we were halfway to my in-laws'.

T, who'd been grinding his teeth, unhinged his jaw. "On one of our deployments to Sarajevo, we figured out pretty quickly that we were not going to get anywhere with the tribe we were trying to infiltrate. It wasn't worth the fight. In Valdivia things were going pretty well until we asked for too much, too soon."

"Then I would say Griff's analogies are accurate," I informed him. "I know you're only trying to keep us safe, but I refuse to introduce unnecessary fear into Olivia's world. I won't do it."

42

T-BYRD

That was a bunch of bullshit, but I didn't know if she knew she was lying to herself so I didn't respond. Olivia would've been thrilled to stay at my house. She would've thought it was a big, fun adventure. It was Maddie who was afraid. It was Maddie who refused to give up control of her environment, and since it was entirely my fault that she was in this situation, I had no choice but to go along.

My phone rang. Hoping someone had something to tell me about Finch's whereabouts, I answered quickly. It was Smith. "Finch was just caught on a security cam at a bank in Denver."

"What the hell is he doing in Denver?"

"He must've left Maddie's house and booked it out there. That's a seven-hour drive. If he flew out there, he used an alias to buy the ticket."

"Then let's go get him." My mind immediately started putting together a plan on how to capture Finch.

"I thought the same thing, but I have no idea where he went after the bank. We're chasing our tails, T. I've got him flagged everywhere. If he books a flight in his own name, we'll know. If he heads back here, we'll sure as hell know."

This was getting ridiculous. Either the CIA needed to snatch him or I was going to. Chasing his traitorous ass all over the US was not happening. Knowing I was going to be relegated back to sleeping on Maddie's couch did nothing to soothe my fraying nerves. Finch needed to pray that Roman got to him before I did.

I tried to mentally prepare myself for seeing Chris's family again. The last time I'd been around them had been at his funeral. Honoring Maddie's request that Olivia not know about our relationship yet, I reminded myself to keep my hands by my side instead of wrapped around her, which is where they belonged. "I'm so glad you're here with me. Seriously, thank you for this. I promise we'll tell Olivia soon." She hugged me before we got out of her van. Okay, I could deal. My savior side was satisfied even if my warrior side was still bloodthirsty and pissed the fuck off.

There was one of those gold star flags hung in the window. I got it. I really did. Absences couldn't be erased. You could only learn to exist around them.

"Uncle T!" Olivia erupted as soon as I walked in the door. Her tiny feet barely touched the ground before she was up in my arms. There was a reason she was one of my favorite people on the planet. Maddie beamed which added to the effect.

"Hey, baby girl. Did you have fun," I had no idea what she called these people so I went with, "here?"

"Yes. Did you know that Mommy has seen your kneecaps?" Her expression was hilariously serious.

Griff choked back laughter. "I'm assuming Mommy saw more than your kneecaps," he spoke so low only I could hear him. I might've given him an exaggerated smirk complete with an eyebrow waggle.

"Olivia, not now, okay?" Maddie squeezed her eyes shut.

"Why?"

"Because... why don't you tell us what you did while Mommy was away."

Chris's father joined us in the entryway, offered Griff his hand,

and then made the same gesture to me. "She talks about you two constantly."

"Well, we really are the best at what we do." But Griff's joke went over about as well as a lead balloon. I didn't let it shake me. Griff's sarcasm was lost on some people. They couldn't really help that. Maybe Chris's supreme intelligence hadn't come from his father.

"Where's Delores, Cad?" Maddie sounded war-weary as she posed the question.

"Oh, uh, she's lying down. Seeing Chris's subordinates is hard on her. Maybe you could've let us know you'd invited them."

"Subordinates?" Griff coughed out. "That's what we're going with? Okay then. That's... interesting."

We'd been in actively hostile environments with people who aligned American Soldiers with Satan's harem where I'd felt more welcomed.

"I'm so sorry," Maddie whispered to me. She sounded bereaved.

I shook my head. "Don't worry about it, sweetheart. It's just a thing."

Panic flared in her eyes. It took me a half second to realize my misstep. *Sweetheart.* Fuck.

"Uh, why don't you both come in and have a seat? Maybe Delores will be up to talking in a little while," Mr. Mitchell spoke like someone was actively driving nails through his vocal cords.

"Oh, we really should be going. "Let's go get your stuff together, Liv." Maddie also spoke like she was being strangled.

The warrior deep inside of me snarled and yanked at his chains. I wanted to take her away from here. I tried to remember that these people had meant a great deal to Chris. I needed to get over myself.

Olivia tapped her little index finger on the palm of her other hand, just like Maddie did when she was listing things out. "I put Howie and my sparkle toothpaste and my Rapunzel nightgown in my bag, but can Uncle Griff help me with my princess tent? I tried to put it away but the sticks won't get in the bag even though I pushed very much."

Griff grinned. "Army tents, princess tents, I can do it all, Short

Stuff. Come here." He held out his hands, and Olivia traded my arms for his.

I'd seen Griff Haywood terrified twice in my life. The first time was a split second before he was shot at point-blank range. The second was at that moment when the ghost walked through the front door and stood right in front of him. This guy looked so much like Chris Mitchell my heart faltered. Same gait, same height, same wiry frame, same eyes. Everything was almost identical right down to the broken tip of the ivory handle of an old Desert Fox knife Chris always carried that was peeking out from the pocket of his jeans.

Griff methodically shifted Olivia away from the ghost, putting himself between her and the apparition. His jaw clenched. His hand hovered at his right leg. His foot slid to the side ever so slightly. I knew he wasn't strapped since he let Liv jump into his arms, but I'd bet my ball sac he had a tac knife in his right boot that he planned to pull before the ghost could blink.

"You're Griff, right?" The guy offered his hand.

Griff nodded twice but did not shake the guy's hand.

"I'm Carl," he reminded him.

"The brother. That's right." Griff managed a breath and shook his hand.

"Yeah. I'm the brother."

Maddie shuddered and scooted so close to me the backs of our hands touched. No wonder she hated coming over here. Poor baby. That was creepy as fuck.

"Uncle Griff is going to help me pack my princess tent into my bag," Olivia explained. She was unaffected by Carl's appearance. She'd only seen her father in photographs. It wasn't enough for her to make the connection and that killed me. It fucking killed me.

"I can help you, Olivia," Carl offered.

She studied him but then shook her head. "Thank you very much. Uncle Griff can do all of the things. Thank you."

I grinned. Clearly, she had no doubts. Even Maddie chuckled. "She knows thank you is polite, so she adds it in when she doesn't want to hurt someone's feelings," she explained.

Carl nodded his understanding and came farther into the entryway to stand with us. "Tom?" he asked me.

"Call me T," I awkwardly instructed.

"I'm sure Mom will be out in a minute. You want a beer or something?" he offered. Mr. Mitchell gestured for Maddie to come into the living room. I followed right behind her.

My mouth fell open. Damn. The entirety of the Mitchells' living room was a freaking memorial to Chris. On the bookshelves, in prominent display, were photographs of Chris and Maddie's relationship. His parents appeared to have photographed and framed Chris on the daily. I felt certain there was photographic evidence of his first shit somewhere.

Nope. Did not want a beer. Did not want to sit. Just wanted to get my girls and get the hell out of the house of horrors.

Maddie seated herself on a plaid sofa circa 1995. Guess we were sitting then. I settled beside her and discreetly propped my arm on the back of the sofa. Not around her per se but over her shoulders.

"Thank you," she whispered.

Since Carl and Mr. Mitchell were looking right at me I didn't respond.

"You okay, Maddie?" Carl asked. "You seem upset."

"I'm fine. Thank you so much for watching Olivia for me. I really appreciate it," Maddie offered Mr. Mitchell.

I marked the distance to the exit doors in my mind. Ten paces due south to the sliding glass door to the yard, but there was a fence to consider. Twenty, maybe twenty-two, paces due west to the door off the kitchen but safe bet it would get us to a closed garage. Front door was our best escape route even at forty paces.

Mr. Mitchell sighed. "Oh, it was no problem. She's such a sweet girl. Reminds me of Chris. That's probably why it's hard for Delores."

It was hard for Delores to be around her own grandchild? I was unaware grandmothers were even allowed to feel that way. As my gaze fell back to the shrine on the bookshelves, it hit me that there was not one single photograph of Olivia up there. Only Chris and then Chris and Maddie. Dear God. What the hell was wrong with these people? Did Olivia not matter because she'd never gotten to interact with Chris? Did Maddie only matter because she had? There were also no photos of Chris with us. If we were going to construct a temple to the memory of Chris Mitchell, I'd say his SF team should've at least gotten a footnote in the program.

Before Maddie could respond to that insanity, Delores was upon us. She had a gold star pin on her bathrobe.

I was a good boy growing up. My mom dragged us all to church most Sundays. I had vague memories of Bible stories about wailing and gnashing of teeth, but it was not until that moment that I understood what it looked like. Besides, wasn't it supposed to be the widows that wailed?

Maddie made no effort to hide her eye roll. Delores made a show of using the shelves with Chris's pictures to walk. When she ran out of shelves, she made it to a chair with no aid at all.

"Cad was just explaining that having Olivia here is difficult for you, Delores. If that's the case, I won't bring her over." The stagnant air lit with challenge.

I tried to hide my grin. "I love you so fucking much," I reminded her under my breath.

"Well, some of us cared about him enough that moving on isn't so easy."

Ho-ly fuck. This woman was certifiably insane. So, that was it? Maddie didn't love him enough. Damn. That was a low blow.

"Griff, can you hurry, please?" Maddie called.

"One sec. This thing has four dozen pieces," bellowed down the hallway.

Delores seemed to have realized I was sitting there. She heaved herself up from the chair and came to sit beside me. *Chris, man, I loved you but your mother is batshit crazy.* The thought formed in my mind before I could stop it. I mean, he had to know that, right?

"I think it was good for mom to see Olivia though. She really should get to spend more time with her," Carl urged. Yeah, because I was frequently in the habit of letting my baby girl take a long stroll through the psych ward.

Another photograph on the table beside the couch caught my attention. Chris and Carl stood side by side both in uniform. Of course, Chris was in his BDUs and Carl was in some kind of service tech coverall thing, but at least he'd made it in a photograph.

Mercifully, Griff appeared with Olivia, her backpack, and her neatly folded princess tent stuffed in a bag. Maddie and I both flew up off of the couch so quickly I was mildly worried it was going to flip.

"You aren't allowed to take your tent home, Olivia," Mrs. Mitchell scolded. "That's a toy Pops bought you, and you can only play with it here."

Back the fuck truck up. I seethed.

Olivia's face fell. "Oh, I'm sorry."

"You bought her a toy but you're not going to let her have it?" Griff sounded almost as disgusted as I felt.

Maddie narrowed her eyes at Chris's father. "Did you tell her that she wasn't going to be able to bring it home when you got it for her?" Oh, Mama Shark was circling.

"Uh, well, no," he shook his head. "I didn't know she couldn't," he admitted.

"Well, she can't," his mother huffed.

"Hey, Liv, it's fine," Griff soothed. "I'll get you a tent."

"It's okay," Olivia laid her head on his shoulder, and I wanted to destroy my best friend's parents. How fucked up was that? "Can I please have Howie, please?"

"Sure." Griff set the tent down, dug in her bag, and handed over Howie. She covered her face with him and then buried herself in Griff's neck. Her little fingers went to town on Howie's ears.

"It is not fine," Maddie snapped. She was in Delores's face a split second later. "You let her go to the toy store, let her pick something out, not something she gets to do very often, and now you're taking it away. Is that how you want her to remember her time with you? Because this will color everything else that happened this weekend."

"She needs to learn that you don't get everything you want. I certainly had to learn that when Christopher married you."

"Unbelievable," Maddie shook her head and rushed to Griff. "Come here, baby." Olivia quickly clung to her mama who marched her out the front door and slammed it shut behind her.

Griff and I stared after her for a split second before our eyes met.

He shook his head. "Look, I don't know you people all that well, but I did know your son, and I can tell you this, that bullshit right there would never have happened on his watch."

"And it isn't going to happen on ours. You're not going to emotionally fuck with your granddaughter. She's a little girl." I grabbed the tent bag and headed to the door. I shouldn't have done it. I knew better, but I turned back. "Chris was right — you are a manipulative bitch. He isn't here anymore but I am, and I can assure you, you'll never see either of his girls ever again. Not on *my* watch."

Griff's cell phone chirped while I drove Maddie and Olivia back home. He blew out an exaggerated breath as he read the text. "Smitty says Finch just chartered an undisclosed flight out of Colorado Springs. He's still trying to get someone at the airport to talk, but so far no one's being too agreeable."

"We have any friends down at Peterson?" I tried to think of anyone I knew at the air force base but came up short.

"Hannah's dad might. I'll get Smith to make some calls."

43

MADDIE

I had no idea what T had said to my in-laws after I'd stormed out. I also didn't care. He'd marched out with her tent cementing himself as our hero once again. His record was still perfect. He'd never let me down.

He'd lied through his teeth to Olivia and told her that Nana and Pops had changed their minds. According to him, they'd decided she could have the tent after all. Then he'd constructed it in the corner of her room, which helped distract her from the fact that we hadn't quite gotten all her toys back to their correct places when we were cleaning up from the break-in.

"You were amazing today," I whispered as I snuggled against his chest on my couch after we'd put her to bed.

"She's not going back over there," he ordered.

"No. She isn't." I should've reminded him that it was really my decision, but I didn't even want to. It was nice to have someone else be a shield between me and Chris's parents. I'd already fallen for him. He was ready to become a permanent romantic fixture in my life. He was already permanent in every other capacity. So, he should have some say in things that involved Olivia. Besides, I'd never trusted anyone else with her the way I trusted him.

"Thank God you agreed. I was half expecting to get my ass chewed for telling you what to do."

I grinned against him. "No arguments on that one." I remembered that her toothpaste-covered nightgown was still in the kitchen sink. I was heavy with exhaustion but I forced myself off of the couch. "I forgot the toothpaste."

"Seems to me asking a four-year-old to pack herself up might've been a lot to expect. You sit. I'll scrape toothpaste."

I followed him to the kitchen instead. "It was kind of refreshing to see the house through your eyes. I know they loved him but those pictures have been up like that since we were in high school. Chris hated always being photographed, but he wanted to make her happy. My brother-in-law isn't much better. He bought the house across the street from her because she told him to. I really think she needs to see someone that can help her."

"Daily," T agreed. "But she doesn't want help, so I doubt there's a shrink in the world that can get through to her." He stared me down while he held the nightgown under the faucet. "I noticed there were no pictures of Olivia. Why is that?"

My role in Chris Mitchell's life clogged in my throat, but I ordered myself to tell him the truth. "Because she never got to become a jewel in his crown. If he'd gotten to meet her, there'd be pictures of him with her, but neither Olivia nor I have ever really mattered. It's only who we were to him that made any difference to his family."

He dropped the nightgown, dried his hands, and wrapped his arm around me. "Honey, he adored you. He loved you more than life itself but you, unto yourself, are so much more than the pinnacle of his achievements. You know that, right?"

"Oh, I was never the pinnacle. That was Team Seven. I was just," I searched for the right word, "a low rung on his ladder, maybe?"

"You were not that to him," he vowed, but I knew better. "And you sure as hell are not that to me. You are everything to me. All of this insanity that's been hurled our way since we started dating has made me utterly certain of two things. I want you, and I want us. That's it. I do not require one other thing to make my life complete."

Unlike Chris's, I had no doubt in T's vows. He was telling me the truth in its most intimate form. Whatever my past had held, I needed my future to be spent holding him. To do that, I had to let go of the railing. "I'm scared." The admission spilled from me in a broken breath.

He leaned back and cradled my face in his hands. "Of what, baby?"

"Of this." The flare of my nostrils brought his wood-smoke scent to my lungs like a dose of fresh cleansing breath, after years of drowning in my own sorrow. "Of you. Of us. I'm so scared to love you as much as I do because people I love get hurt. It's like I'm cursed or something."

"Maddie, that isn't true. None of what happened to Chris or to Olivia had anything to do with you. That's your guilt talking, and it always lies to you."

Maybe so, but as soon as I took one step out into the world of dating again, my home had been broken into and my phone was being traced. I wasn't allowed to have this without consequences. "It seems like it did," I tried to explain.

"Nothing is going to happen to me except that I am going to pick you up, carry you in my arms to your bed, and I'm going to make love to you until you understand that together is the only way this world works for us."

I had to be brave. I couldn't cave to the belief that everything I loved was going to be taken from me. I'd spent years battling that belief. If I allowed myself to believe that again, I couldn't go on.

"Is that safe?" Wasn't he supposed to be my bodyguard along with my boyfriend?

He grinned. "I'm SF, baby. I'll improvise. As long as I'm on top I can get a shot off and go right back to making you moan."

That sounded good to me, but I wasn't through with my confessions. "I was scared to go stay at your house. Olivia would've loved it. It was me who was afraid to leave here. This is the only place I've ever felt completely safe after Chris died. I think I've been using Olivia as an excuse for my own fear for a while now, and I think we should tell her about us. I refuse to be afraid anymore."

"Part of me wants to wake her up and tell her right now, but much larger, harder parts are willing to wait until tomorrow, so I can get on with my original plan."

"Larger and harder, huh?" I teased as I traced my fingertip over the rapidly hardening bulge of pure heat at his zipper line, loving that I could draw those hungry grunts from him.

"My cock has been craving your tight wet pussy all damn day, baby."

Well, when he put it like that who was I to deny him or his cock anything at all? I yanked his T-shirt out of his jeans, desperate for his skin. I plastered my hands to his abs, anxious to feel the way he always came alive at my touch.

He lifted me to the countertop and set me on the edge. Stepping between my legs, he latched his hands on my backside and slammed me against his now raging erection. Yes. This was what I'd needed all day. I couldn't think anymore. I needed him to take it all away.

A desperate moan wrenched from my lungs. Ever attuned to my body, he rocked against me, drawing a gasp when he hit just the right place. His lips crashed down on mine taking brutal possession of my mouth. I became nothing more than pure sensation, a slave to the way he made me feel. His right hand closed over my breast. My back arched, desperate for more. A tremor of unadulterated hunger quaked through me.

He lifted his head from my mouth. The darkened edges I loved were back in his gaze. "I'm going to take you just like this. Hard and fast. Make you ache with it and you're going to be nice and quiet for me," he demanded.

"Now," I whimpered softly.

He made quick work of his snap and zipper pulling them low enough to get the job done. "I know what my baby needs. This is only the beginning."

My head fell back. My body rolled. His hands were on my breasts again, and I rode against the exposed head of his cock. My panties slid to the side when he rocked. My swollen folds craved his heat, but it wasn't enough. I whimpered. I needed to be full of him.

"Uncle T, why are you licking Mommy's mouth?" Olivia yawned.

T froze. His eyes flashed open. Panic blared from him. I wanted to die a thousand deaths. My entire body, which had previously been on fire for him, felt like I'd been doused in ice water. Keeping his now rapidly fading erection pressed against me, he lifted his head from my mouth. My father had caught me and Chris making out once, but this was much worse.

"If we don't act like this is weird, she'll probably forget about it," I spoke through my teeth. He nodded, turned away from her, and zipped up while I quickly righted my sundress.

"Olivia," my voice shook. "Why are you out of bed?"

"I got this," T turned back looking decidedly more put together than I felt. "I was kissing Mommy."

Straightforward and without fluff. Decidedly a Special Forces answer. I sighed.

"That is not how kissing goes," Olivia informed him. "It goes like this." She whisked to him and held up her hands. When he lifted her, she planted a kiss on his cheek free of all tongue, of course.

"It can go like that, but I was kissing Mommy a little differently — the way a guy kisses a woman when he's in love with her."

"Like when Flynn Rider kisses Rapunzel?" Another yawn contorted her face.

44

T-BYRD

Maybe after the credits rolled and Flynn had Rapunzel up in that tower all to himself. "Uh, yeah, let's go with that."

"Does that mean you're Mommy's prince now?" She sounded almost as thrilled with the idea as I was.

"How about if I'm the king and mommy is my queen and you get to be the princess?" I baited.

Her eyes became the approximate size of plates. "This is amazing!"

Maddie hopped off the counter, brushed a kiss on Olivia's cheek, and then one on mine. "I think it's amazing, too."

"Are you going to marry Mommy and be my daddy 'cause I had one but I didn't get to meet him so I don't have one and my friend Allie has a mommy and a daddy but I also still wants you to be Uncle T."

This kid. Man, when she shoots, she hits you square in the chest. "Uh..." I glanced at Maddie. It seemed all she could manage were rapid blinks. If she couldn't answer, I'd make do. "Marrying Mommy sounds like an excellent idea to me, but I think you'd have to help me talk her into it."

"T, are you serious? You can't tell her things like that." Maddie's voice returned. "You can't possibly know that after one week."

"I know that after four years, honey." I was weary of being told what I could and couldn't tell Olivia, but I kept that to myself.

"Mommy, you should marry Uncle T because he loves you like Rapunzel, and you can be a queen even though I don't think queens teach school, and they also prolly let princesses have chocolate milk sometimes."

"We will talk about getting married and chocolate milk in the morning. Now, why are you out of bed, little princess?"

"My pajamas are itchy. I need my Rapunzel nightgown, and Howie heard a noise by my window."

Fuck. How could I have been so stupid? Once again my cock needed to remember my primary job here. For the time being, I needed to be her protector, not her lover. I hated Marcus Finch more and more with every passing moment.

"What kind of noise did Howie hear?" I asked Olivia.

"A scratchy kind of noise." She shivered in my arms for effect.

"It's the chokecherry tree outside her room. Howie hears lots of noises when Olivia doesn't want to sleep," Maddie whispered.

"I'll go check it out just to be sure." I kissed Olivia's cheek and handed her off to her mama. I lifted my phone to my ear and headed towards Olivia's room.

"Still circling the block and still haven't seen anything," Ryder reported.

"I was just checking. Liv thinks she heard something outside her window." I didn't want the guy to think I didn't trust him. He was a hell of a Ranger.

"That's on the back of the house, but still, unless they dropped down out of the fucking sky in the ten seconds it takes me to loop the eastern side, I don't see how anyone could've gotten back there. We could step this up. Let me be a little less obvious."

I knew he didn't agree with my plan. He didn't have to. He just had to follow orders. "I want you to be obvious. I want every fucker in a fifty-mile radius to know Tier Seven is here, and we aren't leaving," I explained.

"Yeah, I know," he wanted to argue but thought better of it.

If Ryder circled constantly, Finch would assume we had more men and more firepower in more discreet locations. I wanted him to believe we had men in all of the places he couldn't see and that they all had their eyes and their laser sights on him. Feint Strategy was Chris's go-to tactic and one of Team Seven's preferred maneuvers. If you had to let the enemy know you were there, make them think you had the whole fucking United States Army with you and that the Navy and Marine Corps were behind them and the Air Force was flying directly above. Basically, go big, scare them shitless, or go home in a body bag.

"You keep circling. I'll check the perimeter."

"Yes, sir."

I flipped on the lights in Olivia's room. Nothing looked out of place. On the floor was her Little People hospital I'd gotten her during her treatments and her firefighter dress-up jacket, but that was it. Stalking to the window, I stayed low and scanned the moonlit sky from the top of the tree line down. The standard Nebraskan breeze did ruffle a few leaves on the chokecherry tree but nothing seemed odd. I stalked methodically from room to room scanning the perimeter of the house.

I stood and shined the light from my phone directly down to the ground. No footprints. Nothing but dirt. I returned to the living room. Liv was lolling on Maddie's shoulder, rubbing Howie's ears. I exited the front door and scanned east to west then north to south. No one there. I performed the same search on all sides of the house. There were lights on across the street and in both of her next-door neighbors' houses but nothing out of the ordinary.

When I returned to the living room, Maddie and I carried on a silent conversation. Her eyebrows lifted. I shook my head slightly. Her sweet grin reached through my chest and squeezed. "Want Uncle T to carry you back to bed?" she soothed.

Olivia nodded against her chest. "And lay down with me because my pajamas are itchy."

I scooped her up. "Itchy pajamas seem like a good enough reason for Uncle T to lie down with you."

Maddie rolled her eyes as I carried Liv out of the room. God knows I didn't want to disappoint her, but we were going to have to go back to G-rated interactions until I had Finch by his sac. No more distractions, which wasn't going to be easy. She was the most beautiful distraction I'd ever laid eyes on.

It took less than ten minutes for Olivia to be sound asleep once again. Typically, it's easier for a Christian missionary to slip out of North Korea than it was to exit a sleeping toddler's bedroom when you're supposed to be lying down with them, but she was sound asleep. I grinned and brushed another kiss on her cheek before I made my way out.

"You spoil her rotten," Maddie didn't sound too upset by that fact when I returned to the living room.

"I like to spoil both of my girls."

"If we really do get married, you're going to have to stop that." I was pleased she was already thinking about it.

"I will do my best, but I make you no promises. When she does that lip-poking-out thing, I cave. I'm a weak-ass bastard for both of you."

She shook her head at me. "Which means we don't get to go back to what we were doing because you're beating yourself up for getting distracted, right?" She knew me far too well.

"Does it help to know that I'm going to have a case of blue balls so bad the only way to recover is to be sucked off constantly for days after this?"

Her mouth dropped open before she dissolved in a fit of laughter.

"Already opening wide, my little cougar. I like it," I harassed her.

She swatted my chest. "You are terrible."

"That is not what you said at the lake, baby."

"If the blue balls get too bad, I definitely volunteer to help you recover."

I gave her the rumbled growl she seemed to be after. "Oh, yes, honey, you will. You'll do exactly as you're told," I informed her to see what she'd make of that.

She gave me the fucking sexiest smirk I'd ever seen. My cock threatened to take a machete to the zipper of my jeans on its own so it could cross the picket line. "Do you seriously think I don't want you to take control in bed?" she laughed in my face. "I'm in charge of everything. Every single thing is up to me. Literally, nothing is not my responsibility. You being in charge is one of the most seductive things I could ever imagine. Nothing could possibly turn me on more." Killing me. She was fucking killing me slowly, torturously. She nuzzled against me, making everything fucked up in our world currently not seem so bad. "And I really hate Finch."

I cradled her closer to me. "Not near as much as I do, but I promise you I'll make it up to you. Let me get him locked up, and I'll take you to my bed and keep you there. Indulge myself in you. You want to be a good girl for me and let me own your pleasure? Done. My ultimate plan for you is to make you sensually helpless to me. Make you drip for me. Get you so sloppy wet on my cock the neighbors know my name from your moans. Rip your fucking clothes off, spread your thighs, take you so deep and so hard you're nothing more than a screaming, sticky mess begging me for more. And I'll give you more when and where I decide." The need for her consumed me. It took on its own pulse between us. It filled my lungs with every breath. Had taken position directly between my shoulder blades. Resided under my skin. A scratch I longed to claw but could never reach. It surged through my bloodstream with every beat of my heart. Rubbed me raw. "He may have gotten to be your first, baby, got to have your innocence all for himself, but I intend to be your last."

She lifted her head from my chest. Shock and intrigue fought for placement in her eyes. Dammit. Where the hell had that come from? What was I even saying? I started to apologize, but she shook her head.

"There is nothing innocent about the way I want you, T. God, I burn with it. It hurts... it physically hurts me. I feel... so empty. I crave you. I can barely stand it. I'm so hungry for your hands to be on me, in me. The things you say to me... they drive me wild. I just... need you."

I tried to steep myself in her words, but I was appalled at my own. The plan was not to let her know I had moments of rampant jealousy. I'd get a handle on it. I was supposed to force it away by the might of my fists. Instead, it had free-flowed out of my mouth.

Maybe it was the glimmer of heat in her eyes and the hunger of her arousal when I tempted her that had me blowing my plans all to hell. Maybe.

Before I could respond, her timid hand glided over the distinct bulge in my jeans. I grunted, half from frustration and half from rampant need. I allowed myself one second to revel in the caress before I put a stop to it all. My eyes closed. My jaw clenched. Her fingertips drifted down my shaft. When her palm trapped the fevered greed and rubbed, a low curse slipped from my lips.

Popping the snap on my jeans, I freed my cock and pressed her hand to the head. I wrapped those shy little fingers in the strength of my own. "Like this, baby. I don't need gentle. I fucking need to feel your hands on me."

Her sweet little gasp cinched around my cock tighter than her fingers. Her thumb traced up and down the thick vein that ran the back of my shaft and I damn near came right then and there. I swore she touched me like she'd never seen a man before. That couldn't possibly be the case. Her fascination ignited my blood, scorching my good sense. She slipped down to her knees. Oh, fuck yeah. When her tongue swirled over the bead of pre-cum at my head, I choked back a roar of pleasure.

"Stop," I mustered the single word I had to insist on.

"Why?" she fussed.

Damn, now she wanted other words. It had taken everything in me to manage the one. I forced myself to breathe. "Finch," I ground out.

She pouted. Fuck me. She was pouting, her lips flushed and full, her eyes alight with her own need, because I wouldn't let her give me a blow job. When I found Finch, I was going to castrate him... before I killed him.

45

MADDIE

I did not want to stop. I didn't want to think about Finch or anything else. I wanted to tempt him into really letting go with me. He'd held back at the lake. I could tell. Maybe I'd needed him to then, but I no longer required his caution. I wanted to see T in full form. I wanted to hear his panty-melting demands. I wanted to obey them. If he'd offered to tie me to the bed, lock the door, and spend all night torturing me in all of the best possible ways, I would've driven to the store to get him rope.

My desperate desire for him to satisfy me was punctured by the blare of my cell phone. I grabbed it from the kitchen counter. My heart hammered out an SOS. Why did this guy keep doing this? I held it up to show T that, according to my cell phone, he was calling me again.

Before I could answer it, he texted something to Smith. When he reached for my phone, I shook my head. "I'm answering this time," I insisted. This had to stop. Clearly, this guy wanted to talk to me.

He looked at me like I'd suggested that I set myself on fire. "Fine," he spat. He answered Smith's call. "On speaker. Answer now, Maddie."

I made the same move with my phone he'd made with his and

turned it on speaker. "Hello? Who is this?" The vicious fury I'd hoped to summon missed its mark. My voice shook despite my direct orders to myself not to do that.

Haughty laughter shot a frigid chill down my spine. "You don't get to know that yet."

T's lip curled. His biceps flexed and rage lit in his eyes.

I thought I recognized a few tones of the guy's voice. I hadn't talked to him that much at the gala, but it did kind of sound like him... I supposed. Something else about his voice was familiar, but I couldn't place it. "Why do you keep calling me?" I sounded moderately less affected that time and mentally congratulated myself.

"To keep you from doing something you know you shouldn't and him from taking advantage of your fragile state."

Bile churned far too high in my gut. My tongue felt entirely too large. I was going to be sick. Frantically, I glanced around my home. The curtains were all drawn. Had someone been watching us? That seemed impossible.

"I'm not in a fragile state," I spat.

"I'll be the judge of that."

T gripped my countertop with enough force to have ripped it from the cabinets, but he remained silent.

Suddenly, *call ended* flashed on the screen.

"Dammit," Smith huffed.

"Did you get anything?" T demanded.

"Couldn't get any data on the phone itself, but the call was made in Lincoln. He had to have known we were tracking it. He timed it perfectly."

Dread slithered over my skin. "Do you think he's watching the house?" The thought of any one seeing me get down on my knees at T's cock made me lightheaded.

"It sounded like his call wasn't planned," Smith pointed out. "That was agenda in his voice. When she asked why he kept calling, he wasn't lying."

"I heard that, too," T wrapped his arms around me. I buried

myself in his chest, wishing he really could shield us from the world. "I'm taking you to my house. I'll help you pack."

"No!" I shook my head at him. He wasn't thinking, which was very unlike him. I really did undo him. As flattering as that was, now wasn't the best time for him to be off his game. "If he's watching us, we'll lead him directly to your house. We have to stay here." At the moment, though, that was the last thing I wanted to do. I rushed to Olivia's room and stared at her, safe and sleeping, in her bed. Sliding down her doorjamb, I took position on the floor. I wouldn't move all night long. If someone was watching my home, I'd keep my eyes steadfastly on my daughter.

"Smith's on his way over. So are Voodoo and Griff." T soothed as he took station right beside me. "They're going to sweep the area again. If he's watching the house, he has to be nearby. I'm so fucking sorry about this. I hate myself for putting you through this." Guilt flooded his tone.

"Stop apologizing." I laced my fingers through his. "It's just a thing, right?" He gave me a haggard nod, but then, his head snapped to attention.

"Shit!" He leapt to his feet and flew back to the living room.

I raced after him. "What?"

T stared at the approximate location where we'd been seated on the sofa. His eyes moved around the room until they landed on my curtains. He set up the step stool I used for candy retrieval at my windows. Reaching behind the sheers, his eyes widened. Panic pulsed with every frantic beat of my heart.

Coming down the step stool in one quick step, he gripped my hand and half dragged me to Olivia's bathroom. He shut the door, carefully felt along every available surface, and then turned the shower on at full blast.

"What are you doing?" I finally demanded.

"Making sure no one can hear us. He set up cameras while he was here," he seethed. "He isn't outside because he could be watching the feeds from anywhere. How could I have been so fucking stupid?"

Steam poured out of the shower, but a cold rush seeped outward from my chest. "What do we do?" This was entirely out of my league.

"When Smith gets here, I need him to figure out where the hell that feed is going. We find that, we have him."

"T, this doesn't make any sense." Surely, even his testimony against Finch wasn't worth all of this effort to scare me. "Unless you know a lot more than you've told me, I can't understand why he'd go to all of this trouble. Are we sure this is Finch? It was that Maidlow guy that actually threatened you."

He rubbed his temples. "You're right. But it just doesn't feel like Maidlow. I worked with him for years. He's an asshole, an opportunist but not a deviant. I helped Chris gather all of the evidence on Finch. You wouldn't believe some of the shit he pulled. One of his favorites was getting photos of soldiers interacting with the locals wherever we were. Then he'd Photoshop them so they looked far more compromising than they were and threaten to send them to their wives. If they didn't pay, he'd follow through. This is how he works."

The rising tide of panic filled my throat. I couldn't imagine how I would've felt if I'd received photos of Chris like that. "That's... awful."

"He's a monster, and the cameras are a game he's used dozens of times before. I can't believe it never occurred to me to check. Without my testimony, Roman doesn't have a case. The timeline, meeting you at the gala, everything points to him, but, you're right, I do need to consider every possibility. Maidlow could probably build a sat phone out of tin cans and a rubber band, so spoofing a cell phone wouldn't throw him. If he can ever get his head out of his own ass, he's a brainiac. I'm not ruling him out entirely, but the thing he wanted was my sign off on his system. He went to D.C. without my signature. I can't come up with another motive for him. Can you think of anyone else who would want to scare you or infuriate me?"

Somehow, assuming it was Finch felt better than the possibility that it could be some nameless, faceless person. Every step before me seemed like the wrong one. I kept my circle tight. I was friends with a few of the moms from Olivia's preschool, but they usually messaged me on Facebook. They didn't have my old phone number much less my new one. There were my teacher friends from school, but none of them were men. The people I interacted with on a regular basis were the men who'd served on my husband's team. As far as I knew, I had no enemies... until now. "I can't think of anyone." The need to move burst through me. I needed to run. I had to escape. I just didn't know who I was escaping from. "I have to check on Olivia."

I raced out of the bathroom and gulped in breathable air.

Smith and Voodoo let themselves in. One more shred of my dignity and sanity crumbled to the floor. T pretended to calmly mess with his phone. I saw his texts to Smith explaining the cameras and shuddered.

Smith's answer instructed T to take me to bed and pretend he'd arrived to take over surveillance. I started to protest, but the cameras prevented me from arguing.

Smith opened his laptop. The Sevens were much better at pretending to be unaffected. None of them ever glanced up to the camera in the curtains. I couldn't seem to stop looking up there, wishing I could see through it to the cretin on the other side.

"You ready for bed, baby?" T played his role perfectly.

This was insanity. How was I supposed to lie in bed with him and pretend no one was watching us? "Olivia's crying," I announced. She wasn't, but none of The Sevens questioned me. I scooped her up from her bed. She gave me a few long blinks and then cuddled back on my shoulder, fast asleep. I carried her to my own bed. Keeping her safe was all that mattered. If I dedicated myself to that single task, I could remain sane, just like I'd done when Chris died. I'd poured everything I was into Olivia. She'd been my savior. I wasn't certain I knew how to let anyone else fill that role.

I certainly wasn't changing clothes, so I laid her gently in the middle of my bed and cuddled beside her, hiding us under every cover I possessed.

"May I?" T whispered when he entered the room.

I nodded. He slipped in on the other side of her, blocking her from view in case there were any cameras in the bedroom curtains.

His capable hands reached over my little girl and softly stroked my cheek. "I'll always keep you safe," he whispered.

"I know."

"Both of you. I would never let anyone hurt my girls." I knew he would try with everything he was to make certain of that, but someone had broken into my home and set up cameras. They'd been watching us. Besides, I already knew this life wasn't without pain no matter how powerful your strongholds were.

I nodded.

"Smith will find him."

I knew that, too.

"Always, Maddie. I swear to you I'm going to fix this. I hate myself for doing this to you."

"I don't want you to hate someone I love. We'll get through this. I just need to be with her."

46

T-BYRD

"T," Voodoo whispered. "Take a walk with me."

Silently, I eased from Maddie's bed and made certain both she and Olivia were tucked safely under the blankets. The fact that some bastard had seen my baby, down on her knees all for me, bubbled pure hatred in my gut. I wanted to gouge his eyes from his head for what he'd seen.

"Where are you going?" Maddie sat up as well. She didn't appear as frightened as she sounded. Another concrete layer of guilt cemented itself in my chest.

Voodoo's consoling smile was illuminated by the silvery dance of the streetlight outside. "You're not being recorded anymore, sweet pea. Smith took care of it. We've got it all under control. Go back to sleep. I'll bring him back in just a few."

She hadn't been asleep, but I saw no point in correcting him.

Smith was still seated in the chair watching something on his laptop screen. Griff was up on the step stool cautiously removing the camera. Apparently, this wasn't going to be a very long walk.

"Did you find him?" I demanded.

"Yes and no." Smith sighed. "It's not quite that simple."

"Define that."

"The surveillance is being uploaded to a remote cloud server. That makes this more difficult. I wrote a packet analyzer, which, in non-comm-sergeant speak, is basically an interceptor that finds and logs traffic on a digital network."

I fucking needed him to get to the part where he found this asshole. "And?"

"I hacked into the server on the camera end, so I can monitor who accesses the data via their IP address. In theory, that should lead us directly to him wherever he is."

"But?"

"But, the last time the data was accessed was around twenty-one forty-five, right before he called her phone again. They're not recording constantly. He's turning them on and off when he decides to watch what's going on. There's virtually no data being passed from them right now. Obviously, we wouldn't be having this conversation in front of them if there were. The cameras are miked so he's listening as well. Until he attempts to access the feed again, I can't tell you where he is. I created an alarm that will alert me immediately when he turns them on. I'll have a location, and we'll have him."

I ground my teeth. My patience was rapidly dwindling. I turned to Griff. "If we need him to access the cameras, why are you taking them down?"

Smith grinned. "We only need him to access the data, not the cameras. We need to know where the data is going, not where it's coming from. It's petty and rudimentary, but I have a plan."

"And that is?" Since Team Seven's planning was usually done by me, this was an interesting turn of events.

"I called Triple A. He was very amenable. I'm going to get the cameras out to one of his barn stalls. When he decides to check in on Maddie, he'll get shots of horse shit. That's better than him being able to listen or see what's going on here or at Tier Seven, which was my first idea. If you've got something better, I'm all ears. Only complication could be that as soon as he accesses them again, he'll know we found the cameras and are looking for him."

Aaron, or Triple A as we affectionately referred to him, was Team

Seven's intelligence officer back in the day. He'd opted out of Tier Seven Security, deciding to become a cattle rancher instead, but he still always came through for us when we needed him. "That isn't a complication. I want him running scared. People do incredibly stupid things when they know they're being chased. How many cameras are there?" This was where I was likely to lose my proverbial shit.

"Why don't you just let me take them down and you have a beer or something?" Griff urged.

"It's almost sunrise. Why the hell would I want a beer? Just tell me where they are."

Smith cringed. "Based on the signal strength from each source, there's one in the kitchen, and two in her bedroom."

"Fucking sick bastard," I huffed.

"Agreed," Griff slapped me on the shoulder before he eased the living room camera into a cardboard box. "You okay with Maddie knowing about the ones in the bedroom, or do you want me to wait until she's occupied doing something else?"

"She'll want to know, just try not to wake up Olivia."

"Done."

At zero seven hundred, I coaxed Maddie from the bed with coffee, since she hadn't slept any more than I had. Now that the cameras were down, she was more comfortable leaving Olivia snoozing in her bed.

"So, no one is watching us. You're certain?" she demanded of Smith after her first three sips.

"I am beyond certain. I sent Ryder out to Camden Ranch with the cameras. Triple A will take it from there."

"Good. Remind me to thank him the next time I see him."

"He would do anything in the world for you, just like the rest of us," Smith reminded her.

"I know." That got him a genuine smile. "I don't know what I'd do without you all."

I didn't point out that without me no one would've broken into her home to spy on her. "Since whoever is doing this wasn't actually nearby when we thought he was, I'd still really like you and Olivia to come live with me. We can get there without him knowing where we are." I waited until her mug was almost empty to ask. I had a better chance when she was caffeinated.

The Sevens all retreated to the far corners of her living room. Voodoo was trying not to laugh.

She studied me, gave me no answer, and refilled her mug. Three additional sips later, she sank down at her kitchen table. "Do you want us to stay with you or live with you? You said live."

Had I? Good. No reason to say something you don't mean. "I'd prefer live, but I'll take whatever I can get."

"I don't know, T. I'm at my breaking point. I haven't slept. We finally decided to start dating, and our world went insane. I want Olivia safe. That's all that matters to me, but I need some time to figure out the best way to make certain this isn't negatively affecting her."

I searched her face. Weighed every word. She was being honest, or at the very least, she believed what she was saying. If she needed time, I'd make that work, but I wasn't above throwing one more pitch. "The way you feel about Liv, baby, that's the way I feel about both of you. I have to know you're safe. That is all that matters to me."

"I know. I'm guessing we're going to Tier Seven with you this morning." She looked like she'd rather go in for a root canal than hang out at work with me. Fuck. Some boyfriend I was turning out to be.

"If you want to take Olivia somewhere, we can go with you," I offered even though Tier Seven was the safest possible place they could be.

"It's fine. Just let me pack her some stuff to do." She carried the remainder of her second mug of coffee off to Olivia's room.

"Asking her to live with you?" Voodoo chuckled. "When you decide to settle down, you go all in. Know the goal, work the plan, right?" He quoted one of my many phrases back to me.

I wasn't in the mood. Before I could formulate some kind of response to that, Olivia called from Maddie's bedroom. "I didn't wet my panties!"

Maddie stuck her head out of Liv's room and smiled. "That's her new morning greeting. Oddly, it is one of my favorite sounds to wake up to."

The Sevens all bellowed out their congratulations while I scooped her from Maddie's bed. She beamed up at me, and I swore her grins made my entire life. "Will you make me pancakes with chocolate milk?" She nuzzled her head on my shoulder. "I like it when you and Mommy are in love and you stay with me." Her shoulder-length hair stood out at all angles. As a two-year-old, she'd been completely bald because of the chemo. Now, she wanted long hair all the way down her back, as she frequently told us, so every inch she gained delighted me.

"I like it, too, baby girl. You know Mama's not gonna go for chocolate milk, but Uncle T's pancakes can definitely be arranged."

"Wait! I need Howie," she fussed. I dug under the covers and rescued the bunny. "Okay, now I can go potty and help you make pancakes."

I set her on the carpet. "Sounds like an excellent plan."

She raced across the house, but halted at Voodoo and grinned. "Are you all here to play with me? Maybe if we promise not to get it in the carpet we can play Play-Doh." Her little legs crossed and she began to wiggle.

"Go potty, Liv," I reminded her. "They'll be here when you get finished." She continued on her sprint.

Since the moment of its formation, Team Seven had never turned down food, so I prepared approximately fourteen dozen pancakes with one arm since Olivia and Howie were in my other. After that, I took a shower and then loaded my girls and half of Olivia's belongings into the van.

As much as I loved being like this with Maddie, and as many times as I'd driven them around in her minivan, I missed my Vette. When Finch was either burning in hell or on his way there, I was going for a long drive. For now, something else was off. I couldn't determine what it was yet, but something raised the hair on the back of my neck and sped my pulse. Once I had them safely at the office, I'd put more of the pieces together.

A low groan from the engine jerked my attention away from my own pissy thoughts.

"What was that?" Maddie gasped. I tapped the brakes.

A high-pitched squeak followed the groan. The temp gauge crept upward as the air conditioner halted its blast of cool air. "Babe, when's the last time you had the fluids changed?"

Voodoo was directly behind us. Griff and Smith were three cars ahead.

"Three weeks ago," she supplied. She was meticulous about stuff like that. As far as I knew, she'd never even let an oil change go past the recommended date.

I was surrounded by cars on both sides. Fuck. I slowed further and white-knuckled the wheel when the van pulled hard right.

"Liv, hold on tight for Uncle T, okay?"

"Okay." I'd intended for her to hold onto her car seat, but she gripped Howie instead. A high-pitched squeal assaulted our ears and then the belt snapped. It took all of my strength to steer the van at all. Maddie would never have been able to get it to the side of the road. Belts snap on their own every day, but everything about this said it was no accident.

I turned on the flashers and got out. Voodoo pulled in behind us. "What the hell was that noise?" I'd seen the guy operate on four men, doctor a dozen farm animals, and deliver two babies all in one day, but cars were not his thing.

"The serpentine belt snapped," I did my damnedest not to say anything that might alert Maddie to the fact that whoever had done this could've killed them.

Voodoo's eyes narrowed as cars flew past us on the highway. "Snapped... because it's old?"

"No. Van doesn't have enough miles for that to be a possibility, and she just had the fluids changed."

"Shit," he mumbled.

Maddie finished reassuring Olivia that all was well, and then she got out of the car. "Did he do this too?"

"Let Voodoo take you on to Tier Seven. I'll wait on the tow and check the engine," was my non-answer.

"So, yes?"

"I can't think of another reason it would snap, and I don't think you could turn the wheel without power steering."

"You want to wait on a tow? Couldn't you get it to the shop?" Voodoo quizzed.

"Not without destroying the engine. Just take them on to the office. Tell Griff to come back and pick me up once he has his car."

47

T-BYRD

I popped the hood as soon as Voodoo drove away with Maddie and Olivia. I didn't have any gloves on me, and the engine was still too warm for me to pull the remnants of the belt. The tow truck driver pulled it for me when he arrived. "That look right to you?" he asked as he held it up.

"No, but it looks precisely the way I thought it would." Three-quarters of the depth of the belt had a clean cut. The rest was ragged. He'd left it partially intact to play his odds, I supposed. He'd not only had ready access to her home while I had her at the lake, he had access to her car in the garage. Jesus, I was a fucking moron. Whatever he'd been trying to do, the fact that I was driving when it gave probably wasn't his plan. I was going to destroy him as soon as I fucking found him.

"Weird though. Looks like someone had to really saw at it at first." The tow truck driver shrugged.

Griff pulled up right behind the tow truck. I filled out the paperwork, paid the guy, and climbed in Griff's car. He was oddly without comment, and Griff Haywood was never quiet. His sarcastic commentary on life was one of the things that kept me sane. "Just say it," I ordered. "Whatever it is you're not saying, spit it out."

"You still thinking it's Finch?"

"I'm not shutting down any other ideas, but doesn't this feel like the shit he used to do?"

"Yeah, but why? He doesn't do anything unless he's getting paid to do it. What's he going to get out of her? She's an army widow and a teacher. Unless you know a whole bunch of shit none of the rest of us knows, I can't figure this out. Guy was a fucking fobbit. If he had to put his boots on in Iraq, he bitched, unless someone was paying him to do it."

The guy was a fobbit, the coined term for anyone who never left base in a war zone. But he was staring down a lifetime in federal prison, and he knew it. It wasn't funds he was after this time. It was his freedom to keep making money on the backs of soldiers and using that money to keep himself out of trouble. "I know what Chris knew and yeah, it is probably more than you know about him."

"You know shit worse than him being the king of the black market?"

"Yeah, maybe. Chris stumbled on some stuff he shouldn't have, but even I don't know what he put in that final report."

"Finch doesn't know what you can and can't corroborate, I guess. Shit's fucked up, I know that."

It galled me that he'd spoken the very words that were currently haunting my lack of sleep. Whoever was doing this, I was going to find them and end it. I'd never seen the final report Chris had obsessed over for months before his death. I had no idea what we were up against, no idea what Finch was trying to cover up. Chris had been certain he'd be the one to have to testify.

"Oh, the marines have landed by the way." He rolled his eyes.

"What the hell does that mean?"

"Those MARSOC guys we've already hired - according to them - were waiting on you when I went in to get my keys."

I shook my head, which I really needed to get out of my ass, or out from between Maddie's thighs if the truth be told. "I forgot I'd told them to come in this morning."

"Figured that. Olivia was entertaining them when I left."

That made me grin. "I have no doubt."

"I'm just going to remind you of Jalalabad."

Maybe I really was losing my mind, but the night Griff was referencing made me chuckle now that it was long over.

"You weren't laughing then," he was quick to remind me.

"Yeah, I know but, my God, what the fuck were they doing?"

"Beats the hell out of me. Literally, the last thing Chris said to them before I picked the lock on that house for a nice, quiet extraction of a terrorist was not to let anyone know we were there. They were just supposed to be backup. We come out to a fucking rave complete with a fight between two Afghanis and three houses on fire. Marines, man, they're fucking nuts, and you want to hire them."

"Marine Special Ops are a little less volatile." I hoped against hope that was true.

"Whatever you say." He was silent for the length of one blink. "If I find you some more Rangers, will you reconsider this hire?"

"No, but if you find me some more like Mathis, I'll hire them, too."

"You know we were the best of the fucking best back in the day," Griff proceeded to pout. "We didn't need any help."

"I do know that. I also know we can't keep living back in the day."

I flew up to the office to find my girl serving princess tea in her plastic tea set to three of the burliest, most badass Marine Raiders I'd ever met. They were all trying their best to hold a diminutive, plastic Little Tikes cup in their massive hands the way Olivia was demonstrating, with her pinky out, naturally. Voodoo, Smith, and Maddie were all spying from Smith's office and laughing hysterically.

I had to choke back laughter myself when Staff Sergeant Trent Garrison, Special Recon Asset of the fucking 1st Marine Raiders out of Pendleton, apologized to Olivia because he hadn't wiped his mouth with the make-believe napkin she'd given him.

"Sorry, I'm late. Car issues." I offered Rio my hand.

"Sir." He looked beyond relieved that he no longer had to play tea party.

"Liv, baby, go get Voodoo to let you play doctor while I talk to them, okay?"

"Okay," she sounded perturbed, "but they didn't get to have their chocolate, carrot, apple-y, gor-ganic fruity bar cookies I'm baking."

"Organic, maybe?" I offered.

"No."

"Okay, then." I gestured to my office and was nearly plowed over by the marines making their escape.

"She's uh... cute," Trent ground out once my door was closed.

"I can't take credit, but I also won't argue. She was our CO's daughter. He didn't make it back, so we all have a hand in raising her."

Rio was chuckling at him. "Don't get your panties knotted, man. It was just tea. 'Sides, Sergeant Byrd here is playing hard for her mama if I have all this straight. She's looking to become the boss's daughter. She wants tea, you have tea."

Garrison looked like he was reconsidering my job offer.

"I'm not that kind of boss," I assured him, "except maybe when it comes to her."

"I'm all right with kids usually," Trent assured me. "My sister has a few. It's just... why are they always sticky?"

"Pretty sure it's a by-product of being four. Maddie and I try to keep the sticky to a minimum. She's not usually up here. Have a bit of a situation going on. Have a seat," I gestured to the chairs in front of my desk.

"What kind of situation?" Rio asked.

Before I could delve into the long, sordid story, Maddie opened my door. "I'm sorry," she immediately apologized.

"It's fine. What's wrong, baby?" She held up her phone. Tier Seven was on the call screen.

48

MADDIE

As I stared down at the phone in my hand, fear oozed through me like poison straight from a drip. "T, I need this to stop."

Ignoring the three marines seated in his office, he came around the desk and wrapped me up in his arms. "I know, baby. I swear I'm going to put an end to all of this."

"How is he doing this?"

At that moment, Olivia ducked around us and wiggled her way between our knees. "I want to be in the hug, too."

Grinning despite the fear hacking away at my nerves, T and I both embraced her. The phone stopped ringing. Relief washed through me even though I was sure he'd call back. Taking things moment by moment was all I was capable of just then.

"Is this about that Finch guy, sir?" Rio inquired.

"Yeah, but there's more to it than what you heard at that gala," T said.

"Figured that. Anybody who's close enough to rim a senator's ass the way he was is up to trouble."

Rylee scooted into T's office. "Sorry to interrupt, T-Byrd, but Kyle

Maidlow is upfront. Says you're going to want to hear what he has to say."

Griff entered right behind her. Unless Hannah was in his presence, he had a pretty short emotional range that ran somewhere between generally irritated to infuriated. At that moment, he'd crossed his own lines into raw outrage. He glared at the marines. "Look, you're all hired or whatever the hell he told you," he jerked his head towards T, "we'll get you your paperwork in a few. Take a walk down the hall. Pick out an office. There are like fifteen empty ones. Find something useful to do. I need to talk to T and Maddie."

The guys might've spent several years in Marine Special Ops, but when the Green Beret gave an order, they were all quick to comply.

Rylee was an army vet, and she appeared just as bewildered as the marines. "Olivia, want to come with me? I'll play tea party with you," she offered sweetly. "Let's go in the back room though, okay?"

"Okay." Olivia wiggled down out of T's hands and hesitantly took Rylee's.

"Keep her the fuck away from Maidlow," Griff huffed on their way out. The reverberation from Griff slamming the door jarred my rapidly disintegrating nerves. "I'm just going to say it. I don't think this is Finch." His words were clipped with his anger. "Like I said in the car, Finch buys his way out of problems. He doesn't put forth this much effort for anything. Wouldn't surprise me at all if Finch showed up here and offered to send Olivia to college if you forget to show up to testify against him. But this, this is just like Maidlow. He'd pull shit like this and then show up here. He's that ballsy, and he's running a long game. The cameras, hiring someone to track her, that has his name written all over it. He thinks if he scares her badly enough you'll cave and give them our sign off."

He was wrong. I didn't know how I knew, but I was certain it wasn't Maidlow. No one was ballsy enough, or dumb enough, to pull crap like this and then show up in the lion's den. He was a bully and nothing more. He'd talked a big game, but I knew he wasn't really willing to take on T. I could tell when they were talking at the gala. He was scared of T and of Tier Seven.

I shook my head. "I think we all need to remember that Chris is the one who turned all of that evidence over to the CIA about Finch," I reminded them. "Sure, it was all kind of a coincidence that I was at the gala, but you just said he buys his way out of his problems. What if he can't buy his way out of this? He saw an opportunity to get back at us all for what Chris did, and he took it. There is no better target than me right now." That fact sank through me slowly leaving terror in its wake. As much as I adored him, Chris had never grasped that I was the one who had to deal with the fallout of his decisions. "I was married to the man who went straight to the CIA with evidence, and now, I'm in love with the guy who can corroborate it all. That Roman guy finally decided to go after him, and he's coming after me."

"Chris did what was right, sweetheart," T's voice was barely more than a whisper. He didn't want to choose between me and Chris.

"I know that, but he isn't here trying to hold his little girl's life together."

"Can we have a minute?" T's request held the weight of an order. At one time, Chris sat at the top of their hierarchy. Griff certainly carried a great deal of weight, but now, no one defied T. No one should as far as I was concerned. He knew it was Finch, too. I could tell.

Griff gave him a single nod. "Fine. But I stand by what I said. This isn't Finch."

"I told you I'm not ruling anyone out," T reminded him. "I'm following the evidence. I'll hunt down every lead, but everything about this says Finch to me."

Griff saw his way out.

I tried to place the precise moment when being alone with T had gone from comfortable to thrilling. I edged closer to him, unable to resist the magnetism between us. His jaw worked visibly, and then he cradled my face in the strength of his hands. His touch filled me with an electric warmth that touched the deepest, darkest wells of pain and healed them. When he was beside me, the fear evaporated. "Do you get that I want to be here to help you hold life together, both yours and Olivia's? That I want to be right here with you no matter what comes our way?"

"I know that. I really do. I just always need to know that Olivia is safe. That's all that matters to me."

He nodded. "Do you get that I don't just want to be here for you and for Liv because he isn't here? Do you really understand that? For a while, I don't know if I got that. But last night while I was lying there trying to keep you safe, trying to physically block you from whatever was coming, it finally occurred to me that I'd want to be right where I was no matter what. Even if Chris had never gotten to be there before me, I'd want to be the man who stands between you and the rest of the world. I will always want that."

The air in the office was far too still and yet with every inhale I caught the wind. "T, I need to say something that is the truth, but there might be moments when it isn't true. Does that make sense?"

He gave me a half smile. "Try it out and let's see what I can make of it."

"I won't choose my memories of him over you either. I want to live in the present with you and have a future with you. I just need to know that it's okay for me to visit the memories when I need to."

In two quick steps, I was in his arms. Solid walls of muscle and heat surrounded me. I'd never had the luxury of counting on anyone else. It was simultaneously thrilling and terrifying, but he had never let me down and he never would. "I would never have it any other way, sweetheart. I want to help you keep his memories alive."

"Thank you."

His hot breath caressed my ear and lifted a few strands of my hair. I shivered from the proximity. Every fragmented piece of me wanted to be beside him with nothing between us. I wanted nothing else to exist except for us. Maidlow, and Finch, and cameras, and all of the insanity that kept trying to dismantle this — I needed for it to be scoured from my life.

"Stay with me tonight," he coaxed. "Please. I need to know you're safe. I need to have you again. I need to see you in my bed, wet and needy for me. I need to show you what it's like to have a man dedicated to bringing you pleasure for hours. Let me have you like that. Let me make everything else go away."

I smiled. Maybe he really could read my mind. The promise of what my night might hold stoked the fire he kept constantly tended low in my belly. I had to trust him. I had to step outside of my own habitat. "I'd really like that." Searching my mind, I decided that was true. Being nervous wasn't the same thing as not wanting to go. I could get through the nerves if he was on the other side of them. He was the only man strong enough to make the world disappear.

49

T-BYRD

"**Y**ou sure as hell don't have any brains, but you've got balls showing up here," I snarled as I stomped into the lobby of my company. I had a plan. If Maidlow was behind this, I'd know by the end of this conversation. I needed him startled.

I chuckled when Maidlow's eyes darted from me to the door. His hands shook.

"The fucking CIA showed up at Coldwell this morning," he huffed. "They questioned me for hours. They took my laptop and my phone. What are you playing at, T?"

Interesting. I held out my hands. The truth was often the best way to begin an interrogation. "I have no idea what you're referring to."

He was on his feet pacing in the next second. "What the hell do you know about Finch? He hasn't been to work in days. There's a file on his computer with Chris Mitchell's name on it. He did nothing but talk about Mitchell's wife before he left for Korea. Said you were dating her now. He was pissed about it. You must know something about why the CIA was looking for him."

This was easier than I'd originally planned. Maidlow wasn't lying. He had every marking of a man who'd gone several rounds with Roman Becker. He might've been having Maddie followed, but he wasn't the one making the bogus phone calls. She'd gotten the last call ten minutes before he arrived. I remained silent. The easiest and most effective interrogation technique would always be to let the silence suck out the truth.

And just like a good little soldier Maidlow quickly filled the void. "I mean, I know Finch has had it out for Team Seven since that thing with Chris back in Iraq, but I didn't know you went to the CIA with it. My God, what were you thinking? Finch knows a lot of people."

"Meaning what?" I demanded.

"Meaning... he's not always a nice guy or whatever." His words were truthful. He stared me down, imploring me to listen, to believe him.

"Yet, you have him working for your company."

"That wasn't my choice. He's good at what he does. That's all the board cares about. As long as his side dealings don't affect our bottom line, no one says too much." He scrubbed his hands through his hair. Sweat beaded along his upper lip, and he tugged at his tie like he was being strangled. His eyes sought the floor instead of my gaze as he shrank in on himself. Guilt was not attractive on anyone.

I shook my head. "And your bottom line is all that has ever mattered. That's precisely what Maddie said." My test hung between us for less than half a second.

"Who the hell is Maddie?" His head lifted rapidly. His brow furrowed.

There was my answer. I'd never introduced them at the gala. He'd never known Chris. Finch must've been referring to her as Mitchell's wife, and that was all Maidlow knew of her. Referencing a person as a belonging of someone else is classic deviant behavior. Still I remained silent.

"Doesn't any of this interest you?" he insisted.

"Literally nothing that goes on over at that farce of a weapons company you're running interests me. The last time we spoke, you threatened me and the woman I was with, so why the hell are you here, Kyle?"

"Was that Mitchell's wife? I didn't know. I swear. She just looked like someone who got you going and... I was desperate." A look of horror shadowed his face. So, threatening a widow was bad, but employing someone who readily committed treason was okay as long as he was making you money. I supposed I should be thankful he'd drawn a line in the sand somewhere that he didn't want to cross. He shook his head. "You pissed me off that night. I'm still pissed at you, but I didn't know you had the CIA in your back pocket. Why didn't you tell me that?"

"What makes you think I sent the CIA your way?"

"They kept asking about you. Where was I on the day your team was attacked? What did I know about it? Did I have any contact with Finch at any time six months prior to the attack? Why the hell do you think I had something to do with that? I'm the good guy, T," he vowed. He was not a good guy, but his vow told me he believed he was. The rest was the truth without margins.

He had me. I was officially intrigued, and I sure as fuck wanted to know what the file on Finch's computer contained. Safe to say if Roman had taken Kyle's laptop, they'd also taken Finch's desktop computer.

Something had driven him straight from a CIA interrogation to Tier Seven. He wanted something. He always did. "Why are you here, Kyle?"

"I need you to help me find Finch. Coldwell Harding is not going down for his shit. I didn't even have anything to do with it." He squeezed his eyes shut. His jaw tensed visibly as he tugged at his tie again. Clearly, a confession brewed on his tongue. I waited. "I'm out of money, okay? I can't bail the company out again. I either need Tier Seven's sign off on the comm system so the DOD will give me a second chance, or I need you to find Finch for me. I can't afford a legal defense capable of taking on the CIA right now. They made it pretty clear that if I don't help them find Finch, I'm going down for the stuff he does."

I refrained from reminding him that there were no legal defense teams capable of taking on Roman Becker, no matter how much money he offered up.

"Please, man. I'm begging," he concluded.

"As it so happens, I am already looking for Finch, so if you know anything about him, anything at all, start talking."

"Thank God," Kyle breathed out in a relieved huff. "He has a house in Phoenix. I don't think he has any close family members. The guy he met with in Korea's name is Jae-Sun. Uh... I think that's all I know. I don't like Finch. It's not like I have drinks with him after work."

"Leave," I directed. "I'll call you if I find anything."

"Are you sure? Maybe I could help you do this."

"You just told me you and Finch aren't close. How are you going to help?"

"I don't know. I just...." He shrugged.

He was scared to leave. Dear God. Roman had really done a number on him. I almost felt bad for him... almost. I needed him to go. I had shit I needed done, and time was definitely of the essence.

"I doubt the CIA will come back for another meeting today. You'll be fine." I stepped forward well aware he would step back. Closer to the door was the direction he needed to go. "It's just a thing, Kyle. It's going to take me some time to find Finch." Another step. He eyed the door like it was the only thing holding back a monster. "I'll call you when I know something."

Defeat settled on him as he nodded. Finally, he opened the door and headed down the staircase.

"Smith!" flew from my mouth as soon as I was certain Maidlow was gone.

He stepped out of his office just long enough to motion me inside and then sealed the door shut behind me. "You're about to ask me to try to access a file on a computer, that has firewall security all on its own, and that is now in the possession of the CIA. To that, I say, you're insane."

"Look, I know it's unethical, but that file has to be about us."

"It is somewhat unethical," he assured me, "but it is also completely impossible."

That isn't what I wanted to hear. "But it isn't currently at CIA headquarters. It's being transported."

He rolled his eyes. "It being transported is yet another reason this is an impossibility. It has to be on a network to be hacked. It's like you fuckers think I can hack anything with electricity. I can't make your toaster fix you breakfast from here. That isn't how this works."

A harsh breath escaped my lungs. "So, there's no way."

"The moment that Roman plugs it in, it will officially be on a CIA network. No one hacks the CIA. That does not happen. I sure as hell want to know what's on that file, too, but unless you can get me physical access to the computer itself, it is impossible."

"Guess I could try to get Roman to tell me what's in the file." As soon as I said it, I knew how stupid I sounded.

Smith rolled his eyes. "You are all about the impossible today. I do think I have something figured out on the Maddie situation, if that helps."

"She's a situation now?"

"I'm talking about the situation with her fucked-up phone calls. I don't know how he's doing it yet, but I know he has to be using her phone to track her. I figure if you talk a big enough game you'll be able to convince her to stay with you tonight. Before you take her out to your place, talk her into leaving the phone with me. I want to see what happens."

I spent several hours retrieving my truck and boat from Maddie's house, taking the boat back to my house, and then returning to Tier Seven. It gave me time to think. If Finch was the one scaring her, why was he doing it? Maidlow had commented a few times on Finch's anger that we're dating. What the hell was that all about?

Maddie readily agreed to give her phone to Smith for the night. In fact, she seemed relieved to be without it. Before we left, even with all of the precaution, I drove all over Lincoln before heading home to make absolutely certain we were not being followed. There had been no more spoofed phone calls that day. That both relieved and bothered me. Finch hadn't shown up on any of the radar systems Smith had put in place. He'd gone underground, and that was far worse than him hopping flights constantly. There was a decent chance he knew Roman had shown up at Coldwell that morning. Was that what had driven him underground? I had no idea, but far too many things can be planned when you know you're done for.

I headed down the dirt road through the cornfields to the five acres I'd purchased at the back of the Higgins family's massive farm. They couldn't grow corn on it, so the back field made an ideal place to build my home. The Higgins were pleased to have an SF soldier living nearby, and I was happy no one could find my house unless they knew precisely where they were driving.

Olivia swung her legs into the back of my seat as I drove. I didn't mind. "Remember last year when I dressed up like corn for my play?" Maddie and I both grinned. She'd been the cutest little cornstalk ever, in the preschool production of Nebraska's founding.

"I do remember that. You sang your corn song," Maddie assured her.

"Yes, but I didn't like that song because it doesn't go like Elsa."

"I know." Maddie giggled. "But you still sang it very nicely."

"And you puts dots on my face." She continued on with her recollections.

"Yep, I did."

I laced my fingers through Maddie's, wondering just how much staying with me was costing her. I had to prove to her that I could give her the same stability she had at home.

"And Uncle T, and Uncle Smith, and Uncle Voodoo came and clapped very loud and Uncle Griff whistled very, very louder and my teacher laughed."

"You know it, sweet girl," I took my turn responding to her thoughts.

"Do you think my daddy could see me from heaven?"

Just as soon as I removed that fist from my gut, I could respond. Maddie's eyes closed.

"He saw you, Liv. I promise," I spoke around the boulder in my throat.

"Do you think he clapped loud, too?"

"He clapped and whistled even louder than Uncle Griff," I assured her.

That seemed to satisfy her. She settled back in her seat and played with Howie.

"I keep thinking someday she'll ask me about him and it won't render me speechless." Maddie sounded disappointed in herself.

"You have a knack for apologizing for being human — did you know that?"

Her brow furrowed. "What does that mean?"

"You demand an awful lot of yourself. It's okay to feel any way you need to feel, baby."

"Maybe."

I'd make a deeper dive into her cryptic answer later. I pulled into my garage and lifted Olivia from her car seat. "I get to spend the night at your house," she reminded me.

"I know. You and Howie can have your very own room."

"I want to sleep with you and Mommy."

My mouth opened and then closed. That was not happening, but I also wasn't so good at telling her no.

Maddie shook her head at me. "I think you can sleep in the bedroom very near to the one Mommy sleeps in."

"But that's not how a sleepover party is pu-posed to go and last night I gots to sleep with you."

This child was entirely too smart. Maybe I should've laid off getting her all of those STEM toys she loved so much.

"I think Uncle T is going to make you cheeseburgers on the grill, and then we can watch a movie, but then you have to go to sleep in your bed, little princess," Maddie laid out how the evening would work. She was so much better at this than I was. Making the switch from Uncle T to stepdad was completely unknown territory. I'd never even considered it until recently. I needed a plan.

They'd both been to my house before, but it had been a while and they'd never stayed over. I typed in the ten-digit code that powered down the exterior alarms and then did the same thing with a different code inside the kitchen. I reset it as soon as we were all inside. There was some motherfucker out there who thought he could scare my baby, and that bullshit stopped right now.

Olivia spied the massive plastic bin on my counter where I kept all of her favorite candy, so I could always take some with me to her house. "Wow!" she rocked back and forth on her tiptoes. "Can I please have some please?"

"After dinner," Maddie reminded her. Disappointed with that answer, Olivia slouched off into the sunken living room. "Do you really eat all of the yellow and green Skittles so she can have the purple and red ones?" She studied the bin.

"Obviously." I winked at her. "Come on, I'm Uncle T."

She beamed at me. "Part of me is pretty sure you're the best man on the planet, and part of me is worried you're going to spoil her so much she'll rot."

"Let's go with the best guy on the planet thing. I like that one."

I leaned against the black granite countertops and grinned when she eased closer. "Thanks for bringing us here. It's nice that no one knows where we are."

Cradling her hips in my hands, I drew her to my chest. While Olivia was distracted pushing random buttons on my glut of remote controls, I worked my mouth up Maddie's neck reveling in the shiver that always elicited from her. "When she goes to bed, baby, be ready for me. This time it isn't going to be slow, and it sure as hell isn't going to be gentle. I'm going to spend hours showing you who you belong to. Teaching you and tending you. Tonight, I'm going to make you mine."

She lifted her head from my shoulder. Those huge doe eyes heated. Her nipples strained against the cotton fabric of her T-shirt, needy for my hands, for my mouth. "Good. That's precisely what I want to be. Believe me, I'll be ready."

I gripped the soft curves of her ass and pressed her body to my erection. The cradle of her thighs did nothing but amp the desperation as it lit through my veins. I wanted to slam myself into her, feel her sexy ass jiggle against me as I rode her hard. And in a few hours, I would have her just the way I wanted her.

A timid moan escaped her lips.

"Needy, baby?" I continued to tempt her with my cock.

"Very."

"Good. I want you so fucking needy for me you're dripping down your thighs. I want my sheets covered in your sweet cream. I want you filthy all for me."

She shook in my arms. Her hands fisted my shirt. "Please," spilled from her lips in a whispered plea.

My baby had every single sign of needing a man who knew how to be dominant in the bedroom, knew the give and the take that would set her at ease and also set her on fire. I'd show her precisely what it was like to be fucked by a man who knew how to make her fly.

50

MADDIE

T tipped the beer bottle back slowly. I watched the gentle flex of the ropes of muscles in his arms and the strength of his jaw and throat as he swallowed. Olivia was lying between us on his massive leather sofa watching Rapunzel and fighting sleep with everything she had. I grinned. She'd gotten a hearty dose of stubbornness from both me and Chris.

T's home was all rough-hewn woods and stone fixtures. It was entirely T-Byrd - an outer testament to the strength and endurance of the man it housed. I allowed myself to imagine actually getting married again. It wasn't something I'd ever even considered as a remote possibility. Would he want me to live here? The tranquility held a great deal of appeal, but I couldn't just leave my home, could I? I'd built our whole life there.

If you got married again, did you invite your first husband's family to the new wedding? I tried to envision actually telling Delores that I was going to marry T. Dear Lord, she'd use that for a century of pity.

Was there some kind of etiquette book for things like this? Was I supposed to get married at the courthouse because I'd already had the big fancy West Point wedding, so now I didn't get to do another one?

After news of Chris's death hit the media, people tended to regard me like the whole of my life had ended as well. For a while, I'd agreed with their assessment. But, being married to a soldier, then the soldier not coming home, and then nothingness wasn't how life worked. I was still here, still breathing, still trying to figure out how to go on. I was fairly certain there were no rules on what has to happen after the flag is folded.

I was tangled in knots of anticipation about what would happen after the movie. He was too far away from me. I needed his warmth, required his touch. Guilt pricked at my skin for willing Olivia to go on to sleep. Surely other moms had the same desire on occasion. As if he really could read my mind, he held out his hand for mine. Always there when I needed him. I had no idea how I'd gotten to where I was sitting, but I clearly owed someone up in heaven something for this. Maybe since he couldn't be here, Chris wouldn't mind me falling for T. He'd always wanted me to be happy, just so long as my happiness wasn't dependent on him being home.

Silently, T gestured his head to Olivia. A deep yawn overtook her, and she finally allowed her blinks to extend long enough to be qualified as closing her eyes. Just a few more minutes and she'd be out. I raked my bottom lip against my teeth. A soft grunt sounded from the man seated close enough to touch but not near enough to devour. A mischievous grin lifted my cheeks, and I returned my lip to my teeth.

"You'd tempt a saint," he rasped. Olivia lifted her head, and he clenched his jaw tight once again.

Being desired should be classified as a controlled substance. It was a heady thing. Wildfire spilled through my veins from the look in his eyes. It both filled me with strength and simultaneously made me weak. It catapulted raw feminine power through me and made me long to be at his mercy.

I prayed he'd keep his earlier promises. I no longer wanted to have anything to do with slow caution or gentleness. I required him in full force. I wanted to feel the roughened edges of his desires scrape against my skin, own the brutal possession I could taste in his kisses, experience the raw power of his thrusts when he finally allowed himself to own me. And I wanted it now.

By the time Rapunzel was becoming a brunette, Olivia was out. I started to lift her, but T shook his head. "Five more minutes just to be safe. Once I start, I have no intention of stopping."

Five minutes sounded like an eternity. I was too old to stomp my feet and whine, so I tried to count the seconds. My mind continued to spin. What might my Sergeant want from me? What might his preferences include now that he knows I have no need of his gentlemanly behavior? I'd always been an excellent pupil. It was one of the reasons I'd become a teacher. Tonight, I wanted nothing more than to learn how to please him, to learn how to render him weak the way he always undid me.

"Screw it. God owes me a few favors. I'm too far gone to skip tempting fate." T eased from the couch. With adept skill, he cradled her in his arms without jostling her enough to awaken her. I grabbed Howie and tiptoed behind them turning out lamps on our way. He'd already plugged her Peppa Pig nightlight into the wall of her room.

With dedicated gentleness, he slipped her expertly into bed and pulled the covers over her. I nestled Howie beside her and brushed a kiss on her cheek. T wrapped his arm around me when I stood. "I love her more than life itself, but I need some time alone with her mama," he whispered.

"Looks like you just got your wish."

He took my hand and guided me to the master bedroom and closed the door. The double click of a lamp echoed in my head as the soft glow of light spilled over the king-sized bed. If it weren't for the tattoo on my backside, I might not have minded his insistence that we always have the light on. One quick look at the intensity locked in his gaze and the determination in the ropes of muscles that comprised his arms, and I knew better than to even ask. I'd momentarily forgotten his warning. I was the student to his master.

"What are you thinking, baby doll?" He stepped in front of me as if to infiltrate my thoughts by his proximity. His eyes were heavy-lidded, a slight blockade to the storm of need in their deep-blue depths.

Unable to hold his gaze while I answered him, I stared at the thick wool rug covering the floor. "I guess I was wondering what you think when you see my tattoo."

His fingers lifted my chin until I had no choice but to stare at him. "It's on you so I think it's beautiful. I have no desire to erase him from our lives, sweetheart. But right now, I'm going to make you all mine. Your past belongs to him. I want your future."

The endless line of patience I'd been forcing myself to extend all evening long disintegrated at that. The insanity that had become my life the past few days, the fear, the confusion, the constant ache when I was away from him - I needed him to absolve all of it. Over me, inside of me, I needed to be entirely surrounded by him.

Tired of waiting, I yanked his T-shirt from the waist of his jeans and splayed my hands over the solidity of his abdomen.

He sucked in a breath. His eyes closed. "Stop," he commanded. His hands folded over mine. The forcefulness of his tone as soon as we were in the bedroom still surprised me, more at my own reaction to it than anything else.

"No," I defied. "I need you."

"I'm going to give you precisely what you need, baby, but you're going to do as you're told."

If he were really going to give me what I needed, he'd already be inside of me, but I was curious enough to see where this led. The man did always have a plan. Who was I not to let him lead me wherever he wanted me to go?

"Take two steps back and take your shirt off nice and slow for me," he ordered. "Now."

I made certain he saw my eye roll as I eased back from him and removed my top with no fanfare. But the fire burning in his eyes roared to a blaze burning away a few of my inhibitions. "Do you not fucking see how damned beautiful you are?" His low growl stirred the need brewing deep within me. "Answer me."

"No. I don't see it."

He stepped to me and turned me to face the large mirror on his dresser. With one adept move, he popped the front clasp of my bra. My breath hitched when the lace caught on my nipples. They stood at attention, raw and throbbing for his hands. A low growl sounded in my ear as he eased the bra down my arms. "They hurt, don't they, baby?"

"God, yes!" Finally, we were getting somewhere.

"I'm going to make them feel all better." But apparently that was not what he was going to do right then. He caught my chin in his right hand again, forcing my line of sight to the mirror. His left made quick work of the snap on my jeans. "So fucking gorgeous. My God, how do you not see it? Watch me." He released my face. His hands encapsulated my breasts. My nipples skimmed between his fingers making me whimper. He didn't bother with a tender exploration. There was no gentleness in his touch, only driven greed. "Feel me," was his next command as he ground against my ass. "Feel how fucking hard I get for you." Keeping one hand on my chest, he let his other dip low into my panties and drew me back against the tantalizing promise of his erection. I couldn't look away from the ecstasy chiseled on his features, couldn't deny the reaction he had to me, couldn't refute his evidence.

My breasts filled his palms. He sank his lips to my shoulder with suckled kisses as he rolled my nipples between his fingers making me groan.

"That's it, baby. Moan for me."

51

T-BYRD

I'd dedicate the rest of my fucking life to showing her how beautiful she was inside and out. She would no longer go a day without me reminding her of her beauty or a night without being worshipped. I'd fantasized about her tits more times than I could count. Clearly, I needed to show her how alluring they were.

Stripping her jeans and the wet satin panties down her legs, I traced my fingertips over her mound. A shiver quaked through her, driving me wild. She stepped out of her jeans. Her breaths shuddered as she turned back to me. I made quick work of my own T-shirt and popped the snap on my jeans. "Please let me touch you," she begged.

As soon as I allowed that, I was likely to lose it all. She had no idea that her touch was as intoxicating as hell. Hesitantly, she dragged her short nails down my pecs drawing a strangled groan from my lungs. Her eyes lit as she realized just a fraction of the power she held over me. I stripped out of my boxer briefs and settled back against my wooden headboard. I summoned her with my finger. Like the sex kitten she was meant to be, she crawled low on her hands and knees to me.

"Up here, sweet baby." This time she obeyed with no contention. Her thighs split over my own. Her swollen tits danced in my face. She was perfect. I gripped her hips and rubbed her pussy against my hard-on. Her eyes closed. Her body rolled. "Feels good, doesn't it? So fucking hard for my baby." I brought my lips to her right nipple, flushed and ripe all for me. I drew her into the heat of my mouth, listening to her harsh gasps of breath. Her hands tangled in my hair. Her body bowed back, begging me to take more, so needy for my mouth.

I scraped my teeth along the underswell of her breast, fucking loving the desperate whimper it drew from her. My hand found purchase on her left breast, leaving only that needy little slip of heaven between her thighs without my attention. Soon. I'd make up for it all too soon.

I switched my mouth to her left watching her as she undulated in my lap. I loved that the shy excitement she'd had in my living room had only been the smoke that had blazed into a wildfire of uninhibited desire when I had her like this.

She was soaked. Her cream coated me as she pressed down my cock driving me insane.

"Please, T," she whimpered. "Please, I need more."

"Oh, baby, I'm gonna give you more. I'm gonna rub your greedy pussy until your legs fucking tremble all for me, until your juices run down my fingers, until every time I breathe I inhale the scent of you aroused. Then I'm gonna spread your thighs nice and wide and fuck you until you want nothing as badly as you want my cock to give you release. But first I'm gonna fuck that sweet little mouth." I traced my fingertips over her swollen, soaking lower lips, listening to her needy little gasps of shocked breath at my promises. Then I slid my fingers to her mouth to trace those lips as well.

"Suck," I commanded.

She readily complied. Her little tongue darted out to stroke the tip of my finger. Her own dark eyes reflected the carnality in my own. "I said suck, honey." She drew my index finger into her mouth and did as she was told.

Of her own accord, she moved her lips to my shoulder then worked her way across my collarbone. "Keep going," I ordered.

Her tongue feathered down my chest awakening nerve endings I'd forgotten I had.

The swollen tips of her breasts grazed against my thighs as she found her place between my legs. I grunted out my own pleasure.

She spun her tongue over the bead of pre-cum at my slit in a quick teasing swipe that made me fucking weak for more. "I crave this," she whispered. Her hot breath over my damp head was a lash of pleasure that tore the breath from my lungs. Her fingers traced the thick veins on the sides of my cock. I cursed as I pressed her hand over me, forcing her to grip me, as if that would ease the tortured pressure constantly rising through my flesh.

"Then take it," I urged. My own voice was thick and harsh. I strangled over the lust that rode me constantly. Her rosy lips closed around me. I'd jumped out of a proverbial fuck-ton of aircraft in my time. But before that moment, I'd never actually flown.

My hand tangled in her hair as she gave me an exploratory suck. Then she took me deeper, indulging me in the velvet heat of her mouth. When her fingernails gently traced over my sac, I gripped the fucking sheets of my own bed. "Holy mother of god," I roared.

She managed a quick smirk with me in her mouth. Her moan reverberated down my shaft. And her face, holy fuck, her face glowed with satisfaction. Her eyes were heavy with her own hunger, staring up at me. Her lips were raw from her suction. Every fantasy I'd had of her like this held nothing on living the reality. I branded the image of her face at that moment in my mind. My body lifted of its own accord. I pushed myself deeper into the sanctuary of her mouth.

She tended the blazing ache in the head of my cock. I swore there was an electric connection between her tongue and my balls. Every nerve ending between the two sizzled. I wasn't going to last. Her delicate hand wrapped tight around my shaft. Every flick of her tongue, the suction of her silky mouth, the caresses of her fingers beneath my sac now, her hums of need - all proved to fucking destroy me.

I managed to force out some kind of encouragement. "Sweet baby. So fucking good," came out in a strangled groan. It likely wasn't sensical. I swore she was sucking my mind out the tip of my cock. She robbed me of any sanity I'd ever possessed. I decided it was an acceptable sacrifice. Delectable torment ripped through me. Sweat beaded across my chest. My vision clouded. Every muscle in my body seized. My sac drew tight. I was going to come.

I gripped her hair the way she'd gripped my heart, with no reprieve. She took me deep, all the way to her throat. "God..." a guttural groan robbed the next words from me before I managed, "baby...mmm...drink me." For a moment, I was convinced the rapture occurred there in my bed as her greedy little mouth consumed the fiery pulses of my cum that seemed unending.

When she lifted her head, lust and laughter glimmered in her eyes. I should have been free of the ecstasy, should've at least been able to formulate thought, but that didn't happen.

I was still hard, still ached, still fucking burned for her. Grappling for sanity that wasn't coming, I jerked her to me and in one quick move rolled her underneath me.

"Yes!" she gasped as her body twisted in need. She was so damned wet I sank my fingers through her swollen tissues, in and out, once, twice, watching her writhe. Then I rubbed at the opening of her sweet, narrow slit so hungry for my cock. I toyed with her, refusing her the penetration she required. "T, please."

"Fucking love to hear you beg for me. What do you need, baby? Tell me."

"You," she whimpered out her strangled plea. "All of you. Please."

"That's right, honey. You need *me*." I was a lying son of a bitch. Some malignant part of me hated him for having this first. When I had some kind of grip on my own mind, I could keep it at bay, but not now, not here, not after what she'd just done to me. She'd shattered through my practiced reserve and accessed nothing but raw instinct and driven hunger.

There would never be enough to satisfy me, never enough of her, of me, of us together. Rearing up on my hands, my thighs widened her own as my cock parted her, and I sank to my hilt. So fucking tight. I pulled back and slammed inside of her again, tearing away anything but the two of us right here, right now.

Her back arched. My force robbed her of breath, momentarily. When she regained it, she begged, "T, mmm, harder."

The demons roared inside of me like a rising tide of destructive determination. She'd get it harder. I pounded into her, praying for the sanctification that might silence the demons once again. My body became a battleground between the love I had for her and the jealousy I hated myself for feeling. With every thrust, she tore parts of me away, parts I'd carried for so damn long I wasn't certain how to be whole without them. The demons fought for their placement. They had no interest in losing ground.

As if her little body understood that she was the only heaven I would ever possess, her pussy nursed at my cock. "That's it, honey. Milk the cum from me," I demanded.

She trembled against me. Her lips parted on a moan of my name. Her body flushed. The angel in my arms I'd never deserve. Her arms wrapped around me, bringing my strength to her, melding our skin. I cradled her to me as the rhythmic pulses began to overtake her body. "That's it, sweet baby. Let it go for me." My sanity seemed to reside in her satisfaction. "I've got you." The destructive thoughts settled on her. The demons inside me recognized their master once again.

She shook in my arms as her climax broke over her in waves. I eased my strokes and stayed with her through it. Not until she stilled did I withdraw. Wrapping my hand forcefully around my cock, I jerked. Her eyes goggled. Another moan made a breakaway from her lungs. "Watch what you do to me. I'm so fucking weak for you." I pulled harder desperate for the friction, for the pleasure that bordered on pain. My shuddered groan echoed around the room. I soaked down her swollen mound, the holy land the beast inside of me insisted that he own.

52

MADDIE

I traced my fingertips up and down T's chest as we caught our breath. I was quite certain I had never had sex like that before in my entire life. Just like our first kiss, it had been a claim of ownership, a demand I had no issue complying with.

"I love you so fucking much," he whispered against my hair. I grinned. I wondered momentarily what it would be like to sleep with someone who didn't love me the way Chris had and T did. I decided I never wanted to know, but there was a note of apology in his vow.

"I love you, too." I snuggled closer reveling in the scent of him after sex. "What's wrong?"

He chuckled. "Not a damn thing in the whole world, sweet baby. My God, how could anything be wrong after that?"

That's what I wanted to hear, but I wasn't so sure it was the truth. Exhaustion tugged at my eyelids. I needed to go check on Olivia, but getting out of the bed required my muscles and bones to move, and I hadn't yet located them inside my body. Besides, not being tucked in T's arms with our legs tangled beneath the sheets felt akin to being tortured.

His right hand tracked down my back and massaged my backside.

"I need to go check on Liv. You get so nice and loud for me we need to make sure we didn't wake her."

I giggled and raked my teeth across his nipple. I loved the fact that he was also worried about her. He shivered. "I just came twice, baby. I'm an SF soldier, not a god, although I see how you could've gotten confused. You're gonna have to give me a few before I can go again."

"You really are terrible." I located enough muscle in my belly to laugh.

"You really are amazing."

The momentary strength I'd found melted once again at his vow. "I kind of think *we* really are amazing."

"I happen to agree. Stay right here, and I'll go check on our girl."

I had no qualms about staring at his delectable ass as he yanked his underwear and a pair of shorts on. It went right along with the rest of him. Firm planes of muscle pulled taut against his skin, every dip chiseled to perfection.

I let my arms extend out over his silky sheets, warm from our love making, and turned my head to inhale his scent in his pillow. Yep, if I got to stay right there for the rest of my life, I'd have precious little to complain about. A rogue band of shock tried to prod that thought from my mind, but I clung to it. I may not have any idea how to mesh our lives, but I wanted to exist in his arms forever.

When he returned to the bedroom, I saw a storm in those cool blue eyes. Something was definitely up. I tried to sit up, but his force had left me rubbed deliciously raw. "Is she okay?"

"Hmm?" He yanked off his clothes and crawled back in bed. "Oh yeah, she's perfect just like her mama. Sound asleep. Howie had apparently decided to HALO jump to the floor, but I restored him to his previous location."

I grinned at my own HALO jumper, one of two I'd ever had a claim on. Other women might know how to fall for men who didn't feel the need to fling themselves out of perfectly good aircraft. I must've been born without that ability. I decided I was okay with it.

He switched off the lamp and drew me back to his haven of heat, muscle, and that intoxicating scent that was all T. I should've asked again what was wrong, but my eyes closed without my permission.

I didn't move until hesitant sunlight peeked around the blinds, and my little girl asked, "Mommy, did you forget to put your night-gown on because you're not pu-posed to sleep with no clothes."

If that little announcement wasn't enough to awaken me from the best night's sleep I'd ever had, T jerking the covers over himself certainly was. I wasn't the only one who'd *forgotten* to put on pajamas. When I blinked in the situation before me, I sighed. He'd covered us up to his neck. My mouth was under the comforter.

"Olivia," he cleared that sexy, sleepy gravel from his tone. "Why don't... you go down to the kitchen and uh... you can have five Skittles from the container." The Skittles were all at the bottom of the jar. It would take her getting the kitchen stool and reaching way in to get to them. He really was a genius.

"Can I really?" she bounced on her toes.

"Yep, you really can," I assured her. Desperate times called for desperate measures.

"Okay!" When she whisked from the room, T and I moved like we were on fire. It took us approximately three point seven seconds to locate clothes and throw them on.

"If I talk you into marrying me, I'm assuming my days of sleeping naked are over?"

"Once she's more comfortable with you being in bed with me every night, and there's not some kind of deranged loon after me, we can insist she knock on our door before just barging in." T loved plans, so I provided one.

"I can work with that." He'd just pulled on a Polo when Olivia reappeared with Skittles precariously balanced in her hand. "Is this five?"

T grinned. Now that he was fully clothed, he lifted her onto the bed. "Let's count them." She missed seven and got a few numbers out of order, but she did pretty well. "You have twelve plus the one in your mouth, so thirteen, which is like eight more than five, but we'll work on that later. So, Mommy said you can have these." He put five in her right hand. "But you probably have to put these back in the jar."

If I'd told her to do that, she would've fussed, but Uncle T said it so she went along. Not that I could blame her. I had a hard time turning him down as well. When she headed back down the stairs, I gave in to the constant desire to be near him. I laid my head against his chest. His arms wrapped around me, easing that ache that had taken up residence in my soul, the one only he could soothe. "Do we go back to Tier Seven with you today?" I'd prepped for the night at T-Byrd's. That had occupied all of my available brain space. I wasn't sure what the plans were for the day.

"If you don't mind, I intend to find Finch and get this put behind us today. If it isn't him, I'll know by close of business, but I need to be at the office to accomplish it. After I have him, we can take Liv and do something fun without me living in a constant state of panic."

"I don't mind. I do have to go back to work in a few weeks though." I tried to envision my life during the school year involving him on a daily basis. Other than the long hours apart, it was highly appealing.

"I'm not going to let someone terrorize you for the next month, baby. I'm ending this now. But since we're talking about the relative future, how much talking would I have to do to get you to move in with me?"

"You do know we've been dating for like a week, right?"

"Four years. When I figure something out, I see no point in not working the plan."

"You could move into my house," I reminded him while I pulled my hairbrush through my hair.

"You're out of bedrooms. What happens if we decide to make Liv a big sister at some point?"

Shock wrung the brush from my hand. It tumbled to the dresser with a loud clatter. "Are you serious?"

"Yeah." He laughed at me outright. "That such a crazy thing to ask?"

"After a week, yes, it is, and stop saying four years. You have not been in love with me for four years."

"True, but like I said why not work the plan?"

Because there was not a plan yet. That's what I'd intended to tell him, but thoughts of having another teeny-tiny baby to cuddle, feed, and raise swelled from my womb and sank into my mind. Having him there with me to do it all got my heart in on the game as well. I could see it. He'd hold my hand in the delivery room and rock the baby. The fantasy took center stage.

I'd never had that before. I'd always imagined it that way, though. I didn't get to wake Chris up in the middle of the night and tell him it was time. My mom had been in the room with me, but that wasn't at all what I'd wanted. Olivia was a week old before he even knew she'd been born. "Maybe I would like another baby," I allowed.

"See, it wasn't a crazy question." Victory lit his gorgeous eyes, and his cocky smirk formed readily on his features.

"It would need to be pretty soon," I challenged. "I'm not getting any younger."

He shook his head at me. "I don't scare easily, my little cougar. You know that."

"I'm not trying to scare you," I lied and he knew it.

"Uh huh. Lie down right now. I'll take care of it all before work this morning."

A rash of heat spread from my cheeks to points below. "You know it does take more than just deciding to get pregnant to actually achieve pregnancy." The army bred rampant pride and confidence into their Special Forces soldiers. It was necessary for their survival. They needed to believe they were the best of the best to be the best of the best, but he was getting a little full of himself.

"Maybe for some people." He laughed.

A loud crash came from downstairs. Didn't take a genius to figure out that the candy bucket was no longer on the counter. "Uncle T," rang up the stairs. She sounded panicked. He stopped me from flying down there.

"I got it. You get ready. And I know it takes time, baby, but I promise if you want to make a kid with me, I'll make damn sure you enjoy the process."

53

T-BYRD

I could do the baby thing. Hell, I'd already done it some. I hadn't been there to hear her cry the first time or to hold Maddie's hand or whatever, but I'd gotten there as soon as I could. I could do it all again. In fact, I wanted to. At least that's what I kept telling myself while I kept constant watch over Maddie's van, the road, all other cars, and anything that might even inadvertently do her harm. I'd taken them to my mechanic's to pick up the van. Since the belt had been replaced, the van was running fine.

Every decision I made was now weighed through the lens of Chris. Did I only want to have a baby with her because he had? Was I that much of a motherfucking asshole? Maybe. I couldn't really be sure.

I parked beside her at Tier Seven, and decided it was beyond time that I pay the money to gate off the parking lot and hire an attendant to guard the cars. I'd take care of that as soon as I got inside. After that, Roman and I were going to have a little chat. I wanted to know what was on that file, and either the CIA got Finch or I did. I was more than happy to make it a race to the finish.

Smith met us in the lot. Once he'd extracted his massive form from his truck, he handed over Maddie's phone. "I was right about the phone. My number came up as the person calling you twice last night. Of course, it wasn't actually me, and when I answered, they hung up."

Maddie stared at the phone like it had fangs. "So, we still have no idea who's doing this." She sighed.

Smith shook his head. "We don't, but I took the child tracker app off of the phone. It seems impossible that someone could be using it to follow you, but having tracking software on your phone in the middle of all of this rubs me the wrong way. T's not going to let either you or Liv out of his sight until we figure this out. I promise we'll keep you both safe."

"I know you will." Maddie turned and gave me her tender grin. It served to both enliven me and to make me double down on catching Finch or whoever was doing this.

I carried Olivia up to the office admiring Maddie's delectable little ass as she climbed the stairs ahead of me. I was greeted by two men I'd never seen before. Since this was my company and I had a plan for my day, I wasn't particularly pleased. "Who the hell are you?" I demanded.

"T," Maddie gestured to Olivia who had her head on my shoulder and was making Howie play with my hair. I set her down.

Smith glanced from the men, to me, and then back to Rylee. "These Griff's friends?"

Rylee nodded. "I'm going to let Haywood make introductions, but I am so glad I have a front row seat for this."

"Yeah, you enjoy this. I need to check something in my office," Smith nodded to our guests and then disappeared down the hallway.

"Sir," one of the men cleared his throat and stepped closer to me. "I'm Reid Cantori, former Det Commander out of SFOD-D. This is Dean Hudson. We served together. Sergeant Haywood said to meet you here for an interview this morning."

"Did he?" I was going to kill him. "Delta Force, of course he did. Griff!" I roared.

Olivia covered her ears. "No yelling," she scolded.

Griff strolled out of his office looking entirely too pleased with himself. "Come on, T, you can't ask for more than Delta Force, now can you?"

I simpered. "How did you find them?"

Cantori chuckled. "Haywood and I go way back to our infantry days. We've been out for a year. Civilian life isn't all we'd hoped it would be, and Tier Seven is making quite a name for itself. If you're interested, we'd love to offer our services."

I'd have to scalp Griff later because I was very, very interested. "I'm interested," I assured them. "Just let me get them settled. My office is the last door on the right."

As they turned and followed orders, Griff chuckled.

Maddie pointed to the empty conference room. "Olivia, let's go play with your Magna-Tiles, while Uncle T yells at Uncle Griff." She spoke the last half under her breath and gave me one of those grins that made everything good.

Breath rushed back into my lungs. "I'm not going to yell... yet."

"No SEALs," Griff taunted as I stalked past him.

"Fine, but your job today is to play parking lot attendant. Supposed to be a balmy eighty-seven. Have fun."

"Fucker," he huffed as he headed out the front doors.

I stopped by to make sure Rio, Trent, and Derek Kingston, our marines, were finding their way around their new offices. By the time I got to my own office for an interview I did not have time to conduct, Olivia was regaling our Delta Force hopefuls with her morning. "So, I didn't wet my panties because I'm a big girl, and then I wents into Uncle T's bedroom, and Mommy forgot to wear her pajamas to bed last night and I think Uncle T did too because his leg didn't look like he had on pajamas but when he stays at my house he does wear them. But now he's Mommy's prince so maybe that means he doesn't gots to wear them at my house. And also Mommy said that she can see Uncle T's kneecaps which are very private." She shook her little finger at them. "Do you know if you have kneecaps?"

Voodoo and Smith were across the hall in Smith's office clutching their guts, doubled over laughing. Both Cantori and Hudson were using their supreme self-control, probably mastered during Operator Training, to keep from joining them.

I leaned into Smith's office. "The likelihood that one of you fuckers is going to get maimed today continues to increase." I scooped Olivia back up into my arms. "Where's Mommy?" I ground through my teeth.

"She wents to the bathroom."

"You go get your Magna-Tiles and you can play on the big table in there, okay?" I pointed into the conference room.

"Can you play with me?"

"I need to talk to them right now." I gestured to the men in my office still choking back laughter.

"I could talk to them, too. I'm good at talking."

"Oh yeah, baby girl, you are good at that." I sighed.

"Come on, Liv," Smith decided to come rescue me. I really needed to give him a raise. "I'll play Magna-Tiles with you until Mommy gets back."

"We can build a castle," she instructed.

"I'm no good at castles. How 'bout a fort?"

"But maybe a castle."

I shook my head at their exchange. Hagen was going to be building a castle, and everyone in the office knew it.

Maddie made her way down the hall. "Why is everyone laughing?"

"Trust me, baby, you do not want me to answer that."

She cringed. "I had a feeling you were going to say that. Where is she?"

My phone buzzed in my pocket, but I decided to leave it until later.

"Hey, T, check that text," Voodoo called.

I pulled my phone from my pocket assuming Voodoo had sent me something crude. But Smith came back into the hallway grinning, and Griff burst back through the front door. Everyone was staring at their phones. "I'm assuming this means I no longer have to babysit cars."

It was a text from Roman. *A gift to Tier Seven from the CIA.* The picture was of Finch with his hands in cuffs surrounded by federal agents.

"Thank God," Maddie breathed.

A hint of relief eased my shoulders, but irritation was buried deep in the darkest pits of my soul. He'd seen her on her knees, seen what was mine. He'd terrified my baby. I wanted to be the one to find him. I wanted a full confession. There was just enough doubt in me to need to hear that he was the one giving us hell, and then I wanted to know why. The file on his computer continued to tighten the screw of tension in my chest. I needed to know what Roman had found, and perhaps more importantly, we all deserved to know.

54

T-BYRD

Maddie hadn't gotten another bizarre phone call in the last week, not since Finch had been arrested. That was apparently all of the confession I was going to get.

We'd agreed that we could not jerk Olivia back and forth between houses night after night. We'd disagreed on where we'd set our home base as a couple, however. I was slowly winning her over, and reminded myself often that all I really wanted was to be in her presence constantly.

That was precisely why I'd brought my girls along to the Hi-Way Diner for a celebratory lunch to welcome the new guys to Tier Seven.

Currently, Olivia was seeing how much ketchup she could get on one french fry, and I was eating with my left hand so I could hold Maddie's with my right.

I'd called Roman no fewer than a dozen times in the last week to ask about that file. I never got a return call. Maddie kept telling me to let it go, but that wasn't something I did well. Giving up on anything had never been an option.

Griff continued his story, "So, we come out of the house with the target and, I swear, two guys were fighting, half the fucking town was on fire, and most of the men who were supposed to be our backup were having their own rave. What the hell?" he asked our new marines.

Rio smirked. I was fairly certain he had Griff's number. "Sounds about like the time we landed in Baghdad, radioed our positions, and went to kick in a door. Some army moron failed to listen to his radio, and his battalion fired... on us. Also let the guy we were there to get know we were coming."

"Baghdad was nuts. There were too many of us trying to do too many things," Griff argued.

"Which is why we radioed our position," Rio came right back.

That shut Griff up. Maddie and I shared a quick grin.

Before I could play peacemaker, my phone rang. I released Maddie's hand as soon as I saw Roman's name on my screen. "'Bout damn time," I huffed into my phone.

"T, listen to me. I have a situation," Roman wasted no time.

That damned screw in my chest continued to tighten. "What's wrong?"

"He escaped."

"What? How the hell did that happen?"

"That's my question as well. He obviously had assistance. Someone on my team had to have helped him, which means I am out here in Phoenix like a sitting duck. I tried to have him stopped at the border patrol. They let him through. Whoever Finch is working for has more power than I do. I have no idea who I can trust. Think about that. I need your help. I need a team I know is not working for Marcus Finch, and I need you now."

"Any idea where he went?"

"Caught him on a street cam at the Wells Fargo in Tijuana. He had a Mexican woman with him. That was two days ago. I was in the middle of an internal investigation trying to determine who the fuck on my team was no longer under my control. He could be anywhere by now, but we're starting with his last known. I'm crossing the border now. I left my team behind and didn't provide a forwarding address.

The agency is sending me some help. Supposedly, these are operators who don't know me and don't know Finch. We'll see just how far his reach extends. Meet us at the Motel Zona. Place is a shithole, but the owner knows when to talk and when to keep his mouth shut."

"You sure you can trust him?"

"I'm not certain of anything. There's one more thing I need to tell you, the reason I never returned your calls."

The icy grip of dread continued to twist my gut. "What's that?"

"I wanted to tell you in person. God, you deserve better than me telling you like this."

"Just fucking say it," I demanded under my breath. Somehow, I already knew what was coming.

"Finch delayed our intel getting to you in Najaf. He's the reason half your team is gone. He went as far as to have you held at knife point. I don't know why yet, but T, be careful. He despises you."

Vomit and bile roiled in my gut. I couldn't respond. Nothing about the day of our attack had ever made any sense. My mind rejected the reason Roman had provided right along with every other possibility I'd ever considered. I'd spent the last four years certain it had been my fault. The only thing that made any sense at all was to find the man responsible and to destroy his malignant network piece by piece.

If he hated me enough to want me to watch my team be slaughtered, surely it was enough to want to terrify Maddie. I centered my thoughts on her. The time I'd be away from her would be to keep her safe.

"I'll see you tomorrow," was Roman's parting line.

"T?" Maddie leapt as soon as I set the phone on the table. "Who was that?"

Rage and some form of raw despair sank through me. Finch was the reason Chris wasn't here. Finch was the reason I had Maddie in my arms, in my bed, instead of Chris. I couldn't force the facts to align. The reality I currently lived and an entirely different one had all been held in the hands of one piece of human garbage. How could that possibly be the way the world worked? It couldn't. I wouldn't allow that to be how I earned Maddie's love.

"It was Roman. He needs our help. Finch escaped custody. We need to go back to the office," I managed. "We're heading out as soon as we have a flight," I informed the table at large.

Rio stood. "We all going?"

"This is a Team Seven deal, and we aren't talking here. Let's go."

55

MADDIE

I swore my stomach turned itself inside out as I watched them stand and leave the diner. *No, no, no, no, no.* I was not doing this again. I couldn't. I was not watching them all board an airplane to some place they couldn't name, to do things no one should ever have to do, while they turned down help. If Roman had lost Finch, then he needed to find him.

Every single time Chris had regarded my concerns over him with indifference struck a sharp blow, threatening to take me back to the frightened girl who willingly shelved her feelings for those of her husband. I wasn't that woman anymore, and I refused to go backwards in time. I wasn't doing this again.

I bit my tongue and listened to more details of this chase all the way back to Tier Seven. I respected him too much to call him out in a restaurant. I left Olivia in Rylee's care and followed him to his office.

"T," I snapped as soon as we were alone. "This is insane. You said Roman didn't even know if he was still in Tijuana. Is your plan really to chase this man all over the world?"

His eyes no longer held their customary glimmer when he turned to stare at me. A blank darkness had eroded their normal ocean blue. "Marcus Finch delayed instructions from our CIA Op about what happened in Najaf. He told them to make me watch, Maddie. The intel is what we were waiting on. He's the reason Chris isn't here."

"And you expect me to just be okay with you going after a man capable of that?"

"What would you have me do? The phone calls stopped as soon as he was in custody. Roman needs our help."

"Then tell Roman to come home and regroup. Go about this with some intelligence. This is outside the scope of Tier Seven, anyway. This isn't what you do anymore. You can't go backwards in time."

The flare of anger in his eyes said I'd struck a chord. "Didn't you hear what I said? He is the reason Chris isn't here."

Realization rocked me to the core. "Oh, I see, this has nothing to do with keeping us safe. It has everything to do with the fact that you can't seem to make our pasts and our futures align, and that terrifies you. You can't stand that one decision by one man changed our lives forever. Well, let me tell you something, that's how life works. One quick decision can change every single thing. It happens every day. I decided to take the bet from Bianca and Jenn. I chose the men I went out with because I knew I'd hate them. And I knew I'd hate them because you were the man I wanted, and no one else would ever measure up. I could've decided not to go to that gala with you. Every single thing in our world is up to chance, and you hate that.

"Every decision, every phone call, every tear we shed together, they all led us right where we're standing. But you still can't rectify the fact that I was married to him and now I'm in love with you. You want to go after Finch because you can't deal with the guilt. That's why you don't want Rio's team to help. That's why it's a Team Seven thing, isn't it? Because it isn't really about finding Finch. It's about earning me. You want the control. You can't always control life, T-Byrd. That isn't how it works."

56

T-BYRD

She was wrong. She had to be wrong. Dammit! I ground my teeth. My hands shook. Why couldn't she just have been wrong? The truth shattered over my skin. I wanted to claw it from the earth. "He put cameras in your house! What about that? What about the things he saw?"

She shook her head. "Chris would've wanted me to be happy, T." Her voice splintered over the fissure in my heart, the one left by the death of my best friend. "What Finch did or didn't do is between him and God. Let him hang for it. Let him burn for it, but it has nothing to do with you. It will not undo anything that has already been done. You know that. He's on the run, and he isn't stupid enough to come back here now. You know that, too. You're doing this because some sick part of your mind thinks if you've avenged Chris's death, you'll be able to earn me. You don't have to earn me. I'm right here. I didn't *fall* into love with you. I *fell* in love with Chris. It was like I had no choice in the matter. But I *walked* into love with you. I chose every single step. Some of them I didn't handle so gracefully, but I don't regret any of it, not even for one second. I know life doesn't always work out the way you want it to. I know a split-second decision can change the course of your time on this earth forever. I also know that when life gives you the very thing you need to go on, you hold onto it with everything you are. Until you can deal with that, until you can leave the dead to rest, don't call me."

Before I could respond, she was marching out to her van with Olivia and driving away from me. That tear in my chest robbed me of all breath. My bones were suddenly hollow. My heart had just fucking gotten into a van and driven away. She was right. Going after Finch the way Roman wanted to was idiotic. It would never work. I couldn't find a way forward, and I suddenly didn't want the path back to my past that had been provided. I had no plan. I'd only had her, the one thing I needed more than I needed the next beat of the shattered organ in my chest, and she was gone.

It took me more hours than it ever should've, after I'd come home to gather my thoughts, to formulate what I needed to say to her. Three words. That was it. Not the three most men struggle over. No, I'd had no trouble with those at all, but the ones I had to say were bitter. They were brutal.

She picked up on the fourth ring. "Hello?" Her sweet voice quaked, and I hated myself all the more.

"You were right," I pressed the words past the jagged knife that felt like it had been returned to my neck. "I'm jealous about the things you shared with him, and then I hate myself more than I ever knew possible for feeling that way. I just... don't know what to do about it, but we're not going to Mexico. Roman's coming home."

"There's a lot of this I don't know what to do with either. I thought we were going to figure it out together. You stopped talking to me about it after the lake. He isn't here anymore. I loved him so much, but that doesn't mean I can't also love you. You were the one that taught me that. What happened to that guy?"

"I'm right here. I swear. I just... dammit, I hate Finch so much for what he took from you. It's fucked up that I get to be with you now because of him. I can't stand that."

"That's how life works," she reminded me. "I didn't know how to make peace with it either, until I finally figured out that the only way you survive this world is to take the things that matter, hold them in your hands, and cherish them for as long as you can because you never know when they'll be gone."

"I know. I'll get it together, Maddie, I swear."

"Good, because I love you so much, and I don't want to do this life without you."

The memories I'd fought for so long assaulted my consciousness. The last slap of wind in my face when we'd leapt out into thin air. The last poker game around the fire. The last time I'd heard him laugh. The tears in his eyes when he'd finally gotten to talk to her and hear Olivia cry. The last conversation. The last time my life had made any damned sense at all. I forced myself to have the memories even if they would always be twisted and washed in his blood.

"Just...take care of... my girls for me."

57

MADDIE

The blare of my cell phone as soon as I'd ended the call with T vibrated through me.

"Hey, Maddie, it's Carl."

As if I needed the reminder, my past called, via Chris's brother, to say it wasn't going down without a fight. "Oh, hey. How are you?" I forced out. Why? Why had I answered?

"Listen, can you do me a huge favor? My car broke down out on Piedmont. I'm on my way to see Mom at the hospital. I hate to ask but could you come pick me up since I'm so close to your house?"

The guilt already had an opening thanks to my earlier fears over T leaving. "Why is Delores in the hospital?" I had several guesses but thought I should ask.

"I think it's just the stress. You know she hasn't handled Chris's death well, and after what T said to her the other night.... They think it affected her heart."

"Wait. What did T say to her exactly?" I grabbed my keys, still not entirely certain why I was agreeing to this.

"Well, he told us we'd never get to see you or Olivia again. It broke her heart."

T. I ground my teeth. Of course he'd said that. She'd hurt us, and he'd never allow that. "I'm sure he didn't actually mean that." But the guilt centered in my chest and squeezed. "Where are you on Piedmont?"

"I'm down near Scooter's Coffee. Listen, I'm in Chris's old Camaro. I bought it off of him when he graduated from West Point. I try to get it out and drive it every now and then."

How had I not known Chris had sold the Camaro to his brother? I was too swept up in the wedding, and his first deployment, and being his wife. I was caught up in the wind with him. It was no wonder the car had broken down. It was ancient. A relic of a past life his family couldn't seem to bury.

"Okay, I'll be there in just a sec."

58

T-BYRD

Before I left my room, I stood the photo of Team Seven back up on my chest-of-drawers. I wanted the memories, but you can't live inside of photographs.

"I swear I never meant to fall in love with her, man, but how could I not? She's perfect. You knew it all along. I will always take care of both of them. Always."

As I made my vow to a photograph of my best friend, hoping he heard me from heaven or whatever, my gaze caught on the pearl-handled knife Chris always carried. He'd take it out and open and close it over and over again, while he planned. It wasn't worth much for cutting, but he swore it helped him think. I'd never seen him without it. It was in the pocket of his jeans in the picture. I even remembered the story of how the pearl at the bottom of the handle had gotten broken. He'd been playing with it in the parking lot one day at school and it had slipped from his grasp, hitting the cement when he'd set eyes on Maddie Lewis walking out to her car. He'd stayed after school that day to help some guy with math. A split-second, last-minute decision that had changed the course of his life forever.

"It was in the box that was sent back to me along with his effects." He

broke into her house. He took Chris's boxes. He set up the cameras. *Looks like he had to saw it at first.* The sick fucker had cut her belt with Chris's knife.

Holy shit, Carl hadn't had a similar knife in his pocket at Chris's parents. He'd had the same fucking knife.

Frantically, I called Maddie's cell. No answer. The photograph of Chris and Carl in their uniforms blazed through my mind. Carl's uniform. Navy-blue coveralls. There'd been a company logo on the pocket. I cranked the Vette and tried to envision the insignia on the uniform. I'd seen it before. I saw it so regularly it had become mundane, but I was still trained to notice every single thing. The uniform was from Spire Cellular.

I touched her name on my phone again. Two rings, three rings, four rings, and her voicemail picked up. I tried again and nothing. *Dammit!* I called Smith. "It wasn't Finch!" I roared into the phone.

"T, listen to me. I was just about to call you. Someone just tried to access the camera feed, and it wasn't from Mexico. It's from the house across the street from hers. There is no way Finch would chance coming back into the States after he escaped federal custody. He's too calculated for that. I don't care what kind of network he has."

"I know. If someone works for a cellular company could they have been spoofing the calls to Maddie's phone? Could they be tracing her location that way?"

"Sure. If they know what they're doing, it isn't particularly difficult — just time-consuming. If someone had access to her actual account, they could do a lot of damage."

"It's Chris's brother."

"What? Why?"

"Call everyone. Meet me at the house across the street from hers. I can't get her on the phone."

"I'm on my way."

59

MADDIE

"Carl, what the hell are you doing?" I managed to keep from screaming as the barrel of one of Chris's old pistols bore into my spine.

"If you don't want Olivia to see the gun, get back in the van."

"I am not going anywhere with you. What are you even thinking? You're insane." None of this made any sense. It was some kind of horrible nightmare. It had to be. I stared down at the grass searching for anything I could use as a weapon. An old pair of Chris's combat boots stared back at me from his brother's feet.

"Get in the car, Maddie. We're going home."

I jerked away from him and made a break for the driver's side door of my van, but he was faster. He whipped the barrel of the gun across my face.

"Mommy!" Olivia screamed from inside the van. Blood poured from my nose.

"Why are you doing this?" I gripped the van and tried to clear his swaying form from my vision.

"Get in the van or Olivia gets the same. High time the little brat learns some manners, anyway."

Vomit and bile filled my mouth. My God. This was really happening. He shoved me away from the door and climbed in the car with my little girl. I stumbled to the hood and managed to fling myself into the passenger side before he threw the van into drive and took off.

"Mommy!" Olivia sobbed. "Why did you hurt her?"

"Shut up," he snarled.

"How dare you?" I spat. "You can wear his boots and you can hold his gun, but you are nothing like Chris. He was a hero. You are nothing!"

He brought the pistol back across my face. I jerked away that time, but he caught my collarbone. A sickening groan followed a distinctive snap.

"Stop it! Stop hurting her!" Olivia begged.

"I told you to shut up!"

I had no idea where he thought home was, but I tried to watch where we were going. I had to let someone know where we were. My vision continued to swim, but we turned down the road to my in-laws' house. Nothing made sense.

"You should've called me," he sneered. "Why did you never call me?"

I decided to placate until I had some idea what his plan for us was. "Called you when?"

"When you were in trouble." *I'm in trouble now you motherfucking idiot, and I'm sure as hell not calling you since you're the one holding us at gunpoint.* But his voice sounded distant as he flew down the road, like he wasn't fully in the car with us. "When your car broke down and I set the alarm in your house off, why did you not call *me* for help? You should've called me!" he roared. He'd actually lost his mind. We were in the car with a madman I'd known since I was sixteen years old. "You always call him! You never call me! I'm your hero now. Special Forces clearly isn't worth much. They thought getting you a new phone would keep me away. They may have gotten you to delete the app I was using to track you, but I still know it all. I am the only hero you will ever need."

Olivia was thrashing in her car seat, screaming for her Uncle T. I doubted that was helping Carl's fragile mental state, but I certainly wasn't going to stop her. Maybe someone would hear her. Maybe I could get the gun away from him. I tried to remember every single thing Chris had ever taught me about self-defense.

I had to wait until he stopped the car. I wasn't certain if he intended to keep us alive. Wrecking the car might bring on the end quicker.

To my shock, he pulled into the driveway of his house across the street from his parents'. "Now, we're home, where you belong."

I'd never make it to my in-laws for help with Olivia, and I certainly wasn't leaving her there with him. There had to be some other way. I had to get the gun.

He yanked Olivia out of her seat. I flew out of my own, but he held the gun to her head and I froze.

"Mommy!" Olivia screeched. I'd kill him. I would get my hands on that gun and I would kill him if it was the last thing I ever did.

He jerked Howie from her grasp. "You won't be needing that anymore. You have me. Nothing from him. In the house now." He dragged my child inside his home, and I had no choice but to follow his orders.

He dead bolted the door and pushed the key in his pocket all while holding the gun. When he shoved Olivia down on the hardwood floors, I lunged for him. "Don't you dare hurt her!" I raged.

This time his fist landed in my chest, ripping the wind, the very thing that had given me the will to fight him, from my lungs. I stumbled backwards.

"Mommy!" Olivia rushed to me. "Why do you keep hurting her?"

"Make her shut up, and get into the kitchen. Make those beef tips you used to make whenever Chris came home."

When he went to make sure the garage and back doors were locked, I grabbed my phone from my purse. There were seventeen missed calls from T.

"I... want... Uncle...T," Olivia convulsed.

"I know, baby, listen to Mommy. I need your help, okay?"

She scrubbed her little hands over her face and nodded. "I'm... a... good helper."

"I know you are. Be brave for Mommy, okay? We're going to be okay." I turned the phone to my favorites list of numbers and slipped the phone into the pocket of her jumper. "Do you remember how you called Uncle T on the phone when Mommy was sick and they all came to play with you?"

She nodded.

"Go into the bathroom, turn on the sink so he can't hear you talking, and call them again. Tell him we're in the house across from Nana and Pops' house, okay?"

"I can do it." She gasped for breath, and I renewed my vow to kill my brother-in-law at the first available opportunity.

"Go now."

She raced to the bathroom, and I prayed this would work. The only numbers on that list were The Sevens. It didn't matter which one she reached.

As I managed to stand, my blurry vision centered in on the bookshelves in Carl's living room. Instead of photographs of Chris, like the ones in his mother's home, the shelves were choked with framed pictures of Carl. Cub Scout badges, second-place spelling bee certificates, and little league trophies were wedged between pictures of himself. But there, on the mantel, was the most concerning thing of all. My wedding photograph from the West Point Chapel had been Photoshopped. It was no longer Chris standing beside me. It was Carl.

60

T-BYRD

"We're in," Griff's voice was low and menacing as he popped the lock on the vacant house across from Maddie's. The laser sight on Smith's M-4 moved swiftly along the carpeting. I followed with my Glock.

Ryder and Rio entered from the back. "Clear, sir," bellowed in a low Alabama accent. "But y'all need to see this."

We cleared the front two rooms and met them in the living room. The house was empty.

"Ho-ly fuck," Voodoo spat. There were dozens of computer-printed photos on the walls, all of Maddie and Olivia. Vomit launched from my gut to my throat when my eyes landed on a wall full of images of my girls, some from the recent past, some as far back as Maddie's high school days. He'd added himself into every photo.

"When I find the sick motherfucker, I'm going to destroy him," I vowed.

"We'll find them," Voodoo vowed. "Maddie told me when I came to talk to her that day that Chris used to have a Camaro like the one we saw pulling out of this driveway. He thinks he's Chris. He's fucked in the head."

Griff's lip curled. "This is why we couldn't find him after he broke into her house. He wasn't ever out on the roads. He came here."

My phone buzzed in my pocket. "It's Maddie!" I answered instantly. "Maddie, baby, where are you?"

"This is Olivia," she panted. She sounded like she'd been sobbing. I'd break every single bone in his body slowly and meticulously.

"Olivia, baby, do you know where you are? Are you with Mommy?"

"Yes. I'm in the across house." The across house. Where was the across house? "And Nana," she tried so hard.

"Okay, listen to me. I'm going to find you. Where is Carl?"

"He's with Mommy. He keeps hitting her, and he took Howie away."

I'd castrate him and feed him his own sac before I murdered the bastard. "Where are you right now, sweetheart?"

"In the bathroom. Mommy said to come in here and turn on the water and call you. I did that."

"You're being so brave. I'm going to find you. I promise. Is there a window in the bathroom?"

"Yes."

"Can you see out of it?"

"No. But maybe I can." I heard her set the phone down on something. She must've been climbing up on the toilet. "Okay, I can see now."

"Can you tell me everything you see?"

"I see Mommy's van and the street. I see Howie by the van!"

"Do you see anything else?"

"I see a house with a window and a door. And another window with a star."

He bought the house across the street from her because she told him to. The gold star in the window. I glanced heavenward. Chris's gold star was quite literally leading me on. "Okay, Liv. I'm on my way. I promise you. I'm on my way."

"Where are we going?" Griff demanded.

"Fucker has them at his house. Maddie's hurt. Let's go."

Smith shook his head. "Hold on, T. We have to do this right. I guarantee you he's armed or Maddie wouldn't still be there. We need you thinking. We need you sane. We need a fail-safe Sergeant T-Byrd plan."

Rage spilled constantly into my bloodstream. I couldn't breathe. I could barely see through the red haze of fury. I had to get to her. I had to save her. "We go in non-illuminated," I began my strategy. "Smith, find me the address. Carl Mitchell owns the home."

"On it." Smith pulled out his phone.

"House was built in the nineties. Breaker box should either be in the garage or in the back. When we get there, Griff will pick the lock from the exterior door into the garage. Rio, you cut the lights. Get Garrison and Kingston out there. Tell them to cordon off the street and any optional escapes on the back of the house without being seen."

"Yes, sir." Rio lifted his phone to his ear.

"Voodoo, call Rylee. Tell her I need the rest of the M-4s from the office vault, along with the night-vision googles, and the therm scope. Tell her to bring the vests, too."

"Already on it." Voodoo pointed to the phone by his ear. "She's loading up now."

"Griff," I started but he held up his hand to stop me. He was already on his phone. "Fucker's got her in his house across from his Mommy's, right? I got it." He paused while someone answered his call. I continued to plan. "Hudson, this is Griff. You and Cantori still at the office? Good. Help Rylee load the trucks and get on the way. I'm texting you an address. Cordon the front of the house without being seen, and wait for me."

When he lowered his phone, I continued, "Once Rio kills the power, he's going to start to panic. We need inside faster than even you can pick a lock. I want a therm scan of the house. We're breaching whichever door has the fewest heat signatures near it. Bring the 12-gauge for the hinges and the Hooligan tool."

"They're in my Jeep with my kit," he assured me.

"The address is 684 Marsdale Avenue," Smith called. "I'm texting it to everyone."

"When we get in," I ordered, "he is mine. Clear the house. Do not fire until we have the girls safely outside. But the motherfucker that hurt my baby belongs to me."

61

MADDIE

"Put these on," Carl demanded. He dropped my rings onto the counter. I watched my past bounce and slide over cheap laminate.

"Why did you take these?" As much as I wanted to have them in my possession, I never wanted to wear them again. My resentment for him increased ten-fold with every passing moment. How dare he tarnish what Chris and I had?

"Put them on. You're mine now."

With that revolting thought, a workable idea formed in my mind. If he wanted my beef tips, who was I to disagree? I shoved the rings back on my right hand and located the largest iron skillet I could manage. Pain seared through my neck and chest as I lifted it to the stove.

If I couldn't get to the gun, we'd do this Rapunzel style. With every terrified tremble of Olivia's body beside me, I hated him more. There was dried blood all over my face. I was fairly certain my collarbone was broken. My chest burned with every breath, but I wasn't going down without a fight.

"What do you think you're doing with that?" he huffed.

"I thought you wanted beef tips." I came right back as I poured vegetable oil in the skillet and turned the flame on as high as it would go.

"Oh. Right. Yeah, okay." He kept firm hold of the pistol. "Glad you finally wised up and listened."

I couldn't lift my arms over my head thanks to whatever he'd done to my chest. He was significantly taller than me, the same height as his brother. Hitting him anywhere above the chest wasn't a possibility. I was going to have to improvise.

When he brushed the hair from the back of my neck and started to kiss the skin he revealed, I fought not to vomit. Revolt slithered over me. I shuddered in disgust.

"You can get nasty with him in the kitchen but not with me? You're nothing but a little whore, aren't you? I'm the only man you need now. Think of how happy Mama will be when we get married."

Just a few more seconds and the oil would be hot enough. Thinking quickly, I grabbed a stack of napkins from the counter. "Olivia, can you go put these at everyone's places on the dining room table for me?" My daughter looked at me like she was quite certain I'd lost my mind right along with her uncle, but she did as I asked.

As soon as she was gone, I gripped the handle of the skillet. When his hands roved over my backside, I decided now was the time. I flung the skillet and hot oil at his crotch. He doubled over.

"Shit!" he snapped. "What the hell, bitch?"

Before he could retaliate, every light in the house went out. Carl had already closed every curtain and set of blinds. It was pitch black.

"Mommy?" Olivia screamed. "I can't see!"

I flew to the dining room. "I'm right here. Stay right beside me." I couldn't lift her. "No matter what you hear, stay right beside Mommy." I guided her towards the front door.

Three rapid-fire shots sounded. The door shuddered from the impact. The hinges. Thank God.

I heard the distinctive sound of Carl cocking a pistol. His knees pounded against the carpeting. Could he not stand? Another round of vomit shot from my stomach to my throat. I had no idea who'd been assigned to knock down the door, but I knew why they called him the fatal front.

"He has a gun!" I screeched and jerked Olivia underneath me. A thundering boom shook through the house. Another boom echoed around me followed by the splintering of wood.

"Please, please don't hurt them," I begged Carl.

Two shots split the air. Olivia screamed.

Someone chuckled. Staying as low as I possibly could, I lifted my head.

"Were you aiming at me?" Griff taunted. "That's hilarious. Clearly your brother is the only marksman in your family, shit-stain. Someone should've warned incoming out in Omaha."

"Don't look now, motherfucker, but you're lit up like a Christmas tree. Your dick so much as twitches we'll blow you to hell and save Satan a trip," Voodoo snarled.

Carl did indeed have eight green and red laser sight dots on his chest and head. All of Tier Seven was in full gear. I couldn't see T. Men swarmed all around us. "Clear," rang out from several of them as they made passes through the rooms of the house.

"Put the gun down, fuckstick," Smith ordered. "You took on the wrong team."

"Where is Maddie?" he roared. T. His voice rushed the missing air back into my lungs. The thunder of his boots as he raced towards us shook the terrorizing fear from my understanding.

"We're okay," I tried to yell but the weight of the day seemed to compress my chest.

"Baby." He gathered both of us in his arms. He scooted his gun away from us and handed Olivia Howie. "Are you hurt?"

"A little."

When Olivia broke down in convulsive sobs, he cradled her to him and helped us both outside. An ambulance pulled up. They seemed perfectly happy to let Voodoo handle most of our care though. "Pretty sure she's got broken ribs and a broken collarbone. We're going to have to get her x-rayed." He shook his head.

"I'm fine, really," I continued to insist.

"Take them to the hospital. I'll be there as soon as I can," T ordered the ambulance driver.

"T?" I had no idea what to say to him when he kissed the top of my head. "What are you going to do?"

"There are a few things I need to figure out. I get that he's sick, okay? But he hurt you, and I need to make certain that never happens again. I'm just going to talk."

As many times as I'd told myself that I'd kill Carl, now that it was over, I didn't want T to have to live with killing his best friend's brother.

"I'll be at the hospital as soon as I can."

62

T-BYRD

"You can't just keep me here," I heard Carl huff.

"We *can* do pretty much anything we want since we're the ones holding the guns," Griff informed our captive.

"Bitch burnt me. Aren't you going to help me, too?" he whined to Voodoo next.

Voodoo laughed at him outright. "Let me explain how it works here in the land of the sane. The bad guys, that's you in this particular scenario, don't get medical attention until after the good guys, that's Maddie. Also, you hurt my sweet pea, so I'd say I'll get to your burnt, shriveled dick sometime between now and the next millennia."

Rio had clearly had enough of Carl's mouth. "You keep calling her names, Leroy, I'll cut your tongue out of your face. That'll give the good medic even more to do so if were you, I'd shut it."

Smith had traded in his M-4 for his laptop, his weapon of choice. He shook his head as I made my approach. "So, Spire Cellular owns an app development firm called Intelix. They developed the child tracker Maddie used for Olivia. He was able to tap in from her account and follow her through the app, while she was keeping up with Olivia with the tracer portion."

With the snap of every puzzle piece into its place, my rage grew.

The rip of the Velcro from my gloves reverberated through the air. I tossed one on the ground and performed the same task with the other.

"Oh shit, man, when the gloves come off you're screwed," Voodoo informed Carl. "Even I won't be able to fix you after this."

"Who was with you at my lake house?" The rest of Tier Seven took a step back as I took a step forward.

His defiant sneer was his first mistake. Spitting at me was his second. The satisfying crunch of bone filled me when my fist connected with his face. "When I ask you a question, fucker, answer me."

His eyes lit with shock. He stood and lunged at me. I drew my fist back again and shattered his eye socket. He went down with a thud. When he finished thrashing and groaning, he decided to talk. "You think you're so smart. Chris taught me a thing or two about war."

"So, that was your attempt at a feint, right? No one was with you. That's why it took so long for you to shut the second door. That's what I figured. Now, what was the point of all of this? Surely you knew I'd come for her. Surely you knew you'd never get through your brother's team. I honestly can't believe you thought she wouldn't fight you. Looks like you've got yourself one hell of a third-degree burn. Trust me, that was just the first thing she had planned for you. What was the fucking point?"

"She should be with me," he defied.

"T, man, he's fucked up," Voodoo warned. "He's not going to give you a straight answer because he doesn't have one."

"Fine." I nodded. "But get this through your fucked-up head." I was in his face. "You ever come anywhere near her or Olivia again it will be the last thing you ever do. Do you get that? I'll destroy you."

"I really think this is probably my fault," Chris's father hesitantly stepped into his son's home. He had his hands up. To be fair, he was staring down the barrel of several M-4s so I couldn't blame him.

"We're not going to shoot you, sir," Griff assured him. "Unless you'd like to get in on Carl's little kidnapping gig."

"No, I have no interest in that. My wife is not an easy woman to deal with. I worry she made him think this was a way to make her happy. After Chris's death, it's been impossible. I'm not sure what to do, but please assure Maddie that I'll make certain Carl is never near either her or Olivia ever again."

Smith cleared his throat. "The Lancaster County Sheriff's Department is going to make sure of that, sir, but maybe you and your wife could seek some counseling for dealing with... all of this."

"Yes. That's probably best." His eyes were pleading as he turned to me. "Did you mean what you said when you told us we could never see Olivia again?" Was he seriously asking me for favors?

"He took her," I spat. "At gunpoint. And then he hurt her. Do you get that? The love of your son's life. The love of my life. He took her and injured her and had plans to do other unspeakable things to her."

"I know." Chris's father blinked back tears. "But he's not in his right mind."

"I don't give a damn where he is. If he ever tries to hurt her again, I will kill him. As for you and Olivia, get in touch with me in several months. We'll see how I'm feeling about you being around her again, under my constant supervision."

63

T-BYRD

I could hear Olivia regaling some medical personnel with the story of her afternoon when I arrived at the hospital. "And then Mommy says for me go into the bathroom and call my Uncle T because he's a superhero and so that's whats I did." I shook my head as I slipped into the small ward set up for trauma victims in the ER.

"Sounds like you were a very brave little girl," the nurse informed her. When I eased past the curtain, Maddie was seated on a bed topless since the nurse was wrapping her chest in a bandage.

Voodoo had cleaned her face. Even bruised and swollen, I swore I'd never seen anything more beautiful. "Hey, baby." I took post beside her and offered up my hand. "Feeling any better?"

She took it readily. "I am now."

"I'm so fucking sorry I wasn't there. I should've come after you as soon as you left the office. I thought I had some time to work through it all and then this happened."

"T, you deserved time to work through this. I'm fine, or I will be soon. I just don't want to think about it anymore." Tenderly, she traced her fingertips over the split skin on my knuckles from beating Carl. "Where is he now?" she whispered.

"Carl is on his way to prison. Revenge isn't going to earn me you so... I just needed to make certain he was working alone. After that, I let the Sheriff have him. All I need is you and us."

"No Carl and no Finch, you promise?"

"If Roman needs my help, I'll do what I can, but not if it means leaving you."

"I like that plan." She leaned her head on my shoulder. "When you got that phone call, it reminded me so much of your deployments. Go off somewhere dangerous because someone said to go there and do terrifying things that someone needs done. I freaked out. I'm sorry I left you standing there to deal with it all. I'm a little clingy, maybe, and I let my fear rule everything. I'll work on it. I swear. I'll figure out how to do this right. He was just never home and..."

"Hey," I tenderly cradled her bruised face in my hands. "You're not clingy, and even if you were, I have no interest in ever leaving you anywhere alone again for a very, very long time, so it works. We have to figure this stuff out together. I won't forget that again. We've lived through hell, honey. We can be in love even if we don't have everything figured out. Good days, bad days, days when we say or do things that we know we shouldn't, moments we aren't proud of, I'm here for all of it. You and us, that's all I want."

"Thanks for loving me in all of the spots I most need it," she vowed.

My heart fucking swelled until I swore that rip in my lungs that had come from Chris's death was covered by her love. I could draw a full breath.

"I love every single part of you, sweetheart, even the parts you don't love as much as I think you should. But thanks for showing me that maybe I can leave things to chance on occasion. The universe did pretty well by me when it gave me a shot with you. And thank you for letting me have the good memories again. I'd shut them out because I was so afraid of the last one, the worst one, but even it deserves to be remembered on occasion. It happened. Me pretending it didn't or trying to repair it doesn't change the reality of it. I also owe you an apology about Finch, and not the one about wanting to take Roman up on his offer. I wanted it to be Finch. God, I wanted it to be the guy Chris hated. I wanted to be the one who put him behind bars because I felt like it would somehow make Chris forgive me for falling in love with you. I might've missed something because I let my hatred of him cloud my vision. It makes me crazy to think that I might've made a mistake, that I could've caught Carl before it came to this."

"T." She shook her head. "Everything about this was calculated. When Smith took that app thing off my phone, that's when he decided to take me."

"Yeah, I know. It did finally occur to me that I don't need Chris's forgiveness because I didn't do anything but fall in love with you. Surely that's something he understands."

"All right, that's done." The nurse stepped back. "The clavicle fracture is minimal. You'll only need to wear the sling for two weeks, and I gather by the lovely things you just said to each other that he'll be around to help you with the rib bandaging. You only need to wear it until it doesn't hurt to draw a deep breath. Coughing and laughing might be tender for a few days. Ice on and off your face will help the bruises and reduce the swelling."

"I'll be there to do anything she needs," I vowed.

Maddie gestured to Olivia. "She keeps rubbing her eye. With everything that happened, that's what's scaring me right now." Olivia's fingers rubbed back and forth over her eye constantly.

I told myself it had to be the stress, that she'd be fine once we had her settled. "Is there a pediatric ophthalmologist here?" I asked the nurse.

"I can get you a pediatrician, but specialists are going to be harder to come by. Let me see what I can do."

The nurse knelt down eye to eye with Olivia. "All right, brave girl, can you help me help Mommy get all better?"

"I can help! I'm a good helper."

"I figured you were just the girl for the job." The nurse grinned at her. "I think we need to let the doctors check your eyes just to make sure all of that yucky stuff that happened today didn't hurt you."

"It didn't," Olivia insisted.

"I think you're right," the nurse assured her, "but we do have to check."

Olivia extended her arms up to Maddie.

The nurse looked almost as devastated as I felt. "Mommy can't pick you up and carry you places for a few weeks."

"But maybe just if I really need her to because I gets scared, and the doctor..." Olivia tried. I accepted my fate. She was always going to be my girl, capable of crushing me in just a few sweet words.

Maddie's eyes closed. She hadn't yet cried over the whole fucking thing. Strongest woman on the planet. Gently, I eased my arms around her.

The nurse wrinkled her nose. "Maybe not. But you are such a big brave girl I know you can do it."

"Maybe Uncle T can carry me just if I get scared and to the doctor."

"Uncle T will definitely do that," I promised her.

"That sounds like the perfect solution," the nurse agreed.

"Uncle T really is a superhero," Maddie's eyes blinked open, and I brushed my lips over hers.

"All right, Ms. Mitchell, I'll get the paperwork ready and you can head home. I'm releasing you to his care for the next few weeks, so I'm going to implore you to let him take care of you. The more rest you can get the quicker this will all heal. I'll find Miss Olivia a pediatrician to check that eye before you go."

"Thank you. I promise I'll let him take care of me," she vowed.

"Can I get that in writing?" I teased.

A few minutes later, a pediatrician swooped into the room. "I heard there was a little girl in this very room who could fly." He winked at Olivia.

"I can't fly." She giggled.

"I bet Dad over there could make you fly up onto the bed so I can check that eye."

Dad. The word whipped through my head. Other than those few intense moments I got to share with Maddie when I lost my mind, I did not want to replace Chris. But the world just kept on turning and there were roles that had to be filled.

"He never really got to be that," Maddie reminded me.

"I know," I choked. I vowed to myself then and there that I'd learn to exist sharing the roles I'd been given alongside my best friend. "Come here, baby girl." I lifted her up, flew her around the room, and reveled in her squeals of delight. "All right, red nine, we have one jumper," I did my best army radio voice. Olivia laughed hysterically, the best sound in the whole damn world. Maddie beamed at me. "You're in zone." I flipped her over my head and then landed her on the bed in my lap.

"See, I told you, you could fly," the doctor chuckled. He made quick work of checking her right eye. "I don't see anything that concerns me. Let's let her talk about what happened today and see how she's going to process it. Definitely take her for a check with her oncologist, and maybe a few sessions with a therapist would be a good idea. Right now, I'd try to keep everything pretty low-key at home and let her work through it all."

"Low-key was our plan," I assured him.

"We will." Maddie nodded.

"Speaking of taking you home, there's one more thing I have to tell you about today and *Carl*," I spat his name like the curse it was.

"What?" I despised the frantic distress that immediately formed in her eyes.

Since I had to know where I was taking her, there was no putting this off. "He had a whole setup in the vacant house across the street from yours. Cameras, photos, computers even Smith is afraid to go through. I don't want to push anything on you, but will you and Liv please move in with me? I can't fathom any judge setting his bail at anything remotely accessible, but I can't guarantee you that. If you hate it there, we can look for something different once he's behind bars."

She stared up at me with those huge brown eyes, her face covered in bruises, and grinned. I swore the gates of heaven couldn't possibly be more beautiful. "I don't hate it there. I love it there because you're there. If I learned anything today, it's that being afraid doesn't keep you safe. It doesn't keep horrible things from happening. It just keeps you from really living. I kept thinking if I didn't get out of there, there was so much I would regret. Being afraid to fully embrace this thing we finally admitted we have was right there at the top of my list. So, I will miss my house, but it's time for me to accept that change is a part of life. If you're sure you're ready for your home to be invaded by girls, I'd really love to move in with you. I'm ready to live again."

64

MADDIE

If one more person carrying boxes into T-Byrd's house told me to sit down, I was going to scream. Just because I was in a sling and could barely breathe didn't mean I couldn't do anything.

T had helped me go through the boxes of Chris's things. Before we'd gotten rid of most of it, he'd told me the story of each thing Chris had saved and why he'd saved it. At the very bottom of the boxes we both found something we hadn't been expecting. We'd found healing.

Hannah and Olivia came down the stairs, smiling. "Aunt Hannah is going to paint my room with a pink stripe like Sofia the First's!" Olivia twirled around me on the sofa and then whisked into the kitchen to see what was being unpacked in there.

"Wow! Did Aunt Hannah ask Uncle T if that was okay?" He'd handled everything really well so far but I wasn't certain how a pink-striped princess room was going to go over.

Hannah laughed. "Aunt Hannah will get Uncle Smith to hold Uncle T down until he says it's okay." She waggled her eyebrows. "It's all about who you know."

I giggled and then cringed. "At some point laughing won't feel like I'm being stabbed, right?" I'd picked the wrong moment to say that. All of The Sevens, Rio, and that new guy, Reid, came to check on me.

Even though breathing was difficult the wind had returned at gale force speeds to my chest, and that made everything bearable.

As it turned out, Delores was never in the hospital. I'd spent so long letting either guilt or fear rule my decision-making I'd been ripe for the picking when Carl had leapt off the deep end. He was currently spending his days under twenty-four-hour criminal psychiatric observation. I had no idea what was coming next, but I'd face it when it came and T would be right by my side.

Carl had been able to start spoofing calls to the last phone T had provided me, when I gave the new number to my in-laws, before leaving Olivia in their care while we went to the lake. He'd been able to get into my house because Chris's birthday had always been our security code in all of our houses. As soon as he was finished going through all of my stuff, he'd intentionally set off the alarm again. According to the psychologists, he'd been certain I would call him to go check on the house. When the call hadn't come, he'd escalated his plans. I'd felt bad using a different code when I moved in. No more doing things out of guilt.

If they weren't going to let me help them unpack, there was something else I'd been wanting to do. I eased off of the couch, and headed up to T's bedroom. *Our* bedroom, I mentally corrected myself.

Stepping carefully around piles of boxes, I made my way to the safe in T's closet.

Spinning the dial, I opened the safe and slipped off the rings Chris had given me. I wanted to be able to visit them, but I no longer wanted to wear them.

"You okay, baby?" T leaned against the doorjamb.

"I'm good. If I could hug you, I'd be perfect," I admitted.

Grinning, he stepped to me, and wrapped his arms around me, tenderly, so he didn't disturb my healing ribs. "I love you."

"I love you, too. I guess I just needed to really put them away for good."

"I get that. Listen, we have to go to D.C. next week. We're

providing extra security for a visiting dignitary. I could send one of the new teams, but it occurred to me that it would be the first time in a long while that Team Seven would be back near Arlington. Why don't you and Olivia come with us? I think I'd like for us to visit him together."

His offer of closure was the very thing I'd been searching for by putting up the rings. He really was my superhero.

65

MADDIE

T carried Olivia in one arm and had his other around me as we made our way through the sea of crosses. An occasional breeze taunted the stagnant heat swallowing D.C.

We didn't need the cemetery's new app to find the grave. We knew it all too well. The last time I'd come had been because his parents told me I should. This time I eased solemnly towards his cross of my own volition. His mother came because she wanted to be recognized. We came because he deserved to be honored.

I understood so much more that day than I had on the day of his service. I knew that grief is really love with no place to go. I knew that life went on even when you were certain it would stop. I knew that he'd loved me the best way he knew how, and I knew that T loved us both. I also knew that love can change from friendship to romance to passion, but the love that remains always retains the element of the friendship we had at the beginning. Most importantly, I knew that Chris would never begrudge me falling in love with T. He'd want me to be safe and happy.

The rest of The Sevens were already at the marker, cold beers in hand. When we arrived, they handed us both one. And just like so many days and warm evenings back at Fort Carson, we spent a few hours together, talking, remembering the good, and forgetting the bad, with a team who'd been the best of the best, but wouldn't truly be reunited until the final Seven drew his last breath.

I knew Chris would be there to meet them. If heaven had Special Forces, my husband was most certainly the commanding officer.

66

T-BYRD

THE LAST WEEKEND IN AUGUST

"Are we doing the saber thing?" Voodoo teased as he tipped back another bottle of beer at a bar in Ogallala.

"Who the hell let you have a saber?" Smith laughed. "That has all the makings of an international incident."

I shook my head at them and willed it to be fourteen hundred hours, the precise moment when she was supposed to walk out of my lake house, down to the dock, to marry me. "She's already done the saber thing. She wanted this to be relaxed," I reminded them. "Plus, she was afraid one of you jack-offs would skewer her with one. I just got all of the bandages off of her. I'd like her to remain intact."

"What's Little Miss think of all of this?" Griff asked.

I grinned. "She likes her dress and has asked me several times if I'll marry her, too. I plan to remind her of that when she's about fourteen."

"You nervous?" Smith asked me with a knowing look in his eye.

"Nope."

"Liar."

"Think you're mistaking nerves for being ready to get this show on the road," I informed him. The fact that I couldn't feel my hands was irrelevant.

Roman Becker took the stool beside mine. "I see I didn't miss the pre-wedding festivities." He offered me his hand.

"Glad you made it. How did the story float in D.C.?" I asked.

"Everyone, save the agency director and a few key people in NSA, believes that I've left to take your job offer at Tier Seven," he assured me.

"We could make that a reality," I reminded him.

"I'm aware, T. There are things I have to take care of first, things that are far too delicate for me to discuss in a bar before your wedding."

"Things you can't accomplish if there's a mole in the CIA, I'm assuming."

He gave me a single nod and gestured for a beer from the bartender.

"I promised Maddie I wouldn't go off chasing after Finch. I intend to keep that promise. She lived a life wondering where her husband was and if he was coming home. I won't do that to her again. But that doesn't mean that I don't want to know why he kept talking about the two of us dating. If you're using Tier Seven as a cover, we get to know what you find when you find it."

"Understood."

Smith joined our conversation. "We're eager to help, if we can."

"I intend to take you up on that, Sergeant Hagen. In fact, I have a mission for you starting in a week or two."

"You name it. I'm there."

"It's about that time," Voodoo informed me.

I'd waited all fucking morning for this, and now, I wondered where all of the hours had gone. But, I was ready. It certainly hadn't been my original life plan, and there had been dozens of split-second decisions that had gotten us here, but sometimes, if you're insanely lucky, life intervenes on your behalf.

"We need to go," Griff urged.

I followed The Sevens down to the dock. The winds picked up when we arrived at the house. The water rippled and the few spare clouds moved further away. I hoped he was there, flying high, free falling, and loving it. I hoped he was there because he was my best friend and as odd as it was, I knew since he couldn't fulfill this role anymore he was pleased I could. From where he was, I knew he was happy for us.

There were maybe twenty people in the folding chairs Smith and Aaron had set up that morning. We didn't need anything more than that. When she stepped out of the house holding Olivia's hand, I swore all of the wind in the Midwest took up residence in my lungs. She filled me full. She'd carefully stitched the tear in my lungs. I could breathe.

We made it through all of the I dos and then I knelt down and grinned at Olivia. "Come here to me," I beckoned. She flew into my arms. "You know I love you like crazy, right?"

She nodded. "You love me a bunch of a lots."

Every single person in the audience swooned.

"I do love you a bunch of a lots. I promise you I will always love you, and always take care of you and of Mommy. I may not always do everything just the right way but, baby girl, you will always mean the whole world to me and Mommy, do you know that?"

That got me another quick nod.

"I wanted to promise you all of that, and I wanted to tell you thank you for sharing Mommy with me and thank you for letting me be your Uncle T. I've had a bunch of titles in my time, but that one is my favorite."

She rocked up on her tiptoes and planted a kiss on my cheek. "I'm a good share-er," she reminded me. The audience was eating it up with a spoon, and Maddie was beaming at us.

"You're the best."

"I love you, Uncle T."

"I love you, too, baby girl, so much."

As soon as Maddie got that ring on my finger, I knew it was right where it belonged.

While everyone enjoyed burgers and beers after the ceremony, Roman made his way over to us. He smiled at Maddie. "It's been my job for many years to be able to discern every possible outcome of any scenario. There were no other possibilities for the two of you. It takes a very special woman to love truly great men into superb ones. You, my dear, have that gift. You've done it twice, now." He lifted a wine glass to her. "Just don't try to love the savior out of him. It's who he is. It's who this world needs him to be."

EPILOGUE

MADDIE

T was beaming. "Know the goal, work the plan. You told me to put a baby in your belly. I followed orders," he teased me as I stared down at the pregnancy test with a bright blue plus sign glowing back at us.

"You're not at all freaked out?" How was he so calm? I was certain I was going to vomit. Of course, that could've had more to do with the pregnancy than my nerves.

He wrapped his arms around me. I melted into the wall of muscle that always steadied me. "If I were the one that had to actually give birth, I would be all kinds of freaked out, but I'm excited."

"I've never had anyone with me while I was pregnant. And... sometimes bad things happen when I'm pregnant." There. I finally verbalized the thing that had robbed just a little joy from this moment.

"Hey." He tipped my chin up so I was staring into those deep-blue eyes. "I will be right here for every single thing. I'll hold your hair back and clean you up if you're sick. I'll go get you weird food. Hell, I'll probably even eat it with you. I already can't keep my hands off of you, so I'm all over the belly rubbing. I'll even do those class things if you want. I'll read books. I'll paint... no, scratch that... I'll pay Hannah to paint fighter jets on the walls of his room. You name it, I'm there."

That did it. I laughed and let myself enjoy his thrilled excitement. "So, you think it's a boy, do you?"

"I was teasing you. I have no preferences. As long as it's okay and you're good, I'm a happy man. I would definitely not mind giving Liv a baby sister. She'd be thrilled."

"We can't tell her yet," I reminded him. This time I wasn't using her to shield my own fear. This was for her own good. Nine months is a long time when you're four years old.

"The last time we tried not to tell her something huge I lasted like four days."

"I remember." I shook my head at him.

"Can we tell The Sevens?"

"Yes." I beamed. I'd told all of them I was pregnant the first time via video chat. Doing it in person would be even better.

"Can we tell them tonight?"

"Yes again." I laughed at his exuberance.

"Then let's go."

A half hour later, I swore the winter winds of Nebraska blew me into the Hi-Way Diner. My wind-pricked cheeks burned as I unwound the scarf from around my neck. Snowflakes found their place on the window panes. I grinned down at my belly wishing the baby was already big enough to feel moving around. Olivia was spending the night with my parents for the first time since the summer before. I was pleased I'd gotten to bring one of our little ones with me, and that he or she was warm and safe tucked in my belly.

I slid into the round corner booth The Sevens occupied every third Thursday. T ordered and brought our food to the table. "How do you want to do this?" he whispered.

"Let's just see how conversation goes."

"How long have you known me?" he harassed.

"A very long time, honey."

"So, you already know *let's see how conversation goes* is not going to work for me. I need a plan."

"What are you two mumbling about back there?" Smith asked before he devoured half a burger in one bite.

"Nosy much?" T countered.

"Yeah." He shrugged.

"T wants a plan," I informed everyone.

"He always does." Voodoo tossed an onion ring in his mouth.

"A plan for what?" Griff asked.

"A plan for how to tell you all that we're going to have a baby."

The table erupted in congratulations.

T wrapped his arm around me. "That was impressive as hell."

"Thanks. That was my plan."

ABOUT THE AUTHOR

Bestselling author Jillian Neal likes her coffee strong and sweet with a shot of sinful spice, the same way she likes her cowboys. In fact, her caffeine addiction is quite possibly considered illicit in several states as are a few of the things her characters do. When she's not writing or reading, you'll find her in the kitchen trying out new recipes or coming up with ~~excuses~~ reasons to purchase yet another handbag or make an additional trip to Sephora. Though she'll always be a Bama girl at heart, Jillian hangs up her hat and kicks up her boots outside of Atlanta with her hunk-of-a-husband and her teenage sons.

For more information...
jillianneal.com
jillian@jillianneal.com

ALSO BY JILLIAN NEAL

Broken H.A.L.O

Camden Ranch

Gypsy Beach to Camden Ranch

Gypsy Beach